EMBERS
BURNING

Also By Eden Hart

The complete *Girl on Fire* Series:

Girl on Fire Book 1

Ashes Falling Book 2

Embers Burning Book 3

Phoenix Rising Book 4

EMBERS BURNING

EDEN HART

PHOENIX FLAME
PRESS

For my dearest sister, Jane Moore,
who always believed in me.

1

DAY 423—January 21

NEW YORK

A SHARP CRY SLICED the graveyard hush of the cruise ship. I paused on the top rung of the ladder, gripping the metal railing on either side as I listened.

Silence.

After a moment's hesitation, I stepped onto the deck.

Terra vines smothered the nearby walls, their leaves briefly whispering in a gust that carried the chill of midwinter.

The wind died down.

Nothing moved on the overgrown deck. No eyes peered from the shadows.

A hush shrouded the vessel again, its presence heavy, expectant, as though waiting for ... what?

In the pale red sky, a familiar eagle wheeled and soared above the murky waters of the Hudson River. I watched WindLord for a few seconds. Why was the silver-eyed bird so far from its usual hunting grounds in Manhattan?

Hurriedly, I refocused on the deck. This old cruise ship—seemingly abandoned and peaceful—held hidden dangers that could kill us.

"What was that sound?" I asked, adjusting the gun tucked into my belt.

Asher Weston shifted his attention from our speedboat, bobbing on the waves far below. Hand resting on the sword at his hip, he scanned the deck. "What sound, Kass?"

"I thought I heard a cry."

"From where?"

"I'm not sure. It might've been nothing."

The remaining members of Liberty and Trident Teams climbed the ladder and joined us. None of them had heard a cry.

Asher addressed the small group gathered before him.

"We need to be extra careful, guys. This ship has been un-inhabited since the arrival of the Mist. Terra plants are all over this place. Some are harmless. Others are lethal." He paused. "Plus there might be xans."

Xans.

People glanced around uneasily.

Asher detailed their assignments, finishing with, "Okay, let's get going. Start at the front and work your way back. Seal off or destroy any terras that might endanger our scavenging teams. Most importantly, stay alert and stay alive."

Everyone partnered up, checked their weapons, and set off.

Asher, Harlem, and I headed to the pool area.

Yesterday, one of our scavenging teams had sighted this cruise ship off Ellis Island. Since *Siren of the Seas* had carried over five thousand passengers on its final voyage, Kennedy Team had boarded it, hoping to discover stockpiles of canned goods and medical supplies. At the sight of the dangerous terras next to the pool cafes and the main kitchens, they'd hastily retreated.

We paused near a deck chair and studied the crimson plants that filled the concrete pool.

"Stranglers." I shuddered at the shifting, leafless vines. "No wonder Kennedy Team got spooked."

Stranglers were the first terras I had battled when I'd joined the Weston Battalion six months ago. I still had nightmares about them choking me.

From the pool, a long crimson vine whipped out, intent on snaring the nearest person: *me*.

I darted aside. Felt its tip trail down my arm. Narrowed my eyes, about to mentally remote-push—

With a scrape of steel, Asher unsheathed his sword and swung it at the outstretched vine. A severed piece dropped to the deck where it writhed like a cut snake, spraying the air with blood-red droplets.

"Why didn't you use your sword, Kass?" He pointed to the blade hanging at my hip.

No way could I admit that I preferred to mentally remote-push instead of physically wielding a weapon. "I was about to."

"Be quicker next time." He surveyed the pool area. "Lots of tiles. Good. They should stop the fire from spreading."

"Yeah." Harlem eyed the clump of writhing terras with his usual wariness. "Let's *not* turn this ship into a floating inferno."

The two boys stood on opposite sides of the stranglers. After switching on their portable flamethrowers, they began burning the terras.

I withdrew my sword, watching for xans.

On this shadowy rear deck, terras grew everywhere. Orange rope-vines carpeted the boards. Leafy stink terras clogged the spa. A clump of purple bushes with spiky leaves grew between the outdoor furniture.

I flinched as something scurried across my boots. Just a rat.

Not a xan.

Had it only been eight weeks since the Night of the Blue Meteors? It felt like years.

That evening, thousands of blue lights had arrowed downward from the darkening sky, triggering fear and panic in the remnants of humanity.

Huddled on the flat roof of a high-rise, my team and I had watched several "meteors" strike a skyweb terra that we'd fled only moments earlier. Within minutes, the blazing structure had been reduced to scraps, then ashes.

To me, it had felt as if the scraps of humanity's future—our threadbare hopes and tattered dreams—were also being reduced to ashes. We were barely surviving the terra plants brought by the Night of the Red Mist over a year ago. How were we going to survive the non-terrestrial animals?

Every day since the blue meteors, we had watched. And waited.

So far, no one had seen a single xan.

But we suspected they were here.

Countless thousands were rumored to have arrived with the blue meteors, released in the Second Wave of the Chi'az's terraforming plans. These non-terrestrial animals—*xanimals* or *xans* for short—would probably coexist with the non-terrestrial plants that'd arrived in the First Wave. If their ecological linkup occurred, our world would soon belong to *them*. The Chi'az.

On the deck of the cruise ship, a darkness shifted in the deep shadows that huddled beside an outdoor bar.

Asher and Harlem circled the pool, gazes riveted on the thrashing strangler-vines, their flamethrowers roaring bright streams of death.

Headlamp on, I crunched across a layer of rope-vine terras, checking on the bar area. Beneath me, the boards snapped and crackled—

—then abruptly gave way.

I dropped into a void.

2

"Kass!" Asher yelled.

Desperately I flung out my arms as I fell—

—and snagged a thick vine that stretched across the hole.

Clutching it, I jerked to a halt and dangled in the dark cavity, legs flailing. Around me, plastic deck chairs crashed to the floor below.

Squeaks ripped the air, the high-pitched notes piercing the gloom. A heartbeat later, dozens of tiny bodies exploded from the blackness, wings beating upward in frenzied flight. Within moments, I was engulfed in a whirlwind of sharp claws and leathery wings.

Xans?

No. Bats.

Their panicked cries stabbed my brain like needles, and their claw-tipped wings brushed my hair.

"Kass!" Fifteen feet above, Asher peered over the edge of the jagged hole. Waving off some agitated bats, he cried out, "Are you okay?"

The last of the creatures squeaked upward and flapped away.

"Fine," I replied, dangling from the terra vine. The beam of my headlamp revealed more vines crisscrossing overhead; others trailed down the hole in leafy lengths that brushed dining tables and chairs in the room below.

"Hang on." Asher shucked off his flamethrower. "I'll climb down and get you."

"Thanks, but I don't need rescuing." I let go of the terra vine, dropped a few feet, and scrabbled off a table.

"I'll get a rope." He disappeared and I heard him shouting, "She's okay, Harl. Hey! Watch out for that strangler."

On the floor around me, broken deck chairs lay amid splintered boards, smashed plaster, and twisted electrical wires that hadn't lit a globe or powered music for over a year. My headlamp swept the dimness. Brown-eyed bats blinked in the light. Terra plants swayed in a breeze that gusted through the hole in the deck.

No sign of any xans.

Yet.

Windows bracketed the enormous dining room, their glass panes meshed with velvet-vines that blocked most of the sunlight, creating a dim cave. The floor, tables, and chairs were flecked with stinking bat droppings; when I'd been hiding in the subway tunnels with my twin, Olivia, I'd become so used to their stench that I'd barely noticed it. But my tolerance had faded after my return aboveground six months ago, and nowadays the sharp reek of ammonia stung my eyes.

A shadow passed over me, dark and somehow furtive. I glanced up at the gaping hole. Nothing moved at its edges. The red sky was cloudless.

A strange sensation trickled down my spine like cool flames, then flared across my skin. My muscles tensed against the cold fire. An instant later, the sensation vanished.

Weird.

One end of a rope snaked down from the side of the hole and landed nearby. Moments later, Asher slid down and joined me.

He scanned for injuries, then gathered me into his arms. "You could've been killed."

"Nope, still here." Despite the Red Fever and my terminal leukemia, despite the dozens of terras and the wild animals that had tried to kill me over the last year, I was still alive. For now. "What about the stranglers?"

"Burned and dying. Harl can finish them." Asher stared at the hole in the leaf-lined ceiling. "The terras must've weakened the plaster and the deck." Frustration edged his sexy Aussie accent, along with a touch of resignation.

"Probably," I said. "Those spike terras have tendrils with long spikes. They can anchor the vines to almost anything, including ceilings."

"Where did you hear that?"

I didn't answer. It had been eight weeks since the Night of the Blue Meteors, but I still couldn't say Lynxx's name aloud or acknowledge his existence.

Yet I continued to drink the Lazarus tonic he left for me each week.

If I didn't, I would die.

"Lynxx told you about the spike terras, didn't he, Kass?"

"He gave a lecture on them."

Asher gently took my hands. "What's going on with you two? Why aren't you talking to him anymore?"

I pulled away so he couldn't read the anger and sorrow and confusion in my eyes. "Everything's fine."

It wasn't fine. I'd been avoiding Lynxx since the blue meteors, unable to forgive his shattering betrayal.

Asher sighed. "I guess you'll tell me when you're ready."

I swallowed a bitter laugh. If I told anyone at the garrison the truth about Lynxx—that he was a hybrid and thus our enemy—I'd be signing his death warrant.

Another cry rang out, spiraling upward into a shriek of terror.

It stopped, the notes severed with guillotine suddenness.

Asher and I glanced at each other. Clearly, terra plants, rats, and bats weren't the only things living on this ship.

Our headlamps swept the surrounding darkness, their bright beams stirring twitches of protest from some roosting bats in a corner.

Asher whispered, "I think the cry came from the deck below us. We need to check it out."

Cautiously, we passed through a corridor lined with photos of *Siren*'s last passengers. The smiling people were frozen in happy poses, all blissfully unaware of their oncoming fate.

We entered an area where sunlight streamed through a cracked side window, highlighting a patch of young Lazarus-vine terras growing in the floor. Scowling, Asher stomped through the harmless seedlings, crushing the precious leaves beneath his boots.

Stifling a protest, I turned away. Lazarus terras weren't common, and it was painful watching Asher destroy the only plant in the world that could keep me alive.

He pulled me back. "Careful!"

I'd almost trampled on a pile of gray decomp-dust. "Thanks."

Countless mounds of decomposition dust were still scattered across New York, making them difficult to avoid. Still, I hated walking through the remains of dead people.

We padded down a staircase that grew dimmer with each step. By the time we reached the next level below, we'd been swallowed by a blackness only penetrable by our lights. Squeaks and the stench of rat urine indicated a large rodent population on board.

Asher muttered, "This place really needs some rat-rod terras."

We entered a wide concourse whose length was greater than the stretch of our lights. Something crunched beneath my boots and, jerking back, I saw bone fragments. Human? Animal? Impossible to tell.

Lynxx's warning from the Night of the Blue Meteors once again echoed in my mind. *Our world has just become a lot more dangerous.*

Another cry rang out. Sharper than earlier. Closer.

We paused, listening.

Silence.

Was something crouching in the inky darkness beyond our beams?

Headlamps blazing paths of light, we continued down the concourse and past adjoining stores. Further ahead, a faint glow flickered in the blackness. Guns drawn, we crept toward the orange light that streamed from an open doorway topped with a projecting sign: Siren Theater.

We stopped, ears straining.

In the hours since *Siren of the Seas* had been sighted, had that elusive hybrid Bone and some of his Brethren recruits boarded the vessel? Or had a crew member or passenger survived the Mist?

Asher moved in front of me, ever protective, ever brave.

Heart thundering, I followed him through the glowing doorway.

3

With a gut-twisting screech, something slammed into me. Black and yellow feathers. Huge rainbowed beak.

The bird squawked in panic, darted around us, and disappeared down the corridor.

"Toucan," Asher whispered.

"Maybe that's what I heard up on the deck."

"Unlikely. Their cries aren't very loud."

Guns raised, we moved through the backstage area of the Siren Theater. Crates, equipment, and racks of costumes cluttered the floor. Scattered among them were piles of decomp-dust, plus a dozen shrubs whose flowers hazed the air with a glow—an *orange* glow.

Asher lowered his gun. "The light's coming from these perfume-globes." Bending, he reached for a plump flower. "I almost like these terras. They release an amazing scent when you touch them."

As I leaned toward a blossom, it puffed up, doubling in size. Hastily, I backed away. "Asher, be careful. They're not—"

Too late.

With a sound similar to an old man hawking up phlegm, the blossom spat a stream of orange blobs at Asher's face. Appalled, he staggered back, wiping the foul-smelling globules from his cheeks and forehead.

"Cripes!" He tossed his soiled handkerchief away. "Lynxx warned us about spitters. He forgot to mention they look exactly like perfume-globes!"

"They're harmless."

"Harmless? They spit and they stink!"

I suppressed a laugh at his outrage.

We pushed through the crimson curtains at the front of the stage. Before us, the audience seating rose in tiers that once held hundreds of passengers, and for a moment I could almost hear the echoes of laughter and conversation.

A blink later, the echoes faded into the hush of forever.

Instead of people, the seats were covered by glowing terras. Luminescent wheat terras mingled with glittering shrubs and hundreds of shining spitters. A seagull flew through an open rear doorway, swept across a patch of bright Mozart flowers, and landed in the branches of a tinkling blue bush.

"This place is incredible," I murmured.

"Yeah. Normally I hate terras, but right now I don't."

Covered in fractured rainbows, we gazed at the shimmering garden, reveling in this sliver of beauty in our increasingly bleak world.

"Willow would've loved this." Asher's words were so soft that I wondered if I'd imagined them.

"When's your next search?"

"There won't be any more." In the past two months, he had led multiple searches north of New York, looking for his former girlfriend. "Commander Powell won't risk our remaining chopper, or any more members, on another Hail Mary."

"He told you that?"

"Well, he used kinder words. The message was the same." A sigh slipped from his lips. "He also told me that *wanting* and *believing* are two different things. And he's right."

"How?"

"I want Willow to be alive. Yet deep down I believe she's dead."

"I'm sorry." My heart ached at his pain. "I know how much she meant to you."

Enveloped in rainbowed fragments of light, Asher drew me close. His lips pressed against mine, tender and warm and trembling—and in his kiss I sensed both a farewell to his lost love and an embracing of his new relationship with me.

A howl rang through the cavernous theater.

We jerked apart. Raised our guns. Glimpsed movement above us.

Something was swinging across a mesh of terra vines that covered the ceiling. A fast-moving shape, black and threatening.

What the—?

Our headlamps spotlighted a creature a few feet long. It had a furred body, short snout, and jaws lined with sharp teeth that glinted in the light as it uttered another ferocious howl.

"Xan!" I gripped my gun tighter.

"No, it's one of ours." An Earth animal. "Howler monkey. Stay still. It's warning us to get out of its territory."

Not moving, I murmured, "How did a monkey get aboard this ship? It's been drifting at sea for over a year."

"*Siren* was returning from Brazil when the Mist struck. My guess? Crew members were smuggling exotic animals into the country to sell on the black market."

Above our heads, leaves rustled.

Slowly, I looked up.

Two more howler monkeys clung to the vine-meshed ceiling. At their bared teeth and fierce eyes, my heart stumbled a beat. "Where—?"

With enraged roars, the two animals dropped on us. Their attack was a blur of thrashing black arms and hairy bodies, mixed with deafening cries. Asher struggled beneath a howler as it battered him, shrieking its fury with each blow. I tried to dodge the other animal. Couldn't. It lashed out with sharp nails that blazed pain down my arm.

I screamed, and within my mind something shifted—then burst forth in an invisible blast.

The two monkeys tumbled back. They toppled over the edge of the stage and loped away, howling.

The first monkey was still clinging to the ceiling. Eyes round with fear, it turned and swung across the terra mesh, retreating as quickly as its overlong arms, legs, and tail would permit.

All three howlers disappeared through the rear doorway.

Grasping his bleeding shoulder, Asher stared after them, open-mouthed. "What just happened? Why did they suddenly run away?"

"No idea." But I was lying.

For two weeks after the blue meteors, I had refused to use the mental powers I'd inherited from Lynxx's hybrid blood. By ignoring the alien part of me—denying it even existed—I'd told myself that somehow I was a normal human. Not infected. Not an outsider.

However, I'd soon reconsidered my decision. The world had changed. So had I. Every day, I fought terras that tried to kill me. Since I didn't have my teammates' health, strength, or reflexes, I needed to use whatever power my leukemia-ridden body possessed.

So I'd resumed secretly practicing the mind techniques that Lynxx had shown me before the blue meteors.

At Asher's groan, I rushed to him. He clasped his shoulder, blood streaming down his ripped sleeve. "It got me." His eyes shadowed at the blood that dripped down my arm, onto my hand. "You're hurt too."

"A scratch. Your injury's much worse." I grabbed a first aid kit from my backpack and tore open a gauze pad. Just as I was about to press it to his slashed shoulder, I pulled back with a sudden gasp.

"What's wrong, Kass?"

I heard Asher's voice but didn't see him.

Instead, I saw myself leaning over Lynxx in a courtyard near Grand Central Station. It was six months ago, the day I'd left the bunker in search of my missing sister, Olivia. Lynxx and I had been injured by an exploding buckshot terra pod and, as I'd sewn up his ripped thigh, his blood had soaked into a deep cut in my palm.

At the time, neither of us had realized that his blood would make me different.

"Did you hear something?" Confused, Asher scanned the glowing plants for more attackers.

On my arm, the gash from the howler monkey dripped a steady flow of blood. Shuddering, I pressed the gauze pad to my injury.

I'd almost infected him!

"You need to get another pad," I said, hiding my panic beneath a sharp tone. "Press it to your shoulder."

"I thought you only had a scratch."

"Well, it stings." Even to my ears, the excuse sounded weak and selfish.

When I fumbled to wrap a bandage around my injury, he moved forward. "Let me help."

"I'm fine." I stepped back, putting more distance between my infected blood and him.

In a hurt silence, he clumsily patched and bandaged his injured shoulder.

Tensely, we gathered our gear and traced the passage of our beams down the corridor, then up a new staircase. I searched for a reason to explain my reluctance to help him, but every excuse sounded hollow.

Back on the upper deck, he radioed the others and warned them about the howlers.

Lapsing into a strained silence again, Asher and I turned into a sunlit hall that led to the pool area. Our steps slowed as we came to a long wall covered in pages ripped from passports, all showing photos.

I tried to break the tension between us. "There are thousands of pages up there."

"It's like a wall of remembrance for the dead." Asher's tone was normal and, relieved, I remembered that he didn't hold grudges. He examined bits of the tape used to stick the pictures to the plaster. The once-clear adhesive had aged to a faint brown. "They've been up there for a long time."

The photos were a patchwork of frozen lives, and I could almost feel the somber faces staring at me in mute reproach. *Why are we stuck up here, reduced to images that no one remembers? Why are you alive while we're dead?*

He ran his fingers over the rungs of a nearby ladder. "Someone must've survived the Red Fever. Look at these rungs, Kass. No dust. Someone's been using this ladder to keep the velvet-vines off the wall, away from the pictures." Ripped green leaves littered the floor, their faint scent of lavender suggesting they'd been broken only recently.

Cautiously, we continued down the hall, past its rows of dead faces.

"Where's this survivor?" I murmured.

"I wish I knew," he said. We moved into an art gallery where the velvet-vine terras covered most of the pictures. "He or she might be—"

We stopped.

A woman in a blue dress lay facedown on the carpet, her gray hair haloed by dark blood.

"—dead," I whispered.

4

Gently, Asher rolled the woman onto her back.

A pair of brown eyes gazed sightlessly from a wrinkled face—

—and a bloodied hole gaped in her forehead.

"She's been shot," Asher said, voice low. "Most likely in the past couple of hours." He pointed to the dark puddle on the dusty floor, explaining, "It's still wet."

I glanced around the art gallery with its whispering wallpaper of velvet-vines. "Do you think she was living on this ship?"

"Probably."

"So another passenger or crew member shot her?"

"Maybe. Or it could've been someone who boarded the ship earlier today. The Weston Battalion isn't the only one with scavenging teams."

I nodded. The Wilders, Manhattan's resident biker gang, also scavenged for food and supplies. And so did Bone's cult, the Brethren.

My gaze moved to a small bloody handprint on the woman's blue dress. "That looks child-sized."

Asher picked up a grubby princess doll from the floor. "Maybe a little girl was also on board."

"So where is she?"

"If Wilders or the Brethren killed this woman, they could've taken her with them."

I swallowed, sickened at the thought of a terrified child being dragged off the vessel by strangers. "Or she might still be on board. Hiding."

"Yeah. This ship's enormous. You can bet a kid knows a hundred different hiding spots." He radioed Harlem and the others. Briefly, he filled them in on our gruesome discovery and the possibility of an armed shooter on board, as well as a missing child.

I turned at a loud flutter of wings. A familiar golden eagle with silver eyes flew through the art gallery and landed on a couch.

Clicking off his radio, Asher raised a brow at the former Bronx Zoo resident. "What's WindLord doing here?"

"No idea."

"He must be looking for food." Dismissing the bird, he crossed to a pamphlet stand and passed me a deck plan of the ship. "We'd better try to find that kid."

As we left the art gallery, I threw a last glance at the dead woman on the floor. Despite the millions of decomp-mounds in New York and the billions more around the world, her death still upset me. Perhaps it was because she'd been murdered so close to being rescued.

Or had she welcomed death as an escape from the endless battle for survival after the Mist?

Quietly, we moved down a hallway matted with velvet-vine terras. Beneath my boots, the broken leaves released faint lavender smells, stirring memories of my early childhood: sunny gardens, sleeping cats, warm cookies from my grandmother's oven.

What memories would the missing child have? I wondered. The smell of fresh blood? The horror of being kidnapped by a stranger? Or the despair of being alone in a floating graveyard?

"We need to split up, Asher, so we can cover more ground."

"Bad idea." He swept his light over a patch of white angel-vine terras. "There could be xans on board. Or the shooter."

"We've been watching out for xans since the blue meteors arrived, but no one's seen any. And hopefully the shooter's long gone by now."

We arrived at a lobby bordered by restaurants and stores. Our beams revealed trash, spiderwebs, and more patches of angel-vines. Nothing sinister.

"If we split up," I said, "we can search this area in half the time."

"But—"

"What if the kid's injured? Or shot, like that woman?"

He scanned our surroundings again, saw nothing suspicious, then sighed. "Okay. Be careful. Radio me if you have any problems."

"Same with you."

He began searching the restaurants on the left.

I headed to the stores on the right. Before entering each one, I stopped in its doorway and swept my beam around the dimly lit interior, looking for danger or signs of life. If the room appeared safe, I searched it. If it contained dangerous terras, I marked the location on my copy of the deck plan, then moved on.

Asher and I kept in contact via our radios, and as I walked through the dark abandoned rooms, the sound of his voice comforted me.

Strangely, I was also comforted by the presence of Wind-Lord. The silver-eyed eagle swept in and out of the boutiques and stores ahead of me. Asher was right. The bird was looking for food—yet it completely ignored the rats that scurried across the floor. Didn't eagles eat rats? I made a mental note to ask Lynxx the next time I saw him.

Then I remembered.

Lynxx was no longer my guide, my companion, my friend.

He was a hybrid.

Warily, I entered a clothes boutique. Limp dresses hung from garment racks, and rows of dusty shoes lined the back wall. WindLord flew over to a tall cabinet in a far corner. Squawking and fluttering its huge wings, it tried to pry open the carved door with its beak.

I turned away. "Sorry, WindLord, even if you can smell a tasty critter in there, I don't want to know what it is."

The eagle stopped squawking, and in the sudden silence I heard a faint noise.

A whimper, like a frightened puppy.

WindLord flapped off as I hurried to the cabinet. Wary of a trap, I stood to the side. "Hello. Is someone in there?"

Silence.

Louder, I announced, "I'm a friend."

A faint sniffle from within. It didn't sound like a wild-eyed adult hiding in wait, gun drawn, ready to fire a bullet through the wooden door. Was this the missing child?

Resting a hand on the pistol clipped to my belt, I stepped closer.

"My name's Kass Madison."

More silence.

Time to try some child-speak. "I'm seventeen and a bit. How old are you?"

Another sniff. Then, "Gwen says I'll be eight next week." A little girl's voice.

"Eight's an excellent age. What's your name?"

"Zoey Richards."

"Nice to meet you, Zoey. You must be squashed in there. Can I open the door?"

"Okay."

Inside the cabinet, a small child huddled in a corner, blinking up at me. Strands of greasy blond hair clung to her tear-stained face. Her pink top and frilly yellow skirt were filthy, and she reeked of urine.

"Let's get you out of here, sweetie," I said, picking her up. She wrapped her dirty arms and legs around my body and clung to me with the desperation of a child drowning in a flood of horror.

Murmuring comforting words, I carried her from the boutique. In the hallway, I balanced her on one hip as I contacted Asher.

His reply crackled from the radio. "Good work in finding her, Kass. I'll let the others know. Where are you?"

"At Siren Boutique."

"How did you get there?"

"I'm not sure." I swapped the whimpering Zoey to my other hip. "It sounds weird, but I think I was following Wind-Lord."

I looked around for the silver-eyed eagle.

It had disappeared.

"Let's meet at Seashell Serenade," Asher said. "The restaurant's on your map."

"Okay."

Zoey and I were already seated at a table when he arrived, and his face lightened with relief at the sight of the child.

A broken window streamed sunshine into the restaurant, along with the tang of the ocean. At a flurry of sharp cries, I looked outside and saw seagulls fleeing in panic as WindLord flapped past, ignoring them.

Under Asher's gentle questioning, the girl told us a story we'd already half-guessed.

Zoey and the dead woman, Gwen, had lived alone on this drifting ship since the Night of the Red Mist.

"Was Gwen a member of your family?" Asher asked. "Your mother? Or an aunt?"

Zoey shook her head. "We met after those red sparkles came down from the sky." Her lower lip trembled. "And after everyone started dying."

He hastily steered the conversation to recent events.

Earlier today, Zoey and Gwen had seen four armed men board the ship and start hauling off their remaining sacks of supplies. After telling Zoey to hide, Gwen had gone to talk to the group—the first people they'd seen since Brazil.

From her hiding spot, the child had heard a loud gunshot.

Tears trickled down Zoey's grimy cheeks. "As soon as the bad men left, I tried to help Gwen. She was on the floor. Her eyes were open, but she wasn't breathing."

"Are the four men still on board?" I asked, glancing uneasily at the open restaurant doorway.

"No. They stole our food, then got into a boat. I saw them go away."

Asher placed a gentle hand on the child's shoulder. "Do you know who they were, Zoey?" When she shook her head, he described the jeans, T-shirts, and vests favored by the Wilders.

Again, she shook her head. "The bad men wore gray pants and gray shirts. One had a red armband."

Brethren.

She continued, "I heard one of the bad men say that he hated Gwen."

"Did he say why he hated her?" I asked.

She nodded. "Because she was a member of the spear. No ... the *sphere*. They said she was a member of the sphere. I didn't understand it. What's a sphere?"

"It's a round shape," I told her, "like a globe. Earth is a sphere."

The Sphere. Asher and I exchanged glances. Who was this new group? Were they human or hybrid?

More importantly, were they our allies or enemies?

5

Tumbleweed terra.

Seated on a stone bench in the garrison courtyard, I watched the ball of branches drift past me. This thing, as small as a baseball, would grow into a massive and dangerous floating plant.

Wearily I looked away, too tired to chase after it.

It had been two weeks since Asher and I had found Zoey on the cruise ship. Two weeks of relentless missions, fighting new outcrops of dangerous terras, hacking and slashing and burning them. Dodging death by day—and dreaming about it at night.

"This looks like a sunny spot." Our head chef, Einstein, sat down next to me. He'd gained his nickname because of his resemblance to the famous physicist. Wild gray hair. Bulging gray eyes. And a kind, grandfatherly manner.

I smiled at his flour-smeared white apron. "Been busy?"

"Always. People insist on eating every day." He raised his age-lined face to the watery sunshine. "Ahh, that vitamin D feels good."

"Vitamin D?"

"Sunshine makes it in our bodies. It's necessary for old bones like mine." He looked across the busy courtyard. "That poor child is finally settling in, thank goodness."

I followed his gaze. Zoey sat at a cluttered outdoor table, helping some solemn-faced kids clean swords, guns, ropes, and knives.

"She seems to like her new guardian," I said. Judith's family had all died from the Red Fever. Last week, after Commander Powell asked her to foster Zoey, the woman's grief-dulled eyes had sparked with life again.

A pager on Chef Einstein's belt chirped. "Already?" Sighing, he stood and rubbed the nape of his neck. "Time to get back to the kitchen."

Disappointed, I watched him leave. People in the Weston Battalion eagerly sought the old man's company, finding his friendly conversations a welcome distraction from our growing worries and fears.

In the courtyard, grim adults repaired cars or sweated through battle moves. Others huddled in glum groups or—like me—simply grabbed a few minutes of sunshine.

Thankfully, winter had been unusually mild this year. No snow. No frost. Just cold days and colder nights.

Overhead, the cloudless sky remained a watery red that resembled diluted blood.

New faces were appearing in the garrison every week. Most were locals responding to Commander Powell's latest warnings about the hybrids and xans. He had also posted warnings throughout New York and via shortwave radio messages beamed across the globe: Earth was being terraformed, its vegetation changed to suit a non-terrestrial species called the Chi'az.

Along with a flood of unfamiliar faces, a sense of dread had also spread within the garrison. People were tense and nervous, and many hurried through their chores with hunched shoulders, as though expecting an axe to slam into them at any moment.

At the corner of my eye, I noticed a white mouse poking its head from a pile of boxes. It scampered across the pavers, drawn by the crumbs from my lunch. Nearby, the small tumbleweed drifted through the air, still hunting.

I fought down a familiar nausea. It had been seven days since Lynxx's last Lazarus tonic. Unless he dropped off a new bottle tonight, I'd be sick and throwing up by tomorrow morning.

The tiny tumbleweed sprang.

It shot through the air and landed on the white mouse. The rodent squeaked in fear as the small ball of branches scooped it up—and I glimpsed black front paws.

Memories sparked through me.

I bolted upright, my nausea forgotten.

Mousy?

A glance around the courtyard. No one was watching.

Good.

Eyes narrowing, I mentally focused on the floating tumbleweed with its squeaking prisoner.

Come here, you awful ball of branches.

The tumbleweed shook. It veered off, circled back, and landed on my cupped palms. Scowling, I mentally pushed the branches apart.

The white mouse scurried to the far side of my palm and huddled there, quivering, unhurt. I recognized the familiar ripped pink ear, black front paws, and pink nose.

"Mousy," I cried, delighted. "Where have you been? How did you get all the way to Lower Manhattan?"

Asher appeared in front of me. "Who are you talking to?"

"A much-loved old friend." I showed him Mousy, still cupped in one palm. Casually, I dropped my other hand to my side and crushed the tumbleweed. Its sharp branches dug into my flesh, but I ignored the pain and kept my voice steady. "This little furball used to be my pet. He disappeared from my subway bunker months ago. I thought he was dead."

"You had a pet mouse?"

"Cheap to feed in post-apocalyptic times."

"True."

I noted Asher's outfit. Dark cargo pants. Tan shirt. Multipocketed vest. A rifle hung from his shoulder; a sword was strapped to his hip. Battle gear.

"Don't we have this afternoon free?" I asked. Since the Night of the Blue Meteors, Commander Powell had reduced everyone's leave. Instead of two breaks a week, we now had only one.

Asher shrugged. "Some of us are dropping by Battery Park to help Trident Team. Harlem says the Lucifer terras there are the biggest he's ever seen."

"How's he doing as Trident Team leader?" I remembered how Harlem had beamed with pride at his latest promotion, his second in the last few months.

"Excellent. He can handle the job. He's come a long way since joining the garrison."

"Thanks to you, Asher."

Another shrug. "He just needed someone to believe in him."

I gestured to his shoulder, injured by a howler monkey two weeks ago. "Are you healed enough to swing a sword?" During our daily missions, he had been avoiding large arm movements because of his injury.

"Pretty much. What about your wounds?"

"Almost gone." The long sleeves of my khaki shirt hid my unscarred skin. The howler monkey's gashes on my forearm had disappeared within a day. I was unsure if my fast healing was due to the weekly Lazarus tonic—or Lynxx's hybrid blood in my veins.

Asher's blue eyes studied me, concerned. "You look ill."

"Just tired. But if you need me ..." I struggled to stand.

He pushed me back onto the bench with a gentle yet firm hand. "Stay here. Rest. The team and I can handle the Lucifers. How about we meet up at dinner tonight?"

"Sure."

I watched him climb into a black Hummer containing the rest of Liberty Team. As the vehicle rumbled from the garrison, I wondered when my luck would run out. At the moment, Asher's feelings for me were blinding him. Eventually, though, he would become suspicious of my weekly illnesses. Plus he'd start to question why I always had less energy and stamina than the other girls on Liberty and Trident Teams.

Opening my right hand, I let the crushed tumbleweed fall to the ground. Its branches had pricked my skin, and bright drops of blood—my leukemia-ridden, hybrid-infected blood—dripped onto the dead tumbleweed.

What would happen when Asher discovered my secrets?

I dabbed my punctured palm with a handkerchief.

Nearby, the former secretary of state strolled around the enormous walled courtyard, enjoying the wintry sunshine. As Samuel Preston passed by, people paused in their work and scowled at the politician, hands balled into fists, postures tense. Some uttered insults or threats.

Their anger was understandable.

This man had been part of a government that had failed us. They had known about the Chi'az's terraforming—as well as the existence of hybrids. Instead of warning everyone, Samuel Preston and the other government officials had suppressed the knowledge. Even worse, they'd shackled our opportunity to fight back. After all, how could we mount a defense if we were unaware that a war had even begun?

Fresh nausea rippled within me. I stared at the ground, fighting a growing urge to be sick. I couldn't—wouldn't—throw up in front of all these people.

"You look like you could use this, Kassia."

The breath caught in my throat.

Kassia.

Only one person called me that.

I hadn't spoken to him for ten weeks.

And I'd hoped never to speak to him again.

6

Lynxx stood before me, holding a potted terra and a small bottle of purple liquid.

His golden eyes regarded me coolly.

As usual, his shirt, pants, and leather jacket were all black, as though chosen to blend him into the shadows.

Was that how he saw himself? I wondered. As part of the shadows? A piece of darkness? If so, my rejection weeks ago had probably reinforced his feelings of guilt. *Good.*

I stiffened as Lynxx joined me on the bench, placing the potted terra between us. Eyes narrowed, I studied him, searching for an alien or hybrid feature in his face, his body.

He looked totally normal.

But I knew he wasn't.

Silently, I watched him unscrew the lid of the bottle containing the purple liquid.

"Here," he said, voice as cool as his eyes. "This will help."

The Lazarus tonic slid down my throat like molten silk, easing my nausea. In a few hours, my symptoms would completely disappear, and I'd have six or seven days of feeling normal.

When I'd finished the last drop, I wiped my mouth and grudgingly said, "Thank you."

His attention shifted to the white rodent still in my cupped palm. To my surprise, his cold expression dissolved into warm astonishment.

"Mousy," he breathed in wonder.

The single word held a strange, almost nostalgic, longing.

I blinked. "How do you know his name?"

He stiffened. Then, carefully, he said, "I call all mice that name. It's more suitable than Mickey or Tiny or Snowy."

"I thought you didn't like mice."

"I don't like *rats*."

"Oh. That's right." I remembered his dislike of the scuttling rats in the passageways of Grand Central Station.

An awkward silence hung over us. I was tempted to get up and leave, but the empty tonic bottle kept me seated. Despite my burning anger and hostility, Lynxx still cared enough to try to keep me alive. The least I could do was to treat him civilly.

Trying to ease the strain, I gestured to the terra plant between us on the bench. "What's with the whipper?"

In the plastic pot, a clump of skinny green leaves fanned out from a central root. The leaves were over three feet long, and as a breeze gusted past, they swayed like seaweed in an ocean current.

"I'm giving a lecture on them in the conference hall later today," he replied.

I regarded the terra with distrust. On our missions, Liberty Team had often fought mature whippers, which used their skinny ten-foot-long leaves to whip prey unconscious before digesting them.

This smaller one on the bench couldn't kill a person, but its whips could rip clothes and slice flesh.

The potted whipper terra suddenly lashed at me.

I gasped. Tried to pull away. Watched its leaves whip toward my face and—

—the leaves snapped back to the center of the pot where they huddled together, trembling.

I looked at Lynxx. Saw his stare focused on the plant. And knew.

"Thanks," I said, grateful my face was still intact.

"For what?" he asked, frowning at the plant, controlling it.

"You mentally stopped the whipper from slashing me."

He turned his frown on me. "You could've stopped it."

"I know. But it caught me off guard."

"Have you been practicing your remote-pushing?"

I nodded.

His eyebrows rose in surprise. On the bench between us, the whipper leaves fluttered, as though surprised as well. "I thought you would ignore your new powers."

I glanced around the huge courtyard. The nearest person was Mavis. The old woman sat on a stool about fifty feet away, reading a picture book to half a dozen warmly dressed children sitting on cushions at her feet.

"I don't want to die," I said quietly. "If remote-pushing dangerous terras keeps me alive for a little longer, I'll do it."

"Is that the only reason you're talking to me right now?" he asked, annoyed. The potted whipper leaves stirred, then jerked from side to side. "Because I make the Lazarus tonic that helps keep you alive?"

"Maybe. I don't know. I'm confused."

"By what?"

The long leaves slowly whipped the air.

"I'm confused as to how I feel about you."

"It's crystal clear, Kassia. You hate me."

The whipper slashed out with sharp snaps—but the skinny leaves stayed away from me, still controlled by Lynxx.

"My feelings are more complicated than that," I said. "You knew about the Red Fever before it arrived. You watched people die and did nothing."

"I'm so sorry. I was a different person back then."

"My family, my friends ... They all died. Billions of people died. Of course I feel angry and betrayed by you."

"You've got to understand, Kassia, that I didn't choose to be born a hybrid." The terra leaves became more agitated, slicing the air with multiple strokes. "I didn't choose to be raised by a sadistic hybrid who brainwashed me into complete obedience." The leaves blurred into frenzied whips. "I didn't choose to meet you," he continued, his voice softening. The whipping leaves slowed, then swayed like streamers in a breeze. "And I didn't choose to fall in love with you." The long leaves stretched out and gently stroked my hand.

Lynxx stared at me, his face neutral, his golden eyes guarded.

I wondered if he realized that the whipper terra was reflecting his emotions.

Flustered, I dropped my gaze to the white mouse calmly sitting in the palm of my hand. Changing the topic, I said, "Mousy's not even trying to get away. He remembers me." At a sudden possibility, I asked, "Or am *I* mind-controlling him without even realizing it?" I didn't know whether to be scared or excited by the idea.

"It's possible you're controlling him," Lynxx murmured. "Or maybe he just wants to be with you. Perhaps he still loves you."

I shot him a sideways glance. Was he talking about Mousy or himself?

The whipper leaves twined around my wrists, their touch as tender as a lover's caress.

Flushing, I pulled free of the leaves' embrace. Hands cupping Mousy, I lowered my former pet to the ground. "Off you go, cutie. You don't belong with me anymore. Be careful."

Without a backward glance, the mouse scampered to a pile of boxes and disappeared.

Now, if only Lynxx would disappear from the garrison as well.

We'd been friends once, and maybe I had even loved him a little. But that was before I had known what he was—and before I'd been changed by his hybrid blood.

Ignoring his reproachful gaze, I coldly asked, "What was your role?"

"Excuse me?"

"During the Mist, what did you do? Help spread the Red Fever? Make sure as many people as possible died?"

His face paled. "No! Never. I was a scribe."

"What's that?"

"I took notes on the effectiveness of the Mist."

"You mean, how quickly—or slowly—people died?"

A nod of shame. "Yes."

I felt a twinge of relief. At least his role had been passive. He'd been a note-taker, not a killer. "Is Lynxx even your name?"

"I changed my given name when I turned sixteen. Every newborn hybrid is named after a hard inanimate object like steel, gun, blade, and so on. It's a dreadful tradition."

My mind flashed to the gaunt-faced, cadaverous Bone. So that was how the hybrid had gotten his name. Ironically, he'd probably been cute as a baby. But he'd certainly grown into his ugly name as an adult.

I stood. "Thanks for the Lazarus tonic. Are you okay with leaving the stuff in our regular spot each week?" A place where I didn't have to see or speak to him. Things were difficult enough without adding Lynxx and his secrets to my messy pile of problems. I needed to try to forget what he was. And for that, I needed him out of sight.

"Um, not really."

"Huh? Oh. Do you want to leave the stuff in another spot?"

Commander Powell and a couple of council members approached our bench.

The Weston Battalion leader seemed to have aged five years in the past few weeks. His previous salt-and-pepper hair was now almost totally gray, and his dark eyes were constantly worried.

The black man gave me a brief nod. "Miss Madison."

Wow. I'd been at the garrison for six months, yet the commander still called me *Miss Madison*. He still disapproved of me.

He addressed Lynxx. "Are you settling in okay?"

"Fine, Commander. I've looked at those locations you recommended. The lab on the eighteenth floor should be suitable."

"Excellent. I'll have some men pick up the stuff from your old place. We'll move you in today."

"What's going on?" I asked sharply.

"Lynxx is finally moving into the garrison, Miss Madison. About time too. It's far too dangerous out there on his own." The commander didn't mention that the Weston Battalion couldn't afford to lose Lynxx's brilliant scientific mind. His experiments with the terras—working out their strengths and weaknesses, and devising ways to kill them—were essential in helping the Weston Cell members stay alive.

Lynxx told Powell, "I need to supervise the packing at my old apartment. Some of my terra specimens require careful handling."

"Of course." Powell looked up as Samuel Preston headed toward him. A muscle twitched at the corner of the commander's temple, but his expression remained neutral. "I'll catch up with you later, Lynxx, so we can discuss your mission to Liberty Island." He and the council members crossed to the former secretary of state.

I waited until they were gone before I turned to Lynxx. "Why are you moving into the garrison? You always said you preferred living alone."

"Things change. People change."

"Are you moving here because of me?"

When he hesitated and avoided my gaze, I blushed. How could I have jumped to such an arrogant conclusion? Since the blue meteors, Lynxx's visits to the garrison had increased. He brought over my Lazarus tonics. Lectured on the terras. Advised on terra battle tactics. Traded supplies. During these visits, he could've begun a relationship with someone living in Weston Tower. Someone who was not me.

"Sorry," I muttered, cheeks burning. "I shouldn't have assumed—"

"Of course I'm moving into the garrison because of you," Lynxx stated. "Since the skyweb terra incident, you've refused to see me. If I'm living here, there's a chance we could be friends again. But if my presence makes you uncomfortable, I'll remain at my old apartment in the Ferguson Complex."

I hesitated, then reluctantly said, "No, it's okay. The commander's right. It's too dangerous living out there alone. You're safer in the garrison."

"Are you sure you're okay with me moving in here?"

"Yes."

"Please don't hate me. I never meant to hurt you."

"I know." I glanced at the whipper plant on the stone bench, remembering how it had caressed my hand and gently encircled my wrist. "You say you want to be friends again. Is that all you want?"

"I think *friends* is the most I can hope for."

Uncomfortable, I changed the topic. "What's this about Liberty Island? Since when do you go on missions?"

"Since I found something strange out there the other day."

"What was it?"

"A crater," he replied.

"Like the ones made by the blue meteors?"

"Exactly."

"We've found lots of those craters across Manhattan. We still haven't seen a single xan."

After the Night of the Blue Meteors, armed teams had scoured New York, searching for impact points. We'd found hundreds of craters in parks and roads and buildings, each one smaller than a car. All had been empty.

"The crater on Liberty Island is different," he told me.

"How is—?" I paused, frowning at a middle-aged janitor who hurried across the courtyard.

Quinn was the sole survivor of a large Texan family and a small Texan town. Since he'd joined the garrison last week, his expression had been dazed and his movements zombielike.

Today, the man's craggy face was flushed with fury. He glared at the group containing Commander Powell and the secretary of state.

What is he—?

As Quinn pulled a revolver from his jacket, I yelled "*Gun!*" and lunged forward with the crazy idea of tackling him.

Lynxx grabbed me. "No! It's too late!"

A series of loud shots echoed in the chilly afternoon air. People screamed and ran for cover. Soldiers bolted forward, weapons drawn.

More shots.

I pulled away from Lynxx and gaped at the carnage.

Commander Powell lay crumpled on the ground, his blood seeping across the pavers. Nearby was Quinn's bullet-riddled body.

The former secretary of state lay on his back, one side of his head blown into bloody pieces. My gaze slid past the fragments of brain and skull and settled on Samuel Preston's arms.

They were outflung on either side of him, as though welcoming death.

7

FOUR DAYS AFTER THE assassination of Samuel Preston, Harlem brought our cruiser alongside Liberty Island Dock.

The famous statue soared above us, her torch raised as though appealing to the heavens for help. A mottled skin of ash terras covered her from head to toe, and clumps of gray vines hung from her frame like tattered rags.

Lady Liberty was dying.

Just like Commander Powell.

I looked across the wind-flecked waters of New York Harbor. The distant skyscrapers of Manhattan added a bleak element to the gloomy day. Some buildings, like Weston Tower, stood defiant and untouched against the gray clouds. Others wore capes of terra plants that were growing thicker and heavier each week.

We left a guard with the thirty-foot boat and cautiously proceeded down the long causeway to the island.

In front, Lynxx walked alone. He didn't look back, uncaring whether or not we were following him.

Or was he continuing to ignore me?

He hadn't spoken a word to me in the past four days. He didn't look at me during his lectures, and he ate his meals alone in a corner of the mess hall.

At first I had been relieved that he was avoiding me.

But today I wasn't. Things had changed for the worse.

On the causeway, Pepper and I trailed at the rear. Months ago, she had been suspicious that I'd somehow controlled a warthog trapped in a tumbleweed with us. Eventually, though, her suspicions had faded and we'd become friends.

The others stretched ahead, a diverse group armed with guns and swords and machetes. Two boys even had portable flamethrowers strapped to their backs, like characters from an old *Ghostbusters* movie.

Pepper's blue hair fluttered in the wind as she studied the looming statue of Lady Liberty. "I'm surprised the council approved this mission."

"What else were they supposed to do?" I asked. "Tell everyone to remain in the garrison just because the commander is … is …" I couldn't get the last word out.

"Ill?"

I shook my head. The truth was far harsher.

Earlier, we had learned that Powell's condition was critical. Nurse Ortiz had repaired the bullet wound in his side, but the antibiotics weren't working. The commander was unconscious, his skin as gray as Lady Liberty's, and his foul-smelling wound was infected.

"He's dying," I finally told Pepper. The second word felt like a stone in my mouth, hard and rough.

"But we need him!"

"I know."

Commander Powell was vital to the Weston Battalion.

Even though Asher had initially formed the cell, he now preferred fighting the terras; he wasn't interested in the endless administrative problems of running the garrison. And none of our councilors had the necessary skills to assume command.

The people in the Weston Battalion needed Powell's firm leadership to survive.

Which was why I was desperately working on a plan to keep him alive—a plan that hopefully *didn't* involve me signing my own death warrant.

At a strange *click-click* from the shrubs on our left, Pepper and I halted. Several terra plants made unusual noises, sometimes for defense, at other times to lure curious prey.

Another *click-click*, this time from the shrubs on our right.

The hairs on my arms stood up.

Hand resting on the gun in my belt, I struggled to identify the thick green plants that bracketed the path. Ten feet tall, they looked like hundreds of massive leaf-covered poles stuck in the ground.

"I don't recognize these terras, Pepper," I whispered.

"They're Earth plants."

"Really?"

"Yep." She slapped at a bug crawling on her arm. "My grandma had some in her yard years ago."

More sharp clicks, as menacing as hammers snapping on gun barrels. Each sound was edged with a faint, unearthly quality.

A chill passed through me. Since the Mist, I'd lived through hell. I'd lost my family, my world, and almost my life. For months, my home had been a subway bunker where darkness reigned and unseen things scurried in the shadows. Aboveground, I'd fought a horrifying variety of dangerous terras—and the occasional wild animal—intent on killing me.

I should've been hardened to fear.

And yet these strange clicks stirred an almost primitive dread in my gut.

"They're hiding in the Earth plants," I muttered through dry lips.

"Who? Terras?"

"Maybe."

Pepper's worried gaze met mine. "Or xans?"

The mysterious, elusive xanimals.

Was this why I felt such fear at the sounds? On a deep subconscious level, did I sense that I was hearing otherworldly creatures for the first time? Xans?

Abruptly, the clicks stopped.

Silence.

Barely breathing, I strained my ears.

No clicks. Only the rustle of leaves as a breeze swept through the shrubs.

Asher and the others were waiting for us down the pathway. Hurriedly, Pepper and I told them of the unnerving clicks.

Asher asked his friend, "What do you think, Harl?"

The black boy shrugged. "We can't look into every strange sight or sound or smell these days, bro. There are way too many. We'd never complete a single mission."

Further ahead, Lynxx pointed to an area near the towering statue. "The crater's over there."

Asher gently squeezed my hand. "We'll investigate those shrubs later. Let's check out the crater first."

I nodded. "Sure." Anything to get away from the creepy clicks.

We joined Lynxx. He stood beside a field of waist-high yellow stalks that swayed below Lady Liberty, their dry leaves murmuring brittle secrets to each other.

Harlem peered at the yellow field that extended around the star-shaped base. "I thought wheat terras were green."

"This is a variation of the species." Lynxx waded into the tall grasses. "These plants are harmless. Let's go."

We trudged toward the center, the stalks crunching and breaking beneath our boots.

I wondered what Lynxx wanted to show us.

People had asked him why this crater was *strange* and *different* from the others. Each time, he had only replied, "You'll see."

See what?

I sighed. Just one more mystery to add to the pile.

In the weeks since the Night of the Blue Meteors, the garrison had trembled beneath the weight of frightened speculation. Although the blue objects hadn't been made of rocks, they'd been nicknamed "meteors."

Some members had believed the blue "meteors" were bringing a deadlier version of the Red Fever. These people had rushed to put on surgical masks and panicked at the first sign of a sniffle or upset stomach.

Weeks had passed. No new virus had reared its ugly head.

Others had believed Lynxx's claim that the blue meteors contained non-terrestrial animals.

As week followed week and no xans appeared, an increasing number of members had declared that *nothing* had come down in the blue meteors. They were an astronomical fluke, and Samuel Preston's claims were those of an unhinged survivor.

But I believed Lynxx.

We paused in the field of yellow wheat terras. In front of us, a long gash scarred the dirt before ending at a depression.

Silently, we stared at the crater. Ten feet wide, it looked like all the others we'd seen around Manhattan in the past month—except this one was only a couple of feet deep.

Our Korean medic, Soo-Yun, blinked at Lynxx in bewilderment. "Why we here? Why crater much special?"

"It's shallow," he replied.

"Shallow?" Asher's eyebrows shot up, along with the disbelieving pitch of his voice. "You dragged us out here to see a shallow crater?"

"Yes. All the others were twenty or thirty feet deep."

"What's your point?"

"Isn't it obvious?" Lynxx stepped into the depression. "This one's faulty." He snapped on a pair of latex gloves and withdrew a trowel from his backpack. Kneeling, he scraped at the dirt.

"What are you looking for?" I asked.

A muscle twitched at the corner of his eye. Ignoring me, he continued clearing away the dirt.

Gradually, he unearthed dozens of small cream-colored objects. Some were the size of pigeon eggs, others a little bigger.

He plucked one from the dirt and held it up. Large as a golf ball, the thing hung from his fingertips, floppy, shapeless, like a small cream balloon half filled with liquid.

"This contains a xan."

8

XAN.

I gasped.

Some people swore.

Others babbled out shocked questions.

Lynxx withdrew several items from his backpack. Sitting back on his heels, he balanced a small metal cutting board on his knees, along with a scalpel, tongs, and specimen containers. He placed the floppy, creamy ball on the metal board and picked up the scalpel.

Asher stepped forward. "Wait, Lynxx."

"For what?"

"Is it safe?"

Lynxx rolled his eyes. "The xan's dead."

"Is it *safe*?"

Lynxx gripped the thing between his fingers, holding it on the board. "I've dissected six of them since I discovered this crater last week. None has sprayed me with poisonous gas or acidic blood, so I'm assuming they're safe ... er, safe-ish. But they're not pleasant."

"Why aren't they—?"

Lynxx sliced open the opaque ball. A small, slimy shape slid out—along with a gush of pus-yellow liquid that smelled like a mix of skunk, rotting meat, and blocked toilets.

We staggered back, gagging.

Through my choking and heaving, I glimpsed Lynxx calmly slipping the specimen into a jar with a lid. Did hybrids lack a sense of smell? Or was he merely controlling his disgust better than the rest of us?

Thankfully, the wind quickly dispersed the foul stench.

When I could breathe normally again, I edged forward with the others and stared at the slimy gray shape in the jar.

It looked like a small embryo of ... something. Big blobby head. Tiny curled body. Four stumpy outgrowths that could've been legs ... maybe.

"What is it?" Harlem's question was muffled by his hand covering his mouth and nose.

"Impossible to tell," Lynxx replied. "It's too undeveloped. Plus it's been decaying for over two months."

Asher coughed as though trying to clear the stench from his throat. "Tell us what you know about these things."

"I don't know anything for sure. I'm simply making guesses."

"Okay. Care to share your guesses?"

Lynxx faced the group, his golden eyes skimming past me as if I didn't exist. "I think each of those 'blue meteors' contained hundreds of embryos." He rotated the jar to show us different sides of the blob.

"Why didn't they burn up as they entered the atmosphere?" Asher asked.

"The embryos were probably encased in something hard, perhaps an enormous flexible s of an unknown material. When the 'meteors' struck the Earth ten weeks ago, they buried the shells deep in the dirt. There, the embryos probably remained for a few days, or maybe a few weeks, or perhaps a couple of months—"

Harlem rolled his eyes. "Gee, vague much?"

"—as they developed," Lynxx continued, giving Harlem an irritated glare. "My guess is the shells acted like cocoons. They provided the embryos with nutrition. Or maybe the shells used osmosis with the surrounding soil."

"That makes sense." Booker pushed his wire-rimmed spectacles up his narrow nose. Broughton "Booker" Bennington was an avid bookworm, seldom seen without a battered paperback in his hand or sticking from a pocket. The thin blond boy seemed to prefer living in the fantasy worlds of his novels rather than in the real, post-apocalyptic world.

Totally understandable, I thought.

"What's *os-cro-mis?*" Harlem asked.

"Osmosis," Lynxx corrected. "In this case, it's where the 'meteor' shells draw in nutrients from the soil for the embryos to absorb."

Beneath the rustling wheat terras, I thought I heard another *click-click*. Too faint to be certain.

Lynxx plopped two more cream eggs into specimen containers. "It's rather clever," he said. "Deep in the ground, hidden from sight, the embryos could develop in peace."

Some of my teammates appeared confused at his explanation, but I guessed what he was trying to say.

"Don't some of our frogs do a similar thing?" I asked. "Not with a meteor or shell, of course." I paused, unable to remember the name of the species that Lynxx had told me about. No matter. "These tadpoles bury themselves in mud. Hidden away, safe from predators or harsh climates, they transform into frogs."

"Exactly." Lynxx finally acknowledged my existence. He even gave me an approving smile. "I think that's what was supposed to happen with these embryos. They were engineered to remain deep in the ground—"

Harlem interrupted, "What about the meteors that fell into the ocean?"

"—or buried in a seabed. Once they reach a certain size, the cocoon or shell disintegrates. The freed xans burrow through the earth or swim to the surface, where they continue to grow.

Or maybe some remain underground, developing further. I'm not sure."

At the corner of my eye, something moved.

I glanced over.

An empty soda can rolled across the crater, driven by the wind.

My gaze shifted to some marks near the edge of the depression.

Asher gestured to the cream balls at our feet. "What happened to these?"

"Bad luck, I'm guessing," Lynxx replied. "This 'meteor' didn't burrow deep enough into the ground. The shell disintegrated too early. All the xan embryos died."

"Maybe not all." I pointed to six drag marks that stretched from small holes in the dirt to the edge of the crater. These half dozen trails extended up the shallow earthen wall and over the top, disappearing into the field of wheat terras.

Asher stared at the drag marks, swore, then pointed to Rusty and Pablo. "You two take point. East and west." The two boys scurried to opposite sides of the crater. Rifles cradled, they scrutinized the surrounding wheat terras.

Soo-Yun moved closer to Harlem, seeking comfort from his presence. "Xanimal on island with us?"

"I don't know," Harlem replied, his head swiveling from side to side. "Could some have survived?"

"Maybe." Lynxx took pictures of the trails in the dirt. Later tonight, I guessed that he would plug his camera into his solar-powered computer and download the pictures. "These trails weren't here a week ago. They look fresh."

A flood of questions poured from us.

"Have some xans hatched?"

"Where are they?"

"What do they look like?"

"How big—?"

"How dangerous—?"

"How can we kill them?"

Lynxx tucked his camera into his jacket pocket. "I don't have any answers. I'm in the dark as much as all of you."

I wondered if that was true.

With the tip of his boot, Harlem nudged a cream ball in the dirt. "They're small."

"The day after the Night of the Red Mist," I reminded him, "all the terra plants were as small as confetti. But they grew larger over the following weeks."

Lynxx paused in packing the containers and equipment into his backpack. "Right again." He smiled at me once more.

Did he think we were resuming our friendship?

No way.

For a moment, I was tempted to walk off and leave him to this unearthly cemetery of dead embryos. Instead, I remained in the dirt crater with Lynxx. For Commander Powell's sake, I had to be strong.

But at the thought of what I was about to do, fear flickered within me in a cold white flame.

9

Swords drawn, alert for trouble, Asher and Booker headed back down the pathway to investigate the thick Earth shrubs with their creepy *click-click* sounds.

As people paired up for their assignments on Liberty Island, I casually crossed to my target. "Do you want to swap partners, Soo-Yun?"

"Much yes." Her almond-shaped eyes gleamed with eagerness. As she hurried toward Harlem, she called to him, "I with you now." Beaming, the pair headed off to search the gift stores and infirmary, alert for dangerous terras—and xans.

The others went to the museum and the remaining structures on the island. Since the Weston Battalion hadn't sent any scavenging teams here before, we were hoping to find canned goods, medical supplies, and equipment.

Lynxx stood beside a thick shrub near the foot of Lady Liberty. Using a pair of pruning shears, he took cuttings of its opaque, marble-shaped leaves. Pearl terras. Harmless.

He glanced around at my approach. "I thought Soo-Yun was with me."

"Change of plans."

"Whose idea?"

"Mine."

"I see." A lock of black hair flopped into his eye, and he brushed it away with an impatient gesture. "Why are you here,

Kassia? You don't want to talk to me. Except for the Lazarus tonic, you don't want me in your life."

"I didn't say that." However, I'd thought it.

"Words aren't the only forms of communication. Whenever you look at me, I can almost feel the chill in your gaze."

"Is that why you've been avoiding me lately?"

He gave a weary shrug. "I've never liked the cold."

I remained silent, confused by my warring emotions. Guilt at hurting him, anger at him being a hybrid ... regret for our shattered relationship.

Grit sandpapered my face as the wind picked up strength; a second later, it calmed down again, its wail softening to a mournful sigh.

Lynxx snipped more cuttings from the pearl terra.

The wind faded away, like the final breath of a dying person.

He paused, pruning shears in hand.

A strange stillness settled over Liberty Island. The wheat terras stood upright and motionless, as though listening.

Slowly he looked up, and I followed his gaze. A tattered terra vine that had swayed from Lady Liberty's arm now hung as limp as a hangman's noose. The squawking seagulls above the harbor had vanished, leaving behind a sullen emptiness.

He scrutinized the heavy clouds. The distant Manhattan skyline. The cluttered Brooklyn shore across the water.

Around us, the hush grew thicker. Heavier.

"What is it?" My words were almost a whisper, yet they sounded sharp-edged in the weird stillness.

For several long moments he didn't answer. Finally he replied, "It's probably nothing ..."

"But?"

"... but there could be a storm coming."

"Now?" Alarmed, I glanced at the sky. The clouds were no thicker than when we'd docked. Their gray had shifted into purple, but that wasn't unusual. Since the Mist, we'd seen lots of clouds in unnatural colors. "It doesn't look stormy."

"Not now. Maybe in three or four hours."

Good. Still enough time to put my plan into action—if I was brave enough. A familiar white flame blazed its cold fire across my skin.

I shivered.

"Are you okay, Kassia?"

"Not really." I took a deep breath. "It's Commander Powell. He's dying." Quickly, I told him about the man's spreading infection and the useless antibiotics. "According to Nurse Ortiz, he'll be dead in the next day or so. We have to help him."

"I'm truly sorry about Powell. He's an effective leader. But I'm not a doctor. There's nothing I can do for him."

"What about that orange powder you used when we first met? We were in that passageway of Grand Central Station, remember, and a buckshot terra pod exploded, injuring us. You used some orange stuff to help heal our wounds."

"The xyroxaline powder wouldn't work on Powell. He needs a super-antibiotic, which we don't have." Picking up a plastic bag of terra cuttings, he began walking away, then trailed to a halt. "Unless ..."

"Unless?"

"*Dipthodine exTerrus.*"

"What?"

"Eye-wing terras. They're rare and hard to harvest. But when they're boiled, they produce a super-antibiotic."

"Where can we get some?" When he pointed up, I blinked in bewilderment. "In the sky?"

"In Liberty's torch. There's a large patch growing on the platform around her flame."

"How do you know?"

"I've seen it."

I squinted at the torch hundreds of feet above us. "If the patch is growing *on* the platform, how could you see it from the ground?"

He watched a lone seagull fly through the open windows that formed a band around Liberty's crown. "I was up there a couple of weeks ago."

"You climbed the stairs to the torch?"

"Er ... yes." The way he avoided my gaze stirred my suspicions. What was he trying to hide? "It's a long climb to the platform and it won't be fun. Do you really want these terras?"

"Absolutely."

With a resigned sigh, he said, "Let's get this over with."

I followed him to the high star-shaped base that supported Lady Liberty. "Where's the main entrance?"

"I know a quicker way in, courtesy of some destructive angel-vines." At the spot where two points of the star met, a ragged gap in the stone wall opened onto darkness. "It's much safer if you wait out here—"

"Forget it."

"—but unfortunately I'll need your help in harvesting the eye-wings. They don't like being cut in half."

"Who would?" I asked with a wry grimace.

He smiled briefly, and for a moment I saw the old Lynxx, the one whose face had lit up whenever he'd seen me. Memories flooded me: Watching movies in his apartment. Discussing books we'd read. Practicing remote-pushing. The candlelit dinner in his conservatory. Soft music. Floating flowers. His kiss. My rejection of him.

A small lump formed at the back of my throat.

He piled most of his gear beside the stone wall, then tucked the pruning shears and an empty plastic bag into one jacket pocket and two rolls of bandages in another. "We'll need to move fast."

"Don't worry, I'll keep up. I still have a couple more days before this week's Lazarus tonic wears off. How long did it take you to climb to the torch before?"

"I didn't time myself." Again he avoided looking at me. "Once we're inside the statue, we'll need to be quiet. No chitchat. We don't know what terras are in there."

"But you've been inside recently," I reminded him, watching his face for signs of evasion.

He met my gaze head-on. This time his voice was firm. "You know that things can change from week to week."

Was he still talking about the terras? Or us?

He switched on his headlamp. "There might even be xans inside."

Xans.

The chill of that one word evaporated my earlier nostalgic memories like dry ice.

I looked over the field of unmoving wheat terras, past the harbor waters and jagged skyline, up to the swelling clouds. The windless world that stretched to the horizon was like a photo. Frozen. Artificial. Not ours.

"Keep close, Kassia."

Nodding, I turned on my headlamp.

He picked his way through a dozen large chunks of concrete that had fallen from the gap in the high stone base. Warily, he stepped through the opening, and I followed him into an enormous room that could've been an old lobby.

Our bright beams swept the darkness.

White angel-vine terras grew everywhere, veiled with cobwebs and long-legged spiders. Lizards and rats skittered from our lights, and I glimpsed the flick of a long scaly tail. Snake?

I muttered, "This is going to be fun—*not.*"

He waved me quiet.

When we reached the stairs inside the pedestal, we began our long climb. Our beams stuttered across patches of velvet-vines that clung to the walls, the terras thriving in the musty air and inky blackness.

Lynxx paused at the spiral staircase that led to the crown. Headlamp dimmed, he whispered, "A hundred steps down. A few hundred more to go. Do you want to continue?"

"Yes. Even if it means my expulsion."

"What are you talking about?"

"If the eye-wing liquid works, the commander will want to know what saved him. No one in the garrison is allowed to eat, drink, or use anything from terras. He won't change his mind just because some terras saved his life. He'll be furious. Don't worry, I'll take the blame. I won't tell anyone you helped me." Within me, the cold white flame of fear grew bigger. Brighter. "I could be expelled from the garrison forever."

I wondered how long I could survive in Manhattan alone.

But that was the problem. I *wouldn't* be alone. I'd be by myself in a city containing Wilder bikers, Outrider hybrids, dangerous terras, wild animals—and now, possibly, xans.

Could I really do it? Could I sacrifice my own safety in the garrison to save Commander Powell?

Was his life worth more than mine? Probably.

Was I brave enough to make the sacrifice? I didn't know.

"Kassia, I think you're worrying about nothing. Powell is a male."

"So?"

"As long as we're not caught injecting him with a terra solution, he'll never suspect anything. He'll think he recovered due to his strong male constitution."

Unconvinced, I hesitated. "Maybe." Then I took a deep breath. "Okay. Let's keep going."

In tense silence, we began climbing the spiral staircase, enveloped by a hot claustrophobic darkness. Cobwebs stuck to my sweaty face. Fat spiders dropped onto my head and shoulders, and I rushed to brush them off.

Strangely, the green velvet-vine terras became more wide-spread the higher we climbed. Uncaring of the darkness, they covered Lady Liberty's skeleton of metal beams and struts, and clumps of leaves stirred as roosting bats and scuttling rats tried to avoid our lights.

As we neared the crown, a faint noise came from the thick vegetation on our left.

Click-click.

I froze.

A couple of steps above me, Lynxx turned. "What's wrong?"

"What was that sound?" I whispered, clutching the staircase railing.

"What sound?"

Around us, the blackness breathed as if alive. Or was I hearing the breathing of things crouching in the darkness, hiding among the velvet-vines? Watching us.

A faint creak of metal from my left. "Did you hear that, Lynxx?"

He nodded. "It could be anything. The wind. Or rats." He glanced at his watch and started up the stairs again. "We need to keep going."

I trailed after him, feeling the weight of hidden eyes on us.

Finally, we reached the ladder that led to the torch. As I climbed the rungs behind Lynxx, I mentally urged him to go faster. The skin-crawling darkness inside the statue was un-nerving. I longed for daylight and fresh air.

But as I followed Lynxx outside, onto the circular viewing platform below the torch, a ferocious wind slammed into us. Hunched over, we crouched beside the wrought iron railing and peered through the ornate rim.

The breath caught in my throat.

10

THICK PURPLE CLOUDS STRETCHED from horizon to horizon. They smothered most of the daylight and saturated the air with menace.

Lynxx raised his voice above the howling wind. "The storm's hitting much earlier than I expected. It's too dangerous up here. We have to go back down."

I was tempted. Even the clicking darkness inside the statue seemed safer than this wild, windswept world.

But I couldn't leave.

Commander Powell had given me a place to sleep, food to eat, a chance to live. And he'd done the same for many others. In the past month alone, the garrison's population had swollen to over five hundred members. Strangers arrived every week, drawn to Weston Tower by fear, Powell's posted warnings, and a need to band together against a new, unseen enemy.

The members of the Weston Battalion needed Commander Powell. Alive.

"We have to get the eye-wing terras," I cried. "Where are they?"

"Kassia—"

"You can go back inside, but I'm finishing the job."

With a resigned shake of his head, he moved forward, hunched against the wind. I followed him, my boots creating footprints in the gray moss on the platform. A vague memory stirred. Pausing, I used my knife to snap off a small piece of "moss" and warily inspected it. The moss was actually tiny plants bunched together. As the wind deflated into a breeze, I caught a whiff of vanilla.

Showing Lynxx the piece of moss, I said, "I saw this stuff a few days after the Night of the Red Mist. It's sharp, so don't touch it."

"I know. It's *Riddiin exTerrus*. Rust-moss terras. They eat metal."

Tiny gray terras that ate metal ... like on the Brooklyn Bridge.

My mind flashed back to a week after the Mist's arrival, and once again I was watching the Brooklyn Bridge crumple into the East River, hearing the terrified screams of people, smelling the smoke and spilled jet fuel.

Shuddering, I pushed the memories away.

Lynxx pointed to a patch of wing-shaped white leaves on the deck, each with a red eyespot in its center. "Eye-wings."

A breeze ruffled the terras, and the leaves shifted and nodded like dozens of eyes watching us.

"Good name," I commented dryly.

He withdrew his pruning shears and handed me a plastic bag. "Here's what you need to do." He detailed the eye-wings' defense system.

When he finished, I looked at him uncertainly. "Are you sure you want to do this?"

"Actually I don't," he replied, withdrawing two rolls of bandages from his pocket. "But they're our only shot at getting a super-antibiotic."

He wrapped his wrists and forearms with the bandages. Then we took up our positions.

Keeping as far from the eye-wings as possible, Lynxx stretched forward and cut the first stem. Two other eye-wings struck. Long tendrils, thin as dental floss, whipped from their eyespots and slashed at him. He jerked back. Too late. The tendrils slashed through the bandages and wrapped his wrist. Squeezing, they cut into his flesh.

I darted forward and severed the tendrils with my knife; Lynxx yanked the remaining pieces from his wrists.

"You're hurt," I said.

He glanced at me, surprised at my concern. Then, wincing in pain, he looked at his wrist. A thin red band encircled it, dripping blood onto the rust-moss below.

"The eye-wings never miss," he told me, disgusted. "They're fast."

"And sharp. They sliced right through the material!"

He returned to the battle, swapping his pruning shears from hand to hand every minute or so. Each time it was the same thing. He cut a leaf. Tendrils darted out and whipped around his wrist. I slashed the tendrils apart. They dropped to the platform, leaving thin bleeding lines in his flesh.

By the time we'd gathered nine or ten eye-wings, the platform was splattered with his blood.

Throughout the procedure, Lynxx didn't utter a single complaint, despite the pain that etched itself deeper and deeper into his face.

My guilt rose with each of his cuts. "I'll take a turn collecting the eye-wings."

"No."

"I'm a fast healer, like you. I can handle the cuts."

"I've never deliberately hurt you either physically or emotionally. I'm not about to begin now." Shears in hand, he resumed the battle.

His words rang in my mind—and their sincerity dissolved some of the anger and betrayal I'd felt since discovering he was a hybrid.

By the time we had enough eye-wings, the gray rust-moss around him was almost red with blood. Guilt-stricken, I pulled a first aid kit from my backpack. Although Lynxx muttered that he was fine, he held his wrists out. As I bandaged them, I pretended not to notice that he was watching me, his face softened by longing.

A mournful blast of a horn startled us.

Tying off the last bandage, I said, "That's the signal to get back to the boat. It's early. Something must be wrong."

I peered over the side of the platform. Far below, people were racing down the wooden jetty toward the cruiser.

Alarmed, I looked around. Heavy swollen clouds darkened the land, and the harbor waters seethed with rough black waves. A savage wind shook Liberty's platform, triggering metallic groans from the statue.

Lynxx tucked the plastic bag of eye-wings inside his jacket. "Let's get off this deck."

We headed for the ladder, pushing against a wind that pummeled us. One savage gust threw me back a step and I staggered, trying to keep my balance.

Beneath me, the mossy gray deck snapped and crumpled.

An instant later, I dropped into a growing hole, my heart jerking in shock as—

—Lynxx grabbed my arm, his grip firm and strong.

Heart hammering, I dangled hundreds of feet above the ground, my legs kicking the air. "Lynxx!"

Slowly, straining with effort, he hauled me up, up, onto the deck and away from the hole. I clung to him, grateful for his fast reflexes, for his strength ... for him.

"Are you hurt?" he cried.

"N-no."

The deck creaked. It began to tilt.

We bolted for the exit. Our beams carved passages in the inky blackness as we clambered down the ladder, then barreled down the winding stairs. I no longer cared about the earlier clicking sounds. All I wanted was to get out of this place. Off this island.

Above the pounding of our boots, I could hear the wind battering Lady Liberty, who uttered creaks of protest.

Finally we reached ground level and raced through the wide gap in the stone base. Outside, the shrieking wind, increasingly vicious, tried to push us back inside. When my steps slowed a little, Lynxx grabbed my hand and pulled me along, into the field of wheat terras.

Above us came a crack, loud as thunder.

I glanced up.

Lady Liberty's upstretched arm was moving sideways. Slowly, it snapped away from her body.

Tons of copper plates and steel beams plunged downward.

11

Lynxx and I turned and dived back through the ragged gap in the stone base, into the lobby.

Liberty's massive arm crashed onto the wide base above us with an earthshaking explosion. Chunks of metal and concrete slammed onto the ground beyond the base, lethal as bombs.

Huddled in the dark lobby, I heard the wind howling in triumph, as though celebrating its mutilation of the famous statue. Seconds passed, then a minute. When nothing else crashed down, we peered through the gap. Outside, huge pieces of gray metal lay scattered among the wheat terras, and I recognized bits of the hand and torch.

The wind's howls grew louder, stronger.

"Let's go," I said, anxious to return to our boat.

"Not yet. We need to stay here until it's safe."

"Why?" Then I remembered the small gray terras that covered the statue from head to toe. "Oh. Right. The rust-moss."

He nodded. "They must've weakened the arm. Probably other parts as well. In this windstorm, the rest of the statue could crash down at any moment."

Click-click.

I whipped around, headlamp scoping the lobby behind us. It looked unchanged. Angel-vine terras still wore their veils of cobwebs. Spiders stalked beetles and bugs. Darkness reigned.

Click-click. Click-click.

The noises were faint. Hard to hear over the windstorm.

Lynxx whispered in my ear, "I think they're out in the corridor."

"So you heard it too?"

He nodded.

Clickclickclickclickclick.

The creepy sounds pierced the blackness, moving closer.

I shuddered. "We've got to get out of here. They're coming." Whoever or whatever *they* were.

Lynxx wrapped his arms around my waist, holding me tightly, and he bent his mouth to my ear. Breath hot on my skin, he whispered, "Don't move."

I stiffened in his embrace.

The wind dropped, revealing a new sound.

Hisses. Inside this lobby with us.

The shadows shifted as shapes emerged from their leafy hiding spots. Twenty. Thirty. More. Rattlesnakes. Most over ten feet long. Black eyes glinting in our beams. Wriggling toward us.

Another whisper in my ear. "Don't remote-push unless you have to."

I gave a faint nod. Even though I longed to mentally remote-push the rattlers away, I resisted the urge. Lynxx had once been my teacher, and in this area I still trusted him.

The scaly bodies slithered closer, closer. Moving fast.

My heart pounded against my rib cage.

I held my breath.

They reached us.

Mere inches from our feet as …

… they kept going.

The snakes poured out through the gap, into the ferocious wind, and disappeared among the churning wheat terras.

Pulling free of Lynxx's arms, I gasped in air, my body shaking. When I could finally talk again, I whispered, "Why didn't you want us to remote-push them away?"

"There were too many to control. We could've ended up triggering multiple attacks."

"So why didn't they bite us?"

Frowning, he scanned the dark lobby. "They weren't interested in us. They just wanted to escape."

"From the storm? But they left this place—this shelter—and went outside, into it."

"They weren't trying to escape the storm," he said. The clicks grew louder in the lobby. "They're trying to escape *them*."

"Xans?"

"I'm not sure. But if full-grown rattlesnakes are afraid of the clicks, then we need to be afraid too." Outside, the wheat terras were straightening up. "The wind's dying down. Let's get out of here."

We plunged through the gap, into the open, and looked back. Above us, the Statue of Liberty still stood, stoic at her mutilated pose. Most of her upright arm lay broken on the wide base, with smaller bits on the ground further away.

We raced across the front of the monument's base and around its side, dodging pieces of broken metal as we headed for the overgrown path that led to the dock.

"My pack!" Lynxx cried, stopping. "I forgot it. My xan specimens are inside."

"Leave them. You can always come back later when it's safer."

"No way. It'll only take a few minutes."

"What about the rattlesnakes? And those clicks?"

"I'll be fine." He began racing back. "Meet you at the boat."

"No, I'll wait here," I called after him. "Yell if you need help."

"Okay." He disappeared around the side of the base.

A shout came from my left as Asher ran up the path, a hand on his sheathed sword.

He grabbed my shoulders and scanned for injuries. "Are you hurt? We saw Liberty's arm come down, and when you weren't on the boat—"

"I'm fine. Lynxx too."

"Good. Where is he?"

"Gone to get his backpack. It's got the xan embryos."

"Everyone's on board, waiting. We need to leave!" He glanced at the heavy clouds. "That windstorm could get stronger again at any second."

Something moved among the thick wheat terras next to him. A heartbeat later, a large rattlesnake slithered from the dry stalks.

Eyes widening, Asher reached for his sword.

Too late.

Mouth gaping, fangs sharp, the snake lunged at his leg.

Instinctively, I remote-pushed.

The rattler flew through the air, as if kicked by a footballer. It landed on a far patch of grass and wriggled off, toward a pile of rocks.

Asher gaped at the fleeing snake. "What the—?"

Hastily, I pretended astonishment. "I know, right? But how? The wind?"

"I guess so." He looked at me, baffled. "Except it wasn't that windy a few moments ago."

I shrugged in fake bewilderment.

When Lynxx joined us with his retrieved pack, we hurried to the cruiser.

The instant we were aboard, Harlem powered the boat away from the dock and across the rough black waters, through the lashing wind.

Slumped at a window, I watched Liberty Island recede into the distance, relieved to be leaving that creepy place.

And worried about what I had to do at Weston Tower.

Please, please don't let me be expelled.

12

AT THE GARRISON, WE unloaded the supplies and equipment salvaged from Liberty Island.

After a hurried meal in the mess hall, I slipped away from the others and took the elevator to the eighteenth floor.

Lynxx's lab occupied a massive space cluttered with benches and equipment. Some of the scientific apparatuses had belonged to labs set up in Weston Tower before the Mist; the rest had either come from his previous lab or had been brought in by scavenging teams.

Lynxx was alone, stirring a beaker of bubbling liquid that smelled almost as bad as the xan embryos we'd found a few hours earlier.

He barely glanced up at my approach. "The eye-wing liquid won't be ready until morning."

"Oh. Okay." Unsure how to make small talk with him anymore, I left.

The night stretched on, each minute an hour. I tossed and turned in bed, unable to sleep. Again and again, I reviewed my plan, searching for flaws. It seemed simple. Pick up the eye-wing liquid from Lynxx. Pretend to visit another patient in the infirmary. Slip into the commander's room when no one was around. Inject the unconscious man with the super-antibiotic.

And hope I didn't get caught.

If I did, I'd be expelled from the garrison.

The thought of leaving Weston Tower was like a vise tightening around my heart. My tiny ex-office cubicle wasn't much, but it was the only home I'd known since Olivia's death. And Liberty Team was my substitute family.

In the morning, I casually strolled into the infirmary, my stomach twisted in knots. In my jacket pocket, the syringe of yellow eye-wing liquid that I'd just picked up from Lynxx felt like a stick of dynamite, its fuse lit.

I greeted the few patients in the main ward and headed down the corridor to the commander's room.

Voices babbled inside.

Oh no. Was I too late? Had he died?

I peered around the doorjamb. Commander Powell sat propped against a pile of pillows, eating the soup that Nurse Ortiz was spooning into his mouth. An intravenous drip poked from one hand, and the infirmary's tuxedo cat, Fluffy, lay curled at his feet. Beside his bed, two councilors babbled about miracles, while Nurse Ortiz declared that Powell's physical fitness plus her dedicated medical care was responsible for his amazing recovery.

I heaved a relieved sigh. The commander was going to live.

But as I hurried from the infirmary, the councilors' words rang in my ears and I scowled.

A miracle? No way.

A few minutes later, I stomped into Lynxx's lab.

He looked up from his microscope. "How did it go?"

"Don't play innocent," I snapped. "When did you give Powell the eye-wing liquid?"

"In the middle of the night."

"Why? It was my responsibility. My risk to take."

"You might've been caught. I'm better at clandestine operations."

"Obviously." Sighing, I withdrew the syringe he'd given me from my pocket. "So, what's this yellow stuff?"

"Food dye and water." He bent his head to the scope's eyepiece, signaling that our conversation was over.

Confused by my conflicting emotions—gratitude for Lynxx's actions, distress at being further in his debt—I left.

Three days later, Commander Powell's condition had improved so much that he was able to return to work. As Lynxx had predicted, Powell simply assumed that his strong constitution was responsible for his recovery, and he threw himself back into his duties. At a reported sighting of the Outrider, Bone, in New Jersey, he assigned three squads to capture the hybrid.

Each returned empty-handed.

Bone and his Brethren recruits had vanished.

Over the next few days, Lynxx and I entered an uneasy truce. We exchanged short greetings in the mess hall. He occasionally called on me during question time at his lectures. And I stopped avoiding him.

Following our trip to Liberty Island, the search for xans intensified, spurred on by the sight of Lynxx's blob-like specimens.

However, despite several return trips to Liberty Island, we couldn't find any living xans, just more dead ones in the crater. And the earlier clicking sounds had ceased.

But I knew the xans were around.

Somewhere.

13

Weeks passed, then a month.

Still no sightings.

By the time March neared its end, most members had started wondering if the blobby embryos had been xans after all. Lynxx still insisted they were, but many were reluctant to believe his unpopular view.

As we entered April, the weather changed to warm, sunny days. Weary from battling the terras, we hoped for heavy rain or super-windy days—anything for a break from our daily workload. But the weather remained fine. No rain. No wind.

Tempers frayed under the endless back-to-back missions.

When there still weren't any sightings of actual xans by mid-April, Commander Powell relented a little. He cut a shift from everyone's schedule, giving us an extra ten hours of free time each week.

Immediately, morale improved.

Some people arranged sporting matches. Others binged on DVDs of their favorite television shows or movies. Avid fishermen took out boats, dropped lines, and pretended they were back in happier times.

On the last Saturday in April, I joined Asher and a large group of teenagers and twentysomethings at Coney Island Beach, south of Weston Tower. As the sunshine dimmed into dusk, Asher posted soldiers at the perimeter and we unpacked wood from our trailers.

An hour later, we had built a huge bonfire of small logs and branches, stacked in the traditional teepee shape. Music blared from an old boom box, powered by rechargeable batteries. A few bottles of clandestine beer made the rounds, barely enough for a couple of swallows each—but as girls giggled and flirted and boys bragged and shouted macho boasts, I wondered if the bottles had been spiked.

Then I realized that my colleagues weren't drunk on alcohol.

They felt as I did: heady with the joy of having fun. We were away from work and the daily battle for survival. For a few shining hours we could be young and carefree.

As fire licked the pyramid of branches, some people sat on the sand, watching the dancing flames. Others played ball or chased each other into the lapping waves, laughing as they splashed in the shallows. Further along the sand, several couples sought privacy in the shadows of some harmless terra bushes.

On the beach, Soo-Yun had laced up her pink satin ballet slippers—a cherished gift from Harlem—and was practicing ballet routines in front of him.

Seated on the sand, Asher wrapped an arm around my shoulder. "I'd forgotten how good it feels to do normal things again."

"Totally." I shifted my gaze to the blazing bonfire. "And I'd forgotten how nice a fire can be."

"What do you mean?"

"Almost every day we handle fire like a weapon, using its brutal flames to destroy terras. This bonfire's different; it's warm and comforting and beautiful."

He leaned closer to my ear and murmured, "It's not the only thing that's beautiful."

Blushing, I nestled against him, filled with a warmth that had nothing to do with the bonfire.

Beyond the stretch of beach, amid the tall buildings that edged the sand, a lion's roar echoed in a street canyon.

People paused. Soldiers raised their guns. Seconds ticked by as we watched. And listened.

Another roar, a little further off.

Asher called out, "It's okay, guys. I think he's a mile or so away."

At the bonfire, Lynxx glanced up from doodling in the sand. "Or it's closer." He looked bored, and I wondered why he'd urged us to come to this particular beach tonight.

"A lion's roar can be heard up to five miles away," Asher said. His face softened, as though thinking of Zimba, his "fur-brother" from the Bronx Zoo.

A third roar, even further off than the last.

Relaxing, people resumed their activities—but I noticed they kept their guns and swords and machetes nearby. I sighed. We weren't quite normal teenagers after all.

At the far edge of the darkening ocean, the red sun slowly deflated below the horizon.

Closing my eyes, I leaned against Asher's firm chest. The salt spray and lapping waves melted the years away, and once again I was a seven-year-old at the beach.

Laughing, Olivia and I play Frisbee at the water's edge, and my parents hold hands as they sit beneath a beach umbrella.

That day, I'd been a happy, healthy child who'd thought the sunshine would last forever.

Sighing, I opened my eyes. A dozen soldiers with semiautomatics patrolled the area, watching for unwelcome guests. In a darkened and near-empty city, the bright light from a bonfire could draw dangerous gatecrashers: bikers, wild animals, tumbleweed terras, or even the mythical xans.

A small crab scuttled across the sand, unnoticed by Asher, and he stretched out his leg, almost crushing it. Idly, I remote-pushed the critter aside, allowing it to scurry away safely.

Asher watched Pepper casually wander across the sand toward Lynxx.

"Finally," he murmured.

"What?"

"I think Pepper's about to make her move." When I looked at him in confusion, he merely said, "You'll see."

14

Ultra-casual, Pepper sat down next to Lynxx.

Her short blue hair gleamed in the firelight, and a sudden breeze flared her locks around her head like a blue halo. Like most of the girls here tonight, she'd swapped her stained work clothes for a pretty dress with spaghetti straps. A line of tattooed red, white, and blue stars trailed down her toned right arm. Brown eyes gleaming in the firelight, she chatted and laughed with Lynxx.

Surprise washed over me. My friend had never mentioned being interested in Lynxx. "How long has she liked him, Asher?"

"A few weeks."

"She told you?"

"It was obvious from the way she watches him. Haven't you noticed how she lights up whenever he enters a room?"

"No." I'd been too busy with everything else in my life. How could I have been so blind? Pepper was my closest friend in the garrison. If she was interested in Lynxx, should I warn her that he was a hybrid? That he was off-limits?

Asher told me, "I've seen Lynxx behave in the exact same head-over-heels way."

"With Pepper?" I asked, a catch in my voice.

"With you. He used to look at you the same way that Pepper now looks at him."

Used to? When had Lynxx stopped? From the way he was smiling at Pepper, their heads close together, he was clearly enjoying her company.

I shrugged. "It's good he's moving on."

"You're not upset?"

"Lynxx and I are friends, that's all." I paused before softly admitting, "Besides, I'm exactly where I want to be. With you."

Asher smiled, his eyes reflecting the bonfire. Something else also burned in them, a heat and passion that blazed brighter than the nearby flames. Slowly, his fingers traced a passage from my shoulder, down my bare arm, to my hand. "Now that Lynxx is occupied with Pepper, maybe you'll notice ..." His words trailed away.

"Notice what?"

"... the way *I* look at you. How *my* face lights up whenever I see you."

"Really?" I whispered, wondering how I'd missed these things as well.

"Really." He bent his head to mine, and his kiss burned with that same intense heat I'd seen in his eyes.

Standing, he held out his hand, and we moved beyond the glow of the bonfire, into the privacy of the shadows.

A few minutes later, our kisses were interrupted by a loud cough.

Lynxx stood a few feet away, his face expressionless. "It's starting, guys."

"What's starting?" I asked him, hastily standing.

He watched me shake sand off my clothes. Like Pepper, I'd swapped my battle garb for a pretty dress, and my auburn hair hung loose and free. As Asher brushed sand from my locks, Lynxx quickly looked away, as though unable to bear the sight of ... what?

Me?

Or Asher touching me?

Again, I asked Lynxx, "What's starting?"

"The reason I suggested this place. I thought you'd like it, Kassia, but you were so … busy … you almost missed it."

On the beach, someone had turned down the music. People no longer laughed or played or chatted. Except for the crackling bonfire, the evening was filled with a strange stillness.

And as I looked around, I realized why Lynxx had wanted to show me this beach.

15

A sea of stars.

Millions of gold stars seemed to have fallen from the night sky. They covered the water and washed to the shore in gold waves that transformed the moonlit sand into a wide glittering ribbon.

Mesmerized, I whispered, "What—? How—?"

Lynxx moved closer, wanting to share my astonishment. "*Denastiin exTerrus*," he said, smiling. "Star-algae terras. Tiny and completely harmless. I saw them last night when I was out gathering new specimens."

"Incredible," I breathed.

"They're prolific but short-lived. They only shine for a few minutes each evening and only last for a few days. By tomorrow they'll probably be gone."

"Then I'm so glad we came here tonight."

Asher scooped up a handful of gold-flecked sand. Grinning, he watched it stream through his fingers in small, sparkling waterfalls. "Nice."

Lynxx's smile remained focused on me. "You look like you're covered in star-fire, Kassia."

I glanced down. Hundreds of gold specks shimmered on my dress and legs. Laughing, I whirled around, arms outstretched, yellow dress flaring—and my twirling sent gold streaks trailing through the air, as if I were on fire and throwing off sparks.

The sand shifted beneath my feet. Suddenly unsteady, I staggered to a halt, wondering if pure joy was as intoxicating as alcohol.

Again, the sand shifted beneath me.

I jumped back. Stared at the sand.

Not my imagination this time. And definitely not caused by joy or alcohol.

Below the surface, a small apple-sized lump was moving quickly, the sand rising and falling in its path. Elsewhere on the beach, people shouted and leaped aside as other lumps traveled beneath the sand.

Lynxx hurriedly stepped between me and the nearby burrowing shape.

The thing stopped a few yards away. It vibrated beneath the surface, then disappeared, leaving the sand flat.

Asher snatched up his sword. "Where did it go?"

"No idea," I said, grabbing a gun from my bag.

The soldiers at the perimeter maintained their positions, alert and ready. The rest of us gripped our weapons as we watched the sand.

"It's got to be xans." Asher scanned for movement. "No Earth animal can travel that fast underground."

Xans.

Please be wrong. Please be wrong.

In the cloudless night sky, a full moon bathed the beach in brightness. Despite my fear of the unseen burrowers, I grieved as millions of the gold specks winked out across the ocean and sand, like fireflies dying en masse.

"There!" Harlem pointed.

A small shape tunneled through the sand, heading for the terra bushes beyond the beach.

Shouts erupted as other shapes burrowed in various directions.

"That way!"

"No, behind you."

"There's another one!"

"Go left."

Booker dropped his paperback and plunged his sword into a lump of moving sand. His weapon emerged unstained. "What's going on? They keep getting away."

"I think they can sense vibrations in the ground," Lynxx explained. "When they feel our footsteps getting closer, they go deeper."

"They're xans, right?"

"Maybe. But terra vines such as stranglers and tentacles can both move quickly through the soil too."

I shuddered, remembering the fighters we'd lost to those particular plants.

Something burst from the sand. It arced through the air and slammed down near Harlem. Warily, he picked up a crushed object. "An old soda can. It looks like it was spat out."

Across the beach, other geysers sprang into life, spurting upward. The loose granules fountained high into the air, then rained down with faint hissing sounds that triggered a memory. A few hours before the Night of the Blue Meteors, Lynxx and I had been climbing a massive boulder in a park when it had suddenly gushed seeds high into the air.

"Maybe they're boulder terra seeds," I suggested.

Pepper grabbed some latex gloves from a bag of supplies, ran to a geyser, and returned with a handful of grains. "They don't look like seeds," she said, holding them out. "It's sand."

"You're right." Lynxx scooped the grains into a petri dish. "I'll confirm it under a microscope later. Thanks, Pepper."

The blue-haired girl flashed him a pleased smile.

My gaze lingered on Lynxx and Pepper. "Sand doesn't jet high into the air like a geyser."

"Hey, guys," Booker called out. "Over here."

We gathered around a hole he'd dug in the sand. A small tunnel, barely large enough to fit a baseball, extended from either side of the hole.

Soo-Yun moved closer to Harlem and slipped a hand into his. Nervously she asked, "Strangler terra make tunnel in sand?"

"Maybe," Harlem replied.

I desperately wanted to believe that terra plants had made the tunnels. I also hoped the terras had produced the spouting geysers and the shifting trails in the sand. The only other possibility—non-terrestrial animals—was too frightening to think about.

A cry broke out, ragged with fear.

We raced to a spot further up the beach. At the bottom of a large hole, a soldier, Brian, was struggling in the loose sand. Like quicksand, it had already swallowed his legs and hips and was gulping its way up his chest. He sank further, arms flailing like a drowning swimmer.

"Help! Get me out. It's eating me!" Brian's desperate pleas dissolved into a shriek of pain.

Asher, Harlem, and a couple of other boys grabbed Brian's arms and pulled.

My skin crawled. Only minutes ago, the evening had been lit by fallen gold "stars," and I'd been warmed by Asher's kisses and passionate embrace.

Now the darkness seemed saturated with a cold, unseen menace.

Grunting, the boys gave a mighty heave and finally dragged Brian from the hole. As the man staggered to the bonfire, the firelight flickered across his shredded pants and bloodied right leg.

Soo-Yun shifted into medic mode and snatched up her first aid kit. Pressing a wad of sterile bandages to the long gashes on Brian's thigh, she cried, "What eat you?"

The soldier shuddered, his eyes squeezed shut in pain. "I don't know. One moment I was standing there, wondering why the sand was moving. And then I was falling into a pit that kept getting bigger and bigger."

Soo-Yun lifted the wad of bandages from Brian's thigh. Strangely, no blood streamed from his injury. She washed his wounds, then wrapped his leg with fresh bandages, her movements confident and practiced after a year of training at the infirmary.

"Interesting," Lynxx said. "Whatever attacked Brian must've used a coagulant. It stops the blood from flowing."

"Why use a coagulant?" Asher asked.

"Rapid blood loss can cause rapid death. The attacker must've wanted him fresh and alive."

Confused, I said, "I didn't know that tentacle terras and stranglers kept their prey alive for a while."

"They don't," Lynxx replied quietly.

His two-word answer skated around a single, unspoken word.

Xans.

Booker shouted, "Look!"

Further down the moonlit beach, several small shapes emerged from holes in the sand. Rifles raised, the soldiers raced toward them, but the rat-sized creatures skittered across the shadows and disappeared into a grove of thick terra bushes.

"What those thing?" Soo-Yun cried.

No one answered.

"We need to get Brian back to Weston Tower." Asher glanced at the somber faces around him. "Let's call it a night, guys. We'll come back here tomorrow morning and search for whatever came out of those holes."

No one argued, and we doused the bonfire in silence.

My earlier happiness at being away from the garrison had vanished. Now, I longed to return to the safety of Weston Tower.

There, no fast-moving lumps burrowed through the ground. No strange geysers spat sand high into the air. And no unseen attackers dug pits to trap their victims.

We gathered our gear and headed back to our vehicles. As we passed a clump of terra bushes, a couple of branches rustled furtively. For a heartbeat, I thought I heard a faint *click-click*, similar to the noise back on Liberty Island weeks ago. When no one else noticed the sound, I shook my head, annoyed at my overactive imagination.

My gaze shifted to Brian's shredded clothes and bloodied wounds. The soldier hopped ahead of me, his arms slung around the shoulders of the two boys supporting him.

The night air grew colder and colder, as if wafting from the Arctic. I shivered, then realized the temperature hadn't dropped at all. My coldness arose from an icy fear that the blue meteors had indeed scattered xans across our planet.

And now these elusive, unseen xans were starting to hunt us.

Hurriedly, I slid across the Hummer's back seat, glad the vehicle's strong metal cabin provided protection from the dangers outside. Harlem started the engine and drove down the empty streets, while Asher began writing a sit-rep about the events at the beach.

Through the windows, I watched the darkened buildings. Some were bare and untouched by terras. Others were wreathed in tattered vines, their leaves twitching in a newborn breeze.

Brian slumped in a corner seat, eyes closed, moaning.

Soo-Yun redressed the soldier's injuries and soothed his moans with gentle assurances, telling him that we'd soon be at the garrison.

Pepper sat next to Lynxx—so close, I noted, that a piece of paper couldn't fit between them. She pointed to a small plaza further up the street. "That's where we had a run-in with some members of Bone's cult." The Brethren.

"When did this happen?" Lynxx asked her.

"Just before the Night of the Blue Meteors."

Incredibly, Pepper shifted a couple of inches closer to Lynxx, pressing her thigh against his. Even more incredibly, he didn't move away from her. Was he actually interested in her? Or simply tired of being alone?

"I wonder where Bone is now," Lynxx mused.

Asher replied, "Far from Manhattan, I hope. We've received a couple of unconfirmed reports of him in Washington. I'd like to think he's dead, but I doubt it. Bone is an Outrider hybrid. Smart. Dangerous. Difficult to kill."

The others murmured their agreement.

After the Night of the Blue Meteors, Commander Powell had formed two groups to operate our shortwave radios. Working in twelve-hour shifts, they'd contacted other groups of survivors around the country and the world. From these far-flung survivors, we'd learned that France's Eiffel Tower had collapsed, Egypt's pyramids were smothered in terra vines, and Britain's Windsor Palace was in ruins.

Over the radio, people suggested ways to kill various terra plants, sent alerts on strange weather phenomena, and posted warnings about Bone and other suspected hybrids.

I threw a covert glance at Lynxx. How would my teammates react if they knew a hybrid was sitting in this Hummer with them?

And not just sitting a few feet away, but sitting ridiculously close to one of their female colleagues.

"Hang on," Harlem cried, wrenching the steering wheel to the left.

Startled, we toppled against each other. Pepper began tumbling toward the floor, but Lynxx grabbed her arm and pulled her back onto the seat. She huddled against him, her posture soft, helpless, like a rescued damsel-in-distress.

Puh-lease! I'd seen her hack a savage tentacle terra into pieces with two blows of her sword.

"What's happening, Harl?" Asher cried as the Hummer screeched to a halt.

"Something's on the road ahead of us."

16

"Nɪx ᴛʜᴀᴛ." Hᴀʀʟᴇᴍ ᴄʟɪᴍʙᴇᴅ out of the Hummer. "Something's *not* on the road ahead of us."

"What are you talking about?" Asher asked, getting out. "What's not ahead of us?"

"The road, bro."

Confused, the rest of us piled from the vehicle, except for Soo-Yun and her patient.

"Careful." Harlem waved his flashlight back and forth. "Yep. Just as I thought."

A hole about fifteen feet wide yawned in the concrete.

"Sinkhole." Asher shook his head, disgusted. "Lucky you saw it in time, Harl." He marked its location on a map. "What's this now? Ten?"

"Eleven."

In the past six months, nearly a dozen sinkholes had appeared across New York, ranging from four to twenty feet across. Three of our vehicles had fallen into them. One fighter had died; five had been injured.

Lynxx swiveled his flashlight across the sinkhole, revealing a latticework of thick purple roots. "*Stephlona exTerrus.* Root terras. They grow out from a central point and burrow through the ground. Sometimes they weaken the earth so badly that it collapses into a sinkhole."

"Okay, guys," Asher said, "we need to block off this hole so no one drives into it." He pointed to some parked cars. "They'll do."

As they crossed to the cars, Pepper joined me.

I forced a smile. "So, Lynxx, hey?"

"You don't mind, do you? I mean, you two aren't together, are you?"

"Not at all."

"Because if you have a problem with it, I'll back off. I'd never let a male wreck our friendship."

"It's okay," I assured her. "You really like him, don't you?"

Her lovely face lit up. "He's beyond amazing. He's not just super-gorgeous, although—wow!—he's stunning. He's also super-smart, thoughtful, and gentle. Most guys who look like him are stuck-up or ultra-full of themselves. But Lynxx is more outward."

"Outward?"

"He's always focusing on things outside of himself: How to kill the terras. Protect people. Help them feel better."

With surprise, I realized she was right. Why hadn't I seen these things in him before?

Suddenly uncomfortable, I glanced across the road. "Asher's like that too."

"Yes, but in a different way. Harlem's occasional nickname for our fearless team leader is spot-on."

"Don Q?"

"Yes," she said. "Don Quixote. A man on a quest to save the world. Asher's like that. He's intent on helping everyone, no matter how dangerous the situation."

I opened my mouth, then closed it again. Pepper was right. Asher was an incredible person in many ways, but he was also impulsive and a little reckless. Would these qualities get him killed one day? Or was he destined to lead a charmed life?

"Anyway," Pepper said, "I'd better go help with the cars."

I remained behind as she and the others unlocked various cars. Despite the thousands of abandoned automobiles in New York, we tried not to damage any of them. No one knew when a particular vehicle—or its parts—would be needed.

As I watched them maneuver a BMW alongside the sinkhole, Lynxx wandered across.

"You're not going to help them, Kassia?" he asked, leaning against the hood of the Hummer.

"I pulled a muscle in training yesterday, so I'm sitting this one out." I flicked him a sideways glance. "Shouldn't you help push the cars?"

He shrugged. "I do brain work, not grunt work."

Click-click-click.

I tensed. *No. Not here.*

"Did you hear that, Lynxx?"

He pointed to a nearby alley. "I think it came from down there."

Another three clicks. No, not clicks, I realized. These were sharper sounds, like metal hitting metal.

Tap-tap-tap. Taaap-taaap-taaap. Tap-tap-tap.

"It sounds like an SOS," he said. "Wait here."

"Forget it. I'm coming with you."

"It's too dangerous."

Indignant, I cried, "I fight *terras*!"

"But—"

Ignoring his protests, I called out to Asher, "Lynxx and I heard something in an alley."

"Don't go too far," Asher called back as they pushed the BMW alongside the sinkhole. "Keep your gun handy."

"Will do."

Lynxx shook his head at me, annoyed. "You're stubborn."

"One of my charms."

He murmured, "Among many." The words were spoken so softly that he probably didn't mean me to hear them. But I did.

We switched on our flashlights and entered an alley cluttered with trash cans, broken glass, and a pair of dumpsters.

"There." He pointed to a clump of rags lying next to a dumpster.

Quietly, we moved down the alley, our beams scoping the gloom.

The lump of rags beside the dumpster turned out to be a bearded old man lying on the hard asphalt. A battered beer can lay inches from his limp hand. Had he heard our Hummer pull up on the street outside? Too weak to call out, had he used the beer can to tap an SOS on the metal dumpster?

Lynxx felt for a pulse. "Dead." He peered at the grimy face. "Oh no. It's Larry Miller."

"You know him?"

"He's one of my long-term contacts. I suggested he join the Weston Battalion, but he preferred living on the streets. Fewer rules."

Larry wasn't alone in his decision. Other survivors also chose their independence over the garrison's rules and regulations.

Lynxx gently placed his hand on the man's dirty forehead. "Rest in peace, Larry."

"I didn't know you were religious." Could a hybrid believe in God?

"I'm not. *He* was." Lynxx touched a tarnished cross on a chain around the wrinkled neck. "Larry was a loner, sure. And an alcoholic. He was also a decent man, always ready to help other survivors if he could. He didn't deserve such an awful death."

"Awful death?" I studied the body. Larry's face was unmarked, his long gray hair was littered with leaves and twigs, and he only wore one sneaker. "Sure, he's dirty, but why do you think he died an awful death?"

"Because he's missing a sneaker."

"So?"

"There are millions of shoes in New York and only several hundred survivors. If you lose a shoe, it's easy to get another one. You'd never walk around wearing just one sneaker." He gestured to the blood and dirt caking the man's bare foot. "That looks fresh, as though he'd been running for hours—which leads to one big question."

"Which is?"

"What was he running from?"

17

Alone, I entered the cemetery.

It had been a month since Lynxx and I had discovered Larry's body in an alley. After Nurse Ortiz couldn't find a cause of death, the commander had ordered the man to be buried in the garrison's cemetery.

"I know Larry Miller wasn't a member of the Weston Battalion," Powell had said at the funeral service, "but many of us had met him. Most of humanity has been reduced to anonymous piles of decomp-dust. Larry, though, died as a man. He should rest beside his fellow humans."

The commander's compassion had surprised me. Usually, Powell was so busy that he seemed distant and hard. Despite this, I knew Asher greatly admired him; I just hoped Asher never became like him.

Today, a mist draped the cemetery in thick white veils.

I'd visited this place many times over the past few months, so it should've felt familiar.

But today it didn't.

The heavy mist had smothered the early-morning sunshine, reducing visibility to a few yards. No birds chatted or squawked in the trees. The eerie silence was broken only by the crunch of dead leaves under my boots and the pounding of my heart against my rib cage.

"It's okay," I muttered to myself. "I'm only a few minutes' drive from the garrison. If anything happens, they'll know where to start looking for my cold dead body."

As usual, I'd left a note on my bed, jotting down my destination and expected time of return to Weston Tower. This was standard practice. Although Commander Powell encouraged us not to wander around the city alone, he didn't forbid it. The arrival of the xans had dampened many people's enthusiasm for solo trips, but others persisted with their outings.

Since I preferred to keep my grief private, I continued to visit Olivia's and Charlotte's graves by myself.

The thick mist hid most of the ninety-four crosses that dotted this makeshift cemetery. The newest grave was only a few yards away, identifiable by its freshly turned dirt.

I withdrew three bunches of harmless perfume-globe terras from my backpack.

"Rest in peace, Larry." I placed a bunch of flowers on his grave.

I headed toward Charlotte's grave.

Today was my cousin's birthday. A few months younger than me, Charlotte would've turned seventeen today—*if* she hadn't fallen from a building, become paralyzed, and died.

No, she hadn't just died. She had been euthanized.

This cemetery held dozens of rough wooden crosses. Each was a reminder that life could be short and dangerous. Death, however, was forever.

I rounded a clump of bushes and stopped.

Lynxx was bending over my sister's grave. He grasped the crude cross that marked Olivia's plot, wrenched it out, and tossed away the splintered branches. A few feet to his right, Charlotte's cross lay in two pieces. Other plots also bore broken crosses.

I gaped at him. In the past month, people had reported several episodes of vandalism at the cemetery. No one—especially not me—had ever suspected Lynxx.

"Stop!" I stomped across to him. "Why are you wrecking their crosses?"

He turned toward me—

—and I saw it.

Next to his feet lay a beautiful wooden cross carved with images, along with the name *Olivia Madison*. The wood gleamed like molten honey, the result of hours spent sanding, varnishing, and polishing it.

"What's this, Lynxx?"

A faint flush crept up his neck and face. "What are you doing here?"

"It's Charlotte's birthday." I placed a bunch of perfume-globes on my cousin's grave. "What are *you* doing here?"

"Warthog."

"Excuse me?"

"A warthog's been scratching itself on the crosses, breaking them. I've fixed Olivia's cross three times in the past few months, but the warthog keeps breaking it. So I made her something stronger and more permanent."

"Why? You hardly knew my sister. I thought you'd only met her a few times."

His face tightened. An elusive emotion glinted in his golden eyes. Sadness? Regret?

"I wish I'd known her better." He withdrew a coil of rope from his backpack and moved to Charlotte's damaged cross. Working quickly, obviously having done this before, he tied the two pieces of wood into their previous cross shape.

Now it was my turn to flush. "Sorry I accused you of wrecking them." I placed my last bunch of perfume-globes on Olivia's grave.

"Only a heartless jerk would vandalize a cemetery." He glanced around, making sure no one else was nearby. "And while I may only be half-human, I can assure you that, physically, I have a heart. Also, I don't believe I'm a jerk."

He returned to the hole left behind by Olivia's old cross. With a shovel, he made it deeper and wider. Focused on his work, he didn't notice the sun emerging from behind a cloud. A shaft of sunlight streamed through the trees and washed over him, sheening his thick black hair and warming his smooth skin. He reminded me of a classical Greek statue. Handsome, sexy, remote.

Sighing, I shucked off my backpack and placed it on the ground.

"Not there, Kassia."

"Why not?"

"Your bag will cover a crabben xan burrow. They'll be cranky."

Quickly, I hung my backpack in a nearby tree.

Crabben xans.

Nasty little things.

Two weeks ago, several species of small xans had appeared in Manhattan. Some resembled bugs like cockroaches and spiders—except cockroaches weren't sky-blue, and spiders had eight legs, not twelve. Lynxx's tests revealed that most of the xan bugs were harmless.

The crabben xans were a little more dangerous. They couldn't kill anyone, but their bite could leave an ugly wound prone to infection if left untreated.

A crabben darted from a hole near Charlotte's grave. Round as a baseball, it had six scuttling legs and six clawed arms that waved through the air.

"What's it hunting?" I asked as the crabben disappeared into a patch of long grass.

"The usual, I suppose. Bugs, spiders, other xans."

"Yay on hunting other xans. The fewer the better."

"Don't get your hopes up. These little xans are just the beginning. Eventually we'll start seeing much larger ones, far more dangerous."

"You mean big bugs and spiders?" I shuddered.

"Not necessarily. Bugs and spiders might stay small. But other species of xans could grow larger."

"So why haven't we seen any larger xans yet?" It was a common question around the mess hall these days.

He gave the same common answers. "They take time to grow. Or maybe they're already grown, but are living in places where there aren't any people."

"That's most of the world these days," I said bitterly.

"Exactly."

The earlier shaft of sunlight had disappeared. Mist again swirled across the grounds.

"Can you hold this in place?" he asked, inserting the carved wooden cross in the large hole he'd dug.

"Sure."

Lynxx tied four lengths of thin rope to the cross, one in each direction, and attached them to the four wooden pegs he'd already hammered into the dirt. "These will hold the cross upright until the cement dries."

After opening a large container, he poured a cement mixture into the hole, then smoothed the surface with a trowel.

My finger traced an image of an arched bridge carved into the cross. "This looks like Gapstow Bridge in Central Park."

"It is."

I shuddered, remembering that fateful day in Central Park when I'd accidentally killed a woman. Guilt-stricken, sick, and alone, I'd stood on Gapstow Bridge. A patch of lethal pink flowers on the water below had offered me a quick, painless death.

And then Olivia had arrived and my world had changed.

Lynxx hesitated. "After the Mist, when Olivia came back to New York looking for you, I told her that I'd seen you on Gapstow Bridge."

Shock slammed into me.

"*You* sent her to me? She told me it was a boy named Rock."

"That was me. My guardian named me Rock as a baby, and the name suited me when I was hard and emotionless. Thankfully, I'm not that guy anymore."

"But she never mentioned Rock having golden eyes."

"She never saw my eyes. I only met her a few times, and I always wore dark sunglasses."

I stared at Lynxx, my heart racing. Because of him, my sister and I had found each other again; because of him, at my darkest point I'd been given a glimmer of hope. "You reunited Olivia and me. How can I ever thank you?"

"You just did." He tightened the four ropes to their wooden pegs in the dirt. "You can let go of the cross now."

Held in place by the ropes, the polished wooden cross stood erect at the top of Olivia's grave.

Something shimmered in the mist beyond Lynxx. Large as a basketball. Red.

A long tentacle reached for his neck.

"Jellyfish terra!" I cried.

A force surged from me in a strong, invisible wave.

18

THE JELLYFISH TERRA EXPLODED, splattering blood and bits of spongy material in all directions. A couple of pieces landed on my face and I hurriedly washed them off with bottled water before they could burn my skin.

"Hold still." I washed several red blobs off Lynxx's hair and neck. "Okay. All clear."

He shook his head, flicking away drops of water. "That was close. You're getting pretty good at that mental stuff."

"Not really. I only meant to remote-push the jellyfish terra away, not explode it."

He poked a stick at the terra pieces on the ground. As he lifted a tentacle, blood dripped from the tube. "It's recently fed."

"Dis-gust-ing."

Softly, almost whispering, he asked, "Did Olivia ever tell you how she got that mark across her neck?"

I nodded. One evening, Olivia had returned to the subway bunker with an ugly red line across her throat. "I thought someone had tried to strangle her, but she told me it was a jellyfish terra."

"Yes. The biggest one I'd ever seen."

"I remember her saying that Rock was there that day. She told me that he ... you ... saved her life."

"The thing almost killed her. I should've remote-pushed it away, but I panicked. Anyway, I blasted it with a shotgun, then treated her wound."

My gaze shifted to another carving on the wooden cross. "This bird with the outstretched wings, is it an eagle?"

"It's WindLord."

"My sister told me that she'd seen the eagle hanging around her lots of times when she was aboveground. She never understood why." When he stayed silent, I asked, "Why put WindLord on this cross?"

"He was a part of her world." The world following the Mist.

My gaze moved across the carvings. "Is this a mouse?"

"Olivia told me about your pet."

"Huh? She told you about Mousy, but she hardly ever mentioned Rock ... *you* ... to me. Why not?"

Another shrug. "I'm not sure."

Reluctant to push him, I moved on to more images. "What's with the can and bottle?"

"Sometimes your sister was unwell or tired when she came aboveground. If I could, I'd leave cans of food and water bottles in the buildings she was searching, just to help her out."

"Oh." I paused, confused by his kindness. Why had he helped Olivia?

I stared at him, unsure what to think or feel.

A bunch of purple flowers lay next to his backpack. Their stems were tied by a thin rope—the same rope Lynxx was using to hold Olivia's cross in place while the cement dried.

"Lazarus terra flowers," I whispered. "Someone's been putting three of them on Olivia's grave once a month since she died. It was you, wasn't it?"

He blinked as though dust had gotten in his eyes. Another nod.

I fingered the soft purple petals. "When we were living underground, Olivia started bringing home three Lazarus flowers every Friday. Just like this bunch. You've even carved a Lazarus flower on her new cross."

"How do you know it's a Lazarus flower?"

"Because it fits. All these carvings represent something in Olivia's life since the Mist—and the Lazarus flowers were extremely important. I didn't realize it at the time, but they helped keep me alive. You told Olivia to bring them to me every week, didn't you?"

"My research suggested their pollen has medicinal value."

"Their *pollen*? Not their scent?"

"The pollen."

"Huh!" I swallowed, almost overcome by emotion. Olivia and I had lived for months in the subway bunker. Unseen and mostly unthanked, Lynxx had helped us survive by providing food, the Lazarus flowers, and probably other things I didn't know about.

"You did all this for Olivia and me. Why?"

He picked up the Lazarus flowers and gently placed them on my twin's grave.

At a sudden thought, I gasped, "Were you in love with her?"

"No! She was like a sister to me."

"Then why go to all that trouble to help us?" When no answer came, I changed tack. "Olivia told you that she had a twin, right?"

"Yes."

"An identical twin sister?"

"Yes."

"So why didn't you recognize me that first day?"

"What day?" he asked, voice shaking a little.

I could tell he knew exactly what I meant. Was he ashamed that he had abandoned me?

"The day I left the subway bunker looking for my sister; the day you and I met in a passageway of Grand Central Station. You pretended I was a stranger. But you knew who I was, didn't you?"

"Well, you didn't exactly look like Olivia back then. You were sick, remember? Weak and pale, plus much thinner than her. And your hair was hidden under a helmet."

"That's not an answer. You knew who I was, didn't you?"

"Okay. Yes."

"Yet you just left me on the street." Despite everything he'd done for Olivia and me, my voice shook with hurt and confusion. "I was alone, scared, desperate to find Olivia. Why did you just walk away from me?"

He grasped my hands, his gesture filled with an urgent need for me to understand. "I was trying to save your life. My guardian, Frost, was nearby, watching us."

"I didn't see anyone else around."

"He was in the passage with us, hiding in the darkness. Later, he followed us from the courtyard, into the street. I had no choice; I had to pretend you were a stranger, someone I didn't care about."

"Why?"

"If he knew how desperately I wanted to help you—a human, an enemy of Outriders like him—he would've regarded me as a traitor. More importantly, he would've punished me by killing you."

I pulled my hands from his grip. "So you just left me there. Alone."

"Only for a couple of minutes. The instant Frost left, I came back."

"I didn't see you."

"I was there, I promise you. I had to stay out of sight in case Frost returned." He paced in agitation. Mist swirled around him, as though reflecting his distress. "I saw the tiger stalking you on that vine-bridge. I was about to attack it when—"

"Asher arrived and shot it," I finished for him.

"Exactly. And during the swarming, when the swarmer seeds were hunting for food, I tried to draw them away from the alley where you and Asher were hiding. Later, when you fainted in the street, I started racing toward you, but Asher carried you to a car and drove to Weston Tower."

Speechless, I stared at him. So Lynxx *had* been there after all. He'd seen the tiger and the swarmers and had tried to help me.

"Asher never mentioned seeing you in the street," I said, struggling with these revelations.

"I'm … I'm an expert at blending into the shadows."

My mind whirled as I stared at the Lazarus blossoms on Olivia's grave.

Lynxx had been placing flowers on my sister's grave every month since she died. I remembered the emotion that had glinted in his eyes at the mention of her. Although Lynxx claimed he hadn't been in love with her—and I believed him—his feelings for my sister were clearly deeper than he admitted.

Earlier, I'd thought the emotion in his eyes had been sadness or regret.

I'd been wrong.

It had been grief.

"Thank you for helping to keep Olivia and me alive." I touched his arm, and he flinched as though I'd burned him. "I'm extremely grateful. I can never repay you for everything you did for us. But I'm confused."

"What about?"

"Why did you help us?"

Instead of answering, he packed up his tools. Brisk and businesslike again, he said, "We'd better head back to the garrison."

"Now? I've still got questions. About those months I spent underground. About Olivia and her life aboveground."

He zipped up his pack and slung it over his shoulders. "I know we've got a lot to talk about. Now's not the time." A familiar hard note warned me not to argue.

Sighing, I bit back my questions.

As we crossed the misty cemetery, he stared straight ahead, lost in his thoughts. From the way he frowned every so often, he appeared to be mentally wrestling with something.

Obviously, Lynxx hadn't told me everything.
What other secrets was he keeping from me?

19

THE FOLLOWING WEEK, ASHER, Booker, and I crouched in the early-morning shadows outside a midtown store.

I studied the xans on the street. The sidewalks of Sixth Avenue were patched with ocher ground terras, white angel-vines, and blue shrubs with sharp angular leaves. It was the perfect spot for crabbens, who loved hunting for bugs and other small xans in the vegetation.

Crabben xans reminded me of mutated gray crabs. Each had six clawed arms and six legs, plus beady black eyes that jutted on stalks above their exoskeletons.

"Crabben xans dead ahead," Asher whispered.

"Vicious little things," I muttered. "How come Liberty Team got this horrible mission?"

"Just lucky," Asher said dryly. "Remember, Lynxx needs at least ten live crabbens."

In front of a dress store, three buzzards squabbled over a dead deer.

Booker reluctantly closed his historical novel and shoved it into his pocket. "Copy that, boss. Crabbens dead ahead." The blond French-Canadian scowled at his bandaged left arm. His elbow was still recovering from an infection caused by a crabben bite two weeks ago. "It was hard enough killing those things when they first hatched. And now Lynxx needs live ones for his research? The only good crabben is a dead one."

"Agreed," Asher said. "But that's not our mission today." He murmured into the radio strapped to his shoulder, "You guys ready?"

Across the wide road, the three other members of Liberty Team gave him a thumbs-up. I frowned at the trio. Although Rusty was competent, he was more interested in playing soccer than hunting xans. Fifteen-year-old Freya would be frightened but eager to prove her bravery; she had replaced Pablo, who'd transferred to Neptune Team. Only Pepper, an experienced fighter, was calmly observing the xans as she tried to figure out ways to capture them.

Asher glanced at me, concerned for my safety. Everyone knew we were a couple, but he tried not to show favoritism during our missions. "Be careful, Kass."

"You too."

I pulled on a pair of thick workmen's gloves that stretched up my arms. Across the street, Pepper did the same thing. Partially protected, we herded some crabbens toward a mesh net out-stretched between Rusty and Freya. Asher and Booker waited nearby, holding small metal cages.

Three crabbens darted around the net and took off down the street.

Booker yelled, "Don't let them—"

A loud crack interrupted him.

Ahead of us, the road shattered. Something long and brown and covered in suckers shot from the ground and scooped up the three crabbens. An instant later, it disappeared back into the earth with the xans.

We bolted for the sidewalk. Pulled out our weapons. Gaped at the broken ground.

"What was that?" I gasped.

"Tentacle terra?" Rusty croaked, his red hair slicked to his scalp with perspiration.

Asher shook his head. "I don't think so."

Behind his wire-rimmed glasses, Booker's eyes bulged. "Well, it sure wasn't an Earth plant, boss."

"Let's put a bit more space between us and whatever it was," Asher said.

Keeping to the sidewalk, we hurried down the block.

"Perhaps it was just a tentacle terra," Pepper suggested.

Booker muttered, "A long, thin terra-plant that smashes through the pavement and lassos three savage crabbens? Sure. It's a possibility."

"There's another possibility," I reluctantly said.

"Xan." Asher uttered the word we'd all been thinking. "It could've been a xan."

"So Lynxx was right." Rusty's freckled face creased with worry. "He told us there could be larger xans around." He threw an accusing glare at Pepper. "Your boyfriend didn't warn us they might burst up from the *ground*."

"How could Lynxx possibly know that?" Pepper snapped.

I frowned. Would she be so defensive if she knew the truth—that the boy she was dating was a hybrid?

Over the past couple of weeks, I had wondered if I should tell my friend about Lynxx. However, the more people who knew his secret, the greater the chance that someone would kill him in anger or revenge or fear.

I knew that the hybrids had been created by the Chi'az, an alien race. But Lynxx was also human. The grief he'd shown at Olivia's grave had definitely been human. So, too, was the love he felt—had felt?—for me. He'd helped keep Olivia and me alive after the Mist. He was still keeping me alive with his weekly Lazarus tonics.

I owed him gratitude, not a death sentence.

In the distance, a droning noise broke the morning hush.

Stunned, I stared at the sky.

"That sounds like a plane," Pepper gasped, gazing up-ward.

"Or our chopper," Booker said, distracted. His worried gaze continued to alternate between the shattered road and the open ground around us.

"It's a plane," Pepper insisted.

"The Weston Battalion doesn't have a plane."

"I know."

I pointed to the sky. "What's that?"

20

A BROWN HAZE SPREAD through the air, growing darker and darker.

The droning noise grew louder as the brown haze moved overhead. Part of it split off, and thousands of tiny spots angled down, diving past the buildings and heading for Sixth Avenue.

"Locusts!" Asher yelled. "Take cover!"

Freya paled and hastily brushed her thin hair back into a ponytail. "Please, no! I hate bugs! Their scratchy claws. Their icky wings."

We looked around. The stores behind us were locked, as well as the ones across the street. We ran down the sidewalk, searching for sanctuary.

In a deafening drone, the whirring locusts descended and swarmed over us. Shouting and staggering, we tried to beat them off, push them away, stop them from getting into our mouths and noses.

As I fought the insects, I remembered a similar battle with a swarm of locusts. It had been Day 47, and I'd been helping some people burn a field of glow-lotus terras in Central Park.

Did Asher also remember that incident? Did he remember a sickly teenage girl who'd accidentally knocked a young woman into a patch of deadly glow-lotus terras? Luckily, he had never realized that *I'd* caused the death of poor Sophie. No one had told him my name that day—plus I'd been unrecognizable due to my large sunglasses and the aviator hat that hid my hair.

Freya's screams drew me back to the present—

—to Sixth Avenue and its whirlwind of locusts.

Tiny stinking bugs skittered over me. They crawled across my face. Snagged their pronged legs in my hair. Tried to push into my nose and mouth and ears.

Asher and the others fought off their hard-shelled attackers. Above the boys' shouts and swearing, I could hear Freya's horrified screams. I'd heard the same horror in Sophie's screams at Central Park that day, and in myriad nightmares since then.

Enough.

A force surged from me like a blast of air. It struck the locusts crawling over my body and threw them back.

Abruptly, the swarm took off in a whir of dry wings.

"Are they gone? Are they gone?" Freya cried, frantically brushing down her hair and clothes.

"Yes," Asher said. "I think they're looking for more food."

The sky no longer teemed with a living brown haze. The heavens soared above us, pale red and clear.

Except another droning noise shredded the silence.

Freya's eyes widened in horror. "They're coming back."

Booker swore in a mixture of French and English.

Asher pointed at the sky. "There. Near those tall buildings covered with terra vines."

A small white plane flew above the buildings.

We gaped at it, our excited comments stumbling over each other.

"Is it ours?"

"No way. We only own a chopper."

"What about another resistance group? One from up north?"

"The nearest one is in Vancouver. That plane's too small to fly from Canada to New York on one tank of fuel."

"So who are they?"

"Why are they here?"

"What do they want?"

The small plane coughed and spluttered.

"What's happening?"

Asher watched the aircraft with the unblinking intensity of a hawk. "I think its engine is failing."

"But why?" Freya wailed, no longer trying to be a brave fighter. From the looks on the others' faces, we all shared the girl's bitter disappointment.

Asher said, "It could've been caught up in that swarm of locusts earlier."

"Maybe the locusts are clogging the engines," I suggested.

The plane disappeared behind Bains Tower.

We held our breaths. Hoped the plane would reappear, intact and smooth-running.

Then—

—a loud bang.

The plane had crashed.

21

WE PILED INTO OUR Hummer, sped down Sixth Avenue, then braked opposite Bains Tower. We jumped out, onto a road littered with pieces of concrete, twisted metal, and terra plants. Further up the side of Bains Tower, the rear end of a small white plane jutted from the vine-covered building like an arrow embedded in an archery target.

Asher peered through his binoculars. "It looks like a Cessna. Six-seater, maybe eight. No signs of smoke or fire."

Booker asked him, "How come the plane didn't explode, boss?"

"It might've run out of fuel. Or the pilot dumped the fuel before they crashed."

"Do you think the pilot survived?"

"Hard to say. The back of the Cessna looks reasonably intact. The terra vines on the building might've cushioned its impact." Asher raised a hand. "Quiet, everyone."

We listened. A hyena's frantic laugh echoed in a side street. Parrots squawked in a cathedral-dome terra. Terra bushes rustled beneath a breeze.

"No cries of help," he said. "But that doesn't mean anything as the plane's high up. We need to get to it."

Freya nervously eyed the entrance to Bains Tower. Past its open doorway, the lobby was thick with red plants that glimmered in shafts of sunlight. "The place is clogged with scarlet-needle terras. Isn't that a strict no-go zone?"

"Yes." Asher surveyed the building's exterior, layered with red and green terra vines. "Here's my plan." As he outlined it, I struggled to hide my alarm. When he finished, he said, "It's risky, guys, so I'm open to other suggestions."

Freya stared longingly at the red plants inside the lobby. "I think I prefer going through the scarlet-needle terras."

"Not an option." Asher waited as we desperately tried to think of a ... saner ... plan. "No other suggestions? Okay, let's do this."

We drove down the street, stopped outside the Spencer Center, and grabbed some equipment from the Hummer.

Asher told Rusty and Freya to return to the garrison. "Find Commander Powell. Tell him about the plane crash."

The pair quickly left, relieved not to be a part of the upcoming rescue.

Asher, Pepper, Booker, and I entered the Spencer Center. Its moldy lobby contained a few small patches of flammable Hades terras, easily avoided. Inside the closest stairwell, the beams of our headlamps revealed bare concrete walls and steps. No terra plants or xans.

"I think the terra is anchored on the twenty-fifth floor," Asher said, sword in hand. "Let's go. Stay alert and stay alive."

Lapsing into silence, we trudged up the stairs.

My anxiety rose. I wanted to help those people in the plane—if they were alive. But in a corner of my brain, I almost hoped we'd run into some unfriendly terra plants or xans in this stairwell. That way, we'd be forced to turn back. We wouldn't have to go up to the twenty-fifth floor where—

I shuddered and forced myself to focus on climbing the stairs.

On the twenty-fifth floor, we entered an open-plan office almost filled with the end of a vine-bridge terra. Dozens of roots—many as thick as a man's arm—plunged into the floor and anchored themselves to metal beams. Thinner ones encircled the solid columns that studded the area.

Cautiously, we moved to the far side of the room, where a shattered wall allowed in wind, rain, and birds. The vine-bridge started at this floor, stretched over a couple of low buildings and ended at Bains Tower. The Cessna had crashed near the far end of the vine-bridge, but a couple of floors higher.

Booker studied the distant building through his binoculars. "I can't see any scarlet-needle terras on the walls above the twentieth floor, boss. Just green vines."

"Good. Hopefully, that means there are no scarlet-needle terras *inside* the offices on the higher floors. Still, we'll need to be careful." Asher turned to Pepper and me. "Are you ready?"

Pepper gave him a bright smile. "Absolutely." Ever confident. Ever brave.

I gulped. "Sure." Inside, I was screaming *no*.

I'd always been afraid of heights—yet I'd gone hang-gliding with Asher a few months ago. At that time, my grief at Olivia's death had outweighed my fear of heights, plus I'd felt safe with him. Weeks later, when a tumbleweed terra had stranded me on the side of a tall building, my fear of being eaten alive had been greater than my fear of heights.

Today, though, my stomach knotted at the thought of walking across this woody vine-bridge. Almost four feet wide, it was made from several thick vines that had twisted together to form a solid gnarly mass.

Asher gave my shoulder a reassuring squeeze. "Stay behind me."

He scrambled onto the vine-bridge. After taking a deep breath, I followed. Then Pepper.

Bringing up the rear, Booker whooped excitedly. "This is going to be fun."

"Fun?" I shook my head, bemused. For a bookworm, Booker was strangely adventurous. Was he trying to imitate the heroes in his novels? "You don't like spiders, Booker. If I tossed some big hairy tarantulas on you, would you find them fun too?"

"Yuck! No."

"Then please drop the *fun* comments."

He sighed, then nodded.

Carefully I walked behind Asher, keeping a few yards between us. If I fell, I didn't want to take him with me.

The vines felt rough and uneven, yet firm. Small leaves snapped beneath my boots, releasing a foul smell, and I crinkled my nose. "These leaves stink."

"If Lynxx were here," Pepper replied, "he'd probably tell us it's to stop animals from eating them or something."

At the edge of the shattered wall, I paused and looked down. The ground was incredibly far away. Too far. I pictured myself plunging through space, my body slamming onto the hard pavement, my head splitting open—

"Kass." Asher was waiting on the vine-bridge a short distance ahead. He stood in the open air, with only one wide twisted vine-bridge between him and death. "It's okay." His blue eyes held concern, as though he'd guessed my fear. "If you want to wait back in the building, you can."

I couldn't. With the departure of Rusty and Freya, our team was already down two members. "Are you sure this thing is safe?"

"It's strong enough to hold a herd of lumbering elephants."

"What if it gets windy?"

"It's early morning."

"So?"

"The air's calmer early in the morning. Usually, it gets windy as the day warms up."

"Good." Taking a deep breath, I slowly walked forward. "I'll ... I'll be fine." *Focus on the woody bridge*, I told myself. *Don't look down.*

Step by step, Pepper, Booker, and I followed Asher across the vine-bridge, through the space that yawned between the two tall buildings. The vine remained solid and unmoving in the cold windless air.

I'll be fine. I'll be fine.

Finally, an eternity later, the four of us jumped from the woody structure into an upper-floor office in Bains Tower. I fought a temptation to drop to my knees and kiss the carpet with relief.

Asher scanned the vines inside. "I can't see any scarlet-needle terras, but be careful, guys."

He led us through a series of hallways and rooms, all free of scarlet-needles. Many had harmless green vines growing over their mildewed carpets, crumbling desks, and rusting metal chairs. Time hadn't just stopped in these rooms, I realized; it had fled, leaving them to rot.

Two floors up, the broken front of the plane poked through the far wall of an enormous, open plan office. We began hurrying toward it, then stopped.

Scarlet-needle terras.

They layered a large section of the floor like a carpet of blood.

Slowly, we backed away and huddled in the safety of an alcove.

"Do you think they sensed us?" I whispered. Every cell in my body quivered, expecting an attack.

Pepper murmured, "We wouldn't be standing here if they had."

I hated scarlet-needles. Their leaves looked vibrant and innocuous, but at any movement or sound, the highly sensitive plants would fling off hair-thin barbs that pierced the skin like hot needles. Three months ago, I'd been stung by a few barbs. The pain had burned for two days.

"We need to go around," Asher said. "We'll enter by that far doorway. As long as we're fifty feet from the scarlet-needles, we'll be okay. They can't throw their barbs that far."

We made the detour as quietly as possible.

To our relief, the area in front of the plane was free of scarlet-needles—

—and deathly silent.

22

Had anyone survived?

Pieces of the wreckage lay strewn across the office. Snapped wings and broken propeller. Glass shards and chunks of concrete. Across the front of the Cessna's cockpit, debris blocked its window.

Asher scanned the pool of scarlet-needle terras in the office. "We're far enough away to be safe. But just in case, we need barricades."

Quietly, we cleared the tops of three desks, turned them on their sides, and crouched behind them.

From behind his desk-cum-barricade, Asher shouted, "Hello. Is anyone inside the plane?"

We held our breaths and listened.

No clatter of hair-thin barbs striking our desks. No cries from inside the Cessna.

Another shout from Asher. "Is anyone inside the plane?"

Silence.

Still no barbs. The scarlet-needles were too far away to hit us.

A faint voice came from the plane. "*Help us.*" It sounded like a young woman.

Asher crawled from under his desk. "Are you the pilot?"

The rest of us joined him.

"Passenger."

"How many people on your plane?"

"Six, including the pilot."

"Is anyone hurt?"

"Yes."

"Can you get to the cockpit?"

"No."

"Okay. Hang tight. Stay where you are. We'll try to get you out."

I surveyed the Cessna. Almost half of it—the heavier half—was poking through the wall into the office.

"The plane looks wedged in place." Asher placed his sword on a desk. "I need to get inside it."

"Are you crazy?" I gasped. "That wall could collapse at any second."

"Which means I don't have a second to lose."

I sighed. "Then I'll go with you."

Booker and Pepper volunteered as well.

Asher agreed to take Booker with him. "If people are trapped," he explained to Pepper and me, "I'll need his strength."

The pair climbed onto the plane's nose, shoved off the concrete chunks that blocked the smashed window, and crawled inside. Moments later, Asher called out, "The pilot's dead. Broken neck."

They disappeared into the cabin, whose rear was sticking from the far side of the wall, hanging outside. I tensed. What if Asher's and Booker's weight caused the Cessna to snap in half? It would plunge twenty-seven floors to the ground.

I scowled. Asher's reckless behavior was worrying. He should never have placed Booker and himself in such danger.

The murmur of voices came from inside the plane, followed by grunts—and the sound of groaning metal.

"Are you guys okay, Asher?" Pepper and I grabbed the nose of the aircraft, hoping it wouldn't topple backward.

The plane wasn't moving. It felt rock-solid. For now.

"We're fine," came his muffled reply.

Over the next twenty minutes, he and Booker worked to free the trapped passengers.

Perched on the Cessna's nose, I helped each survivor crawl through the front window, then passed them down to Pepper. An old man named Albert emerged first, followed by an elderly woman, and a dark-haired teenage girl who looked vaguely familiar. All were bloodied.

Booker wiggled through the window and jumped down to join us, his clothes ripped and dirty.

Asher followed. Blood streaked his face and splotched his khaki shirt. "That's all. Only three survivors."

"Are you hurt?" I asked him.

Wearily, he shook his head. "It's not my blood." He gathered me into his arms and held me tightly, as though I were a rocky outcrop in a roiling ocean.

What had he seen inside the plane?

Asher turned to the elderly woman, who looked about seventy. "It's Isabel, isn't it?" When she nodded, he went on, a faint note of accusation in his voice. "Those two dead children back in the plane had bandaged heads and chests. The blood on the bandages had dried, as though their injuries happened hours before your plane crashed." He waited for an explanation.

"They were injured before they even got on the plane." Isabel's voice was frail. "We were trying to escape—"

The Cessna gave an ominous metallic groan.

"Move, everyone!" Asher shouted.

We hustled Isabel, Albert, and the young girl through the office, avoiding the patch of scarlet-needle terras. At the far exit, I looked back.

The wall rumbled and crumbled around the Cessna as the plane plunged backward and disappeared. I visualized it falling, its broken shell and dead passengers dropping down, down ...

Seconds later, a crash echoed through the city streets.

My body shook, and for a moment I thought the building was shuddering. But it was just me. If Asher had stayed in that plane a minute longer, he would've died.

He stared at the spot where the plane had been. "We'll talk later," he said to Isabel. "After we're safe on the ground."

As we climbed the stairs to the vine-bridge, the teenage girl tilted her head at me. "My name's Rebecca. Have we met before?"

"I'm not sure."

She definitely looked familiar. Long black hair. Dark eyes. Head tilted in a questioning glance.

My mind arrowed through the months to a memory that still lived in my nightmares—

—to the same black hair fluttering in the breeze at Central Park, and the same dark eyes staring in horror at the dying woman sprawled on the glow-lotus terras.

"I did it," I'd blurted out, heartsick, to the youth who'd been burning the glow-lotus terras. "I felt dizzy. I stumbled and knocked Sophie into the flowers."

"You did this?" Asher had asked, horrified.

My cousin's boyfriend, Jase, had snorted. "She's been feeling rotten all day. She's in the final stages of leukemia."

Rebecca eyed me suspiciously. "When Asher climbed into the Cessna, I recognized him right away. He was at Central Park a few weeks after the Mist. You were there that day too, weren't you? You bumped my friend, Sophie, and she fell into the glow-lotus terras. She died."

How had she recognized me? Then I remembered. At the park, I'd briefly removed my aviator hat and sunglasses to brush away some locusts. Luckily, Asher had left by then.

"It wasn't me." The vile lie passed through my lips, tasting foul.

Asher frowned at Rebecca. "That other girl at Central Park was skinny, weak, dying. She was in the final stages of leukemia."

Brow still creased, he asked me, "Didn't you have a friend with leukemia?"

"Yes. It must've been her at Central Park." More foul lies. I longed to admit the truth. Couldn't. The prospect of being expelled from the Weston Garrison was too frightening.

"Okay, that's straightened out," he told Rebecca.

She remained silent.

When we arrived at the vine-bridge, Asher explained to Rebecca and the others why this was our only way out of the building, citing the scarlet-needle terras that clogged the lower floors. Surprisingly, they gave resigned nods.

"Where we come from, we have terras like the scarlet-needles, plus these terra bridges," Albert said. "Often, they're the safest way to get around."

"Where are you from?" I asked the old man. Part of me was eager for answers. Another part wanted to deflect Rebecca's thoughts from that dreadful day at Central Park. "How did you get a plane? You said you were escaping from something. What—?"

"Talk later." Asher stopped at the end of the vine-bridge. "We need to focus on getting across this thing safely."

The elderly woman's thin body trembled. "I don't know if I can make it across."

Asher took Isabel's arm firmly. "We'll go together, ma'am. I won't let anything happen to you. Promise."

Silently, I followed them onto the bridge. My earlier fear of heights had faded a little, outweighed by my worry about Rebecca.

Midway across the bridge, a sudden thought struck me with an almost physical blow.

My reprieve from Rebecca's accusation was only temporary, maybe seconds or minutes at the most. That day at Central Park, Jase had called me by my name in front of Rebecca. A short time later, he'd abandoned me and left with her group. In the weeks and months that followed, he had probably mentioned me in conversations with her.

The moment Rebecca heard someone call me Kass, she'd remember that I *had* been the girl at Central Park.

The one dying from leukemia. The one whose life with Asher and the Weston Battalion had been built on lies.

Trembling, I trailed to a halt on the vine-bridge.

My current life was unraveling with terrifying speed.

23

SOMEHOW, I FORCED MYSELF to resume walking across the vine-bridge.

Why was it so cold out here? Despite the overhead sun, the windless air held a bone-numbing chill, and the pale red sky seemed carved from ice. Every muscle in my body felt frozen.

But I knew my coldness had nothing to do with the weather. I was chilled by despair.

Would I ever feel warm again? And once I was expelled from the garrison, would I ever feel safe again?

A noise penetrated my misery. Pausing on the vine-bridge, I looked around.

"There!" Asher pointed. A brown haze rounded a corner of the Bains Building. With a whirr like thousands of chainsaws, it headed toward us. "More locusts!" He pulled Isabel down and shielded the old woman with his body.

A blizzard of insects hit us.

We crouched down, scattered along the vine-bridge, arms covering our faces as we huddled into balls. The locusts crawled everywhere, their revolting stench making me gag. Tiny skeletal legs snared my hair. Dry wings brushed my skin like dead fingers. Brittle bugs crawled over my face.

I panicked.

Get off!

An invisible wave surged from me, slammed into the swarming insects, and threw them back.

Hastily, I glanced around.

Asher and the others were still hunkered on the vine-bridge, their bodies covered in insects. They weren't looking my way, so when more locusts engulfed me, I remote-pushed them as well. This time, only a few retreated. Dozens of bugs still crawled and dug and scratched at my skin and hair, attacking me in an endless barrage that almost made me scream.

On my right, someone shouted.

I saw Booker dangling below the vine-bridge, shouting as he clung to a long thin vine. Asher leaped up and raced toward him. Pepper, closer, began crawling to him as well.

A scream. From my left this time.

Rebecca staggered along the vine-bridge, brushing at the locusts that covered her.

"Rebecca," I cried. "Get down!"

She kept stumbling blindly, shoving away the insects.

I scrambled up and ran toward her.

She slipped.

Shrieking, she began sliding over the side of the bridge, clawing at the vines.

I dived forward and skimmed along the bridge, crushing locusts into a slimy layer, my arms outstretched and—

—I grabbed her hand.

She hung on, squeezing my hand as she dangled below the thick vine, her face upturned and eyes wide with terror.

"Don't let me fall!" she screamed, kicking the air.

"Stay still." I struggled to hold her. At the back of my mind, in an unspeakably dark corner, something whispered: *If Rebecca dies, she won't be able to reveal my secret. I won't be expelled from the Weston Battalion.*

Appalled, I pushed the terrible whispers away and tightened my grip on the girl's fingers.

"Don't let me die," Rebecca begged.

"I won't. I promise." Beads of sweat popped across my brow, and my arms burned from her weight—but I wouldn't let her go. I couldn't. Those terrible whispers weren't the real me. They'd been born of fear, a desperate longing to survive.

"Help!" I shouted to the others. Muscles on fire, I strained to lift Rebecca. She rose an inch. Not enough. "Help!"

My palms sweated.

Through the blur of locusts, I saw Asher and Pepper struggling to drag Booker to safety. Further away, the elderly woman, Isabel, was still hunkered down, besieged by the locusts with their deafening drone. Had anyone even heard my cry for help?

"I'm coming, miss." The old man, Albert, crawled toward me, through the cloud of bugs.

Below the vine-bridge, Rebecca flailed about, hanging by one arm. She kicked at the air like a drowning swimmer, whimpering.

Her fingers began to slip from my sweating palms.

"Rebecca," I shouted. "Give me your other hand. Reach up!"

"I'm going to die!"

Her fingers slid down a fraction more.

"Hang on! Reach up to me." Ignoring the insects that pelted me like hail, I leaned further over the side of the vine, in danger of falling myself. I didn't care. I had to pull her up, save her—

Her fingers slipped from my sweaty grasp.

She fell.

Arms flailing, terrified eyes gazing upward, she plunged toward the ground far below.

Her screams ripped the air, growing fainter and fainter until they—

—abruptly stopped.

Stunned, I peered over the edge of the vine-bridge, staring down at her body. Around me, the world had fallen silent. No screams from Rebecca. No shouts from Asher and the others.

And no buzzing.

After eating all the leaves on this vine-bridge, the swarm was now disappearing behind a distant building.

I lay there, dazed, unable to process Rebecca's death. Later, in the midnight-quiet of my room, I'd try to deal with it. Right now, I had to keep going.

I forced myself to join the others in the middle of the vine-bridge.

Booker lay pale-faced and grateful. "Thanks for saving me, guys."

Everyone listened in horror as I told them of Rebecca's fall. Then, glumly, we set off again for the end of the vine-bridge.

I noticed Albert trailing behind the group. As Asher continued shepherding the others forward, I hurried back to the old man. He stopped and stared at the pale red sky, his age-weary eyes dull with the desperation of someone caught in a never-ending nightmare.

"What's wrong, Albert? Do you see some more locusts?"

"No, miss," he muttered, voice gravelly with fatigue. "I see nothing."

"Good. We have to go. The sooner we get to safety, the better."

"Safety?"

"Over there." I pointed to the Spencer Center at the end of the vine-bridge.

The man shifted his weary eyes to me, the wrinkles on his face deepened by grief. "There's no safety anywhere." He gestured to the street far below. "At least it's all over for Rebecca now. Lucky girl. A few seconds' fall and now she's at peace."

"She wanted to live," I gently reminded him.

"For what, miss? To mourn the loss of everyone she's ever loved? To watch our beautiful planet change into hell? To live with dread every second of every day? Is that living?"

"What other choice do we have?"

"We're human," he croaked. "We always have choices." I wondered if that was true. "But we need the courage to pursue them."

"What are you talking about?"

"Peace."

He stepped off the vine-bridge.

"*No.*" I lunged for him. Grabbed air.

Albert fell. Silently. No screams of terror. No flailing arms or legs. No anguished eyes looking upward, pleading to live.

He just ... fell.

24

Back at the garrison, we debriefed Commander Powell on the day's tragic events. Later, he and Asher spoke with Isabel, now the sole survivor of the Cessna plane crash; shaken, she hadn't uttered a word to anyone on the drive back to Weston Tower.

I waited outside the closed office door until Asher exited.

"What did Isabel say?" I asked.

"A lot." He rubbed a weary hand across his face. "None of it good."

"Terras?"

He shook his head. "Those two dead children on the plane, the ones with bloodied bandages ... they weren't injured by terras."

"Then who? The Chi'az? Hybrids?"

"Xans." Glancing at his watch, he set off down the corridor. "I have a stack of things to organize, Kass."

I hurried to keep up with him. "What's going on?"

"The commander's sending a squad and two teams down to a small town called Eldron."

"Where's that?"

"A little north of Miami, Florida."

I blinked at him, astonished. "Powell has never sent teams that far before. He's always said the countryside's too dangerous to travel through."

"That's why it's volunteers only. You should stay back here, Kass. I want you safe."

"I want you safe too. Guess we're both going to be disappointed, hey?"

Asher studied my face. He must've seen the determination in my eyes because he sighed in defeat. "Okay."

"Why are we going on a mission to Miami? What's so important?"

He detailed the conversation that had taken place in Commander Powell's office.

The old woman, Isabel, was part of a community that lived in Eldron, Florida. Recently, several attacks by xans had left twenty-one people dead. Anxious to arrange the community's escape, their leader had sent several of them off in a small plane to Manhattan—along with a proposal.

"Why Manhattan?" Commander Powell had asked Isabel.

"We'd heard rumors of a strong resistance cell here," she had replied.

"And what's this proposal?"

"Our community wants to join your community here at Weston Tower."

"But your community is in Florida."

Isabel had cleared her throat. "Our group can travel here, if you lend us one of your mechanics."

"What? Why?"

"We have a trawler, and a captain to pilot and navigate it. Plus a crew. But we need a mechanic to fix the engine."

"I can't send a mechanic all the way to Florida just to fix your engine. He'd need soldiers to protect him, and a couple of resistance teams to fight any dangerous terras or xans. We've heard it's bad in the countryside. Sorry, Mrs. Kean—"

"Isabel."

"Sorry, Isabel, it's just not practical. Tell your people to drive up here."

"We only have enough vehicles to transport half of us. Plus traveling via land is too dangerous." Isabel's age-veined hand brushed a lock of gray hair from her eyes. "Nila's authorized me to make you an offer."

"Who's Nila?"

"Our leader."

"What's the offer?"

"A doctor. Our community has a doctor."

Powell's tired eyes sparked with interest. The Weston Battalion had been in desperate need of a doctor for over a year. "A genuine primary care physician?"

"In the flesh. Dr. Tran's saved many lives since the Mist. He's also delivered three babies."

"How old is he?"

"Forty-three."

"Years as a doctor?"

"Eighteen."

"Healthy?"

"As a horse."

Powell rubbed his chin, thinking. "This trawler of yours, does it have a cargo hold big enough for three or four Templars?"

"Templars?"

"They're armored vehicles."

"Never heard of them."

"They had just hit the market when the Mist struck."

"How big are they?" Isabel asked

"Each is as wide as a Humvee and about five feet longer."

"No problem. There'll be space for them all in the trawler's hold."

"Good. I don't want to lose them."

"You won't. Also, Nila's worked hard to get the trawler fully fueled and stocked with provisions. As soon as your mechanic fixes the engine, everyone can leave. Your teams would have a nice relaxing cruise back to New York."

Powell nodded. "I have an engineer, Bevan, who used to work on a cruise ship. Will he do?"

"A ship's engineer? Perfect."

"You have a deal," the commander told Isabel.

In the hallway, Asher finished relaying the conversation. Blue eyes somber, he told me, "Liberty and Trident Teams are heading to Miami."

"When do we leave?"

"Tomorrow."

25

We left the next afternoon.

Our convoy consisted of four modified Templars, each resembling a cross between a Humvee and a souped-up SUV. Painted in camouflage colors and with reinforced cabins, each solid Templar seated eight people: two in the front, followed by two rows of seats facing each other, each taking three passengers. A rear section held supplies, equipment, and fuel.

Templar 1 led the convoy, occupied by Sergeant Thorne and most of his squad. Liberty Team was in T2, with Asher and Booker sharing the driving. Behind us, T3 contained Trident Team, our medic Soo-Yun, and the ship's engineer Bevan. T4 brought up the rear, the driving shared by two soldiers; this vehicle was crowded with a pair of motorized dirt bikes, more supplies, and spare fuel.

The elderly woman, Isabel, remained at the garrison, deemed too frail to accompany us. Besides, we didn't really need her.

On the first day, we traveled a hundred miles—but it felt like a thousand, as each mile took us further and further from the safety of the Weston Garrison.

I sat slumped at a rear side window of T2, watching the changing countryside. Lifeless shops and homes lined the highway. *No, not lifeless*, I realized with a twinge of bitterness. Living, thriving terra vines smothered empty buildings and vehicles, their leaves quivering in an afternoon breeze.

Among the vegetation I glimpsed raccoons, foxes, deer, and a couple of panthers.

Booker glanced up from his sci-fi novel. "Anything interesting to see?"

"Just the usual terra plants," I replied, "and a few Earth animals."

In T2, our newest recruit, Davey, paused a game on his tablet. Skinny as a whippet, he had been discovered living alone in New Jersey by one of our scavenging teams. A good fighter and highly enthusiastic, he'd been a hasty replacement for Freya, who had been quarantined at Weston Tower with a bad cold.

"I wish I had a pilot's license," Davey said, his thin face bright with excitement. "It would've been cool to fly a chopper down to Florida instead of driving."

"Choppers draw too much attention," Asher reminded him from behind the steering wheel. "Plus there's the problem of fuel. Isabel's group had to search for weeks to get enough fuel for that Cessna."

"Bad luck it crashed into a building. Man, I'd love to fly a plane." Although twenty-two, Davey still had the eager-puppy enthusiasm of a kid. "At least we don't have to drive back home. A trip in a trawler sounds fun. Right, Pepper?"

"Yeah, yeah." Pepper's scowl was focused on Lynxx, seated opposite her in the Templar. Beside him was a large birdcage covered by a black cloth. "That owl stinks." Her voice held a sharp edge, suggesting the rumors were true that Lynxx had split up with her.

T2 bumped over some rocks on the cracked road.

"Your owl *really* stinks, Lynxx," Pepper insisted again.

He didn't bother looking up from his open laptop. "You're imagining things."

"And why'd you give it a stupid name like Owl Freak?" she huffed.

"Not Freak. *Fred.* Owl*fred.* I named her after Alfred Hitch-cock."

"Alfred is a male name. Your owl is female."

"She doesn't know the difference."

For the fourth time that day, I peeked under the black cloth. In the birdcage, a small tawny owl blinked at me with round, yellow eyes. "She's so cute."

"Whatever." Pepper glared at Lynxx. "I still don't understand why you named it after Alfred Hitchcock."

"He directed some great movies decades ago," he replied, "including one called *The Birds.*"

"So?"

"Well, Owlfred's a bird."

Pepper gave an irritated sigh. "Why's it even here?"

"I need her. She'll help in identifying certain dangerous terras."

"It's a bird, not a bomb dog."

"The commander didn't object to her coming along." Last night, Commander Powell had assigned Lynxx to the mission, stating that his knowledge of terras would help keep everyone alive.

"Did he know you were bringing it?" Pepper snapped.

Lynxx shrugged. "Maybe not."

"I knew it!"

Rolling my eyes, I turned away from their bickering.

By the fourth day of our mission, the small towns had given way to farms and fields and grasslands, all forever changed. Even the multilane highway was almost unrecognizable. Clumps of thigh-high weeds mingled with patches of grass terras, turning the cracked concrete into an ancient and timeworn track. Sinkholes pockmarked the road, forcing frequent detours, and patches of gold terra trees lined the berm.

I watched a white-tailed deer bolt into a patch of bushes.

Booker lowered his horror novel. "Are we there yet, boss?"

"Not even close," Asher replied from the front.

"At this speed, it'll take us forever to get to Florida."

"The roads are too cracked and riddled with terras to go faster. We may be driving slower than we'd like, but at least we'll get there alive."

"Do you think there are any hybrids in Isabel's group, boss?"

"No idea."

I was surprised at Booker's question. Usually he lived in the worlds of his novels, ignoring the real one as much as possible.

"Why are you asking about hybrids?" I asked him.

Booker waved an arm at the strange landscape. "Because they're terraforming Earth, that's why."

I glanced at Lynxx and felt a sudden urge to defend his kind. "The Chi'az are the ones terraforming Earth, not the hybrids."

"It's the same thing," Rusty said, joining the conversation. He tossed a baseball from one freckled hand to the other. "If I ever meet a hybrid, I'm putting a bullet in its brain. That's not murder, is it? After all, they're not human."

Lynxx looked up from his laptop. "They're half-human. And besides, how can you tell if someone is a human or hybrid?"

"Hybrids have black marks on their earlobes and—"

"That's incorrect, Rusty," said Lynxx, voice tight. "A myth. Before he died, Professor Doylen told Kassia and me there's only one way to be sure."

I nodded, backing him up. "You have to check the person's DNA under a special microscope—which we don't have."

"Just great." Rusty gripped his baseball. "So anyone here or back at the Weston Battalion could be a hybrid. Remember, no one suspected that pilot, Ridge, of being one, did they?"

Others murmured their agreement.

"That's why we have to trust each other," Asher said firmly.

"Or find one of those super microscopes." Booker returned to his novel.

As the afternoon shadows lengthened, Asher scouted for a place to spend the night. He eventually chose a farm with a brook.

Weapons drawn, Liberty and Trident Teams destroyed three small patches of tentacle terras close to the farmhouse, then declared the area safe.

Sergeant Thorne assigned some soldiers to guard duty.

The sprawling farmhouse was weathered and smelly, but intact. I'd just unrolled my sleeping bag on the dusty living room floor when Lynxx murmured, "Feel like a walk, Kassia?"

I nodded. It was Tuesday, my Day 7.

Asher gave me a surprised glance as I gathered my sword and left. I didn't bother explaining that my relationship with Lynxx was more of a truce than a resumption of our friendship.

A short distance from the farmhouse, we found a spot next to the brook. Bracketed by thick trees and away from prying eyes, I drank the purple tonic Lynxx gave me. "Thanks. How many doses did you bring?"

"Four. It took me hours to make them."

"Thank you. I really appreciate all you've done. Four doses are enough for this three-week mission." After Lynxx's recent revelations at the cemetery, I found it easier to talk to him. I was grateful he'd helped to keep Olivia and me alive during our months in the subway bunker. And I was no longer angry or repulsed by the fact that he was a hybrid. Clearly, he was a humanized hybrid, capable of love and loyalty and compassion.

"It's best not to have all of your doses in one place." He passed me a small bottle. "Hide this in your bag. I'll keep the other two until you need them."

I buried the Lazarus tonic at the bottom of my backpack.

We began retracing our steps through the forest that sprawled between the brook and the farmhouse. Dry leaves crackled beneath our boots, and a deer darted away with a flick of its tail.

I asked, "Where are all the gigantic terras that people say are in the countryside? So far we haven't seen any."

"I'm sure they're around." Lynxx clambered over a moss-covered log. "People tend to focus on the unusual, the outstanding, the different."

"What do you mean?"

"Think about it. A man goes on a trip through the countryside. He sees hundreds of harmless angel-vine terras—and two colossus-tree terras. Naturally, he'll tell people about the colossus-trees he saw. He'll describe them in horrific detail. He'll speculate on their sinister purpose. And he'll rave about their frightening size. He won't even mention the hundreds of harmless angel-vine terras he saw."

"I guess so."

A flock of sparrows settled in an oak, squabbling as they picked their roosts for the evening.

"Of course, there's another possibility."

"Which is?"

"There *are* lots of new and dangerous terras out here. We just haven't seen them yet."

"Comforting thought," I muttered, then gasped as Lynxx grabbed my arm and jerked me back. "Oww!"

He pointed to a saucer-sized plant with spiky leaves. "You almost stepped on it."

"Oh. Thanks." Deceptively beautiful, the glow-lotus terras had razor-sharp stamens that could spear a foot and pin it to the ground.

Grabbing a rock, I smashed the flower into a pulpy mess. We set off again.

A peal of demented laughter startled us. The cackle wove through the forest, rising and falling.

Smiling, Lynxx pointed to a large tawny bird with black markings, perched on an upper branch. As it opened its beak and again cackled like a crazy person, he told me, "Kookaburra. The Australians used to call them *laughing jackasses*."

"They have some strange birds down there." I paused. "Or they did." In the coming years, how many of Earth's plants and animals would survive the Chi'az terraforming? Would humanity still exist a century from now? A decade? A year?

We continued through the forest, listening to the kookaburra's demented laughter and the squabbles of roosting sparrows.

Lynxx paused next to a thin stream. "Excellent." He gestured to some brown plants in the clear water. "*Aquanis exTerrus*. Water terras. Their dried leaves make a powerful painkiller." He fished out some plants and crammed them into a specimen jar.

Abruptly, the kookaburra stopped laughing.

The squabbling sparrows fell silent.

And the stream turned red.

26

Blood.

My gaze traced the stream's path to behind a rocky out-crop.

Weapons drawn, Lynxx and I cautiously rounded the boulders.

A dead deer lay in the shallow water. Its stomach had been ripped open, and the current was washing its blood downstream.

We scanned our surroundings. No one was in sight.

Lynxx splashed across to the carcass and inspected the slashed abdomen. "This was done by sharp claws."

"An animal?" I looked around nervously. "Where is it?"

"It might've taken off when it heard us coming."

We froze as a low moan drifted through the late afternoon air.

Moving quietly, we headed to a thick clump of bushes. Beyond them, a full-grown tiger lay in the middle of a clear-ing, its legs and chest entwined by dark vines. When the animal saw us, it snarled and struggled to get free.

I scowled at the vines from a safe distance. "Grippers." Nonpoisonous, they killed their prey by strangulation, like strangler terras.

"The poor thing's scared," Lynxx murmured. "We need to help him."

I hesitated. The last tiger I'd met had stalked me on a vine-bridge, intent on attacking me. "You saw what it did to that deer."

"I don't think this tiger killed that animal. Tigers grasp their prey's neck with their jaws, severing the jugular. They don't kill by slashing abdomens."

"Then what killed the deer?"

"No idea." He studied the tiger and the tangled vines. "We can't just remote-push him free. Maybe we can cut him loose."

"Not me. I'm not going anywhere near that thing."

"We can try remote-soothing him first."

"What's that?"

"It's like remote-pushing, but gentler. Done correctly, it calms the animal, like a cat being petted." He paused as the tiger lifted its head and roared. "But I haven't remote-soothed an animal this large and dangerous before. We'll need to do it together."

The tiger slumped on the vines again, panting as it gazed at us, yellow eyes bright with fear and pain.

"What do we do?" I reluctantly asked.

"Focus on the tiger. Imagine that your hands are petting his head, calming him down."

"Got it. But if we manage to free Stripy and it rips out my throat, I'm blaming you, Lynxx."

"Fair enough." He took my hand, explaining, "The tiger probably weighs over four hundred pounds, so we need to mentally combine our efforts. Hurry, before anyone hears his roars."

I glanced around. No one was in sight. Yet.

Hand in hand, we mentally focused on the distressed animal. I visualized stroking its head, smoothing its fur, relaxing its muscles. Lynxx's fingers twitched in my grip as he did the same thing.

Seconds passed. Then a minute. Two.

Slowly, a warmth seeped through me, soft as a sun-kissed cloud. Stripy's struggles gradually eased, along with its roars. Now silent, it lay on the gripper terras, calm and exhausted.

When a new gripper started crawling toward the tiger, Lynxx flicked a hand and the vine fell back.

The tiger lay still as Lynxx moved forward and carefully cut away the grippers around its legs and chest. When the last of the severed vines fell to the ground, he hastily rejoined me.

Stripy leaped free of the grippers and paused in the clearing. Its yellow eyes sized us up, as though deciding which of us to eat first.

"Not today, Stripy," said Lynxx. "Keep going." He flicked his hand, and the tiger bounded into the forest.

My shoulders sagged in relief. "Wow, that was different."

"Good different? Or bad different?"

"It was great." Elation bubbled within me. This new power was both unexpected and welcome. "I prefer remote-soothing to remote-pushing. Much gentler."

"But slower," he reminded me. "In a life-or-death situation, Kassia, always remote-push first. Besides, you need to practice your remote-soothing a lot more before you can become good at it."

"Hey, I just used it on that tiger—"

"*We* used it. Actually, mostly me. But you helped a bit."

"A bit?" I blushed in embarrassment. "Fine. I'll practice remote-soothing on smaller, less dangerous animals whenever I get a chance."

"Good idea."

I radioed Asher and told him about the tiger, the gripper terras, and the dead deer with its ripped abdomen. "Okay," came his crackled reply. "I'll let the others know. You and Lynxx get back here ASAP."

"We're on our way."

As I pocketed my radio, a gust of wind swept past like an invisible train, rustling and swaying the leaves.

A branch snapped.

Suddenly uneasy, I looked around.

In a grove of trees beyond the clearing, several dark shapes moved among the shadows. About four feet tall and walking upright, they slunk through the forest as noiselessly as ghosts.

Xans?

The wind deflated—and as a hush settled over the clearing, I felt an ominous quality. Heavy. Menacing.

Lynxx raised a finger to his lips. As soundlessly as possible, we hurried back to the track. By the time we reached the edge of the forest, we were running, uncaring of the noise we made, wanting to be anywhere but here.

At a flash of movement, we turned. Three chimpanzees were swinging through the treetops, leaping from branch to branch. Their size and shape matched the vague outlines I'd seen in the shadowy grove of trees.

"Those other animals were probably just chimps," I puffed.

Lynxx nodded. "Chimps." But he sounded unsure.

We hurried toward the farmhouse, glancing back at the forest every few seconds.

27

A FLOORBOARD IN THE barn's loft creaked.

I glanced at Pepper. She scanned the loft, nodded, and raised her gun.

With the tip of my sword, I pushed an old basket over and jumped back. Rats scuttled out. Squeaking, they disappeared beneath a pile of rusty tools on the floor.

"Good one, Kass." Pepper holstered her weapon. "Way to get the heart racing."

"Sorry." I sheathed my sword. "I guess I'm still jumpy from those shapes that Lynxx and I saw in the forest today."

"Didn't you say they were chimps?"

"I said they were *probably* chimps."

Pepper headed toward the staircase at the far end of the loft. "I'm more worried about the tiger you saw. What if it smells our roasting venison tonight?" Two hours ago, Harlem and others from Trident Team had burned the gripper-vines in the clearing, then hauled the dead deer out of the stream. Usually, we only had meat once a week. Fresh venison was a welcome addition to our canned goods. At Booker's suggestion, Asher had allocated a hindquarter for a barbecue tonight.

"We'll be safe, Pepper. Sergeant Thorne's posting guards outside."

"Good."

My gaze lingered on the line of red, white, and blue stars that trailed down her right arm, from shoulder to wrist. "I like your tattoos."

"Thanks."

"When did you get them?"

"A few weeks after I joined the Weston Battalion." She swatted away a fat spider rappelling toward her face. "Even though the world is changing and disappearing, the stars on my arms remind me that our country still exists as long as some of its people still exist."

"I didn't know you were so patriotic." I followed her down the wooden stairs.

"I never felt especially patriotic—until my homeland was attacked."

We moved to the middle of the barn.

"All clear in the loft," I told Harlem, who was setting up an old metal spit. Above us, a hole gaped in the sagging roof. "Are you sure that's big enough to vent the smoke?"

He snapped, "Would you rather have our barbecue in a stinky farmhouse riddled with rats? Or outside with the tigers and the xans?"

An image of the earlier dark shapes in the forest flashed through my mind. "Er, no. This barn will be fine." Even if it wasn't exactly rat-free. A dozen of the critters ignored us as they squeaked and scurried over bales of hay. Since wild rodents only lived about a year, many of these rats had grown up in a world where they didn't fear humans—because there were virtually no humans around to fear.

Harlem tossed a match onto a pile of kindling beneath the spit. Flames flared high and black smoke gushed upward. Coughing, he turned away, kicked a can across the dirt floor, and swore.

"Are you okay?" I asked, surprised at his mini-tantrum.

"Peachy. Have Alan and Rusty finished cutting up that deer yet?" When I shook my head, he snapped, "Do I have to do everything around here?" He stormed off.

Pepper turned to me. "What's wrong with him?"

"No idea. I've never seen him so snappy."

By the time of the barbecue, Harlem had calmed down. Earlier, he and Soo-Yun had cleared out a few piles of decomp-dust, then positioned bunches of harmless perfume-globe terras around the barn. As night fell, the scented flowers threw off waves of soft orange light that lit the darkness.

We sat on bales of hay around the spit, watching the fire and enjoying the smell of roasting venison. Smoke wafted through the hole in the pitched barn roof, hazing the stars in the night sky.

Asher's arm tightened around my shoulder. "This is nice," he whispered, his breath warm on my ear.

My hay bale felt scratchy, the drafty barn reeked of old manure, and rats squeaked in the cobwebbed rafters. None of that mattered. I was nestled in the crook of Asher's shoulder and his strong arms held me. "It's perfect," I murmured.

A gruff voice said, "Weston, I need to talk to you. In private."

Sergeant Thorne loomed over us. The man had been in the Army before the Mist. In his mid-forties, he looked like a walking threat. He had a shaved head, hard face, multiple tattoos, and the bulked-up physique of a weight lifter on steroids. Whenever he swaggered by, people watched him uneasily, as though afraid he'd suddenly punch them.

I didn't like him. And I didn't trust him.

Sergeant Thorne and Asher moved to a distant corner of the barn where they huddled together.

When Asher returned, I asked, "What did Thorne want?"

"Just work stuff." He tossed a small branch onto the fire, triggering a flare of sparks. "Nothing to worry about."

Thorne and the other soldiers sat in the shadows, separate from the rest of us.

Beaming, Soo-Yun passed Harlem a bunch of DVDs. "I find in farmhouse attic. Much action movie. You play back in Weston Tower, yes?"

Harlem shuffled through the disks, his face red from the heat. "What a load of junk." He tossed them into the fire, then scratched his arm.

The Korean girl's smile faded. "I thought you happy I find action movie."

"Not that junk. Are you an idiot?"

Asher leaned forward. "Hang on, Harl. You're being rude."

"Butt out, pal. Soo-Yun's *my* girlfriend."

"Then treat her with the respect she deserves."

"Why should I listen to you, Rich Boy?" Harlem tried to stand, but swayed, then sank back onto the hay bale. "You abandoned that actress, Willow Grace, the girl you claimed was 'the love of your life.'"

Despite the warm glow of the fire, Asher's face paled. "What are you talking about? I never abandoned Willow. When the Mist came, she was in LA. I was in New York. You remember what it was like. Chaos. No planes or trains. No electricity, no phones—"

"You should've loaded up a tank with cans of gasping ... I mean *gas*." Harlem scratched his arm again.

Tank? Gasping?

"I would have, if I'd had a tank." Asher's voice cracked in long-buried grief.

"You had the money, Don Q, to pay the Army to find her."

"What Army? People in the military were dying too."

"Don't you get it? They were only pretending to die. It was all part of a movie script." Harlem scratched his chest, his fingernails almost ripping through his denim shirt. "It was the Egyptian mermaids, Don Q. The Egyptian mermaids."

Asher gaped at his friend.

Lynxx stepped across and shoved up a sleeve of Harlem's shirt. Oozing pustules covered his forearm. "I thought so." He turned to the rest of us. "I saw some ivy terras outside. Did anyone see Harlem near those plants?"

"Ivy terra?" Soo-Yun nodded. "He pick some with perfume-globe terra. He hold only for few second before dropping much quickly." Worried, she reached for her boyfriend but pulled away at the last second. Nurse Ortiz had trained her well; Soo-Yun knew medics had to stay healthy, no matter what.

Asher frowned at Lynxx. "Ivy terras only give you an itchy, stinging rash like poison ivy. It doesn't cause that." He gestured to the slimy mess on Harlem's arms. "And it doesn't produce brown pus."

Lynxx said, "Remember when Harlem was bitten by that Komodo dragon? I think the dragon's venom made him highly allergic to things like ivy terras."

"Is bad allergy?" Soo-Yun's gasped. "Harlem die?"

"Maybe," Lynxx replied. "He's critical."

"I'm okay—" Harlem crumpled to the ground. His body twisted and shook as violent spasms threatened to snap his bones.

Asher rushed forward. "Everyone stay back," he ordered, struggling to hold down the thrashing boy. "He might be contagious."

"He's not," Lynxx said. "He's convulsing. Dying."

"Quick, Soo-Yun," cried Asher. "Get me an EpiPen."

"EpiPens won't work," Lynxx told him. "I'm sure this allergic reaction is unique to the Komodo dragon's venom."

"What about this?" I grabbed a bottle of purple Lazarus liquid from my backpack, plus a syringe from my first aid kit.

Lynxx drew in a sharp breath. "No! You can't."

I knew what he was thinking. He'd only brought four doses and I'd already used one. If I used another on Harlem, I'd only have two doses left for the rest of our mission.

Two doses were still enough.

"I have to try to save him, Lynxx."

Asher watched me fill the syringe with the purple liquid. "Is that the stuff you used on Harl after the Komodo dragon bit him?"

"Similar."

Voices jumbled over each other.

Soo-Yun's frightened voice: "No let Harlem die."

Asher's worried voice: "That purple stuff could kill him."

Lynxx's agitated voice: "Kassia, stop. I didn't make it for him."

My inner voice: *What if something happens and I need this dose to stay alive?*

Ignoring all the voices, I reached for Harlem's arm.

"Cripes!" Asher yanked the syringe from my fingers.

"What are you doing? He'll die."

"I'll do it." He unzipped his backpack. "Despite what Lynxx said, that brown pus could be infectious." He passed the syringe to Booker. "Hold this for a second." After snapping on a pair of thin latex gloves, he grasped Harlem's slimy arm and carefully injected the tonic into a vein.

Harlem fell unconscious, his body still jerking as though electrified. Asher and Booker carried him into the farmhouse, followed by an anxious Soo-Yun.

The rest of us doused the fire and disbanded.

The night stretched on, long and cold. We listened to the feverish groans coming from Harlem's room. We heard Soo-Yun's soothing voice; at other times, we heard her soft weeping.

No one slept.

We waited.

28

TWO DAYS LATER, OUR convoy had tortuously traveled another two hundred miles.

At the steering wheel, Booker warned, "Hades terras dead ahead."

T2 drove across a patch of gold leaves on the highway. As the vines crackled and ignited, our vehicle plowed through the iridescent flames.

Still weak, Harlem winced at the walls of fire outside the windows.

Soo-Yun gave his arm a gentle, reassuring pat. "Templar no catch alight. Tires are flaming retarded."

"Flame retardant," Harlem gently corrected her. "And I know we're safe, Soo. I was just remembering the cookout in the barn ..." His words faded away in embarrassment.

Asher's eyes gleamed as he teased, "We all know you acted like a jerk, Harl. No need to apologize again."

"Gee, thanks, bro."

Our Templar passed through the flames and then we were clear, with the open highway ahead.

"How are you feeling today?" I asked Harlem. Yesterday, he'd slept for fifteen hours straight, curled on the back seat. Pepper and Davey had ridden with Trident Team, allowing Harlem and Soo-Yun to join us in T2.

"Better. No more itching or delusions. Although I'd be happy if all of this"—he gestured to the huge onion terras outside—"turned out to be delusions."

"No such luck."

Lynxx shifted uneasily. "You're fortunate to be alive, Harlem." He darted me a disapproving glance, still upset that I'd sacrificed one of my Lazarus doses.

Asher frowned at Lynxx and me. "As I told you yesterday, I realize you both used terras after that buckshot pod exploded months ago. The terras saved your life. And I'm grateful they've saved Harl's life—twice. But using terras is strictly against the Weston Garrison's rules. Commander Powell's policy exists for a reason. We don't know what effect eating or drinking terras will have on us."

"This was a rare exception," I replied, mentally crossing my fingers. "It won't happen again."

"It can't," Asher stressed. "You know that."

"Sure." I looked through the side window, hoping he couldn't read the guilt on my face.

Outside the Templar, things were changing.

The weather was warmer, and many of the terras were larger. Colossus-trees studded the land, some of them tall enough to dwarf the giant sequoias of California's national parks. Fifty-foot-high onion-like terras loomed along the highway, each bulbous shape held aloft by long, thin roots that twitched and trembled as our convoy passed by. Even the beautiful but lethal cathedral-domes were oversized versions of the ones back in Manhattan.

Had my father and Olivia encountered similar enormous terras on their drive from Los Angeles to New York? Only my sister had made it home. She'd told me that Dad's death had been peaceful, and I'd chosen to believe her. Now, I wondered if she'd been trying to spare me a more agonizing truth.

Beside me, Lynxx looked at his watch yet again. "We need to pull over soon."

It was only 2:30 p.m.

"What's wrong?" I asked as he glanced at the covered bird-cage beside him. "Is Owlfred okay?"

"She's fine. Tired, though."

"Tired? All she's done on this trip is sleep in her cage. She doesn't even have to hunt for her supper, thanks to all the rats around."

"Can we go faster?" Lynxx craned his neck, scanning the road ahead.

Behind the steering wheel, Booker shrugged. "Sure, if you want to end up in a sinkhole that we don't notice until too late."

"No, thanks. A broken axle or wheel will make us even later."

"Later for what, Lynxx?" I asked. "What's going on? You've been on edge ever since you got up this morning."

"I just want to get moving. I wasn't expecting a four-hour delay because of T4's engine problem. The rest of us should've kept going and let T4 catch up to us tonight."

"We don't split up, no matter what," Asher told him. "There are too many unknown variables out here. We're safer if the convoy stays together."

Lynxx grunted and stared through the window.

Monkeys swung in the branches of a small colossus-tree, watched by a bobcat on the ground.

Ten minutes later, we passed through a small town called Benson. A couple of miles beyond the last building, the owl started screeching inside her covered cage.

"Pull over," Lynxx cried. "Something's wrong with Owlfred." He peered through the side window. "There. That clearing ahead. The one with the cow statue out front. Pull in there. Quickly."

Booker radioed the other vehicles, and the line of Templars parked at the berm.

The moment T2 halted, Lynxx jumped out.

"Hey, what about Owlfred?" I called after him.

"I made a mistake. She's fine." He didn't even glance at the covered birdcage, and when I peeked under the black cloth, the small owl sleepily blinked her yellow eyes.

Had he used Owlfred as an excuse to pull over?

Standing next to the open door, Lynxx said to Asher, "We're due for a rest stop in ten minutes. How about we make it here?"

"Are you okay?" Asher asked him.

"I'll be fine once I take a walk."

"Okay. I'll let the others know."

Lynxx hurried toward the far side of the clearing.

I caught up with him. "Where are you going?"

He cast me an impatient glance. "This is a rest stop, Kassia. Can't a guy have a bit of privacy?"

"We had a stop two hours ago, and you haven't eaten or drunk anything since then." I gave him a cheeky smile. "So, where are you going?"

Not answering, he hurried on, and I followed him to the edge of a strange field.

"*Leginiius exTerrus*," he murmured. "Teardrop terras. They can be extremely dangerous, Kassia. Be careful."

The field was studded with plants that resembled seven-foot-tall teardrops. Each glistened in the afternoon sun, and most seemed to have something inside of them.

"Listen," he said.

To what?

I listened. A couple of birds chirped. Leaves stirred in a breeze. Far off, a lion or tiger roared.

"Nothing." His shoulders sagged. "Stay here while I have a look."

"Forget it. I can't battle these things down the road if I don't know why they're dangerous."

"Okay. But keep close to me."

As we moved among the tall teardrop terras, I peered through their transparent petals. One plant held a wild boar, partially decomposed. The others had different contents including a dead deer, two dead wolf cubs, a pony skeleton, and various other animals too decomposed for identification.

Asher's hushed voice came from behind. "What are these things?"

Sergeant Thorne, Pepper, and others joined us. All stared at the gruesome teardrops.

Dismayed, Lynxx said, "You guys shouldn't be here. These things are dangerous. You need to get out of this field now. Be careful you don't step on any flat petals on the ground; they're almost invisible."

"Hey, I've seen these things before," Davey cried. "One got my friend back in New Jersey. They're killers." Face tight with determination, he withdrew his sword and stomped across a glistening patch of grass.

"Watch out!" Lynxx cried.

A circle of flat petals sprang up and snapped shut, trapping Davey inside a now-upright teardrop terra. Swearing, he struggled to escape as the terra sprayed him with a white substance.

"Quick!" Lynxx cried. "Cut him free."

Asher, Booker, and Rusty withdrew their knives and sliced into the huge petals.

As Lynxx moved away, I asked him, "Where are you going?"

"To the other plants." At a faint groan, he pointed to some distant teardrops. "Over there."

I watched Davey squeeze through a long slice in the teardrop terra. "Will he be okay?"

"He'll be fine."

We hurried toward the teardrops at the far end of the field. Three contained dead animals. The fourth held a woman. She gazed through the transparent petals, her bloodshot eyes numb.

She was alive—barely. A few feet away, the last teardrop held a middle-aged man, also dazed but alive.

I rushed to cut the woman free.

Lynxx halted me with a sharp gesture. "It's too late."

"What are you talking about?"

Asher joined us, sheathing his knife. "Davey's okay. But Lynxx is right, Kass—it's too late for these people."

I stepped closer and finally understood. Both victims were covered in a white gel that had eaten away parts of their clothes, their skin, their flesh. As we watched, the stuff sizzled through muscles on their chests and face, exposing bone.

My stomach twisted. "What can we do?"

Sergeant Thorne arrived and assessed the situation. "This sucks."

Asher caught the soldier's gaze, nodded, then told the rest of us, "Go back to the Templars."

We hesitated, then left Asher and Thorne in the field of teardrop terras.

Lynxx's golden eyes were heavy with distress. "If T4 hadn't had engine problems this morning, we might've arrived in time."

I regarded him, curious. "How did you know they were here?"

"I didn't."

"You insisted on stopping at this place."

"That's because I recognized the cow statue out the front."

"Huh?"

"It was ... um ... in a documentary I'd seen on TV once. I wanted to ... have a closer look at it."

His claim was ridiculous. "You're a terrible liar," I cried, stomping away.

The hypocrisy of my accusation followed me back to the Templar. I'd been brought up to tell the truth, and yet I was hiding secrets in order to stay alive.

Was Lynxx hiding his secrets for the same reason?

Davey slouched past me, dripping water, no longer covered in the white spray from the teardrop.

"Glad you're okay," I said.

"Stupid plants," he grumbled, heading for T3.

A single gunshot sounded from the field of teardrop terras. Then another.

Asher and Thorne returned to the convoy, the sergeant whistling as he crossed to the lead Templar. Asher silently took his seat, face grim.

Dejected, we continued our journey, quietly carrying our secrets with us.

29

LATER THAT AFTERNOON, THE sunlight was slowly fading as we stopped in a small town just off the highway.

Nilster, North Carolina, was silent.

Too silent.

But at first we didn't realize it.

In pairs, we scouted for overnight accommodation and supplies. Asher partnered with Davey, who was still shaken from his close call with the teardrop terra.

Harlem and I were partnered up, and we cautiously moved down Main Street, scanning the stores on either side. Despite seeing only a few harmless angel-vine terras and a flock of parakeets, we kept our guns drawn.

Harlem murmured, "Thanks again for saving my life the other day."

"I'm glad you're okay."

We made a quick sweep through a convenience store with broken windows, empty shelves, and overturned shopping carts.

As we left the store empty-handed, Harlem threw me a glance. "Be careful. People are starting to talk."

"About what?"

"About the bottles of terra liquids that you and Lynxx carry around." He squinted through a broken window of a diner. "We know you only use the stuff to heal injuries. And hey, I'm real glad you used it to keep me alive. But you and Lynxx know the stuff is strictly against the garrison rules."

No way could I admit that I drank a weekly terra tonic to stay alive.

I struggled to find an explanation. "It's ..." I paused, the hair at the nape of my neck prickling.

It felt like something was watching us from the shadows "Kass?"

And then I realized why I was on edge.

The town was too silent.

No birds chirped in the trees. No rats rustled among the trash. No wolves howled in the distance.

Harlem gasped, "Look!" He pointed a shaky finger.

Down the street, an object hung from a curved lamppost. A body, swaying in a breeze. Beyond it, three more bodies dangled from lampposts. All were about four feet tall.

Guns drawn, Harlem and I cautiously approached. Each body had been skinned. Raw muscles and sinews glinted red in the weak sunlight, large eyes bulged in lidless sockets, and the skulls were scalped and misshapen.

We stopped at the first corpse, avoiding a pool of blood below it. Flies buzzed and crawled over the dangling remains, and a rank smell of death filled the air.

Harlem's appalled gaze slid down the row of bodies. "What are they?"

Shuddering, I squinted up at the first body. Its arms were abnormally long, and each hand had four thick fingers. Long claws. Barrel chest. Muscled torso.

And jaws studded with fangs.

Asher and Davey emerged from a side street, bulging bags of supplies slung over their shoulders. At the gruesome display, Davey withdrew his gun. He studied our surroundings, watching for movement, eager to take on any attackers.

I told them, "They're about the size of the animals that Lynxx and I saw in the forest a few days ago."

"These don't look like chimps to me." Asher deposited his bags on the sidewalk. "Not with those skulls."

He was right. Each skull had a flat top. At the back, the bone protruded in a horizontal outgrowth that was several inches long and ended in a blunt point; the shape reminded me of the streamlined helmets some cyclists used to wear in races.

My skin crawled. "I wonder what these things looked like alive."

"No idea," Asher said. "But from their sharp fangs and claws, I'm guessing they were pretty dangerous."

Davey gripped his gun, ready for action. "The blood's still wet." He scrutinized the buildings on Main Street. "The killers might be in Nilster right now, watching us."

A pulse throbbed at my temple. Was that why the town was so silent? Were the birds and animals hiding ...

... from what?

Asher spoke quietly into his radio, telling the others about our discovery. "Everyone back to the vehicles."

On the pavement near the first body, somebody had drawn—in blood—a jagged bolt of lightning. The same red bolt appeared near each of the other bodies.

We hurried down the street, scanning our surroundings. Our theories and fears bubbled forth in a tangle of subdued voices.

"What were those things?"

"They've got to be xans."

"Who killed them? Strung 'em up?"

"Humans?"

"Maybe they were killed by those alien things, the Chi'az."

"We don't even know if the Chi'az are on our planet yet. Besides, why would they kill their own creations?"

"Okay, maybe they were hybrids."

"No. Hybrids look like humans with normal human skulls."

"Or hybrids killed those things."

"Why would hybrids kill xans?"

"The hybrids who've become humanized—the good ones—might not like xans."

After the incident on the massive skyweb terra months ago, I'd told Commander Powell about Bone's claims: that humanized hybrids were regarded as traitors by the Outrider hybrids, who in turn remained fiercely loyal to the Chi'az. The commander had passed this information along to the rest of the Weston Battalion and then to the other communities scattered around the world.

Asher kicked a can, rattling it across the street. "There's no such thing as a *good* hybrid."

I thought of Lynxx and remained quiet.

The tangle of comments continued from the others.

"Did people do this? Kill and skin those xans?"

"But why would they do that?"

"As a warning?"

"Revenge?"

"Sick fun?"

A few minutes later, radio reports started coming in from the rest of our group. A misshapen four-foot body had been found on a driveway of a house. Two more bodies were displayed in the window of a clothing store. A pair reclined on benches in a park. Others were seated in cars or mounted on rooftops. One was crammed into a cage on a sidewalk.

All skinned.

All muscular.

All with four thick fingers and claws, abnormally long arms, misshapen heads.

And all accompanied by red lightning bolts drawn in blood.

30

WE HURRIED ALONG NILSTER'S main street, clumped together for protection.

The shadows around me felt thick with menace. And I could almost feel the dead eyes of the strange, skinned creatures watching our retreat.

A few minutes later, our convoy sped away from the creepy North Carolina town.

Subdued by the day's incidents, we made camp in an old barn, then turned in early. I lay in my sleeping bag, staring into darkness, remembering the scenes from the day. The frightening teardrop terras with their dead victims. The gut-churning skinned creatures in Nilster.

Toward dawn, I fell into a restless sleep.

The next day, we spent long boring hours driving down highways and detours lined with familiar and weird plants.

At 4 p.m., Asher consulted his map. "We'll stop in Devil's Tomb. It's just a few miles ahead."

Devil's Tomb.

I shrugged.

The name had probably been scary before the Mist. Now it barely raised a flicker of concern as we drove through the small South Carolina town. After a quick reconnaissance, Asher selected Three Oaks Inn on the outskirts of Devil's Tomb.

Tired and dejected, I unrolled my sleeping bag in a dusty guestroom. After hours of being cooped up in the increasingly smelly Templars, it was a relief to stretch my legs.

Relief changed to groans, though, when Liberty Team drew water duty.

Glumly, we strapped empty water bottles to our backs. Weapons in hand, we gathered at the top of a hill with a stream at the bottom. The sunlit ground was carpeted with bell-like melody terras that, according to Lynxx, were harmless.

He hadn't mentioned how unique the silver flowers were.

Grouped together for protection, we trudged down the slope of flowers—and our glumness disappeared.

By our third trip, we were almost certain there were no dangerous terras in the immediate area. And the only xans were some crabbens down at the stream.

Relaxing, we spread out, laughing and chatting as we strolled up and down the flower-covered hill.

Beaming, Asher put his heavy water bottle on the ground. "Watch this, Kass." He sounded like a carefree teenager instead of a battle-weary resistance fighter.

Gun holstered, he tap-danced over the tightly packed melody terras, moving with skill and grace. The silver flowers didn't break under his weight; instead, they sprang back with melodious tinkling sounds, their petals and stems intact.

We had discovered that slow, deliberate steps produced low notes, while short, quick steps created bell-like music that matched the patterns of our footwork.

I laughed, delighted to see Asher having fun. "For someone who hates terras, you sure seem to like these ones."

"Who wouldn't? They're incredible."

I was tempted to say that *he* was incredible. Despite the dangers and stresses of our existence, Asher's spirit remained unbroken. His love of life was a flicker of light that helped others bounce back, even after our darkest days.

"Hmm." He paused. "Time for some line dancing."

Grinning, he hooked his thumbs into his weapons belt. Humming a country tune, he boot-scooted across the musical flowers like a born-and-bred cowboy. A sexy cowboy. The muscles that rippled beneath his khaki shirt indicated strength and youth and vitality, and I stood helpless as a wave of heat surged through my body, scorching my neck and cheeks.

Flustered, I glanced away from him—

—and saw someone on the terrace of the Three Oaks Inn.

Lynxx. He sat at an outdoor table, ignoring his open laptop as he watched Asher and me.

A wave of suspicion doused the fire that Asher had lit within me.

I was certain Lynxx had known about the man and the woman trapped in the teardrop terras yesterday, even before we'd found them. How, though? He rode in the Templar with us every day, but at night he always took a room by himself and slept with the door closed. Was this when he used his radio to contact someone? Who? And why?

Asher glanced around. "Where are the others?"

"At the stream."

"Good. That gives us a couple of minutes of privacy." Laughing, he pulled me down onto the silver flowers, setting off a series of low harmonious notes. The blossoms felt springy beneath me, the way I'd always imagined clouds would feel if I were able to walk on them.

He gathered me into his arms, his blue eyes gleaming. "Kass," he murmured. Beneath us, the flowers played their songless music, soft and seductive. His warm lips crushed my own, and I longed to lose myself in their heat and the oblivion of passion.

But I could still feel a pair of eyes watching me.

I sat up, glancing at the terrace.

Lynxx quickly looked away.

Asher followed the direction of my gaze, then gave a resigned smile. "It's hard finding somewhere romantic and private these days."

"True."

The melody-flowers' perfume filled the air, so heavy that I could almost taste it. And perhaps I *was* tasting it. During my months in the subway bunker, Lynxx had regularly given Olivia bunches of Lazarus blossoms. These terras had helped keep me alive, their healing properties hidden within their pollen.

I sighed, realizing I owed Lynxx an unpayable debt of gratitude, not suspicions.

And yet ...

Was Lynxx like the Lazarus flowers? He looked innocent, but was he hiding more secrets?

Standing, Asher pulled me up, into his arms. "Kass," he murmured, stroking my hair. "My Kass." He placed my hand on his chest, and I could feel his heart thudding.

On the terrace, I saw Lynxx push away from the table and shove his laptop into his backpack. He hurried inside the inn, as though unable to bear the sight of Asher embracing me for a moment longer.

Asher's eyes flickered from my somber face to the retreating Lynxx. Releasing me, he took a heavy step back—and the terra flowers clanked like out-of-tune bells. "What's going on with you and Lynxx?"

"Nothing."

"What aren't you telling me?"

"Nothing," I said again, aware of all the secrets I was hiding from him.

His blue eyes dimmed, shadowed by confusion. "Has Lynxx hurt you in some way?"

"No. He would never hurt me!" I shook my head, throwing off the absurd suggestion.

Asher and I moved a few steps across the melodious flowers. The blossoms bent and sprang up again as we passed by, their music growing softer, as though reluctant to disturb our argument.

A drift of laughter came from further down the hill.

Relieved at the interruption, I told Asher, "The others are coming."

His gaze remained fixed on my face, and his next words were whispered, as if afraid to even voice them. "Do you have feelings for Lynxx?"

"Not like that. Never."

"Then what is it? What's going on between you two?"

The only answer I could give him was another feeble, "Nothing."

Asher stepped back, angry, disbelieving.

Then he stopped. He stared down at the silver blossoms. Stomped his boot. Once. Twice. More. The flowers sprang up, whole, undamaged—

—and silent.

31

"Hey, boss," Booker said, strolling across the melody terras, "who turned off the music?"

Pepper, Rusty, and Davey looked at the silent flowers, perplexed.

"I'm not sure." Asher scrutinized the field and the grounds beyond. Nothing appeared suspicious. "Maybe they're just shutting up shop for the day." He nodded at the filled water bottles. "Thanks, guys. I think we've got enough."

As we deposited our bottles on the back terrace, Rusty asked, "Where are the others?"

Through a window, I could see Lynxx at a bench, his back to me as he typed on a laptop. "Lynxx is in the kitchen," I said.

Avoiding my gaze, Asher added, "Sergeant Thorne and some of his men have gone hunting. Most of the others are scouting the town for supplies. No idea where Harl is."

"Actually," Pepper said, "Soo-Yun radioed me a while ago. She and Harlem are taking a break. They were headed to a lookout to practice her ballet routines. But they came across a herd of rhinos instead."

"Really?" Asher's eyes widened in interest. "Where?"

She pointed to three oaks a short distance away. "In a field beyond those trees, about ten minutes' walk."

Asher grinned at us. "Who wants to see the rhinos?"

A chorus of enthusiasm answered him.

As we set off, he took my hand, our earlier argument for-gotten—or at least shelved. Internally, I gave a relieved sigh. Fortunately, Asher didn't hold on to his anger the way I held on to my secrets.

We were just approaching the three oaks when we abruptly halted.

A line of crabben xans crossed our path. The baseball-sized critters had been at the stream earlier, but they hadn't bothered us and we hadn't bothered them.

Now they were only a few feet away.

Booker gripped his elbow, remembering the painful bite he'd received from a crabben last month.

Ignoring us, the crabbens hurried onward, their stalk-like eyes fixed on a nearby woodpile. Previously, they'd scurried on claws and legs that clattered and ticked. Now, each xan rushed across the path on the tips of their front claws, moving soundlessly.

"Are they tiptoeing?" I whispered.

"I think so," Asher murmured. "Strange." Then he stiffened, as if struck by a sudden possibility.

"What?" I asked.

He jerked his arm up, fist clenched. *Stop. Silence.*

Everyone froze, scanning for danger. Except for the tip-toeing crabbens, our surroundings appeared peaceful, almost normal.

A warthog emerged from a bush and dashed across the grass. Its oversized head had long curved tusks, and skeins of saliva trailed from its jaws.

"Stay still," Asher quietly ordered us. "Don't move."

I fought an urge to run. Instead I gripped my sword. The others did the same as—

—the ground split open.

A long brown object shot out, lassoed the squealing warthog, and dragged it down into the cracked earth.

Four more brown things burst from the ground. They jutted a few feet above the grass, swaying like cobras enthralled by snake-charmers. The xans, eyeless as worms, had undersides lined with suckers like octopus tentacles.

Déjà vu. Back in Manhattan, just before Isabel's plane had crashed into a building, we'd seen a similar xan—with similar suckers—smash through the broken road and grab up some crabbens.

The four sucker xans remained upright, their bodies twitching.

As the last of the crabbens scurried into the safety of the woodpile, I finally realized what Asher had already guessed.

These blind sucker xans hunted via sounds and vibrations. This was why the crabbens had tiptoed to safety. It was also why the melody terras had gone silent. Both species must've sensed the sucker xans nearby.

The suckers shrank back into their holes, as though disappointed at the lack of prey. Barely breathing, we watched their retreat. Then we looked at Asher, awaiting his signal to leave.

He shook his head. *No.*

I eyed the distance to the inn. About four hundred yards. The xans were between us and the building. If they were hiding, lying in wait, we'd only get a few feet before they attacked us.

I felt vibrations beneath me, as though the sucker xans were tunneling through the soil. We remained motionless, not moving a muscle—

—except for our newest member, Davey, who shouted, "They're right below me!"

Geysers of dirt exploded as half a dozen brown shapes burst from the earth.

Our silence dissolved into shouts and cries.

One sucker grabbed Rusty's legs and pulled him over. He shouted and kicked as he was dragged toward a hole. Savagely, I remote-pushed the xan away from him with such force that I felt momentarily dizzy. The long tentacle exploded, and I glanced around, alarmed. Had anyone seen what I'd done?

No one had noticed. They were all too busy trying to survive.

Booker pumped half a dozen bullets into a xan, but the thing still lunged at him. Swearing, he grabbed his sword and slashed it to pieces.

Asher hacked and slashed at the xans around him, his sword glinting death with each stroke.

Beyond him, I glimpsed Lynxx racing toward us. He wielded a baseball bat and, as he shucked off his backpack, he shouted, "Kassia!"

Nearby, a brown sucker xan rose behind Pepper. Startled, she slipped on the loosened soil. I grabbed her hand, yanked her up, and we leaped aside as the fat xan speared toward us. I gave it a ferocious remote-push that thrust the creature toward the woodpile. A second later, I staggered beneath a wave of dizziness, and my sword slipped from my weakened fingers.

A terrified shout came from behind.

Turning, I saw Davey being pulled into a hole, the soft soil gulping its way past his chest and shoulders.

"Hold on." Shaking off my dizziness, I bolted toward him, remote-pushing. However, his xan-attacker was underground, out of sight. Nothing for me to remote-push away.

I dived toward Davey, sliding over the grass, my arms outstretched as his head disappeared, with only one arm remaining above the ground. My fingertips brushed his wrist. "Grab my hand, Davey." A heartbeat later, he was yanked beneath the dirt.

Dark blood puddled up, marking his grave.

Davey.

Something squeezed my ankle.

"Oww!" I glanced down. A xan was coiled around my leg, its suckers painful even through the thick fabric of my jeans. Desperately, I remote-pushed it away, but the effort left me weak and dizzy again. The thing relaxed its hold for a second, then tightened its grip again.

I collapsed under a flood of fresh pain.

The xan dragged me toward a hole that gaped like a jagged mouth in the earth.

"Kassia!" Lynxx wove and darted through the attacking xans, slamming his baseball bat left and right while remote-pushing others away. "Push it off."

Again, I mentally tried to shove the xan off my leg, but a rush of queasiness left me kitten-weak. "Can't!" Helpless, I couldn't even stop myself from being hauled across the ground.

Further off, Asher yelled, "Hang on, Kass." He slashed his sword at the xans around him. "I'm coming."

I clutched at the soil, trying to slow myself down, but my fingers had the strength of wet spaghetti. Useless. What was wrong with me? It was only Day 6. Did I need an early dose of the Lazarus tonic?

Across the clearing, Lynxx's backpack lay discarded, along with its precious doses of Lazarus tonic. The pack was too far away. And too late to help me. I'd be dead within the next few seconds.

As I watched, the backpack started tilting, then teetered on the edge of a hole. I tried to shout a warning to Lynxx, but my voice emerged as a whisper. "Your backpack ..."

He didn't hear me.

The pack dropped into the hole.

Gone.

Pepper rushed across, swung her sword down, and hacked at the long xan attached to my leg. Reeking droplets splattered my face. When the xan finally relaxed its grip, I pulled it off my leg with shaking hands, and Pepper cut the thing into pieces that twitched and jerked on the grass.

"Thanks," I croaked.

Asher reached my side. "Are you hurt?"

I lifted the leg of my jeans. Red circles covered my calf, oozing pinpricks of blood. Nothing serious. "I'm all right, thanks to Pepper." Surprisingly, I was starting to feel less woozy, and when Lynxx reached me moments later, I assured him, "I'm okay."

"Good," he said. "Because they're still coming."

More sucker xans burst from holes, spraying dirt over us.

"We have to get to the inn," Pepper cried.

"We'd never make it," Asher said. "Too far away. We need a diversion." Withdrawing his gun, he shouted, "When I start shooting, guys, get to those oaks behind us." He fired several times at a greenhouse near the inn. The panes shattered like brittle thunderclaps, and broken shards crashed down.

Vibrations. Sounds. The two things the sucker xans used for hunting.

Like lemmings drawn to a cliff, the xans turned and raced toward the greenhouse, wiggling across the grass with surprising speed.

We ran toward the three oaks.

"They're coming back," Pepper cried.

I glanced over my shoulder. The shattered greenhouse stood broken but quiet. Losing interest, the sucker xans headed back to the only other source of vibrations and sounds around.

Us.

32

WE SCRABBLED UP THE trees, into the branches, desperate to get as far from the ground as possible.

Pepper and Rusty climbed the furthest oak. Asher and Booker perched in the middle one. Lynxx and I were in the third oak.

Rusty clung to a branch, his chest heaving from exertion. As a dozen xans reached the trees, he called out, "Do you think they can climb?"

"We're about to find out," Asher replied.

Sucker xans twisted and wriggled at the bottom of each oak. A couple even managed to stretch partway up the trunks before falling back down again.

We heaved sighs of relief in our overhead perches.

They can't climb.

From his tree, Asher looked across at me. Frowning, he shifted his gaze to Lynxx, who was sharing my branch. "Take care of her, okay?"

"I will," Lynxx assured him.

Normally I would've objected to their male overprotective-ness, but my recent puzzling bouts of weakness kept me silent.

Asher checked on the others. Except for some cuts and bruises, we were all okay. Mostly. Poor Davey was dead.

"Okay," Asher said, reloading his gun. "Let's turn these suck-ers into calamari."

We blasted the wiggling xans.

No effect. It was as though we were shooting rice instead of bullets.

"Don't they have organs?" Booker called out.

"They probably have small ones," Lynxx replied, "difficult to hit."

"So we're trapped in these trees?"

"Until the rest of our group returns." Asher lifted his radio. "I need to warn them."

With Asher distracted, I shifted closer to Lynxx on the branch. Quietly, I told him what had happened when I'd remote-pushed the sucker xans earlier, then asked him, "What's wrong with me? Why did I get so weak?"

"I think remote-pushing is like a muscle. If you don't keep practicing it, you'll have problems like today."

"What do you mean?"

"Before, you've always remote-pushed one animal at a time. Or a bunch of insects like the locusts on the vine-bridge terra. Today, you needed to remote-push half a dozen large xans, one after the other. The first two or three were okay. After that, each push left you feeling weaker, sicker."

"I saw you remote-pushing lots of xans today, Lynxx. You were fine."

"I'm more practiced than you." His gaze flickered to Asher in the nearby tree. With a note of reproach, he added, "You've been busy with other things. Plus you keep changing your mind. One week you want lessons from me. The next week you want nothing to do with me."

"You're right. Sorry," I said, flushing. "So I don't need to increase the dose of my Lazarus—? Oh no!"

"What's wrong?"

I felt sick again, only this time with despair. "Your backpack fell into one of those holes dug by the xans."

"What? Your last two doses were in that pack!"

"I know."

At the tremble in my voice, he hurriedly suggested, "Maybe you don't need them anymore."

"What do you mean?"

"You've been drinking the Lazarus tonic for months now. Maybe, after all that time, it's cured your leukemia."

Cured my leukemia? I felt lightheaded with hope. After years of living in the cold shadow of my illness, I longed to walk in the sunshine once again.

"Anyway," he continued, "we'll soon know for sure."

From the middle oak, Asher called to us, "I've just contacted Harl. He and Soo-Yun are in a minivan. They've got a plan to draw the xans away from us."

"What kind of plan, boss?" Booker asked.

"He didn't say."

A series of far-off gunshots punctuated the afternoon air. Distant feet rumbled. A minute or two later, a herd of stampeding rhinoceroses thundered into view, their leathery feet stirring up clouds of dust that hazed the animals into ghostly shapes.

At the sight of the lumbering rhinos, I felt a stir of guilt. "I hope they're faster than the sucker xans."

Lynxx smiled. "Much faster. Much stronger." His golden eyes widened. "Hey, I have an idea." As the thunder grew louder, he told me his plan, then said, "I can probably manage it by myself."

"No way. I'm feeling better. I should be able to handle a smaller one."

"Are you sure?"

"I think so."

The eyeless sucker xans turned toward the charging rhinos, attracted by their noise and vibrations. A long xan wrapped a coil around a rhino's leg, but the rhino effortlessly dragged the snake-like body across the dirt, and another rhino squashed it.

When the herd approached our tree, Lynxx remote-pushed the largest rhino, and I focused on a smaller one. As the two animals veered away from the group, we used a series of rapid remote-pushes to manipulate them into stomping on the pack of sucker xans.

The rhinos' strong leathery feet crushed creature after creature into stinking brown sludge.

Lynxx's success rate was almost perfect. Mine was low, and I felt weaker with each push.

When all the xans were dead, we released our mental holds on the rhinos and began climbing down. By the time we joined the others on the ground, my head was spinning and I staggered a little. Quickly, Lynxx put a steadying hand under my elbow.

Adopting stunned expressions, Lynxx and I pretended to share the others' astonishment as they stared at the squashed xans.

"What just happened?" Asher gaped at the departing herd of rhinos.

"No idea." Pepper screwed up her face at the sludgy mess on the ground. "Yuck. They stink."

"Let's get out of here," I suggested, my dizziness evaporating.

Lynxx looked at me with a question in his eyes, and I gave a clandestine thumbs-up.

We hurried toward the inn, avoiding the holes in the ground and watching for new attackers. Our distress at losing Davey was muted by a surreal sense of survival. Around me, people shared battle stories of the sucker xans and offered theories about the rhinoceros' bizarre behavior.

Asher shook his head, still bemused. "Kass, did you see the way those two rhinos ran around squashing the xans?"

"Yeah," I replied, wide-eyed with fake innocence. "They must really hate sucker xans."

"I'll say!"

As Lynxx and I fell back behind the rest of the chattering group, we exchanged a small private smile.

33

After the incident at Three Oaks Inn, we were all reluctant to walk across open ground.

However, as the days passed with no further sightings of the subterranean xans, we pushed away our fears. Even before the Mist, life had been precarious. People died in car crashes, boating accidents, even playing football. In these post-apocalyptic days, we had simply swapped one set of risks for another.

A week after the sucker xan incident, our convoy reached North Florida.

The landscape was studded with huge onion-shaped terras, colossus-trees, and other strange plants. Some Earth crops also thrived in the warm weather, and we scanned the land for familiar vegetables.

When Booker spotted some overgrown vegetable patches in front of several ruined buildings, we parked and began harvesting the produce. Trident Team gathered potatoes and pumpkins, while Sergeant Thorne and his soldiers picked cabbages from outside a rundown community center.

Liberty Team cautiously entered an old church. Its roof had caved in ages ago, allowing the wind to gust through the ruins. Pepper muttered that a storm was coming—and I agreed.

A storm was definitely coming.

However, I wasn't worried about the strange purple-tinted sky overhead. I was worried about the potential storm brewing between Asher and Lynxx.

Inside the church, toads hopped away at our approach and parrots screeched from broken rafters. A raccoon scurried outside, growling crossly at being disturbed.

A quick sweep showed only a few harmless terras, mainly velvet-vines. Reassured, people gathered beans from a network of green plants on the crumbling brick walls, the weathered pews, even the broken altar.

Asher joined me in the middle aisle, a half-filled sack of beans slung over his shoulder. He scowled at Lynxx, who was poking around the terras near the stained glass windows. "What's with that guy lately? Every time I turn around, he's there." His low voice couldn't hide his annoyance.

"Is he?" Avoiding Asher's gaze, I dropped a handful of beans into my satchel. "He's just getting terra samples."

"He seems more interested in you than the samples."

"I'm sure that's not true."

But I knew it was.

Back at Three Oaks Inn, Lynxx's backpack had been swallowed by a sucker xan hole. Losing my Lazarus doses had left us both on edge, and since then he'd kept an eye on me, worried I'd get ill again.

My last dose had been thirteen days ago, and I was still feeling fine—except for a growing knot in my stomach. The tension between Asher and Lynxx reminded me of the air just before a storm. I sensed uncharged electricity, an oncoming turbulence.

Asher called out to the others, "Remember, guys, only pick three-quarters of the beans. Leave the rest on the vines."

"Why?" Pepper asked. "There aren't any other survivors around."

"We don't know who'll wander into this place over the next few weeks." He gestured to a family of squirrels on a rafter overhead. "Besides, some Earth animals might enjoy these vegetables too."

I tried to smile at his kindness but couldn't. Fear still gripped me, a sense that my happiness with Asher was about to be destroyed.

Harlem appeared in a doorway, holding up a watermelon. "Hey, bro, check out the huge patch of melons outside."

Asher hesitated. He glanced at Lynxx, who was on the far side of the church, absorbed in gathering terra samples. "Okay." He followed Harlem from the ruined building.

Closing my eyes, I took deep calming breaths. I tried to ignore the squeaking bats in the broken rafters and the distant howl of wolves. Instead, I focused on memories of choirs singing, children whispering behind their hymn books, people chatting as they sat on the wooden pews.

"There's something off about your friend."

I jerked around. Sergeant Thorne stood near me, glaring across the church at Lynxx.

Short and belligerent, Sergeant Thorne had retained the bulky muscles and rigid posture of his Army years. His shaved head, multiple tattoos, and hard eyes added to his threatening image.

"What are you talking about?" I asked.

"Your weird friend, Lynxx."

"What's your problem with him?" I snapped, stung into defending him.

"I don't like him. For a start, he's way too smart for his own good."

"Excuse me?"

"I remember a guy at school who was a brainiac too, just like Lynxx. Didn't fit in anywhere." The corner of Thorne's thin lips curled in memory. "Me and my buddies, we made Chuck's life a misery for four sweet years. Dunked him in the toilet. Trashed his locker. Spread rumors that he liked little girls. Last I heard, he tried to slash his wrists. What a wuss." He gave a slow, satisfied smirk, as though reliving his glory days as a bully.

"Leave Lynxx alone, Sergeant. He's one of us."

Thorne ignored me, his attention still fixed on Lynxx. "He's not just an egghead. There's something different about him. I can't quite put my finger on it." He gave me a calculating look. "Care to share?"

"There's nothing to share. He's—"

Thorne swung up his rifle and fired.

A possum tumbled from a rafter beam, missing Lynxx's head by an inch. Startled, he dropped his bag of specimens and swung around. "Freaking heck!"

"Tut-tut," Thorne called, lowering his rifle. "Such language in a church, Brain Boy. Didn't your mama teach you better?"

And I suddenly realized that Lynxx had never had a mother to socialize him, train him in everyday activities, teach him to be normal, show him love and affection. His guardian, Frost, had been a cruel, savage hybrid, and his Outrider associates had rejected humanity.

In many ways, Lynxx had been raised by wolves.

Thorne grinned at me. "That was fun."

"You killed that poor possum," I fumed, clenching my fists, my fingernails digging into my palms. "And it just missed hitting Lynxx on the head."

"Admittedly not my best shot. I need to improve my aim if I want to brain a brainiac. Hey, brain a brainiac. Good one, eh?" Sniggering, tossing his rifle from hand to hand, he strutted toward the front of the church.

At a flicker of black and white among the leafy vines near the entrance, I slowly smiled. By the time Thorne was near the open doors, I'd already remote-pushed the animal into position.

Two more steps.

Now.

The skunk raised its tail and sprayed Thorne with a cloud of noxious, stinking gas. The man yelled, clutched his face, and staggered outside. Another remote-push, gentler this time, sent the skunk scurrying into the safety of a hole in the wall.

Lynxx appeared at my side, disapproval in his harsh whisper. "What are you doing? We don't use remote-pushing against humans."

"He's a bully. He tried to injure you—and he killed that poor possum."

"I know. But he's also human."

"He deserved to be skunked."

"That's not the point. What if someone had seen you?"

"Seen me do what? I was nowhere near him when it happened."

"Kassia ..." Lynxx's words drifted into a tired sigh.

For the first time, I noticed his fatigue. His shoulders slumped a little and weariness shadowed his face. "Are you okay?" I asked softly.

"I haven't been sleeping much lately."

"Why not?"

"Too busy."

"Doing what?"

He hesitated. "Nothing."

What was he doing at night that left him so tired each day? What secrets was he keeping? Should I share my concerns with Asher? *No!* Lynxx wasn't a threat to the Weston Battalion. Time and again he'd proven he was one of the good hybrids, more human than alien, and an asset to the garrison. I couldn't—*wouldn't*—risk his life.

Lynxx kept his voice low. "Have you been practicing your remote-pushing?"

"I just did." I eyed the spot where Thorne had been skunked. The stench would cling to the man for days, and he'd be forced to drive the supply Templar, T4, alone. *Excellent.*

He gazed at me wearily. "You're being difficult."

"Sorry. And, yes, I've been practicing when no one's around."

"How's it going?"

"Not great."

"You need to be patient."

"I need to improve," I said. "Back at that inn, your rhino killed most of the sucker xans at the bottom of our oaks. My rhino only squished two."

"It takes time and practice. That's why I should be giving you lessons. Helping you."

A quick shake of my head. "I can't spend too much time alone with you. Asher already thinks something is going on between us."

"Fine." Wearily, he walked away.

At the far end of the church, Asher had returned and was examining the floor behind the altar.

Curious, I joined him.

I stared at the symbol on the tiles. "We've seen this before," I muttered. Back in Nilster, the town had been dotted with strange, skinned bodies. Each dead xan had been accompanied by a lightning bolt drawn in blood.

On the dusty floor, someone had drawn a similar lightning bolt, also in red.

"Blood?" I asked.

Asher nodded. "Harl found two more at the school."

"Any skinned xans?"

"None so far."

At a sudden burst of squeaks, we looked up.

Dozens of bats were fleeing their roosts in the broken rafters. Instead of leaving through the hole in the roof, they streamed down the center of the church in a flurry of panicked cries.

We ducked, covering our heads as they raced past.

They streaked through the front entrance and vanished.

34

"WHAT'S UP WITH THE bats?" Pepper called from a far pew.

Within the church, the others looked around, nervous, as if expecting sucker xans to burst through the cracked floor and drag them to their death.

"What's that?" Rusty pointed at the jagged-edged hole in the roof. Beyond it, patches of the purple-tinted sky wavered, as though translucent objects were moving overhead.

"Can you see anything, Kass?" asked Asher.

"Not really. Something's up there, though."

"I agree." He watched the translucent patches shimmer across the sky. "Maybe they're what scared the bats."

"Maybe."

Lynxx joined us. Ignoring Asher, he told me, "They could be air terras. I've heard they're almost invisible, like jellyfish terras."

Asher scowled. "Are they dangerous?"

"I'm not sure. I haven't received enough information about them yet, just descriptions."

The translucent shapes disappeared, leaving the sky clear again.

Curious, I asked Lynxx, "Who do you get your information from?"

"People."

"What people?"

"Other survivors." He shifted uncomfortably. "Come on, Kassia, you know I have contacts across Manhattan. They supply me with information and I supply them with food."

Asher's brow furrowed. "Food you get from the garrison, no doubt."

"So what? Commander Powell doesn't have a problem with the trades. Why should you?" His tone challenged Asher to object.

"Our food's valuable," Asher retorted.

"Information's valuable too." Lynxx's tiredness had vanished. He seemed as irritated as Asher.

Asher glared at Lynxx but addressed me. "Tell him, Kass, that food's more valuable than information."

Lynxx's eyes narrowed. "Information keeps us alive so that we can eat the food. Right, Kassia?"

"This argument's silly," I told them. "Information and food are both important. How about we finish picking the beans so we can get out of this place? What if those air terras come back?"

They ignored me.

"Kass knows that food's more valuable," Asher growled.

"She knows that information's more important." Lynxx almost spat the words out.

I rolled my eyes. "What's going on with you two?"

Asher turned to me. "I could ask the same question, Kass. What's going on with *you two*?"

"What do you mean?"

"I've seen the way you and Lynxx huddle together, talking quietly. And whenever I approach, you both fall silent. At other times, there's this look between you, like you share a secret no one else knows."

At Asher's hurt tone, I flushed with guilt and shame, unable to deny his claims. Lynxx and I were linked by secrets that we couldn't share with Asher or anyone else.

Suddenly, I realized why Asher had been arguing over such a silly matter. In his mind, if I picked his side, I'd be picking him over Lynxx.

Slowly, deliberately, I took Asher's hand. "I agree with you. Food *is* more important than information."

Relieved, he squeezed my hand.

From the hurt on Lynxx's face, his argument with Asher had obviously held the same deeper purpose for him too. His breath came in short shallow bursts, as though he was struggling with his emotions. "Are you sure, Kassia?"

I tightened my hold on Asher's hand. "Absolutely." My stomach again roiled.

And then the long-familiar nausea that I'd been denying all morning finally won.

Turning, I vomited into a patch of weeds, heaving until my stomach was empty.

Around me, the ground started swaying. The church walls surged forward, swallowing the air. I couldn't breathe. Couldn't stand straight.

As I crumpled to the floor, I realized that the impending storm hadn't been about Asher and Lynxx after all.

It had been about *me* and the return of my leukemia.

Blackness rushed in and I fell into nothing.

35

I VAGUELY REMEMBER BEING carried from the ruined church.

Then more blackness, mixed with brief periods of consciousness.

Someone put me in a musty bed, where I tossed from side to side, hot and feverish. The unfamiliar room blurred beneath painful memories.

Charlotte and I are picnicking in Central Park, celebrating my sixteenth birthday. I kiss a mysterious, gorgeous boy in front of my grinning classmates. None of us realize that the Night of the Red Mist is only hours away.

Charlotte and I are running, running, trying to escape. People scream. Cars crash. Further behind us, a passenger jet slams into Brooklyn Bridge in an explosion of noise and billowing smoke and flames.

I'm in a subway tunnel, trembling in the shadows, watching as a psycho in a zebra-skin cloak cuts chunks of flesh from the body of a man he's just killed.

Gasping, shaking, tears wet on my cheeks, I bolted upright—"*No!*"—and saw that I was in the musty bed again, my backpack on a nearby armchair.

Asher dabbed a cool wet cloth on my forehead, murmuring, "It's okay. You're safe."

Shuddering, I pushed away the memories. "What happened? Where am I?"

"You fainted. We're in a house near the ruined church."

Two oil lamps threw circles of light into the dusty room. Beyond a window, darkness pressed against the cracked glass.

"How long have I been here?"

"Since yesterday." Asher stroked my hand, his touch light, as if worried about breaking me. He looked exhausted. "How do you feel?"

"Bad." Around me, the room swayed like a ship caught in storm-tossed waves.

"When did you start feeling ill?"

"Yesterday morning."

The bed creaked as he sat on the edge of the mattress. "Soo-Yun says you've got a fever, probably from a bad case of the flu. Do you have joint pains? Loss of appetite?"

"Yes," I answered truthfully. I didn't tell him those symptoms were also signs of the return of my leukemia.

"Hopefully you're over the worst of it. Soo-Yun's given you some pills from our first aid kit, but she didn't have any for flu. Still, she thinks you'll recover in a few days. You're young and healthy."

He was half right. "How long have you been here?"

"Since you fainted." He hesitated. "Lynxx's been stopping by every few hours as well. He insisted."

"Okay."

"Sorry, but I can't let the others enter this house, not even to visit you for a few minutes."

"I understand." These days, without medication, the flu could spread and kill with frightening speed.

Except I didn't have the flu.

"I'll tell Soo-Yun you're awake. Back soon." He kissed my forehead and left.

A minute later, Lynxx slipped into the room and hurried across to my bedside. He looked even more tired than Asher, and his black clothes were rumpled and dirty. "You're as pale as a ghost, Kassia."

"Gee, nice to see you too," I muttered weakly.

He placed the back of his hand on my forehead. "You're burning up." He launched into the same questions that Asher had just asked, and I gave him the same answers.

"It's your leukemia," he pronounced. When I nodded, he went on, "Don't worry, I won't let you die."

"We don't have much say in that."

"Wrong. We've kept the Grim Reaper away before and we can do it again."

"Without the tonic?"

"I would've made more if I knew you were going to give some away." He paused, his words thick with reproach.

"I don't regret using a dose to save Harlem's life," I said, meaning it. "I'd do it again."

"I know you would. And that's just one of the reasons why I ..." He drew in a deep breath and changed tack. "I have to make some more tonic."

"Don't you need a lab?"

"I found an old one in the area. That's not the problem." He ran an agitated hand through his thick black hair. "In between seeing how you were every few hours, I've been searching for Lazarus-vine terras."

"Any luck?"

"None. I have to tell Asher about the Lazarus plants. He's already decided the convoy will remain in this town until Tuesday while you recover. With his help, we can have a couple of dozen people looking for the terras tomorrow, not just me."

"No." When I tried to sit up, a fresh wave of dizziness sank me back against the pillow. "Promise you won't tell him."

"I can't make that promise."

"Please."

He hesitated. "I'll hold off for twenty-four hours. If I don't find any Lazarus plants by then, I'm getting Asher's help." He cut off my argument by leaning forward and whispering, "Bye, Kassia. I've found a car that works, so I'm going AWOL."

"You're leaving?"

"I need to expand my search if I want to find some plants. And since I don't have time to make up explanations for Asher, or to seek permission, I'm just going."

"You can't roam the countryside alone. It's too dangerous."

"I'll do whatever it takes in order to keep you alive." He gazed at me, golden eyes bright with fear and love. "I'll be back soon. Promise."

And then he was gone.

The next morning, when Lynxx's absence was noted, I told Asher, "He'll be back ... before we leave Tuesday." My voice wavered, weak and dizzy. "He's found ... working car. Looking for ... pills to help me."

Asher frowned. "I'm annoyed he's taken off, and I'm worried he'll get himself killed out there—but mostly I'm hoping he'll find the flu pills you need."

Over the following hours, my nausea and pain grew steadily worse, and I only escaped them when I fell into a restless sleep.

On the second night, Asher left my side to answer a radio call from Commander Powell.

I lay in the bed, staring through the window at the night sky. A purple-tinted moon hazed the land with pale beams, softening the overgrown yard outside my room.

Where was Lynxx? Was he okay? Surprisingly, I was worried about him, even though I knew he was extremely good at surviving. Lynxx was not as physically strong as Asher, but his hybrid powers would keep him as safe as any sword or gun. Even so, I wished he hadn't gone off alone.

I glanced at my watch.

Midnight.

A curious sense of déjà vu stole over me.

I'd been in this situation before, a day after joining the Weston Battalion. Unable to save my cousin, Charlotte, I had lain on her empty hospital bed and waited for my leukemia to kill me. It had been midnight then too.

Now, as I stared at the purple-tinted moon, a deep sadness filled me. Without my meds or the Lazarus tonic, I would suffer a slow, painful death over the coming days.

When I'd been in Charlotte's hospital room, I'd lost my family and friends, and my world. I'd wanted to give up and die.

This time, I wanted to live. Desperately. Passionately. Completely.

I had a new family—the Weston Battalion—and new friends. True, the world was changing in dramatic and often frightening ways. Terra plants. Xans. Hybrids. A possible invasion.

But it was still my home, with Earth animals and trees, warm summer nights, sunrises and sunsets ... and maybe even a future with happiness and love.

"Kassia. Kassia." The words floated on a whisper.

With a start, I realized I'd fallen asleep, dreaming of a better world and a happier life. As I tried to sit up, nausea surged through me and I sank back again, shaking.

Asher slept in a moldy armchair by the door. Sometime in the night, he must've returned to my room, where he'd finally succumbed to his exhaustion.

Lynxx was climbing through an open window. Beyond him, a red glow flowed upward from the horizon, heralding sunrise.

He padded across the dimly lit room. His face was lined with weariness, his clothes were muddy and torn, and he walked with a limp. His hands were empty—no bottle of purple liquid—but I didn't care.

He was back. Safe.

"Lynxx, are you okay?" I spoke softly, reluctant to wake Asher.

He flicked a glance at the sleeping boy in the armchair and whispered, "I'm fine."

"I was worried about you."

"Worried?" The single word won a pleased smile. "Really?"

"Of course." An invisible giant slowly tightened a clamp around my chest, making it hard to breathe. "You're limping. Is your leg hurt?"

"I'll heal." Gently, he slid an arm beneath my back and sat me up against the pillows. "I could only find enough Lazarus plants for a single dose. I'll keep looking for more. But for now, this is it." He withdrew a small bottle from his jacket and I eagerly drank the purple liquid. As he brushed the sweat-slicked hair off my face, he murmured, "Unfortunately, you're so sick that a single dose won't be enough."

My heart sank. So I was going to die after all.

"For the next few days," he said, "you'll need an extra supplement, something gentle but effective. They kept you alive in that subway tunnel, so they should work again."

"They?"

He grabbed a burlap sack from the shadowed floor beside the window and withdrew a bunch of familiar flowers on long stems. "Take deep breaths, Kassia."

Trembling, I buried my face in the satiny purple petals and inhaled. I used to think the Lazarus flowers smelled like roses.

But on this red-purple dawn, they smelled of hope and possibilities and the chance of a future.

The sweetest scents of all.

36

By midmorning my nausea, burning pain, and the other symptoms of my leukemia had vanished. My swift recovery was put down to the "flu" pills that Lynxx had "found."

Leaving the others to pack the vehicles, Asher and I wandered down to a nearby lake. After three days of immobility, we both needed to stretch our legs before traveling inside a cramped Templar for hours.

By the time we reached the lake, red-tinted clouds veiled the sun, and a thin mist stretched in all directions. As we headed to some boulders along the shore, I saw Lynxx in a rowboat on the water. He paused, gave us a brief wave, and returned to scooping his net through a patch of floating terra leaves.

Asher scanned our surroundings, placed his sword within reach, and sat beside me on a boulder. "Still all clear." At my puzzled expression he explained, "The others have already scoured this area for dangerous terras and xans over the past couple of days. It's safe."

"That's a relief."

"And so is your recovery." Gently, he ran his hand down my cheek, his touch warm. "I was really worried. You were getting worse and worse. I desperately wanted to help, but there was nothing I could do."

"You stayed with me. That helped."

"Not enough. Lynxx and I don't always see eye to eye, but I'll always be grateful he found the pills that made you well again."

"Me too." Back at the ruined church, Lynxx had seen me choose Asher over him—yet he'd put aside his hurt and had risked his own life to save mine. Sighing, I glanced at the purple Lazarus blossom clutched in my hand.

Asher squinted at Lynxx's rowboat. "Owlfred's back." The tawny owl was perched on the vessel's bow.

"I hadn't realized she'd gone missing."

"She disappeared the same night Lynxx went walkabout. Strange. Why would he take his bird while searching for flu pills?"

"No idea."

Two chipmunks chattered on an overhanging branch, and quacking ducks paddled past our boulder. I gave a faint smile. It was wonderful to feel healthy again. Almost normal. Lifting the purple bloom, I inhaled its healing terra pollen.

A single high-pitched cry came from the forest on the far side of the lake. It spiraled upward, hovered in a drawn-out wail, then snapped off.

"What was that, Asher?"

"I don't know. We've heard the sound a few times over the past two nights. This is the first time I've heard it during the day."

"Why didn't our convoy relocate?"

"You were too sick to move. Besides, it might just be a bird. If we jumped at every strange noise, we'd send ourselves crazy."

"I suppose." Guilt weighed on me like an invisible leaden shroud. The others had stayed here because of my leukemia. Had my illness put them in jeopardy?

Asher frowned at my Lazarus blossom. "You haven't let that out of sight since Lynxx gave it to you this morning."

"It's a beautiful flower with a lovely scent," I hedged.

"It's a terra."

"Not all terras are bad."

"Why's this one so important? Is it because *he* gave it to you?"

At the hurt that shaded his words, I realized we were back in the same emotional triangle as before. Asher. Lynxx. Me. Secrets and misunderstandings. Hurt and jealousy and mistrust and—

"Lies," I blurted out.

"What?"

"I didn't have the flu." The admission poured from me, unplanned and unchecked. As it fled my mouth, the invisible leaden shroud around my shoulders became lighter. "And I didn't have a friend with leukemia."

"What?"

Gathering my courage, I finally admitted the secret that had been weighing me down for months. "I have leukemia. I would've died a long time ago if it hadn't been for Lynxx. He's been making a tonic from these Lazarus plants that keeps me alive and makes me feel normal. But I need to drink a dose of it every week."

"*What?*" Asher seemed stuck on that word, as though it was the only one his stunned mind could form.

"Anyway, we lost my last two doses during that sucker xan attack. When I started getting sick again, Lynxx went AWOL, searching for some more Lazarus terras. He managed to find enough to make me a single dose, which I drank this morning. This Lazarus flower is a supplement." Another deep breath of the purple blossom. "Its pollen helps me feel better too."

"Kass—" He stopped. Held up a warning hand. Pointed left.

Half a dozen spiky-ball xans raced toward us along the edge of the lake. Each resembled an orange basketball covered in porcupine-like quills. We'd seen these xans before, but their sharp barbs had always kept us at a distance—except for Lynxx. After studying a few, he'd pronounced them harmless unless alarmed.

Had that strange cry earlier alarmed these spikey-balls?

Not moving, we watched their approach, aware it was too late to retreat. The xans were only a few feet from us, within striking distance. They stopped, sniffed the air—and their quills vibrated.

Uh-oh.

Could I handle six at once? Holding my breath, I focused my mind and remote-pushed left to right in a strong sweep of energy.

Quills flattening against their bodies, the spiky-balls bolted away.

"What just happened?" Asher asked, puzzled.

I hid a satisfied smile. "Maybe we scared them off."

"Something sure did."

Our earlier conversation hovered in the air, an axe ready to drop. Frowning, he returned to it. "Why didn't you tell me the truth before?"

My answer poured out in a waterfall of emotion. "Have you ever been ill, Asher? Or rejected? You were the healthy son of a billionaire, privileged and pampered all your life until the Mist. Do you know what it feels like to be an outsider just because you're sick? Treated as different? Judged for your illness and not for yourself?"

"Kass—"

"No, let me finish. I was scared of dying from my leukemia, even before the Mist arrived. But once the Mist started killing people everywhere, I was terrified in too many ways to count. I was alone and the Weston Garrison offered me sanctuary. I had no family or friends, and your community offered both. Everyone I loved had died. And then I met you and I had a future again."

His mouth opened and closed as he struggled to find the words to say.

I waited a moment before continuing softly, "Have you ever wanted your life to have purpose, to mean something? With the garrison, I had both. I didn't want to die. I wanted to live. The Weston Battalion gave me that chance. I hid my secret because I was afraid of being expelled from the garrison." Pausing, I drew in a deep, trembling breath. "I lied because the truth would've cost me too much."

"And now? Why are you telling me the truth now?"

"Because lying would've cost me too much."

Silence stretched between us, wide and deep. Even the noisy ducks and the chattering chipmunks had quietly left. Only our breaths disturbed the mist.

Finally Asher said, "I don't care."

37

AT THE DREADED WORDS, pain sparked in my heart. "I understand. I'm so sorry that I ruined things between us by—"

"No." Asher took my hand. "I don't care that you've hidden your leukemia or that you drink a terra tonic every week. I just want *you*. Alive and healthy and by my side."

"Do you mean that?" I blinked back tears.

"Yes. I'm sorry."

"For what?"

"For making you too scared to admit that you were sick and needed help." He gave a rueful grin. "I can't believe I'm saying this, but I'm grateful for Lynxx and his determination to keep you alive. And now that I know what's been going on between you two—thankfully not a mutual love—I feel a lot better about him." He paused. "Is that all, though? No more secrets?"

This was my chance to tell him about my—and Lynxx's—hybrid powers. I bit my lower lip, hesitating. Concealing my leukemia had put my colleagues at risk, so I had needed to reveal that secret. However, my remote-pushing was different; this secret didn't endanger anyone—but revealing it could get hybrid-Lynxx expelled or killed.

"Kass?"

"No more secrets." My invisible shroud of guilt grew heavier once again.

He paused, thinking. "Okay. We won't tell anyone about your leukemia."

"Thanks," I said. "What happens when we get back to New York though?"

His face shadowed. "If Commander Powell learns that you have leukemia and drink a terra tonic every week, you'll be expelled from the Weston Battalion."

"That's what I'm afraid of."

"I hate keeping secrets from the commander—"

"I know."

"—but I can't bear the thought of losing you, Kass. So I won't tell him."

"Thank you. One more request."

"Yes?"

"Don't treat me any differently than the others. Don't watch my every move or study me as if I'm about to die at any second. Treat me like I'm healthy. Normal."

"That won't be easy. I'm worried about you."

"Don't be. I'm fine as long as I have the Lazarus flowers or the Lazarus tonic. They've kept me alive for months and they'll keep doing it. Lynxx will see to that."

"I suppose so." His brow knotted. "But if you start getting sick again, tell me."

"Promise."

"Okay."

Another high-pitched cry came from the forest beyond the lake. It didn't sound like a bird; then again, neither did the kookaburra I'd heard last week. At a sudden flap of wings, I looked up and saw Owlfred flying across the water, headed for the dark forest. Back in the rowboat, Lynxx was lying across the wooden seats.

In an attempt to lighten the mood between Asher and me, I nodded at the drifting vessel. "Guess who's taking a nap?"

"Huh! He looks uncomfortable. And exhausted." Guilt tinged Asher's words. "Understandable, since he spent day and night searching for the terra plants to save you. And what did I do?" His words turned bitter. "I sat in an armchair by your bed."

Quietly I told him, "I remember tossing and turning and waking up in a sweat from nightmares. Afraid. Alone. Every time, *you* were beside me, cooling my face with a wet cloth, soothing me with soft words ... and I'd relax a little, comforted that I wasn't alone after all. In your own way, you helped keep me alive too."

"Really?" He gathered me into his arms, and I lost myself in the warmth of his embrace and the heat of his kiss.

The crackle of a radio interrupted us. It was Harlem. "We'll be ready to leave in a few minutes, bro."

"Okay, Harl. Kass and I will head back. Have you contacted Lynxx?"

"I tried. He's not answering his radio."

In the middle of the misty lake, Lynxx still lay asleep in the rowboat.

"I'll tell him, Harl. We'll be there soon." Asher cupped his hands to his mouth and yelled, "Lynxx."

Multiple cries answered from the distant forest, sharper than before, more menacing—and closer.

Definitely not a bird.

We withdrew our binoculars. On the far shoreline, a dozen shapes were hurrying through the shadow-draped forest. They were about four feet tall, moving upright on two legs. Large misshapen heads, pointed at the back. Overlong arms. Long sticks gripped in hands or paws.

I glanced around, suddenly understanding why the ducks and the chipmunks had gone silent. They were hiding.

Lynxx's sudden shout came from my radio. "Get back to the Templars, Kassia. They're coming!" Awake and sitting up, he began furiously rowing toward us. Owlfred clutched his shoulder, her wings fluttering in agitation.

Asher turned on his radio. "Who's coming, Lynxx?"

"Krols! Get Kassia away from here." He powered the boat across the mist-covered water.

I spoke into my radio. "We're not leaving without you, Lynxx." Hastily, I shoved the Lazarus flower deep into my jacket pocket and withdrew my gun.

"I'll be fine, Kassia. Go!"

Asher grabbed his sword. "What are krols?"

"Xans," Lynxx cried. "Remember those strange, skinned bodies strung up in Nilster? They were krols. They hunt humans. They're strong. Vicious. Fast too."

His boat was still fifty yards away.

"There are over twenty people in our group, all armed," Asher reminded him. "I'm sure we can handle them."

"You can't. There are dozens of them."

"How do you know?"

"They travel in large packs. Can't you hear them?"

We listened to the shrieks in the forest, the number of cries racing my pulse.

Asher switched on his radio. "Harl, we've got trouble. Get everyone into the vehicles and start the engines. *Now.*"

"Yo, bro!"

Lynxx finally reached the shore, Owlfred still on his shoulder.

Asher raised his sword, legs astride. "Take Kass and go, Lynxx. I'll buy you both some time."

"No," I cried. "You'll die."

Lynxx insisted, "We *all* need to go." He dismissed Asher's objections with a wave of his hand. "Kassia will never leave you behind. Don't you get it? Your team needs you. *She* needs you."

Asher hesitated. Then he grabbed my hand, and the three of us turned and ran, Owlfred still clutching Lynxx's shoulder. I didn't look back, mostly because every muscle in my body was focused on running—but also because I didn't want to see *them*.

Their shrieks grew louder. Closer.

We reached the convoy and piled into T2.

A worried Booker gripped the steering wheel. "What's going on, boss?"

"Go, Booker!" Asher turned on his radio, shouting to the other drivers, "Leave. Now!"

The four vehicles screeched away, tires squealing, gravel spraying.

Finally I looked back. Dozens of dark shapes flooded onto the road far behind us, all running upright, all waving sticks.

Our Templar rounded a corner, blocking them from view.

Heart hammering, I sank back in my seat.

Krols.

And we were in their territory.

Our journey had just become a lot more dangerous.

38

Our Templars left the shrieking, aggressive creatures far behind.

In the front passenger seat, Asher shook his head, stunned. "Cripes! They were krols, Lynxx?"

"Yes," he replied, gently returning Owlfred to her large cage.

"How do you know what they're called?"

"Survivors have begun warning about them over my shortwave radio. Someone called them *krols* and everyone else started using the name."

"Are they widespread?"

Lynxx nodded as he covered the cage with the black cloth. "In the last couple of days, radio reports have been coming from all over the country."

"Why didn't you tell us about them sooner?"

Lynxx glanced at me. "Kassia was dying. I was focused on keeping her alive."

"Oh. Right." Asher lapsed into silence.

That night we bunked in a gas station, posting extra guards outside.

Taking Lynxx aside, I relayed my conversation with Asher about my leukemia and the Lazarus tonics.

"And he'll keep our secret?" Lynxx asked, surprised.

"Yes."

"But you didn't tell him about our mental powers?"

"Not a word."

My sleep that night was fitful, broken by dreams of Lazarus plants and krols.

At dawn, our convoy headed off again.

Just before midday, Lynxx pointed to a huge patch of purple plants growing alongside the road ahead. "Pull over. They're what I'm looking for. Lazarus plants!"

After our convoy parked, Asher handed around sacks, telling the others, "We're harvesting these terras for research purposes."

At dusk, Lynxx drove to an old lab he'd found on a map. Hours later, he returned, a relieved smile on his face and six bottles of Lazarus tonic carefully packed in his bag.

The next afternoon, T4 broke down again. When our mechanic said that the repairs would take several hours, Asher gave the rest of us time off.

Some people hung around the vehicles, cleaning weapons or napping. Lynxx gathered samples of terras from the grounds. Harlem opened a thick medical book and quizzed Soo-Yun on various diseases, as she had recently started studying to become a doctor.

Three soldiers gathered their rifles and went hunting to the east.

Asher and Booker decided to go hunting as well, and the pair headed west, into a forest. Pepper and I tagged along. After yesterday's krol incident at the lake, Asher had ordered that no one was to wander off alone.

Pepper and I trailed the two boys through the forest, carrying their lunches, backpacks, and swords.

I adjusted Asher's pack on my shoulders, grumbling, "Does this feel sexist to you, Pepper?"

"Sure does."

Asher turned and threw me a smile. "You're welcome to take the first shot when we find some game."

"Er ... no thanks! I'll carry your gear." I touched the Lazarus blossom in my jacket pocket. Still there. Good.

Ahead, Booker waved us quiet and pointed.

We caught up with him—

—and my eyes widened.

A field stretched before us, thick with thigh-high weeds. In the center was an extraordinary terra that resembled a massive, fifty-foot-tall onion bulb. This gigantic bulb was suspended high in the air; its fat bottom was supported by a thick central stem surrounded by dozens of thin rigid roots, all about forty feet tall.

"Onion terra." Lynxx's voice came from behind as he caught up with us. "We've seen them in the distance, but they're even more incredible up close."

Asher asked, "What are you doing here, Lynxx? You're not supposed to wander around alone." His voice was reproachful but friendly; his whole attitude to Lynxx had changed since my leukemia confession yesterday.

"I can take care of myself." Raising an arm, Lynxx watched his tawny owl land on his hand. "Besides, Owlfred needed to stretch her wings."

I stroked the small bird's feathered head. "I thought she slept during the day."

"Not always." He shifted the owl onto his shoulder, then withdrew a digital camera and began photographing the enormous onion-shaped terra. "Don't get too close to that thing, Kassia," he called out, moving further back as he tried to get the entire terra in his picture. "It could be dangerous."

"Don't worry. I'm staying right here."

Asher radioed our location to Harlem at the convoy, spoke to the mechanic about the repairs to T4, and made sure the other members were okay. Satisfied that things were under control, he signed off.

"Ready, boss?" Booker asked eagerly. An avid carnivore, he hated eating meat only once a week. The chance of several nights of fresh pork or venison left him eager to go hunting.

"Yep," Asher replied, rifle in hand. "Let's go. Everyone watch out for krols and sucker xans and dangerous terras and hybrids and ..." Wearily, he shook his head. "Just watch out for everything."

Pepper gave a playful salute. "Will do."

The tall weeds in the field swayed as a boar with curved tusks shuffled through them, grunting and snorting.

Asher grinned at me and mouthed, *Fresh meat.* Behind him, Booker gave an excited thumbs-up. The pair separated as they stalked the animal through the weeds.

The boar's head jerked up, snout twitching. Curved tusks glinting in the sunlight, it charged at Booker as—

—something long and thin darted from the weeds and snatched up the boar.

The squealing beast rose through the air, gripped by a thin gray tentacle.

No, not a tentacle, I realized, unsheathing my sword. It looked like one of the roots that supported the onion terra, but it was far longer. It carried the boar up, up, and dropped it into the pursed top of the terra. The squeals descended, as though the boar was falling through a hollow cavity. Then I heard a faint splash. Had the animal landed in some liquid at the bottom of the onion terra?

Squeals echoed inside the hollow terra, followed by screams. Human screams. Terrified.

Stunned, Asher and I glanced at each other. From the far side of the field, Lynxx shouted and began racing across to us.

Booker cried, "Someone's inside that thing, boss." He started toward the onion terra.

"Wait," Asher yelled. "We need to—"

Another long skinny root whipped up from the tall weeds and lassoed Booker's waist. Shouting, we raced toward him. As Booker rose into the air, I gave a frantic remote-push. The root sprang open, dropping him to the ground. A second root lunged at Asher. Another snaked out for Pepper.

No!

Heart slamming, I remote-pushed in a desperate one-two punch that paused the roots for a couple of seconds. I kept running, remote-pushing the roots again and again. The effort left me weak and dizzy, and my sword slipped from my hand.

The attacking roots finally pitched backward and thudded to the ground.

Pepper pulled a winded Booker to his feet. Asher shoved them both away from the roots, shouting, "Go!" He swung toward me and—

Something yanked me upward, strong and fast. The terra root tightened around my chest, almost suffocating me as I rose through the air. Far below, Asher and Lynxx stared up, their expressions anguished, helpless.

With breathtaking speed, the terra root tossed me into a hole at the top of the onion terra.

I plunged through a hollow dimness ripped by more terrified screams.

39

A DEEP SLUDGE BROKE my fall. Spluttering, I clambered to my feet, chest-deep in the foul stuff. My chest and shoulder ached, but nothing felt broken.

Where was the boar?

I grabbed for my sword. Gone. Shaking, I wrenched a knife from my belt and whirled around.

I was in a large cavity, its dimness lit by a thin stream of sunlight from the distant hole at the top.

A gravelly voice echoed in the hollow space. "Quick! Over here, lass."

No time for questions.

I waded toward an old bearded man and a teenage boy standing at the side of the pool. In the sludge, unseen things crunched beneath my boots, and a rank smell filled the air. Grasping the man's outstretched hand, I climbed onto a woody ledge that ran around the inside of the onion terra.

"Where's the boar?" I cried, gripping my knife.

The old man pointed to a crumpled shape halfway out of the foul sludge. Muscular body. Curved tusks. "It's dead."

"Not right away, though," the boy muttered. His face was smeared in dried blood from a shallow gash on his forehead. Leaves and twigs clotted his long dirty hair, and his dark coveralls were torn. "It swam to the side and began climbing out of the pool, eyes red and crazy. I shouted, sure it was about to attack us. Then it just died."

"A flat-out miracle, Panny," the man said, his tone gruff but affectionate. "I didn't fancy dancing with them pointy tusks." The man's wild gray hair, bushy beard, and old clothes reminded me of a hillbilly. Turning, he addressed me earnestly. "That pool is flat-out foul, lass. You'd best wash out your mouth and your eyes, if you can."

Sheathing my knife, I pulled a water bottle from Asher's backpack and splashed its contents over my face. "What about the rest of me?" I asked, gesturing to my sodden clothes.

"I'm thinkin' you'd have to be in the pool for over an hour 'fore your skin starts sloughing off like a snake," the old man replied. "You got out after a few minutes. You should be a-okay."

"*They* weren't," the boy said, glancing sideways.

I followed his gaze—and gasped.

Skeletons cluttered the edge of the pool. Horse, dog, snake, other animals, plus two humans. Back when I'd been in the pool, had the crunching beneath my boots been bones?

"What happened here?" I asked. "Who are you people?"

"I'm Xavian." The man gestured to his companion. "This here lassie is Panny."

Lassie? I peered at the teenager's face. Beneath the smeared dried blood and dirt, I saw gray eyes, a delicate nose, and full curved lips. She looked about my age.

"I'm Kass," I said.

A silver-eyed pigeon flew down and settled on a crimson fern that sprouted from the onion terra's wall.

Withdrawing a flashlight from Asher's backpack, I swept its beam around the enormous cavity. The place—around a hundred feet wide, fifty feet high—was like a living cave. Bats clung to the roof, watching us with upside-down brown eyes. Fernlike terras studded the walls, their leaves crimson and spiky. Insects whirled and swirled in the weak sunlight that streamed through the distant hole in the roof. Squeaking rats and clattering crabben xans darted over the skeletons beside the pool.

With a whirr of wings, the silver-eyed pigeon launched itself from the spiky fern. As it flew up to the sunny hole, I envied its ability to escape this strange place so easily.

My waterlogged radio beeped and Asher's agitated voice crackled from it. "Kass, are you okay?"

"Fine, although I could use some painkillers." I rubbed my sore shoulder. "What about you and Lynxx and the others?"

"We're all fine. What happened to the boar?"

"Dead."

"Good. Can you climb out of there?"

I studied the inside of the onion terra. Apart from the spiky fern terras, the walls were smooth and curved upward. Nothing to grip in a climb. "Negative."

"Don't worry, Kass. We'll get you out."

"You need to stay away from those long skinny roots." I winced at the skeletons piled around the pool. "This terra's really good at catching animals and people. There are lots of bones in here, and a pool that's a few feet deep."

Xavian leaned toward my radio, calling out, "Dollars to dog biscuits, the pond's one gigantic digestive pit. It's like them pitcher plants me cousin used to love. Jad would drop flies into the cup of the plant and watch 'em get digested. Weirdo."

"Who's with you?" Asher asked me. When I explained about the two people trapped with me, he said, "Okay. We're going to get you all out. Give us a few minutes to figure out a plan. Stand by."

"Okay." Lowering my radio, I turned to Xavian. "What is this thing?" I gestured to the ledge. About three feet wide, it ringed the inside of the onion terra.

"It's just me guess here, but it could be some sort of water level. When the digestive juices get too deep and reach this ledge, maybe it's a signal for the terra to stop making more juice. If this plant becomes too top-heavy, the whole thing could collapse faster than me cousin's Christmas onion soufflé." With a low groan, he rubbed his chest.

Panny leaned toward Xavian, worried. "How are you feeling?"

"Finer than frog hair, lass. Just a touch of heartburn."

I asked him, "Are you sure it's just heartburn?"

"Yeppo. I've had it before. Me and Panny, we was eating roasted rabbit when some wolves happened by earlier today. Eating and running ain't a good mix at me age. And then we got grabbed up by this stinkin' terra. Sizzling sugar beets, if that weren't the cherry on top of our day."

"How long have you been in here?"

He looked at his battered watch. "Nigh on five hours."

I swept my flashlight around the onion terra again. The bright beam revealed curved walls covered in thick ropelike filaments or ribs, too thin to use as climbing aids.

With the butt of my knife, I smashed a small triangular hole in the tough wall. Air and light gushed in, and I widened the opening, hoping to create an escape route, but the ropelike ribs were as strong as steel. Only my head could fit through the triangular gap.

In the field far below, beyond the reach of the skinny terra roots, I saw Asher, Lynxx, and Pepper huddled together, talking.

I waved my hand out of the makeshift window. "Hey, guys. I'm up here. Don't come closer, though." When they waved back, I turned on my radio. "Where's Booker? Is he okay?"

"Yes," Asher's voice crackled in reply. "He's gone to pick up supplies and reinforcements. Lynxx has a crazy plan he wants to try."

"What is it?" As a groan sounded behind me, I told Asher, "Stand by."

I turned. Xavian sat on the woody ledge, clutching his chest.

Panny bent over him, distressed. "Are you getting those pains again?"

"It's nothing, lass." He pointed a shaky finger at the far side of the cavity. "Can you have a look in that old backpack we saw earlier? Maybe it's got some aspirin that'll settle me guts."

She hurried along the ledge.

"Be careful," Xavian called after her. "Don't fall in." The moment she was out of earshot, he motioned me closer. As I kneeled beside him, he whispered, "I know we just met and all, but if anything happens to me, Kass, please look after Panny. She's like me daughter." He swallowed, overcome with emotion.

I couldn't guarantee Panny's acceptance into the Weston Battalion, so I hedged my reply. "I'll do my very best." My answer satisfied him, and he sat there, breathing a little easier.

Overhead, a shadow flittered.

I looked up.

A skinny terra root tossed something into the hole at the top. It splashed into the dark green pool and disappeared.

Warily, I watched the liquid.

A long thin shape rose to the surface and swam through the sludge, headed for Panny. In the downfall of sunlight, I saw an enormous snake. Almost twelve feet long. Thick as my arm. Light and dark scales in a distinctive pattern.

Diamondback rattlesnake.

Aggressive and lethal.

40

ON THE FAR SIDE of the cavity, Panny stopped rummaging through the backpack. Frozen, she stared at the oncoming rattler.

Xavian croaked, "She's terrified of snakes." Eyes narrowing, he jerked his chin up in a sharp motion and—

—the snake jerked too, as though touched by a tiny bolt of lightning. It sank from sight, joining the other dead animals at the bottom of the pool.

I threw Xavian a startled glance.

Panny called out, "Is it dead?"

I met Xavian's pain-filled gaze. Saw his sweat-beaded forehead. And I knew what he'd done.

"It's dead," I told her.

"Good." Across the cavity, the girl emptied the contents of the pack onto the ledge.

Quietly, I said to Xavian, "You're a hybrid, aren't you?" When he didn't answer, I hurried on, "It's okay. Your secret is safe with me. Is Panny a hybrid too?"

"Nope." His voice was weaker than before, his breathing more labored. "I found her two months after the Mist. Alone, afraid, hungry. I took her under me frail wing." He peered at me. "Ain't you afraid of me?"

"No. You're a *good* hybrid."

"How can you tell, lass?"

"Because of the way you love and protect Panny. She's human. You would've let her die if you were an Outrider."

"Those evil bastards," he muttered.

"Does she know you're a hybrid?"

"Sure. It worried her big-time at first. After a bit, she realized I weren't evil and she settled down. I ain't never told her nothin' about me mental powers, though. She's fragile and it would've cracked her mind like a walnut." He cocked his head, mustering his energy. "How'd you know I was a hybrid? You're not one."

"No, I'm not. But I'm pretty sure you somehow killed that snake."

"Yeppo. It was big, angry, poisonous. The worst combo. And it was fixin' to bite Panny."

"What about the boar?" I gestured to the dead animal halfway in the pool.

"No choice. It was mega-aggro. I had to remote-kill it too."

Remote-kill.

41

STUNNED, I SANK BACK on my heels, rocked by the frightening concept. Remote-pushing and remote-soothing were one thing. But remote-killing? Could Lynxx do it? *Could I?*

"Found it." Across the pool, a triumphant Panny began hurrying back to us.

A sudden possibility made me gasp. "Xavian, can you use your powers to smash a hole in the side of this terra? If you make it big enough, we could—"

"No can do." Wearily, he shook his head. "I've tried a baker's dozen times since me and Panny got snatched up. But I'm too sick. It's harder to use me powers."

"But you just used your mental powers a few minutes ago. Twice."

"Had to." Sweat trickled down his face. "You heard them stories about mamas lifting cars off their kidlings?"

"Sure."

"In emergencies, adrenaline can give folks extra *physical* strength for a few secs."

"Is that what happened to you?"

"Sort of. Panny was in danger, and some chemical in me brain gave me a brief burst of *mental* strength so I could save her." He wiped beads of sweat from his forehead.

"Hang on a little longer, Xavian. One of our team members has a plan to get us out of here." I left out the part where Asher had called Lynxx's plan *crazy*.

205

We fell silent as Panny rejoined us.

"This will help you, Xavian." She handed him two aspirins from a pill bottle.

I sniffed the air. The foul scent from earlier had been replaced by a new odor. It smelled like crushed ants—pungent, reeking—and I gagged.

At a clattering sound, I turned.

A group of crabbens emerged from a nearby pile of skeletons. They clattered across the bones on their claws and dropped into the green sludge.

Weird. Why would the xans swim in the digestive juices?

Panny anxiously grabbed Xavian's arm. "They're doing it again."

"What?" I asked.

Xavian grunted, "Watch."

My beam skimmed the sludge, following the trail of ripples created by the submerged crabbens. A couple of minutes later, the xans left the pool, dragging a dog's skeleton in their claws.

"Are they cleaning the pool?" I asked, incredulous.

"That's me guess," Xavian said. "This here terra we're in—"

"My team calls it an onion terra."

"Fittin' name. Anyway, the ... onion terra ... and them critters act like buddies. Both get the goods they need. The onion terra's juices dissolve its prey's flesh and guts. But it don't dissolve the prey's bones—or the critters. So the critters hang around the pool, waiting for the go-ahead."

"What go-ahead?"

"That stink. Didn't you smell it?"

"The one like crushed ants?"

"Yeppo."

"Are you saying this terra communicates with the crabben xans by smell?"

"Crabben xans? Huh. Another good name. And yeah, that's me guess. When this onion bulb thingy lets off that stink, them crabben-xan-critters hustle into the sludge. They grab up a skeleton and haul its sorry ass out of there."

A new smell wafted up, similar to burned rubber.

Xavian sniffed. "Chow time." He pointed to the dog skeleton, now piled on top of some older bones. The wet crabbens scuttled over it, using their claws to rip scraps of flesh from the skeleton. Rats snatched up fallen pieces from the floor. "It's what them city folks call a win-win. The crabben-xan-critters and the rats get their chow. And the onion terra's pool don't get clogged with good-for-nothing bones."

I gestured to the partially submerged boar. "Why aren't the crabbens eating that animal? It's got far more flesh on it."

"Probably verboten until the onion terra dissolves the bottom half still in the pool. That might take days. Once it's finished, though, the fleshy head and shoulders will be a finger-lickin' buffet for the other critters. Par-tay time."

I swept my beam around. On the walls, bugs crawled over the spiky fern terras. Bat droppings splotched the ledge. Centipedes skittered over dried bones, their myriad legs fluttering. Fluorescent slugs left slimy trails on an old skull. Crabbens and rats gnawed at bits of decaying flesh hanging from the dog skeleton.

This place was a mini eco-system.

"Fascinating," I murmured. Then I blinked, surprised at my description. In the past, I would've simply said *dis-gust-ing*. These days, I saw things differently. Was Lynxx's scientific fascination with the world rubbing off on me, at least a little?

Panny huffed at Xavian and me, disapproving. "Fascinating? Par-tay time? You're both forgetting something."

"What, Panny-lass?"

"We're part of this terra's buffet."

Oops. She was right.

Outside, a distant roar of engines grew louder.

Hurrying to my makeshift window in the terra wall, I watched two dirt bikes approach. Both had been stored in T4, the supply Templar, and were used for getting into tight places that the larger vehicles couldn't enter.

Soo-Yun sat behind Harlem on the first bike. Sergeant Thorne and another soldier rode the second one. Further back, I saw Booker and more soldiers running toward the onion terra.

Dismounting, Thorne drew his semiautomatic gun and yelled at his men to fan out. "And stay away from those freaking skinny roots!"

Carrying bulging bags, Harlem, Soo-Yun, and Booker hurried across to Asher's group.

"What's going on?" I asked into my radio.

"The soldiers are going to stand guard," came Asher's crackled reply. "The rest of us are trying to figure out a way to rescue you, Kass. We need to sever the onion terra's roots without bringing the whole thing crashing down."

"What about Lynxx's crazy plan?"

"It's well named. We're trying to think of something safer. Or less crazy."

"And?"

"Nothing yet."

I lowered my voice. "The old man trapped with me is having chest pains. He says it's just heartburn. What if it's more serious? We need to get him out of here now, not later. What's Lynxx's plan?"

A familiar voice came on the radio. "Let me tell her." The radio clattered as it changed hands. "Kassia?"

"I'm here, Lynxx."

"Remember how we trained Owlfred to fly to you whenever you sang 'The Star-Spangled Banner'?"

"What?" We'd never done that. Was he actually crazy after all?

"Remember? You sing it and Owlfred flies to you."

At a strange note in his voice, I gasped in understanding. "Oh. Right," I said, playing along with his lie. Was he going to remote-push Owlfred to fly to me? But he was too far away to control the bird. "Why do you want Owlfred to come to me?"

Asher took the radio and explained the plan. I listened, heart sinking. *Definitely a crazy idea.* I glanced at Xavian. He sat slumped on the ledge, breathing with difficulty. The sooner our medic treated him, the better.

"It's really dangerous," I said to Asher. "I can't decide for all three of us. Stand by."

When I explained the plan, Xavian gave a quick nod. Panny also nodded, scared but anxious to get her guardian some help.

Returning to the triangular hole, I said, "Okay, let's do it." On the ground, Lynxx hurried toward a grove of trees, the small owl perched on his shoulder. I spoke into my radio again. "Where are you going, Lynxx?"

"Owlfred gets stage fright. She needs privacy for this to work."

"Huh? She needs privacy?"

Lynxx called to the others, "Stay where you are, okay? Don't come over here or you'll ruin everything. Understand?" They shrugged their shoulders and nodded. He disappeared behind some bushes.

A foul odor suddenly filled the terra cavity. It smelled like sewage mixed with skunk.

My nose crinkled. "What's that stink?"

Panny said, "The onion terra wants some more skeletons gone from the pool. Xavian thinks the different smell means a different area to be cleaned."

"Charming."

Lynxx's voice came from my radio. "Owlfred's ready. You can start, Kassia."

Feeling foolish, I poked my head through the gap and started singing "The Star-Spangled Banner."

Owlfred shot from the bushes and winged her way toward the onion terra. Still singing, I darted back inside the dim cavity, my radio emitting a chorus of *oohs* and *ahhs* as my colleagues watched Owlfred fly up to me.

Great remote-pushing, Lynxx!

The owl flew through the triangular hole and landed on my outstretched arm. Her head swiveled from side to side, taking in the strange surroundings and my companions. In the dimness, her eyes looked silver instead of her normal yellow.

Xavian frowned at the silver-eyed bird.

Carefully, I unhooked the small device slung around the feathered neck. "Good girl. Now off you go."

The owl flew back to the gap in the wall. She perched on the edge, her silver eyes looking at me for a long moment. Then she darted off. *Impressive.* Maybe one day I'd be able to remote-push as well as Lynxx.

But remote-kill like Xavian? My skin crawled.

I gingerly held the smooth black object that Owlfred had brought. Flat bottom. Curved top. Recessed LCD.

A small bomb.

<h1 style="text-align:center">42</h1>

Bomb cupped in my hand, I spoke into the radio. "Now what?"

"Position it over the thick central root," Asher replied.

"Yuck. That's in the pool of digestive juices."

"If you can't do it, Kass, we'll try something else." He was still protecting me. Treating me differently. Fretting about my leukemia.

Xavian's face creased in pain and he grasped his chest.

"I'll do it," I hurriedly told Asher. "Stand by."

At the edge of the pool, I drew in a deep breath—*seriously, how can anything smell this bad?*—and waded into the sludge. It felt like a massive bowl of cold porridge. Bones snapped beneath my boots. Human? Animal? A few steps later the stuff beneath my feet felt spongy. *Oh no.* Was I walking on flesh?

I forced myself onward, stopping in the middle of the pool. "I'm here," I said into my radio. "Now what?"

Following Asher's directions, I set the timer for five minutes.

The LCD screen began counting down.

Five minutes.

Three hundred seconds.

"You're nearly finished, Kass," he said. "Place the device on the bottom of the pool. Make sure the timer is facing upward, not down."

Two hundred and eighty seconds.

Something nudged my leg.

A triangular head bobbed to the surface, along with a thick scaled body. *The rattlesnake.* Instinctively, I remote-pushed it away—then remembered it was dead. Remote-killed by Xavian.

Two hundred and thirty seconds.

Eyes squeezed shut, I pinched my nose closed and crouched down in the sludge. Blindly, I shoved the device onto the bottom of the pool, timer facing upward.

Unable to see the numbers, I continued mentally counting down.

One hundred and fifty seconds.

Standing up, I gulped in rank air.

"Hurry!" Panny cried, hands outstretched.

I waded toward her, more bones snapping beneath my boots.

One hundred and three seconds.

At the edge of the pool, I hauled myself onto the ledge, helped by an anxious Panny.

Sixty-three seconds.

I splashed my eyes and face with water from a bottle.

Crabben xans scuttled over the skeletons around the edge of the pool, oblivious to the oncoming destruction.

I wondered if these were the last few seconds of our lives. The small bomb was a directional device. When it exploded, the force would be focused downward into the central root. Hopefully, it would kill the root without destroying the rest of the plant—or us.

But what if it caused the whole onion terra to crash to the ground?

Wiping my face, I bent over Xavian. "How's your chest?"

"I'll be fine and dandy soon as we get out of here."

Forty seconds.

He reached out a blue-veined hand to Panny, and she clasped it gently. "Panny, the Mist was a soul-breaking abomination. Still and all, it brought a ray of light into me life. You."

Tears trailed tracks through the dirt and dried blood on her cheeks. "No, Xavian, don't say goodbye. I need you."

Thirty.

I clutched my wet radio. Should I be saying goodbye to Asher and Lynxx?

"I love you, Panny." Xavian struggled to get the words out. Was his pain emotional or physical? "You're like me daughter."

Twenty.

"Get down, Panny." I lay along the ledge and wrapped my arms around my head.

Fifteen.

She threw herself on top of Xavian, shielding him with her body.

Sheesh. I'd promised Xavian that I'd protect her.

Ten.

I leaped to my feet—

Five.

—and flung myself on top of Panny.

One.

43

An explosion rocked the onion terra.

Cold digestive juices cascaded over us in a shower of bone fragments and bits of rotting flesh. Something sharp cut my cheek, spilling warm blood.

Terrified bats fled in a flurry of beating wings. Rats squeaked and crabbens clattered as they ran across the skeletons, onto our narrow ledge. Tiny paws and hard claws scrabbled across my head and body. *Dis-gus-ting!*

The shaking stopped. The ledge stilled. A new sound filled my ears.

Rushing water. No, not water. Liquid.

I peered from under my arms.

As the pool's level slowly dropped, I visualized a dark green waterfall cascading to the ground, through a hole in the base of the onion terra.

Hurriedly, I stood and shook myself, throwing off the critters on my back. Kicking a stray one aside, I wiped away the sludge and bits of bone that splattered my clothes.

Panny rolled off Xavian.

He grunted, "You lasses ain't no bags of feathers."

She kneeled and hugged him. "You're okay! You didn't die."

Gray-skinned, he managed a faint smile. "I ain't dying yet, Panny. Who'd whop you in cards every night? Or be your guinea pig for your latest super-supper-of-the-week? What was it the other night? Brussels sprouts, beets, and pigeon stew?" He gave a comical wince.

My anxiety eased. Xavian was breathing better and talking easier. Perhaps he'd merely had a bad case of heartburn after all.

Sitting up, he frowned at my injured cheek. "You're bleeding, lass."

"It's just a cut," I said, washing the injury with bottled water. "It'll heal."

I crossed to the triangular gap in the terra wall. Outside, Asher, Pepper, and Booker were retreating as the terra liquid flowed across the ground. Animal skeletons bobbed in the current or clung to the weeds, floating like bony islands.

Asher's agitated voice crackled from my radio. "Kass! Are you all right?"

In this strange and dangerous terra, the sound of his voice was like a lifeline, and I grasped it eagerly. "I'm fine. Look up." I waved from the window. "We're all fine."

"Good." His one word held massive relief.

"Did it work?" I asked.

"I'm not sure. The top part of the thick central stem has been blown up. But the skinny roots are still supporting the onion terra."

"Be careful," I said, watching from the window. "The skinny roots might still be alive and hiding in the grass. That's how one got me."

"I should've stopped it. Kept you safe." Asher retreated a few steps as the dark green lake grew wider and wider.

I rolled my eyes. "Can you say *hero complex*? As much as you want to, you can't save everyone."

His voice grew quieter, more intense. "As long as I can save you."

I blushed, aware the others—*Lynxx*—were hearing these private comments on their radios. "Thanks. But right now, I just want to get out of here." The digestive juices had drained through the gaping hole. I swept my flashlight's beam across the empty pool and over the woody veins that lined the bottom. "It looks like the thick stem supplied nutrients to the thinner roots."

Lynxx's voice came on. "That's what I was counting on, Kassia. With the thick stem dead, the skinny roots will gradually die too. The same thing happens to the branches of an Earth tree once its trunk dies."

"That could take days," I said, chilled by the idea of being stuck in this cavity for so long.

"Right," Lynxx agreed. "But terras are different from Earth plants. Those skinny roots might already be dead."

Asher said, "I'll find out. Stand by."

I waited impatiently, unable to see what they were doing. Finally, Asher returned with the good news. The skinny terra roots seemed dead.

Following Lynxx's instructions, I again sang "The Star-Spangled Banner."

Moments later, Owlfred flew through the gaping hole in the emptied pool, a thin line clutched in her beak. Even in the brighter light, her eyes still looked silver instead of yellow. *Strange.*

I looped the line around the steel-strong rib that edged the small triangular window. Pulling on the line, I hauled up a harness, a mesh bag filled with bottled water and granola bars, and a long thick nylon cable that I fastened to the rib.

As Xavian and Panny ate and drank, I splashed some more water over my face, washing off any remaining digestive juices.

Panny and I supported Xavian as we carefully moved toward the hole.

When I went to put the harness on Xavian, he waved me aside with a weak hand. "Panny first."

"Absolutely not," she cried. "You're going first, Xavian. No argument."

I heard the inflexibility in her tone and saw the resolution on her face. So did Xavian. With a resigned nod, he slung his battered backpack over one shoulder.

Quickly, I harnessed him up, ensuring he was secured to the thick nylon cable. Wrinkled hands gripping the rope, he descended through the hole.

Asher radioed me, "Soo-Yun's waiting to check everyone out as soon as you get down."

"Good. Make sure she knows about Xavian's chest pains."

"Will do."

We watched Xavian safely descend to the ground via the harness and rope.

Panny went next.

A few minutes later, the empty harness returned. "You're next, Kass," came Harlem's voice from my radio.

"Where's Asher?"

"Talking to Sergeant Thorne. Some new problem, I guess."

I strapped myself into the harness. Pushing away from the crumbling edges of the hole, I began my descent to the ground.

Beyond the soaring terra, the earlier sun had vanished behind thick clouds. The onion terra loomed above me, supported by dozens of vibrating terra roots.

Vibrating?

I stiffened. Were these skinny roots still alive?

A gust of wind wailed past, strumming the skinny roots like strings on a guitar, causing them to vibrate. I relaxed. As I was hauled downward, I pulled out my binoculars.

On the left, beyond the lake of digestive fluids, Xavian lay on the grass. Soo-Yun and Pepper were kneeling beside his motionless form.

Oh no! Was he alive? Dead?

Panny raced across to them, but Booker stopped her. She struggled in his grip, pointing to Xavian. Booker shook his head and held her back.

Off to the side, Asher was still talking to Thorne, their gestures agitated.

I descended past the broken central stem, which poked from the ground like a jagged tree trunk. Only the bottom half of the forty-foot stem remained. Dark sap trickled from its shattered top like blood seeping from a dying body.

I aimed my binoculars at Xavian again—and my heart leaped.

He was sitting up, smiling weakly as Panny hugged him.

He was alive.

Something wet and spongy rubbed my neck. It was a skinny root. Thick as a thumb, it stretched from the ground to the base of the onion terra, reminding me of a giant black worm, slimy and revolting.

Dozens of roots surrounded me like a forest of upright worms. One of these things had snatched me from my world and had thrown me into a frightening realm of skeletons, snakes, and critters that scratched and squeaked in the dimness.

My breaths grew quicker, shallower. Cold panic clutched at my throat—

—and then my boots touched the soggy ground and a pair of strong arms encircled me.

"Kass, I was so worried." Asher gently touched my bloodied cheek. "You're hurt."

My panic dissolved in his warm embrace. "It's just a cut."

Harlem and a couple of others began unclipping the cables.

"Make sure you put some disinfectant on it," Asher said.

"I will."

"Any other injuries?"

"Sore shoulder. It'll be fine in a couple of days."

Reassured, he showered my face with kisses, avoiding my injured cheek.

Laughing, I unstrapped my harness. "Careful. I'm filthy and wet. Believe me, you don't want to know what's on my clothes."

"Are you sure you're fine?" he murmured in my ear. "Your illness hasn't returned?"

"I'm fine, truly."

Lynxx trailed to a halt a short distance away, ankle-deep in the foul sludge. From the way he stared at me—longingly, despairingly—I guessed he'd been rushing to my side. He stood there, alone, watching Asher embrace me.

Then he turned and walked away.

Over Asher's shoulder, I saw Panny hurrying toward us. She squelched through the shallow green lake, ignoring the islands of skeletons as she focused on us, her face alight with gratitude.

Again, Asher touched my cheek with a gentle hand. "When I thought I'd lost you, it felt like my world was ending. Again." His words shook with relief, as though he'd been pulled back from a dark abyss.

Panny faltered a few steps away. A hand fluttered to her mouth as a small cry escaped her, ragged with disbelief.

Asher looked around. He stared at the grubby teenager, at her blood-smeared face, her filthy hair.

His eyes widened.

He seemed to stop breathing. To freeze on the spot.

What was going on?

And then Asher spoke ...

... a single hushed word with the potential to shatter my world.

"Willow?"

44

Willow.

The love of Asher's life.

Dazed, he released me—and the parts of my body that'd been warmly pressed against him suddenly felt ice-cold.

The girl stumbled into Asher's arms, crying. He threw me a confused look, saying, "How ...?" She clung to him and he stroked her hair with a trembling hand, as if afraid she'd disappear at any moment. "Willow! I thought you were dead."

"Xavian found me. Kept me safe."

"You're alive." A quiver swept him and his arms tightened around her. He buried his face against her neck and uttered a cry that seemed wrenched from his soul: long-buried grief threaded with dawning wonder.

I stared at them, my mind flashing back to the first time I'd seen them together. It had been a few days after the Night of the Red Mist, at a busy New York airport.

A familiar couple stood nearby. The seventeen-year-old girl was Willow Grace. Breathtakingly beautiful, she had long blond hair, porcelain skin, and stunning violet eyes.

The boy embracing her was Asher Weston.

His hands cupped Willow's face as they gazed at each other, clearly in love.

I struggled to match that stunning actress with this filthy, bedraggled girl. Torn coveralls clothed a body more skinny than slim. Her long hair was muddy and matted, its color drab. Her face was smeared with dried mud and blood.

She turned to me. Inside the dimly lit onion terra, her eyes had appeared gray, but here in the afternoon sunlight, they were a rare and glorious violet.

Willow gazed at me—and her violet eyes shimmered with questions similar to my own. *Who is this girl? How important is she to Asher?*

Harlem paused in rolling up a cable and gaped at Willow. "When that old guy reached us, he told me to make sure *Panny* got down safely."

"That's his nickname for me."

Brittle noises sounded behind us, like branches being crushed in a giant's hand.

I whipped around. The skinny roots that had supported the towering terra were buckling and snapping.

The massive "onion" began tilting.

"Run, Kass!" Asher cried. He grabbed Willow's hand and pulled her after him. "Come on."

People scattered as more skinny roots snapped.

Alone, so alone, I raced across the shallow lake of digestive juices.

The ground shuddered as the onion terra crashed down behind us. Broken bits of terra shell shot through the air, and bones arrowed past like javelins. Something whacked my back. I stumbled. My boot snagged on a bone in the green slush and I toppled forward.

For a moment I lay in the foul liquid—and then a strong hand pulled me up.

"Are you hurt?" Asher gripped my shoulders, searching for injuries. Nearby, Willow's brows were knotted with concern. For me? Or because Asher was fussing over me?

"I'm fine," I said.

A flurry of movement caught my attention.

Hundreds of small crabbens darted from the surrounding forest and dived into the green lake. Tiny legs paddling furiously, they headed for the shattered onion terra.

Willow gave a disgusted cry and stepped closer to Asher.

Ankle-deep in sludge, we sloshed across the stinking lake. We skirted islands of skeletons, dodged swimming crabbens, and avoided sodden rats fleeing the toppled onion terra. Here and there, crabbens and rats met in battle, splashing in deadly whirls of sharp teeth and forked claws.

Wet and dazed, we rejoined Xavian and the others.

Our convoy had parked beside a small public school. As we washed off the reeking terra liquid in a nearby stream, the three soldiers who'd gone hunting finally returned, triumphant. They set up a spit in the schoolyard and started roasting a leg of wild boar.

By the time we changed into fresh clothes—Willow borrowing garments from the other girls—dinner was almost ready.

I sat on a swing away from the campfire. On the other side of the schoolyard, Asher and Willow perched on an outdoor table, heads together as they talked.

Above the trees, a red-gold sunset ushered in a new night. Sighing, I wondered if *I* was also approaching a new night—one empty of Asher's warmth.

Lynxx took the adjacent swing. "How's your cheek?" He nodded at the large Band-Aid below my right eye.

"It's fine. Doesn't hurt anymore."

"Good." He glanced at the cozy couple across the schoolyard. "I heard about Willow Grace. Are you okay?"

"They've got a lot to catch up on."

"You didn't answer my question."

Shrugging, I changed topics. "Have you ever met that old man, Xavian, before?"

"No. Why?"

"Are you sure you've never met him?"

"Positive. Why?"

"Can you remote-kill, Lynxx?"

"*What?*"

Quietly, I told him about the incident with the rattlesnake in the onion terra.

"Xavian's a hybrid?" Lynxx blinked at me, shocked. "And he killed the rattler with his mind?"

"Yes. Can *you* do it?"

"No. I've heard of hybrids having that power, but I've never tried it. Not sure I want to."

"Same here." I shuddered, visualizing the snake jerking in the pool as its neck snapped.

Remote-killing was scary ...

... but effective.

45

AFTER DINNER, MOST PEOPLE took their sleeping bags and trudged to various classrooms, tired from another long day. Soldiers patrolled the schoolyards, rifles clasped to their chests.

As midnight drew closer, a core of us sat around the campfire's dying flames: Asher, Willow, Xavian, Harlem, Lynxx, and me.

Except for a slight tremor in his voice, Xavian showed no sign of his earlier weakness in the onion terra. Stroking his gray beard, he looked at us. "Who owns the owl that flew up to the onion terra today?"

Lynxx stiffened. "I do. Why?"

"I used to own an owl when I was a lad. Cute bird. What's his name, son?"

"*She's* called Owlfred."

Asher fixed his gaze on the old man. "Willow tells me that you're a hybrid, Xavian."

"Yeppo. Born and bred, though not in that order."

"Hybrid?" Harlem gasped. He tried to peer at Xavian's earlobes, covered by his long wild hair. "Where are your black marks?"

"That's a stuff-and-nonsense myth, lad. There ain't no easy way to tell a hybrid from a full-fledged human."

Asher's eyes narrowed. "So we've heard."

"What kind of name is Xavian?" Harlem asked. "Is that a hybrid name?"

"Shoot, lad, me hybrid name is Hammer. Hammer! What kind of fool name is that for a babe?"

Harlem grimaced. "Why Hammer?"

"All hybrids babies are named after hard inanimate objects, lad. Things that ain't got no emotions, no humanity. Stuff-and-nonsense names like Gravel and Axe and Wire."

"So you changed your name?" I asked, remembering how Lynxx had rejected his cold hybrid name, Rock, when he was sixteen.

"Yeppo. When I was four-and-ten, Mr. Xavian was a teacher at school. Actually, he was the only teacher at school."

"You weren't homeschooled?" Lynxx asked, surprised.

"Naw. Me guardian couldn't be bothered with home learning, so he sent me to school for two months a year. We lived off the grid down in Louisiana, but there was a one-room school a mile and a bit away as the crow flies. Mr. Xavian MacGavin was the teacher. A Scot. Kind, fair, and compassionate—everything my guardian wasn't. Everything I wanted to be. Eventually, I done decided to borrow my teacher's first name, figuring it were a better fit for me than Hammer. Sweet frogs in mud, any name's better than Hammer!"

Asher shifted uncomfortably on his seat. "I appreciate everything you've done, Xavian. Truly. From what Willow's said, she's alive because of you."

The old man patted Willow's hand, his wrinkled skin dotted with age spots. "Panny saved me life as well."

"How?"

"Most of me life, I was an outsider. I ain't belonged to one world or the other." His gaze paused on Lynxx and me. "Odds on, some of you know what that's like." He cleared his throat. "Later, I married me Maryanne and we had a son, Charlie. Them twenty years were the happiest in me life. Then the Outriders decided to punish me for becoming 'humanized.' Anyways, they murdered me family, and I was alone. An outsider once more."

He looked at Willow, his eyes glittering with tears. "But when I found Panny, I had a family again."

Willow squeezed his hand, her own eyes glittering.

"Why do you call her Panny?" I asked.

"When I first found Panny—Willow—she was a sick, scrawny lass. I couldn't just leave her to die, so I took her under me old wing. A week later, after we got to trust each other a smidge, she mentioned the movies and TV shows she'd made." He beamed with the pride of a father. "Me Panny's beautiful, famous, and talented."

Everything I wasn't.

Willow blushed. "Xavian hadn't seen much of my work, but he'd watched a few episodes of *Pandora*."

I remembered the paranormal show, a massive hit. Willow had played the title character, Pandora, a feisty kick-ass heroine who battled the evil forces she'd accidentally released from a wooden box.

"From then on," Xavian continued, "whenever she got frightened by some noise or spooked by a shadow, I'd call her Pandora. It helped her big-time. Instead of itchin' to hide, she'd straighten her shoulders, lift her chin, and face her fear. She *became* Pandora. Over the weeks and months, I shortened her name to Panny."

Willow gave Xavian's hand another squeeze.

Covertly, I studied Asher's former girlfriend across the campfire.

Her borrowed T-shirt, jeans, and denim jacket were a better fit than her former baggy coveralls. Instead of appearing skinny and gaunt, she now looked slim.

More dramatic, though, was the transformation brought about by soap, shampoo, and a long scrub in a stream. Butterfly bandages covered the gash on her forehead. Her face was no longer layered with dried blood and dirt. Now, the warm glow of the campfire highlighted her delicate features, porcelain skin, long-lashed eyes—and full lips that Asher would've kissed again and again in the past.

I wondered if he'd kissed those lips since his reunion with Willow this afternoon. Had he stroked the hair that now fell in shiny blond waves down her back? Embraced that slender body?

When she glanced at me, I hurriedly studied the fire, as though the answers to my questions lay within its writhing flames.

Harlem cocked his head at Willow. "Did you ever live in Felton after the Mist?"

"Where's that?" she asked.

"A hundred miles north of New York."

She shook her head. "Xavian and I never got that far north."

"Figures." Harlem rolled his eyes. "Mavis was wrong."

"Who's she?"

"An old lady. She told me about a rumor of you living in Felton."

"No, it wasn't me."

Click-click. Click-click.

My head jerked up, stomach tightening.

I'd heard that sound before, at the Statue of Liberty.

From the adjoining dark forest came more sharp clicks, like bones snapping.

The others stared at the dark forest for a few seconds. Then, apparently unconcerned, they resumed their conversation.

"I'm sorry, Xavian, but you can't stay with us," Asher said regretfully. "We don't allow hybrids into our group."

Willow's beautiful eyes flashed. "No, Ash! If Xavian leaves, I leave."

I bit back a snort of disbelief. Every time Willow looked at Asher, her face held longing and relief; a person lost in the desert would regard an oasis with that same yearning.

Click-click. Click-click.

I froze, listening.

Back on Liberty Island, those clicks had stirred a cold fear within me. Tonight, I felt it again.

"Shouldn't we investigate those clicking noises?" I asked Asher.

He gave a distracted wave. "We've got guards for that. It's probably just xan bugs. Or crabbens."

"Yeah. Probably." A flashlight nestled in one of my pockets and a gun in the other. For a second, I considered investigating the clicks myself. Then sanity prevailed. Only a crazy person would search a dark creepy forest alone, hunting unseen creatures that made sounds like snapping bones.

Probably just crabbens.

I remained in the warm glow of the campfire.

"Xavian's not our enemy, Ash," said Willow firmly. "He's on the Sphere's side."

"We've heard of them. Who are they?"

"The good guys," Xavian replied. "Well, at least the good hybrids."

He explained the difference, echoing some of what Bone had told us up on the skyweb months ago. Basically, the Sphere members felt more human than hybrid. Following the Mist, they had united to help humanity—and themselves—survive.

The Outriders were the opposite; loyal to the Chi'az, they were currently attempting to create a virus to eliminate the remaining remnants of humanity.

"We know about their new virus, the Threads," said Asher. "How close are the Outriders to success?"

"Hopefully a good ways off." The old man stared into the dying flames. "Still, it'd be right-smart to stop 'em before they're ready to rock and roll. I sure as heck don't want to live in a world run by the Chi'az and Outriders."

Soft clicks came from the black forest again. Fainter, as though retreating. *Good.* I relaxed a little.

Asher looked from the old man to Willow and back again. "Xavian can stay with us, at least until New York. Then it's Commander Powell's decision."

"Fair enough, lad," Xavian said.

Willow beamed, and I drew in a sharp breath as she kissed Asher on the cheek. "Thank you," she cried. "I knew you'd let us stay."

Asher stared at the dying fire, not looking at me. Willow had been the love of his life. He'd known her since they were in kindergarten, and she was the only person left alive that he'd known before the Mist. Their long history together connected them far more than my relationship with him.

"There's one condition, Xavian," said Asher.

"What's that, lad?"

"You need to tell us everything you know about the Chi'az, the Outriders, and the Sphere."

"No problem. It ain't gonna be much, though. To be flat-out honest, I've been trying to keep out of their battles since I were knee-high to a grasshopper." Xavian paused, thinking. "I got one nugget of info that might pay for me suppers, though."

"What's that?"

"The location of Bone and his Brethren recruits."

"We already suspect they're in Florida."

"I've done heard that Florida's a wild sprawlin' place these days. An elephant could hide in its patches of thick jungle—and probably does. You got Bone's exact location?"

"No."

Xavian gave a faint smile, like a homeless kid eyeing a potential new family. "I do."

46

MONSTERS CIRCLED OVERHEAD. ZOMBIES, werewolves, dragons, and sea serpents hunted each other round and round, whipped by a cold wind that gusted through a crack in the classroom walls.

Alone, I lay in my sleeping bag, staring at the rotating monster mobile suspended from the ceiling.

Sleep was impossible.

Two hours ago, Asher and Xavian had gone to Sergeant Thorne's quarters. I guessed the three of them were still huddled around a map of Florida, working on strategies for dealing with Bone and the Brethren.

The rest of us had lingered by the campfire until the arrival of a grit-laden wind. It had smothered the flames, cracked branches, and barreled trash across the schoolyard. Blinking away the grit in our eyes, we'd scurried to our sleeping quarters. Some people had bunkered together. Others—like me—had sought the privacy of solo rooms.

I wondered where Willow was sleeping tonight.

I tossed and turned, my fears and worries driving sleep away. For the tenth time, I gazed around my makeshift bedroom.

Like most of this school, the walls were dotted with harmless, luminescent moss terras that threw off blue glows. If I half-closed my eyes, it almost looked as if I were in a warm summer ocean, with sunlight streaming through the water.

But when I fully opened my eyes, I saw fading pictures drawn by dead children, abandoned books of fairy tales, lonely toys, and empty desks huddled in cobwebbed corners. An eerie sense of loss hovered like the fading notes of a funeral dirge; statistically, I knew that every child from this class had probably died from the Red Fever.

Outside, the windstorm shook the wooden building and slammed the loose shutters.

Tap-tap-tap-tap.

Startled, I looked at the windows.

They were empty.

Breathing deeply, I tried to calm my churning emotions.

Life as a resistance member was frequently stressful, but this afternoon had been a nightmare.

I'd been grabbed up by a long skinny root. Tossed inside a massive onion terra. Thrown into a pool of reeking digestive juices. Climbed over the skeletons of other victims. Met another hybrid. Watched him remote-kill an enormous rattlesnake. Helped rescue this hybrid, along with a teenager who'd turned out to be Asher's former girlfriend. Fled from the onion terra as it'd crashed to the ground. Watched Asher reunite with the love of his life.

What a rotten day.

I was exhausted but too agitated to sleep.

Tap-tap-tap-tap.

A small shape fluttered outside a window. Owlfred. The bird flapped at the glass pane, dropped from sight, then reappeared, struggling to stay aloft. Again she pecked at the glass.

Tap-tap-tap-tap.

Quickly, I opened the window. "Owlfred, what are you doing here?"

The owl tumbled inside and fell to the floor, too weak to fly. As I scooped her up, she gazed at me with round eyes that should've been yellow. Instead, they were the same silver they'd been in the huge onion terra.

A sudden memory flashed through me.

Mousy.

When I'd been living in the subway bunker, my pet white mouse had kept me company while Olivia was scavenging on the surface. His tiny eyes had sometimes looked black; other times they'd been silver.

Weird.

Owlfred squawked, a weak sound of sorrow and pain. What had happened to her?

"It's okay, Owlfred," I said, holding her gently. "Lynxx will help you."

His room was down the hall, his door closed. Even though he had a strict rule about not being disturbed at night, I cradled Owlfred and knocked several times.

No answer.

I entered, calling his name.

The moss terras on the walls lit the room with a blue glow. Lynxx lay on top of his sleeping bag. Hands clasped across his chest, he seemed as motionless as a sculptured figure on a tomb.

"Lynxx, something's wrong with Owlfred."

Silence.

The bird stirred in my arms, weaker than before, still gazing at me with desperate silver eyes.

"Lynxx, wake up."

Nothing.

Still cradling the drooping owl, I kneeled and shook him with one hand.

No reaction.

And then the air shifted, as though thousands of atoms were suddenly colliding. A whisper of electricity or power or *something* flashed like invisible lightning. Owlfred's silver eyes turned yellow again.

The air fell calm once more.

Had I really felt a shift in the air? Or was I overtired and overstressed?

Lynxx moved. Groaned. His eyes fluttered open, and he looked at me with the unmistakable relief of someone dragged back from the edge of a crumbling cliff. For a long moment, he struggled to speak. Then, finally, he croaked, "Thank you, Kassia."

"For what?"

"Saving my life."

"What do you mean? I'm trying to save Owlfred."

"Owlfred! I almost forgot." He grabbed his backpack. Moments later, he injected the owl with a few drops of a green substance.

The Gamma-6 liquid.

"Do you think she's been poisoned?" I asked.

With a weary nod, he gently placed Owlfred on a soft cloth in her cage. "We were investigating those clicking sounds you heard earlier, Kassia. We got too close and got stung. I didn't think we'd make it back here."

"*You* got stung? How? I thought you were in this room."

"I meant Owlfred got stung. By the click xans."

"Click xans?"

"That's what I'm calling them until I can settle on a zoological name. Nasty little critters; smaller than crabbens; much uglier." He peered in the cage. The small owl was already looking a little better, and she blinked at us with yellow eyes—not silver.

"You just said that *you* got too close and got stung."

"I meant that we ... no, Owlfred ... was stung."

Why was he confusing himself with Owlfred?

A sudden, wild suspicion gripped me.

47

I GASPED. "DID YOU somehow get inside Owlfred's mind?"

"What? No. Of course not." His words rang hollow.

"You're lying."

Lynxx hesitated, trying to summon the energy to argue. Finally, his shoulders slumped with fatigue and defeat. He glanced at the door and windows, making sure they were closed. "Okay. I mind-blended with Owlfred."

"Mind-blended? What's that?"

"It's sort of like remote-pushing, but much, much more. You have to mentally leave your body, which falls unconscious or non-conscious—"

"*What?*"

"—as you throw your mind *into* the other creature. You mentally blend with it, and yet dominate it so that you're in charge."

I gaped at him. "You can do this?"

"Yes."

"A few minutes ago, when you were stretched out on your sleeping bag, I couldn't shake you awake."

"I couldn't wake up because my mind was gone. My body was just lying there, non-conscious." Even in the blue glow of the moss terras, Lynxx looked pale. His body shook as though he'd just run a marathon, and he sank back onto his sleeping bag.

"You're in shock." I sat beside him and waited until he stopped trembling. "Better?"

"A little. I've never had a mind-blend go so bad."

"You've done this before?"

"Most nights on this mission."

"What? Why?"

"How else can I get the information we need? As Owlfred, I can fly around looking for the terras you need to survive, Kassia. Search for labs to make the Lazarus tonics. Scan the roads ahead for dangers. Investigate strange noises like those clicks."

"Is this what you've been doing at night while the rest of us slept? No wonder you're often exhausted during the day."

He shrugged. "When I'm mind-blended, my body falls unconscious. My mind, though, is still active for hours—"

"And the mind needs sleep as well as the body," I finished for him.

"Exactly."

I stiffened as the classroom windows rattled. Outside, the howling wind prowled the schoolyard like a hungry wolf.

"So you were mind-blended with Owlfred when she got stung by a click xan?" When he nodded, I went on, "Did you actually feel the poison affecting her body?"

"When I'm blended with a bird or animal, I control their bodies, feel what they feel, sense with their senses. Usually it works fine, unless there's a problem."

"What kind of problem?"

"I was in a gopher once that was about to be eaten by a leopard. I had to mind-hop out of him pretty quick."

"Where did you go?"

"Into a nearby mouse, then a sparrow, and an eagle."

"Why didn't you do that tonight when Owlfred got stung?"

"No time and, besides, there were no other creatures nearby. I barely had enough strength to fly Owlfred back to the school. But when I got to this classroom, I found my window slammed shut, probably by the wind."

"Couldn't you mind-hop through the glass pane, into your body?"

"Normally, yes, if it's less than twenty yards. Tonight, though, I was too weak."

At the fatigue in his voice, I decided to shelve some of my questions until tomorrow. *Can I mind-blend? How dangerous is it? What does it feel like?* Instead, I asked, "Is that why Owlfred-you came to my room? You hoped I'd take her to your body for the mind-hop?"

"No. I was trapped in Owlfred's body, fading quickly, barely able to breathe. I thought I only had a few seconds left."

"So why did you come to my room?"

"I knew I was dying." He paused. When he spoke again, his words were a whisper. "I wanted to see you one last time, Kassia."

My heart clenched. Tears blurred my vision.

Turning away, I pretended to study a knotted rug on the floor. When I looked back again, Lynxx was stretched out on his sleeping bag, eyes closed. For one heart-stabbing moment, I thought he was dead. Then I saw his chest rising and falling. Even asleep, his perfect features were shaded with exhaustion, and I shuddered at the thought of how close he'd come to death tonight.

This hybrid—no, this *boy*—had been quietly risking his life every night for my colleagues and me. He'd asked for nothing in return. And when he'd been dying in Owlfred's body, he'd fought to get to me, desperate to spend his last moments at my side.

Hand unsteady, I reached out to brush a lock of black hair from his forehead. At the last second I pulled back, his hair untouched.

I cared for Lynxx. I even loved him a little—but it wasn't the kind of love he felt for me. And it was nowhere near the deeper feelings I had for Asher.

But did Asher still feel the same about me? Or had Willow's return stirred up his old emotions?

Stress and worry knotted my stomach.

Sleep would be impossible.

Sighing, I spread a blanket beside the sleeping boy. *I'll just lie here for a few minutes*, I told myself, *to make sure he's okay*.

Lynxx's deep, regular breaths were as comforting as gentle waves on a beach. In. Out. In. Out. The rhythm of life. *His* life.

Moonbeams streamed through the windows, illuminating a display of children's paintings. Elsewhere in the room, the moss terras cast soft blue glows that were curiously calming. The overhead mobile that hung from this classroom ceiling didn't have monsters; instead, a prince, princess, and fairies circled to the tinkle of tiny bells.

No longer alone, I closed my eyes. My agitated breaths gradually grew slower and slower until they matched Lynxx's soothing rhythm ...

... and I slept.

48

WHEN I AWOKE THE next morning, a note lay on top of Lynxx's gear. *Gone for a walk.*

Disappointed, I gathered my blanket and checked to see that Owlfred was okay. She was sleeping peacefully in her covered cage, seemingly recovered from last night's trauma.

A low murmur of voices came from a distant hall where breakfast was being served.

I paused at an open doorway and looked at the school-yard, thick with leaves, branches, broken tiles, and trash.

Asher joined me. "What a mess, hey?"

My skin tingled at his nearness. "I didn't realize the wind had been so strong last night."

"And I didn't realize what a jackass I'd been."

"Excuse me?"

Regret gleamed in his blue eyes. "I'm sorry."

My stomach tightened. This was it. He was about to break my heart.

"I'm sorry I've neglected you since we found Willow," he said. "I was in shock. I couldn't believe she was alive, and then we had so much to catch up on."

I hid a tremble of relief. Maybe he wasn't breaking up with me. "I know how important Willow is to you."

"You're *both* important to me." He drew me close and kissed me—but my fears remained.

Hand in hand, we went to breakfast and sat opposite Willow and Xavian. Her anxious gaze flickered from Asher to me, and she bit her lip. When the old man blinked at us in bewilderment, she squeezed his wrinkled hand, murmuring, "It's all right, Xavian."

After breakfast, Asher announced that T4 wouldn't be fixed until lunchtime. As a result, most of us had a few more hours off.

Asher gave me a quick kiss, then turned to Xavian. "I have a meeting. Can you join us for a while, sir?"

"No problem, lad."

Lisa from Trident Team stepped forward. Her face gleamed with a fan's eagerness as she said, "I'll keep you company, Willow. I super-loved *Pandora*. Is it true that ...?" And she launched into a dozen questions about the show.

Restless, I wandered outside and picked my way through the debris.

Lynxx emerged from the nearby forest. After glancing around to make sure that we were alone, he said, "Thanks for your help last night."

"Huh?" Distracted, it took me a moment to realize what he was talking about. "Oh. Owlfred." And his dying wish to be with me. Why was I blushing? I'd known for months how Lynxx felt about me. "Owlfred seems fine."

"I know. I looked in on her before I left and fed her a dead rat for breakfast."

"Yummy," I said, smiling. "How was your walk?"

"It cleared my head. Mostly."

"Mostly?"

"When I woke up this morning, you were sleeping next to me."

"You almost died last night. I wanted to make sure you were all right."

"Is that the only reason?"

Flustered, I replied, "Maybe. Not really. I don't know." Hastily, I changed the subject. "T4 isn't fixed yet, so we have the morning off. How about some training?"

"You *want* to train?"

"Yes." Anything to quench my restlessness.

"Let's go. I saw a perfect spot during my walk."

We set off. A few minutes later, we stopped at a clearing in the forest. The sun broke through the clouds, unleashing bright sunshine. Dragonflies darted above a glittering stream, and a chorus of croaks came from the grass.

Lynxx pointed to a deer drinking downstream. "If we wait a bit," he whispered, "she might come closer."

"Why do we want that?"

"Right now, she's about thirty yards away. Too far for either of us to remote-push; we need her to be less than twenty yards for it to work."

"Remote-push?" I shifted restlessly on the spot. "I already know how to do that. I want to learn how to mind-blend."

"After what happened last night? You saw Owlfred-me. I nearly died."

"That's exactly why I want to learn. Maybe I can help with your nighttime missions. That way, you can get some more sleep, and you'll be sharper and more careful when you go off by yourself."

"Forget it. Do you think I could sleep knowing you were out there alone at night? I'll handle the missions." His voice held a familiar iron note.

"Fine. But I still want to learn to mind-blend. It might come in handy one day."

"You don't realize how dangerous it is."

"I have a fairly good idea. I was there when you nearly died last night, remember?"

At the determination in my voice, he sighed, "Very well. However, I need to explain a few fundamentals first."

"Okay."

He glanced around, making sure we were alone. "Before you start, always make sure you're lying or sitting somewhere safe. When you mind-blend, your mind completely leaves your body and your physical form is unprotected. You don't want to return after a mind-blend to find that your body's been eaten by a bear or burned in a wildfire."

Alarmed, I asked, "What if that *does* happen?"

"Not good. You'd be stuck living in animals or birds for the rest of your life. If that happens, avoid mice if you can; they only live for three years. Elephants are good as they can live for seventy years."

"So I could survive for years mind-blended with an animal?"

"Yes. If your human body has died, your connection with it dies too. That allows you to live indefinitely in animals."

"What about jumping into another human body?"

"Most of the time they're mentally too strong for us, Kassia."

"*Most* of the time?"

"You *might* be able to temporarily mind-blend if the person is weak-minded."

"Like a baby?"

"Yes. Or someone ill, on drugs, with dementia, or in a coma."

A shiver ran down my spine. "Terrible choices."

"Exactly." His face grew serious. "Listen carefully. This is important. If a host animal or bird dies while you're mind-blended with it, your mind will die too."

I gulped. "Got it. Is there anything else I need to know?"

"Are you claustrophobic?"

"No, tight spaces don't worry me."

"It's different when you're in a host's mind. At first, it can feel like you're trapped or you're being smothered. Don't panic. Harden your own mind like steel. Let the claustrophobia wash over you in a wave. It's not fun, but it's over in a few seconds."

"I'll ... I'll try."

He glanced at his watch. "We only have a few hours. Do you still want to go ahead?"

"Absolutely."

"Okay. You'll only be spending a few minutes mind-blended with an animal host today."

"A few minutes? Huh! What's the longest time you've mind-blended?"

"I try not to go over three hours. After that, my non-conscious human body can start waking up, and if it wanders around without a mind, it could injure me."

"I thought you said we could live for years mind-blended with an animal."

He paused, struggling to explain. "Think of an invisible cord connecting your absent mind and your non-conscious body. If your human body is alive, this invisible cord will start pulling your mind back into your body after three hours. But if your body has died, the cord is severed and there's nothing pulling your mind anymore. That's why, if your human body dies, your mind can live indefinitely in an animal or bird."

"Oh. Got it."

He pointed at three green frogs in the weeds. "How about we start with Kermit? Or would you prefer Croaky or Hopalong?"

"Who?"

With a faint smile, he asked, "Didn't you know that all frogs have their own names?"

"Huh! You're fickle. You once told me that all mice have the *same* name: Mousy." A wisp of memory hovered just beyond my reach.

Abruptly, Lynxx's face turned serious. "Time to begin." He gestured to a tree. "Sit down and rest against that trunk. Remember, your body needs to be protected when your mind is away. Always sit or lie somewhere safe." He watched me lean back against the rough bark. "Comfortable?"

"Sort of. Now what?"

"Make sure your subject is less than twenty yards away." He gestured to the closest frog. "Now mentally reach out to Kermit, as if you're about to remote-push him. Then, just before you mentally touch him, throw your mind further, *into* his brain."

I stared at the green frog, squinting, focusing. My mind leaped forward. For a split second, I saw pinpricks of light and sensed something soft and squishy. Then my mind snapped back, like a stretched elastic band suddenly released. I jerked upright. "Oww! That hurt."

"Did you get in?"

"I don't think so. Maybe my mind won't fit into Kermit's tiny froggy brain. Is there a size limit to the animals and birds we can blend with?"

"I'm not sure. I've blended with birds of all sizes and animals from giraffes to mice."

Mice.

Mousy.

Why did that name again flicker in my thoughts like an elusive memory?

Silver eyes.

I stifled a gasp as the truth finally hit me.

49

Carefully, I said, "Last night, when you were Owlfred, her eyes were silver instead of yellow. They were also silver when she flew inside the onion terra yesterday."

Lynxx nodded. "I don't understand why that happens, but it's a feature of a hybrid mind-blend."

"So you didn't remote-push Owlfred to fly inside the onion terra with that small bomb?"

"No. The distance to the top of the onion terra was over thirty yards. I can only remote-push or mind-blend with an animal if it's less than twenty yards away. So I took Owlfred behind the bushes where we couldn't be seen, mind-blended with her and flew up the device as Owlfred-me."

"If an animal's eyes are silver, does that mean it's being mind-controlled by a hybrid?"

"Yes."

I stared at him, conflicted. Long moments stretched together.

"Are you okay, Kassia?"

Ice crystals expanded in my chest, sharp-edged and hard. Unable to voice my suspicions, I took a deep breath and said, "Continue with the lesson."

"Are you sure?"

"Yes."

"Good." He pointed to another frog. "This time, focus as you throw your mind forward into Hopalong."

With difficulty, I tried to concentrate on the task. Over the next hour, I shoved my mind free again and again, mentally leaping toward Hopalong. Once or twice, I glimpsed tiny starbursts, and I felt a strange soft sponginess that only lasted a second. Then I was back in my own body again.

Lynxx continued to encourage me, but his enthusiasm lessened with each attempt.

Finally, wearily, he said, "Time for a break."

"I agree."

He drew in a deep breath, bracing himself. "There's something I need to tell you."

"Oh?" My single word was an icicle.

"I've wanted to tell you the truth for a long time. But I was afraid."

"Of what?"

"That you'd think I'd been spying on you like a pervert. You see, when you and your sister Olivia were living in that subway tunnel—"

"You mind-blended with Mousy," I finished for him.

His mouth dropped open. "You knew?"

"Not until an hour ago."

"Are you angry?"

Frostily, I replied, "Not yet. After all you've done for me, you deserve a chance to explain."

"I'll try."

There, sitting on the grass beside the stream, Lynxx told me everything. How he'd first met me at Central Park on Thanksgiving Day, mere hours before the Night of the Red Mist. "You and your cousin were watching a tug-of-war match between two groups of boys. I think Charlotte gave you a dare or something, because you suddenly walked across to me." His voice held a gentle longing, as though he was reliving a cherished memory. "And then you kissed me."

I frowned, remembering that boy from Central Park seventeen months ago.

Tall. Lean. Face hidden by a baseball cap and dark sunglasses. Red plaid shirt, faded blue jeans, and cowboy boots.

"No, I kissed Loner that day—" I stopped as realization slammed into me with the force of a kick to the chest. Lynxx's hair was shoulder-length now, and he'd swapped his country outfit for black clothes. "*You* were Loner."

"Loner?" He winced. "I guess it's a fitting name. I was raised by my guardian, Frost. But until I met you, Kassia, I had always felt alone. And then, that afternoon, you kissed me—and everything changed."

My kiss, he explained, had stirred previously unfelt emotions within him. Over the following months as the world died, he'd fallen in love with me.

"You already know how I'd leave meds and food for Olivia to find."

"Yes. You told me about that weeks ago, at Olivia's grave. You also told me how you saved my sister's life when she was attacked by a jellyfish terra." I paused, remembering. "My sister was also attacked by a psycho wearing a zebra-skin cloak. A silver-eyed lion saved her. Were you that lion?"

He nodded.

My icy heart slowly thawed beneath a warm wave of gratitude and awe. "How can I thank you?"

"Not necessary. Olivia was like a sister to me. And I loved you, Kassia. I did everything possible to protect you both." He drew in a shaky breath. "When you were in the bunker, I never intruded on your privacy. I promise." His words resonated with sincerity. "I always waited until you and Olivia were dressed before I entered your bunker as Mousy."

"I believe you," I said. "But *why* did you mind-blend with Mousy?"

"Most days, Olivia would go aboveground hunting for food or searching for supplies. Since you were too sick to help her, you had to wait in that subway bunker, worried and alone. You needed a companion, even if it was only a small white mouse."

"Why didn't you just introduce yourself to me, in your human form?"

"Too dangerous." He detailed his guardian's ruthlessness and dedication to the Chi'az cause, then said, "If Frost had suspected that I loved you, and cared for Olivia like a sister, he would've punished me."

"How?"

"By killing you and Olivia."

"That's twisted! Evil!"

"Frost was both. He was a fanatic Outrider, loyal to the Chi'az, and indifferent to humanity."

I wondered how Lynxx had turned out so differently from the hybrid who'd raised him.

"Xavian mentioned a similar thing," I said. "He told us how his wife and son were killed by the Outriders as punishment for him becoming humanized."

"It's a common punishment by the Outriders." Lynxx shuddered. "A few times, Frost almost discovered my relationship with you and Olivia. Eventually, I realized I couldn't keep putting your lives in danger. Even though it ripped my heart, I had to stop seeing you and stop helping Olivia. Thankfully, by then your sister knew how to keep you alive without the meds."

"Because you'd told her about the Lazarus flowers." Another thing he had admitted back at Olivia's gravesite.

"Yes."

"And yet when I first met you in the passageway of Grand Central Station—six months after the Mist—you pretended not to know me. You behaved as if you didn't even like me. Why?"

"Frost was watching us."

"Your guardian? You've told me that before, but I didn't see anyone else in the passage."

"He was mind-blended with a bat, and later with a rat."

"Oh." I remembered the silver-eyed bat and rat in the passageway that day. "But how could you be sure? Was it because their eyes were silver?"

"Yes. Also, I *sensed* him. A hybrid can't sense another hybrid if they're both in their normal human bodies. That's why I didn't know that Xavian was a hybrid until you told me, Kassia. However, it's different if a hybrid is blended with an animal or bird. A hybrid-human can occasionally sense a blended hybrid-animal, as some of them give off a vibration like a current in the air."

"I felt that the other night! Only it wasn't when you were in Owlfred's mind. It was during your mind-hop from Owlfred back into your own body."

"Your hybrid abilities are growing." He paused, frowning. "That day I met you in the Grand Central passage, I sensed Frost's presence nearby. I think he was mind-hopping from bats to rats as he spied on us. If he had suspected that I knew you—or even worse, that I loved you—he would've slaughtered you."

"Is that why you abandoned me on Fifth Avenue?"

His shoulders sagged beneath the weight of a long-borne guilt. "Frost was watching me closely. I *had* to walk away from you. But as soon as he left, I mind-blended with WindLord—"

"The golden eagle."

"—and I flew overhead, making sure you were safe. I saw that tiger on the vine-bridge, and I flew down to help you. Before I could do anything, though, Asher killed it with the arrow." Lynxx paused. "I watched him help you survive the animals' stampede in the street and the swarmers in the alley. When I saw him drive you to Weston Tower, I finally relaxed a little, knowing you were safe."

My brow furrowed as more memories surged forth. "I remember another animal with silver eyes. It was a few weeks after the Mist arrived. It was the day Asher played the 'Flower Duet' from the opera *Lakmé* on some loudspeakers."

"I remember that day too."

"You do? Anyway, I was sitting on Gapstow Bridge in Central Park. I was at my lowest. Thinking about ending it all. And then, a few seconds after the 'Flower Duet' finished, a squirrel ran up to me. It sat beside me for a little while, keeping me company, and I felt better." I watched Lynxx. "It had silver eyes, just like Mousy."

A slow nod. "That was me."

"*You* were mind-blended with the squirrel?"

Another slow nod.

I felt angry, torn, grateful—and guilty. Lynxx had been saving my life far longer than I'd suspected. Why couldn't I love him the way he loved me?

Confused by my conflicting emotions, I was suddenly overwhelmed by a fierce need to escape. Scowling, I stared at the frog, Hopalong. I heaved my mind forward. Bright lights exploded in a galaxy of starbursts. The universe spun and whirled as I plunged through a soft gray sponginess.

Multiple green shields soared around me—*no, not shields; they're blades of grass*—and a giant fly clung to a massive rock, the insect a few feet long.

No, not a few feet long.

I was only a few inches long.

I was in the frog.

50

I WAS TRAPPED. COULDN'T breathe. Suffocating. Dying.

Lynxx's words echoed through me. *Don't panic. Harden your mind like steel. Let the claustrophobia wash over you in a wave.*

I tried to calm myself. *I'm okay, I'm okay, I'm okay.*

Fear swept me, harsh and dark. A moment's pure terror—

—and then I was actually okay. No longer in a panic. Still alive.

And still in the frog.

A shadow blocked out the sun and I froze ... no, Hopalong froze ... *frog-me* froze.

Lynxx's gigantic face loomed above frog-me, worried. "Kassia?"

Wow! His voice sounded weird, as if it had layers. Frog ears obviously heard sounds differently than human ears.

"Is that you, Kassia?"

I tried to nod. Instead, fresh panic lanced through frog-me and I fled. Huge hops. Through the air. Up. Down. Up again. Away. Through the grass shields. Toward the glittering water.

Oh no. Hopalong was bolting for the stream.

Stop. Stop.

The frog ignored me.

The water loomed closer with each enormous hop.

"Kassia, take control. Push hard. Push!"

I mentally pushed. Something invisible resisted me. Another push. A final desperate all-or-nothing push.

And then emptiness. The resistance vanished.

Stop, I mentally ordered the frog.

It stopped hopping.

Turn.

It turned.

Look up.

Frog-me looked up.

Lynxx's gigantic face appeared overhead, his smile enormous. "You did it." His smile faltered. "It is you, isn't it?"

Frog-me nodded.

"Excellent," he said.

I felt excited, nervous, awed. I was in a frog. Controlling it.

Lifting my front right foot, I brought it closer to my bulging eyes. Four long skinny toes; shiny green skin. *Eww!* No, no, Lynxx wouldn't say *eww*. He'd say *interesting*.

Okay, my frog-toes were interesting.

I poked my tongue out. *Wow. Long.*

A sudden thought struck me.

Where was *I*? My human body?

A series of super-hops brought me to the top of a boulder—or maybe it was just a large rock. Whatever, I could see over the grass shields. And there I was. A giant girl slumped against the trunk of a tall tree. Head drooping. Eyes closed. Auburn braid dangling over one shoulder.

A loud crack rang out.

Halfway up the tall tree, a huge branch snapped off. It plunged down, down ...

... right toward my non-conscious body.

"*No.*" Lynxx bolted across the grass, grabbed up my body, and stumbled off.

Behind him, the branch crashed onto the ground, shaking it like an earthquake.

I gaped at the spot where my human form had been resting mere moments ago. If Lynxx hadn't—

Oww!

Something sharp grabbed my frog-body. A critter snatched me off the rock and scurried across the clearing, holding me up. Shocked, I struggled to escape the claw. Couldn't. The thing had me in a tight grip.

Twisting my frog-head, I gazed down at a hideous sight.

My captor vaguely resembled a crabben xan, only smaller and much uglier. Round body covered in short black spikes. Eight long segmented legs, each topped by a pincer claw. Dark, soulless eyes on either side of its angular head. Long scorpion-like tail.

Gripping Hopalong-me in one claw, it scuttled up the trunk of an oak, moving quickly.

"Kassia, where are you?" At the bottom of the oak, Lynxx was scanning the rocks and grass, still holding my limp human body in his arms.

Terrified, I tried to scream. A loud croak emerged, followed by another and another.

He looked up the trunk, his eyes widening. "Hang on. I'm coming."

Hurry.

He placed my non-conscious body on the grass, then lay down beside her ... um, *me*.

By now my xan-captor was near the top of the oak. It uttered a series of familiar sharp clicks.

Oh no! Hopalong-me had been caught by a click xan, one of the creatures that had almost killed Owlfred-Lynxx last night. They were highly dangerous, with fast-acting venom. When the clicker reached its destination, it would probably sting me. Since I lacked Lynxx's mental strength, Hopalong and I would be dead within moments.

Panic swelled within me but I tried to fight it down. *Mind of steel.*

Could I mind-hop into another animal? The only creature nearby was this click xan. Could a human mind-blend with a xan? What if my mind bounced out of the ugly critter and landed in nothing? I'd die.

The clicker scurried along a horizontal branch to a bowl-shaped lump of mud and twigs. It held me over the structure, and I saw a clump of eggs at the bottom.

I felt sick.

It was a nest.

The clicker grasped one of my legs with another pincer claw and squeezed. My leg bone snapped. Agony flared through frog-me like fire.

The claw released my body.

Hopalong-me fell, landing beside the eggs. I struggled to stand, to flee, but my broken leg crumbled and I lay there, unable to move.

The click xan leaped into the nest. Again, my mental screams emerged as croaks. Terrified, I watched the clicker's scorpion-like tail and braced myself. Would dying hurt? It really didn't matter. I was already in agony.

The clicker ignored me. It scampered over the clump of eggs, cracking each one with a pincer claw. Then it scurried out of the nest and disappeared.

The surrounding eggs trembled. Minute claws poked through the shells. The cracks widened into holes.

And I knew my fate had just become a lot darker.

Instead of a quick death from the click xan's sting, I was about to be slowly and painfully eaten alive by its young.

51

One by one, the tiny clickers crawled from their eggs. I tried remote-pushing them back, but they kept emerging.

Over the past few years, I had become used to the idea of dying. Once or twice, I would even have welcomed death as an escape. But I'd never wanted to be eaten alive!

The first clicker hatchling scurried toward me like a black spider.

With a beat of wings, a bird swooped down. A falcon. *Don't falcons eat frogs?* Its sharp talons snatched up Hopalong-me, and then we were soaring up, up, away from the nest of creepy little clickers. The falcon darted and wove through a maze of branches, and my frog-heart almost exploded with terror.

Enough already. Just eat me quickly.

The bird landed on my outstretched human body, which was lying beside Lynxx. Standing on one claw, it gently placed frog-me on my human chest.

What was going on?

In agony from my broken frog leg, I looked up at the falcon. For a moment, its silver eyes stared at me. An instant later, the air shook with that same invisible current from last night. The falcon's eyes turned dark and it flew away.

Beside me, Lynxx's body trembled.

He sat up. "Jump, Kassia. Hurry!"

Rallying one last time, I pushed the pain aside and threw my mind from the frog.

Starbursts. Flashes. Electricity.

Familiarity.

I was back home. In *me*.

My own eyes fluttered open. Groaning, I sat up. As Hopalong toppled from my chest, I caught him. The poor frog trembled in my cupped hand, his leg broken and bleeding.

Sickened by his misery, I reached for a rock.

"Let me," Lynxx said softly.

I shook my head. "We were mind-blended. I feel responsible for him."

With a single blow, I put Hopalong out of his misery. Gently, I placed the small green body among the weeds. The frog wasn't in agony anymore. But I still was. Not physical. Emotional.

Sinking onto the grass, I hugged my knees, shaking uncontrollably.

Lynxx kneeled beside me. "Are you hurt? I tried to get to you as soon as I could."

It was a struggle to speak. "I owe you my life—again. Thank you!"

And then I buried my face in my hands. Huge heaving sobs burst from me. Tears ran down my face. My body shook as though I'd been tasered.

"Kassia." Lynxx wrapped his arms around me and tried to soothe me with soft murmurs. "You're safe. You're alive."

Through my sobs, I gasped out, "I nearly died. I was so scared. And then, when the click xan broke my leg ... I mean Hopalong's leg ... I was in agony. Terrified. Desperate to get out of there. Couldn't. That feeling of being trapped, waiting to be eaten alive."

"You were unlucky today. If that branch hadn't been broken by the windstorm last night—"

"But it was."

"—and if that click xan hadn't decided on frog for lunch—"

"It did."

"—your first mind-blend would've been a much better experience."

"It wasn't. It was a nightmare." Panic welled, threatening to overwhelm me once more. "Never again!"

"What do you mean?"

"I can never go through that again."

"The mind-blending? Next time we'll be more careful. We'll do it in a much safer place."

My stomach heaved at the thought of blending with another creature. Gagging, I turned away and threw up on the grass.

After wiping my mouth, I fixed my gaze on Lynxx. "I've made my decision, so please don't argue. *I will never mind-blend again.*"

52

THE CLICKER SPAWN CRAWL through the cracked shells and down the piled eggs. They scurry across the mud nest, onto frog-me. Tiny pincer claws pierce my green skin, setting me on fire with agony and—

"Kass."

—the falcon is eating Hopalong-me. I try to escape, but it rips off my head and blood spurts—

"Kass, wake up."

My eyes fluttered. The clicker spawn and the falcon vanished, replaced by the interior of a Templar crowded with people and equipment.

Beside me, Asher was stroking my shoulder. "I think you were having a nightmare."

For a moment, I blinked in bewilderment. Then I realized I was in T2, continuing our journey through Florida after T4's repair. On the opposite bench, Xavian dozed next to Willow, who was reading an old magazine. Booker and Pepper sat up front. Owlfred napped in her cage beside me.

Scuttling click xan spawn. Tiny creepy legs. Soulless eyes.

I trembled again.

Asher wrapped his arm around my shoulder. "You're shaking. Are you sick?" His worried voice held an unspoken question: was my leukemia flaring up again?

"I'm fine." *Must calm down. Must calm down.* "Just a nightmare. That's all."

Across from me, Lynxx's golden eyes softened with sympathy. Unlike the others, he knew the cause of my nightmare. Yesterday, when I had declared that I'd never mind-blend again, he'd accepted my decision with a gentle, "I understand, Kassia. I won't suggest it again."

And he hadn't. He had chatted about old movies while we'd packed T2 with our gear. He'd fussed over his pet owl as he secured her cage on a seat.

And he'd warned our driver about three large sinkholes in the road before anyone else saw them.

As the others congratulated him on his eagle eyes, I'd fought back the temptation to correct them. Lynxx didn't have eagle eyes. He had owl eyes. He'd probably seen the sinkholes during his scouting missions as Owlfred the previous evening.

"Boss, it'll be sunset in a couple of hours." Behind the wheel, Booker surveyed the thick vegetation that bracketed our road.

"I know," Asher replied. "If we can't find somewhere to camp, we'll have to sleep in the Templars."

A chorus of groans met this unwelcome—and uncomfortable—news.

"Give it a few more minutes," Lynxx suggested. I waited, guessing he'd already investigated this area last night as Owlfred. Sure enough, after a couple of minutes he pointed to a massive tree ahead. "We can overnight there."

Asher stared through the window. "Is it safe, Lynxx?"

"I've researched those terras before. I've never found any dangerous creatures living in their branches."

Our convoy left the highway and bounced down a rough track.

A short way off, a colossus-tree towered fifty stories high. Its lowest branches were far wider than the narrow ones at the top, giving it a leafy pyramid shape. Thick leaves rioted in a kaleidoscope of blue, gold, orange, and red—very different from the green colossus-trees back in New York. It also didn't have the thicket of skinny roots that had supported the one in Feral Tower; obviously this one didn't need them.

Parking next to the massive, wide-as-a-house trunk, we gingerly exited our vehicles. The lowest branches hung several feet above our heads, giving us space to move around beneath them.

"Whoa!" Xavian pressed his wrinkled hands against the trunk and gazed up at the soaring branches. "They sure grow 'em big down here in Florida."

Asher scanned the bare, shadow-darkened ground. "I suppose nothing can grow in the shade of this terra."

"You're half right," Lynxx said. "But the shade isn't the only reason nothing grows." He pointed to the bare land that extended far beyond the wide branches. "The roots of this colossus-tree drain every bit of nutrient from the soil. If Owlfred were to fly over this area, she'd see an enormous patch of land bigger than a football field, with this giant tree right in the middle."

"Huh," I scoffed.

"Excuse me?"

"I'm sure your aerial description is spot-on, Lynxx." Thanks to his pet owl. "But I thought terras could grow on things like rocks, sand, ice, carpet, even on metal. Not a lot of nutrients in those things."

The corners of his lips twitched. "You're correct. However, the colossus-tree hates competition. Its roots release a chemical that poisons the soil for most other plants, whether Earth or terra."

"Most?"

"Nothing's one hundred percent effective. Some plants might be resistant to the colossus's poison. Just as some humans are resistant to the Red Fever."

Trident Team and some soldiers scoured the area for dangerous terras and xans. The rest of us broke into teams for our assigned tasks, including putting up the tents, preparing dinner, digging a latrine, and so forth.

Asher, Xavian, Willow, and I had water duty. Large plastic bottles strapped to our backs, we headed to a small stream beyond the colossus-tree.

Willow pointed to the low green terras that fringed the edge of the stream. "Lynxx was right about some plants being resistant to the colossus's poison. Is he your resident genius or something?"

"He's certainly something," I wryly replied.

Asher stared at the green terras. "Whippers." Two-foot-long leaves fanned out from central roots. "At least these are small. We need to clear a patch along the bank so we can get to the water."

We rolled down our sleeves and pulled on leather gloves.

"Why don't you guys hang back?" Asher suggested to Xavian and Willow. "Kass and I can handle the whippers."

"We ain't sitting this one out, lad," Xavian said. Beside him, Willow nodded. "Panny—I mean Willow—and I have handled these vicious whipper-things before."

"Only ours were much bigger," she added.

"Are you sure you want to help?" I asked him.

"Sure as a turkey hiding from hunters at Thanksgiving."

Willow crinkled her perfect nose. "How do the turkeys know the hunters want to shoot them? Aren't they supposed to be dumb birds?"

Suppressing a smile, Asher raised his hand. "Focus, guys. Even small whippers can hurt a lot."

He was right. As we ripped the whippers from the bank, they attacked us with their long skinny leaves. Our gloves and sleeves gave some protection, but the pain was still sharp and stinging. After the first few lashings, my forearms felt as if they were on fire. Instinctively, I began to remote-push the leaves away.

"Cripes, Kass." Asher raised his eyebrows. "What's your secret?"

"Secret?"

"Those last few whippers didn't attack you."

Oops! How could I've been so stupid?

I yanked some whippers from the dirt, letting them flog my arms. With tears of pain in my eyes, I turned to Asher. "Sorry, what did you say?"

"Er, nothing."

After ten painful minutes, we'd cleared a long section of the bank and started filling our water bottles. A few yards away, the pile of uprooted whippers feebly waved their leaves in the air.

At a soft wheeze, I looked over.

Xavian was breathing heavily.

"Are you okay?" I asked, wiping my sweaty face.

"Just a little heartburn, lass." He popped a couple of white pills under his tongue.

Willow hurried across. "Are you feeling ill again, Xavian? You need to rest for a bit. Let's go. I've heard that T3 has the softest seats." Wrapping an arm around his waist, she gently led him off.

As soon as they were out of earshot, Asher turned to me. "Back in the Templar, you were shaking. Was your leukemia flaring up again?"

"No. Just a bad dream." When he still looked uncertain, I assured him, "The Lazarus dose works for a week. Lynxx has made six more doses. That's enough to get me through six weeks without being sick. So you can stop worrying."

His shoulders sagged in relief. "Okay."

"Good." Arms stinging, face slick with sweat, I continued helping Asher fill the water bottles.

We were almost finished when the hairs at the back of my neck prickled. I froze.

Beside me, Asher tilted his head a little, listening.

A twig snapped behind us.
Slowly we turned.
And stared.

53

THEY STOOD ON THE dirt a short distance away.

Three xans.

About two feet tall, they stood upright on two legs like penguins. Black porcupine-like quills covered their bodies, except for their white chests. Two sets of black eyes blinked on either side of their large heads. Penguin-like beaks protruded forward several inches, their tips curved.

"Penguin xans," I murmured.

Asher whispered, "Dangerous?" His hand inched toward the gun at his belt.

"They're predators, according to our 'resident genius,' Lynxx. Don't make any sudden moves."

"I'm a good shot. I can get them all."

"What about the others?"

"What others?"

My gaze flicked to the edge of the nearby forest. "Them."

A dozen penguin xans stood in the shadows, watching.

"Sneaky," he muttered.

The three closest xans studied us with their double sets of eyes. One scratched the dirt with a long curved talon, as though itching to drag its claws down our abdomens so it could feed on our intestines.

My eyes narrowed. In the past, I'd remote-pushed six spiky-ball xans at once. Surely I could handle these three xans.

If I swept my remote-push from side to side, like a flashlight's beam, it should work.

Drawing a deep breath, I focused. Hard. Harder. Within me, a tingly force exploded out as I remote-pushed.

Abruptly, the three xans jumped back. Black quills unfurling into feathers, they flew off, followed by the rest of the flock.

Stunned, we watched them disappear.

"They can fly," I gasped.

"Bird xans," Asher groaned. "Great. Just great. How did you recognize them?"

"Lynxx has been building a reference collection of photos and drawings of various xans. He gets info from his sources in Manhattan, plus he's in radio contact with other groups around the world."

"Why didn't he warn us about these xans?"

I tried to remember what Lynxx had told me about them. "There have been reports of penguin xans in Russia and Australia, but none in the States."

"They're here now, so we'd better let everyone know." Puzzled, he said, "I wonder what scared them away a few minutes ago?"

I shrugged, pretending ignorance. "No idea."

"Let's get out of here before they come back." Hurriedly, he capped the final plastic water container.

Loaded with the bottles, we began walking back to the campsite.

In the distance, Willow and Pepper were setting up the tents.

"Willow really cares about Xavian, doesn't she?" I asked.

"Deeply. She's always been a kind and caring person. Even after everything she's been through, she hasn't changed."

"Has she told you how she survived this long? She doesn't look very strong."

"Don't underestimate her, Kass. When Willow sets out to do something, she can be incredibly determined."

His words stirred a wisp of unease in me. At the moment, Willow accepted that Asher and I were together. But what if she changed her mind about her former boyfriend?

A fly buzzed around my face. Annoyed, I brushed the disgusting thing away. Thank goodness I hadn't eaten any bugs when I was mind-blended with—

Memories flooded back again, sharp as thorns.

Trapped in poor doomed Hopalong. Waiting to be eaten. The agony of my broken frog leg. The horror of the click xans—

"Are you okay, Kass?"

"Huh?" I blinked. "Sorry." Anxious to think about something else, I asked, "What happened to Willow after the Mist?"

Quickly he summarized her story.

When the planes and trains had stopped running after the Night of the Red Mist, Willow had been stuck in Los Angeles. With people dying all around her, she'd managed to get a lift with three strangers, who'd all died within days. Her next traveling companions had headed south and she'd ended up in Mexico.

Later, Xavian had found Willow in Tijuana—alone, starving, sick, frightened. Weak and dying, she'd begged him to take her to New York. "I know my boyfriend, Ash, is probably dead by now," she had told him. "But if there's the slightest chance he's alive and waiting for me, I have to try to get to him."

The hybrid, Xavian, had nursed her back to health. When she was better, he and Willow had made their way from Mexico to the southern states.

"What was Xavian doing in Mexico at the time of the Mist?" I asked Asher.

"He was on a bus tour."

After months, the pair had just reached the East Coast when Xavian had begun feeling ill. Shortly afterward, they'd been snatched up by the onion terra. Trapped inside, with Xavian too weak to free them, they'd resigned themselves to death.

Asher's face softened. "That's when you came along and saved them."

"It was a team effort."

"I think Xavian's sicker than he lets on. He could have a heart condition."

"Is there anything Soo-Yun can do to help him?"

"Nothing. She doesn't have the training, and we don't have the meds to treat him, especially since ..." His words fizzled out.

Aghast, I stared at him. "Are you saying he's not worth treating because he's a hybrid? He saved Willow's life. She loves him like a father."

"Her own father died when she was a baby, so I understand her attachment to Xavian as a father figure. And I feel guilty not wanting to use any of our meds on him. But we don't have enough meds to treat our own people or any children they might have. How can I justify using up our limited supply to keep an old hybrid alive? They're the enemy, remember?"

"Xavian's sympathetic to the Sphere, the good hybrids."

"So he says."

"Don't you believe him?"

"I'm not sure. Hybrids can lie as easily as people."

"You're being racist, Asher." I paused, remembering how hostile I'd been to Lynxx when I'd first discovered he was a hybrid. My tone softened. "I'm sorry. You didn't deserve that. In fact, I used to think every hybrid was evil too."

"Now you don't?"

"No. I believe Xavian's a good, decent man. And if he can be good, then other hybrids can be good too." *Like Lynxx.* "Up on the skyweb, Bone told us that some hybrids have embraced their human side. And according to Xavian, after the arrival of the Mist these humanized hybrids created a group called the Sphere, whose goal is to defeat the Chi'az."

"You're right, Kass." He sighed. "Humanity has far too many new enemies. We could use a potential ally."

"Like the Sphere hybrids?"
"Maybe."

54

ASHER AND I HURRIED back to the campsite. The tents had been erected, and Harlem and Soo-Yun were cooking steaks on a massive grill.

We joined Lynxx beneath the colossus-tree. When we told him about the penguin xans, he pulled out a portfolio.

"I don't have much information on them," he said, showing us a drawing that matched the creatures, "but I've heard reports of them attacking humans."

"I'll have a chat with Xavian," Asher said. "Maybe he knows a bit more about these penguin xans." He hurried toward the parked Templars.

Lynxx continued taking samples from the colossus-tree, bagging leaves and bottling samples of the sticky droplets that trickled from the higher branches. I followed him around to the rear of the tree, where no one was around.

"Are you still feeling okay?" I asked. "That click xan poison nearly killed Owlfred and you."

"We're both fine. Owlfred is taking a well-deserved break."

I breathed a sigh of relief, surprised at how much I wanted Lynxx in my life. Yesterday, he had stunned me with his revelations about mind-blending with Mousy and WindLord. And months ago, he had gone to extraordinary lengths to protect Olivia and me. Now it was my turn to try to help him. Maybe he didn't need my physical protection—but he needed the community and safety of the Weston Battalion.

Plus I liked having him around.

He watched a squirrel dart up the trunk of the massive tree. "This colossus is a lot bigger than the one we saw inside Feral Tower in Manhattan."

I shivered at the memory of the terrible Feral Tower.

Hyenas.

Two hyenas battling in Feral Tower: Ripped Ear and Black Muzzle.

As I ran my hand across the smooth colossus trunk, another memory surged forth.

Lynxx lying unconscious as the two hyenas battled to the death.

I gasped, "You were blended with Black Muzzle!"

"Who?"

I reminded him of the hyenas' ferocious fight in Feral Tower, then said, "You were blended with Black Muzzle. I'm certain of it. It had silver eyes. So did Ripped Ear, the other hyena. Was it mind-blended with a hybrid too?"

He nodded. "It was my ex-guardian, Frost. He'd been suspicious ever since he saw us together in that passage in Grand Central. He had blended with that hyena—the one you called Ripped Ear—in order to kill you. He gave me no choice. I had to kill him first."

"So that's how your guardian died?"

"Yes. When Frost and I were fighting as hyenas, our battle frightened away every other creature nearby. When Frost's hyena host was dying, there were no animals or birds around for him to mind-hop into. So he and his hyena host both died."

"Good."

"After my guardian died, I was free for the first time in my life! I could openly see you, talk to you, be around you."

"Thank you for saving my life back then ... again."

Gently, he said, "Every time I save your life, Kassia, I'm saving myself as well. If I hadn't fallen in love with you, I would've remained a cold, soulless hybrid."

"Lynxx, I—" At the sound of approaching laughter, I stopped.

Asher and Willow were headed toward us, talking and laughing with an easy familiarity, like long-lost friends—or long-lost lovers.

They crossed to us.

Asher wrapped an arm around my waist and gave Lynxx a friendly nod. "Food's ready, guys."

Lynxx and I exchanged glances. So many things remained unsaid between us, but they'd have to wait.

We joined the others at the plastic picnic tables beneath the colossus branches. As twilight faded into night, small portable floodlights lit the area. People relaxed a little, and even Xavian joined the group, looking better after a nap in T3.

We had almost finished eating when the branches overhead suddenly rustled. A moment later, dozens of small shapes darted from the tree in a frantic blur of wings.

Bats.

We ducked for cover. The bats swept over us, strangely silent, then disappeared into the forest.

Indignant, Pepper turned to Lynxx. "I thought you said no creatures lived in colossus-trees."

"I said no *dangerous* creatures lived in these trees," Lynxx replied calmly. "Bats aren't dangerous."

"Shh." I grabbed a portable floodlight. "Those bats were in a panic, but they didn't squeak."

Asher stiffened in sudden understanding. "Just like the bats at the ruined church the other week, the one with the hole in its roof."

Harlem murmured into his radio, contacting the guards patrolling the perimeter. None reported anything unusual.

I moved to the edge of our campsite and stood below the furthest tips of the branches. Asher and Lynxx joined me as I aimed a floodlight up into the night sky. The bright beam revealed a weird sight. Far above, patches of the air were shimmering. No, not shimmering. Multiple translucent objects were traveling overhead.

Lynxx murmured, "We saw those things back at the ruined church, remember?"

"What did you call them?" Asher whispered. "Air terras?"

Lynxx nodded. "Yes. They're a floating terra plant, like jellyfish terras and tumbleweeds."

Shivering, I lowered my light. "From the way the bats fled, I'm guessing they're dangerous." As we headed back to the picnic tables, I said, "Why didn't those air terras attack us?"

Ever logical, Lynxx suggested, "Maybe they weren't hungry. Or perhaps they only hunt during the day. The bats wouldn't know this, so they simply flee whenever the air terras are around."

Asher and Sergeant Thorne debated moving our campsite to another location. Eventually they decided that, since no one wanted to travel at night, we would remain beneath the colossus-tree, post some extra guards—and tightly zip up our tents.

After a restless sleep, I awoke at dawn and spent a few minutes tossing and turning in my two-person tent. Worried about waking Pepper, I went outside.

I wasn't the only one up this early.

At the stream, Lynxx was taking samples from the pile of uprooted whippers. I guessed he was trying to figure out how long the terras could survive after being ripped from the dirt.

Guards still patrolled the far perimeter, which was edged by a dark forest. Above the treetops, the red blush of a fading sunrise smudged the sky, and the early-morning air held a peaceful hush. I knew the scene was deceptive, like pretty paper wrapping an ugly world of terras and xans—plus the threat of a new virus called the Threads.

At a flutter of wings, I looked around.

A large black crow flew across to T3, a small metal tube dangling from a cord around its feathered neck. The bird gave a soft squawk. The Templar's door opened. A wrinkled and age-spotted hand reached out, removed the metal tube, and quietly closed the door again.

Concealed by shadows, I watched the crow fly away.

It had silver eyes.

The bird was being mind-controlled by another hybrid.

Frowning, I wondered why Xavian was receiving a secretive visitor at dawn.

And what was in the metal tube?

55

LYNXX WAS STILL SQUATTING beside the stream, dropping bits of terras into specimen jars. A pile of uprooted whippers lay nearby, twitching as their leaves turned brown.

At my hurried approach, he stood. "What's wrong?" When I told him about the crow with its metal tube, he frowned. "Are you sure it was Xavian who opened the door of T3?"

"Positive. He's the only one here who has a wrinkled hand with age spots."

"True." He paused. "And Xavian's openly admitted to being sympathetic to the Sphere."

"What if he's lying? What if he's an Outrider? The metal tube might contain their new virus."

"It's possible."

"We need to tell Asher."

"Agreed." He slung his backpack over a shoulder. "Let's go."

We headed for T2, parked beside the campsite. Asher often worked in the vehicle until late at night, sometimes sleeping in it. At the murmur of voices from inside, my heart hammered. Who was with him? Willow? Had she been in there all night?

Lynxx rapped on the window and opened the door. "Asher, we need to—"

Inside, Xavian clutched a piece of paper in his wrinkled hand.

Asher turned, distracted. "Morning, Lynxx, Kass. Can you send Harl and Sergeant Thorne in here? And close the door. Thanks."

Bewildered, we passed on his messages to Harlem and the sergeant.

Then we waited.

By the time they all emerged from the Templar, breakfast was ready. Joining me at a table, Asher murmured, "I need to make an announcement after we eat." He was tense, on edge, his blue eyes worried.

Above his bowl of porridge, Lynxx lifted an inquiring brow at me. I shrugged.

The air felt charged, as if bracing for something.

When breakfast was over, Asher moved to the front of the tables. "Heads up, guys." As the conversation died down, he gestured to Xavian.

The old man gave Willow's shoulder a reassuring squeeze and slowly walked forward, moving with the effort of someone weak or sick.

Lynxx murmured to me, "Maybe that metal tube contained pills or medicine."

Asher addressed the group. "As you all know, we have two newcomers with us. Willow Grace is human. And, as a few of you already know, Xavian is a hybrid—a *good* hybrid."

Angry shouts erupted from the audience.

"The only good hybrid is a dead hybrid!"

"They're killers."

"Murderers!"

Asher raised his voice. "Xavian is one of the humanized hybrids we've heard rumors about. Some of these 'good' hybrids call themselves the Sphere."

"Humanized hybrids are still hybrids," Greta snapped, joining in the discussion for once. Outside of her work with Trident

Team, the nineteen-year-old usually kept to herself, lost in her own glum thoughts. "All hybrids are our enemies."

"I used to agree." Asher paused. "But life isn't black and white. Sometimes we have to accept the gray."

"Why should we accept a murdering hybrid?" Sergeant Thorne growled. "They killed my buddies."

"Many hybrids identify more with humanity than with the Chi'az," said Asher. "The Sphere had nothing to do with the Red Fever. That disease was spread by the Outriders. We believe the Sphere hybrids are actively working *against* the Outriders."

Thorne stood his ground. "This old hybrid should be hanged from the nearest branch. It's time for some payback."

Xavian stepped forward, his lined face creased in sympathy. "I understand your anger, son."

"I'm not talking to you, hybrid."

"Then just listen, son." The old man wiped his sweating forehead with a shaking hand.

Lynxx and I exchanged glances. Xavian seemed sick. Barely able to stand.

Willow rushed forward and led him to a cleared picnic table. "Here, sit on top of this. Everyone can still see you. And if they can't, they can just listen harder."

"You're a good lass, Panny." Xavian perched on the edge of the table and addressed the group. "Nigh on seventy years ago, I was born to serve the Chi'az. But when I was knee-high to a gopher, I began to identify with humanity. Since then, I ain't wavered a bit." He uncapped a small container and swallowed a couple of pills.

"You need to rest," Willow said, worried.

"Soon, lass." He drew in another labored breath and continued, "I met me Maryanne when I was twenty-three. She was one hundred percent human, topped with a hefty dose of angel, I reckon. We got hitched and two years later our son, Charlie, was born."

I stifled a gasp of surprise. Earlier, when Xavian had mentioned his family, I had assumed that he'd married another hybrid. But he'd married a human. And this hybrid and human had a child together.

Xavian's voice caught on an edge of grief. "Our boy, Charlie, was seventeen when he and his mama were shot by a stinkin' Outrider, right in front of me. The Outriders were punishing me for choosing humanity over the Chi'az."

Greta raised her voice. "If you're the good guys, why didn't any of you warn us about the Chi'az and the Mist?"

"We didn't know what was gonna happen. Them Sphere and Outriders are throat-rippin' enemies. Every so often, some Outriders would kill the families of Sphere hybrids as punishment for becoming humanized. The Outriders didn't trust Sphere hybrids, not a whisker, and usually stayed away from us. We weren't weeping, though. We hated them guys more than a hillbilly hates opera." Xavian's thin body sagged a little and sweat trickled down his whiskered cheeks.

Willow gently took his arm. "You need a break."

"Not yet, lass," he said, patting her hand. His intense gaze swept the group as he continued, "Only a few high-up Outriders knew about the Chi'az." His words tumbled out, full of anguish. "When the Mist arrived, the Sphere—and me!—was as flabbergasted as y'all, and as heartbroken."

Asher told the group, "The Sphere hybrids watched their human husbands, wives, and children die from the Red Fever, just like us."

A couple of people murmured sympathetically. Most glared at Xavian. Hate and hostility flowed toward the old hybrid like a foul black stream.

I hid a quick shudder. No wonder Lynxx was reluctant to reveal his secret to this group. If they discovered that a hybrid had been living among them for months, someone could try to hurt him—or even kill him.

Sergeant Thorne snapped, "We heard that the Sphere is working on a way to stop this new virus. Is that true?"

"Yes, son, it's true." A coughing fit wracked Xavian, and Willow hastily gave him a cup of water.

We waited. A sense of expectancy shimmered amid the hostility, and the leaves of the towering colossus-tree whispered anxiously in a warm breeze.

Xavian handed the empty cup back to Willow. "What was I saying?"

"The Sphere," said Harlem tightly. "Stopping this new virus."

"Oh. Right. Well, folks, I received a note from the Sphere this morning."

I sensed hope beginning to blossom in people, including me.

"They believe," Xavian said, "that the Outriders are about to trial their new doomsday virus."

56

SHOCK AND HORROR EXPLODED through the group.

Asher called for silence. When the noise simmered down, he said, "Go on, Xavian."

The old man spoke again, each word a drop of acid. "They call it the Threads virus."

"We've heard of it," Asher said.

"Good. Well, since the Mist, I've been in contact with the Sphere by radio and other means—"

Yeah, like being visited by a crow mind-blended with a hybrid, I thought.

"—so me information is as fresh as a day-old hatchling. The Sphere has moles in various groups of Outriders. One mole claims the Threads will be trialed over the next few days in different spots around the world." At an outburst of questions, Xavian said, "I'm right sorry, folks, but that's all the info I got."

"Listen, guys," Asher said, raising his voice so everyone could hear. "This news about the Threads is bad. Real bad. But you heard Xavian. The Outriders are going to trial it in several locations around the world. The odds of us being infected are incredibly small. And some of us are working on making those odds even smaller." He gave a meaningful glance at the group of soldiers.

Sergeant Thorne scowled. "Yep."

"That's all I can tell you right now." Asher checked his watch. "I've already passed this info on to Commander Powell. Now we need to load the Templars and get going."

People scowled at Xavian as they packed up and took their seats in the vehicles.

Above the revving motors, gunshots pierced the distant silence. Rapid shots. Frantic.

Asher lowered his window. "Someone's in trouble." He listened to the sound of more gunfire, then shouted directions to Booker, who was driving.

Led by T2, the convoy raced down a dirt road, took a sharp turn, and followed a potholed road for a couple of miles. Thick shrubs and bushes huddled along the berm as empty houses gave way to a dark forest.

The gunshots grew louder, closer.

By the time we reached the end of the road, the shooting had stopped. Our vehicles screeched to a halt at a rusty wire gate flanked by two metal poles.

Impaled on the left pole was the skinned, bloodied body of a krol, a gunshot wound in its barrel chest. Beneath it, a dark puddle stained the dirt.

On the other side of the gate, also impaled on a pole, was the body of a naked man. Intestines dangled from his ripped abdomen, and his hands had been hacked off, leaving stumps that dripped blood.

Beyond the gate, a dirt track led to a cabin in a clearing.

Sergeant Thorne pointed to three of his men. "You're with me. Everyone else stay here." Weapons drawn, the trio headed for the building.

We waited at the gate, our attention split between the two impaled bodies and the nearby thick woods. Was anything lurking in those shadows?

Asher studied the skinned krol and the naked man. "Human versus krol. No winners here. I wonder what happened?"

"Maybe the man killed the krol," Harlem suggested, "skinned it, and stuck it on the pole as a warning to other krols. A *Keep Out* sign."

Lynxx nodded. "I've had reports of survivors doing exactly that. It fits in with the skinned krols we saw in Nilster, North Carolina."

I shuddered at the memory of those dead krols displayed throughout that town like grotesque scarecrows. Gesturing to the impaled man, I said, "Maybe the krols killed him in retaliation."

"Yo, here's another of those butt-ugly things." Fifty yards away, Xavian pointed to something behind a large boulder. "Only this one ain't been skinned."

Everyone began hurrying over to him.

"What does it look like?" Asher called out.

"Ugly as a hellhound."

57

Spot-on.

An unskinned krol sprawled on the dirt, its chest riddled with bullet wounds.

Willow paled and clutched Asher's arm.

People turned away or swore in disgust.

The intact krol vaguely resembled a four-foot bat without wings. Large bat-like ears stood upright on its head, as though used for locating prey. Its pug nose was deeply recessed in a face that oozed menace, a threat reinforced by double rows of jagged teeth. A pair of large black eyes glared at us sightlessly, hostile even in death. Mottled black skin covered its hairless, barrel-chested body. Two overlong arms ended in clawed fingers, and its long thin legs had toes tipped with sharp claws.

When Thorne and his men returned—"No sign of anyone else"—we resumed our journey, relieved to be leaving the mutilated man and the two dead krols behind.

At 2 p.m., Asher directed the vehicles into a truck stop. To our surprise, we were told to set up camp. Minutes later, Sergeant Thorne and most of the soldiers left, leaving only a couple of men to guard our camp. We guessed their target. Thorne's squad was using the location provided by Xavian to go after the Outrider, Bone.

Once the campsite was ready, we had the rest of the afternoon off. Asher and Harlem pored over maps and various routes to our destination near Miami. Some people went hunting. Xavian wandered around the campsite, using a branch as a cane. Willow, Pepper, and Soo-Yun chatted about movies.

In an isolated spot in the forest, Lynxx and I continued my training—minus the mind-blending. Midway through remote-pushing a squirrel, my skin started tingling, as though a chill wind were wafting over me. *Strange.* Especially since the afternoon was windless.

Something landed with a flap of wings in a nearby tree. A foul odor drenched the air.

"What a stink!" I cried.

A few feet away, a bizarre creature perched on a branch, watching us. The size of a rooster, it had a brown feathered body and black-and-white streaks on its long neck. Spiked orange feathers topped its small head, and its stink reminded me of skunk spray blended with cow dung.

"Bird xan," I said, disgusted.

"Nope. That's one of ours," Lynxx told me.

"Seriously?"

"It's from South America. A hoatzin, *Opisthocomus hoazin.* Commonly called a stinkbird."

"Well named." My nose crinkled at its foul odor. As the hoatzin tilted its head, its eyes glinted in a stray beam of sunlight. "Silver eyes." My voice dropped to a whisper. "Is that bird mind-blended with a hybrid?"

"Yes. I sensed its presence before I saw it," he murmured.

"I think I did too."

"You did?"

"It was a cold, tingling sensation."

"Your powers are growing."

"Thanks." I felt strangely pleased at the compliment. "Who's controlling the stinky bird? And why's it here?"

"I don't know."

The hoatzin flapped to the ground and hopped over to Lynxx. Its beak grasped the bottom of his black jeans.

I remained still, barely breathing.

The stinky bird tugged at Lynxx's pants. Another tug. A third.

I whispered, "I think it wants you to go with it."

The hoatzin flew awkwardly to another shrub. Perching on a branch, it gazed at us with weary silver eyes.

Frowning, I said, "It looks tired or maybe sick—" I gasped in realization. "Are you Xavian?" It nodded its spiky-feathered head. "Do you want us to follow you?" Another nod. "Okay, lead the way."

With the bird flitting ahead, Lynxx and I hurried through the forest to a pond. Xavian sat slumped against a boulder, his eyes closed. The hoatzin landed beside the man, then flew off, its wingbeats strong again.

Xavian opened his eyes. Grunting, he struggled to his feet with our help. "Holy corgis in the snow, that was a blast from the past. I ain't mind-blended for yonks." He grinned with satisfaction. "And it's good to know that I may be old but I ain't lost all me marbles yet. When Owlfred flew inside the onion terra, I thought I sensed another hybrid mind-blended with the owl. Plus I saw its silver eyes." He studied Lynxx. "It was you, wasn't it, lad?"

"Yes."

"Does anyone else know you're a hybrid, besides Kass here?"

"No," Lynxx replied. "And I prefer to keep it that way. You saw what happened earlier, and how hostile some people became when they heard you were a hybrid—a good hybrid."

The lines on Xavian's forehead deepened. "Yeppo. Half the folks in your group wanted to string me up; the others would've happily watched. Don't worry, lad. Your secret's safe with me. I ain't even told Panny me suspicions."

"Good," Lynxx said. "Did you want something, Xavian?"

"I needed to talk to you away from the others."

"What about?"

"Panny ... er, Willow." The man sank onto the boulder. "She knows I'm sick, but she ain't got no idea how bad."

"Don't hybrids have quick healing powers?" I asked, glancing at the smooth palm of my right hand, scarless after using some terra powder.

"Hybrids can heal fast," Xavian agreed, "but we also age just like regular humans. And we can get terminal cancer, lass."

"Oh. I'm so sorry."

"How can we help you?" Lynxx asked him.

"No one can cure me cancer, lad. I'm too sickly and the drugs are nigh on impossible to find these days. But I've still got a few weeks to live, Lord willing and the creeks don't rise. Till then, you and me can scratch each other's back."

"How?"

From his pocket, Xavian withdrew the metal tube I'd seen the crow carrying earlier. "My feathered visitor this morning brought two things. I already told y'all about the note containing info on the Threads. But I ain't told no one about this metal tube."

"What's in it?" Lynxx asked.

"Life."

58

"Excuse me?" I asked Xavian.

"A month and a bit ago, a Sphere mole in an Outrider group smuggled out a vaccine sample. Some of them Outrider scum had just finished working on it, knowing they'll need protection from their own Threads. The Sphere reverse-engineered the sample."

Awed, I stared at the metal tube. "This is a vaccine to protect people?"

"I'm sorry, lass." Xavian's eyes held a deep sadness. "For humans, it's as useless as rubber lips on a woodpecker. It only protects hybrids."

"Oh." I wasn't afraid for myself; I was used to the idea of dying. But the thought of Asher and the others dying left me almost breathless with fear.

"They only gave me one dose." Xavian turned to Lynxx. "It's yours, lad. You need to drink it all up for it to work."

"Aren't you going to drink it?" he asked.

"No point. Thanks to me cancer, me use-by date ain't that far off. A few weeks, maybe. Then who'll take care of me Panny? She's both as strong as hardwood and as fragile as butterfly wings."

"You should give the vaccine to Panny ... I mean, Willow."

"Lad, with all me heart and soul, I wish I could. But seeing as she don't have a single drop of hybrid blood in her, it'd be useless." A coughing fit wracked him, and a handkerchief pressed to his mouth came away spattered in blood. He waved off Lynxx's offer of water. "I'm fine, lad. I just need you to make sure Panny gets to the Weston Garrison. Once she's there, she should be safe, especially if the Sphere stops the Threads and the Outriders."

"Is that possible?" Lynxx asked.

"They're working on something, real hard-like."

"Why are they bothering?" I asked, confused. "The Sphere hybrids have a vaccine against this new Threads. Only humans will die."

Xavian shook his head. "The Sphere will never be safe until every Outrider hybrid is stone-cold dead, plus all of them stinkin' xans and terras. It's the only way to stop the Chi'az." He fixed his watery stare on Lynxx. "Is it a deal?"

Lynxx hesitated, then took the metal tube. "Yes."

A girl's voice sounded in the forest. "Xavian, where are you?"

"Over here, lass. Next to the pond." The old man's gaze swept Lynxx and me as he whispered, "Lips tight as a cranky clam about me cancer, right?" We nodded.

A minute later, Willow and Asher emerged from a grove of trees and hurried across to us.

"Xavian," she cried. "Someone at the camp said they'd seen you heading into the forest. Why did you go off by yourself?"

He patted her hand affectionately. "I'm old enough to take a walk by meself, lass."

"Not when you've been feeling unwell," she scolded.

Asher looked at Lynxx and me. "What were you two doing out here?" His eyes were sharp with curiosity.

"Bird-watching," Lynxx told him. "We were following a stinkbird—very rare in these areas—and it flew right to this pond."

I hid a smile at his neat way of telling Asher the truth. Partly.

"Kass," said Willow, "I've been meaning to ask for a favor."

"What is it?" My mind whirled with crazy possibilities. *Break up with Asher. Give me back my boyfriend. Transfer out of his team.*

"Can you train me to be a resistance fighter? When we get back to New York, I'm hoping your commander will let me join Liberty Team."

Asher shook his head. "Liberty Team is too dangerous, Willow. You'd be better off helping in the gardens at Weston Tower. Or in the kitchen; Chef Einstein needs another assistant."

"I want to do more than that," she replied firmly. "I want to contribute. Pull my weight. Be useful, even if it's dangerous work."

Despite myself, I felt a grudging respect for Willow. Most people who joined our cell were eager to remain in the safety of Weston Tower and happily accepted non-combative jobs there.

Xavian picked up his makeshift cane. "We can chew the fat on this topic later, Panny, after I take a catnap. I'm mighty tired."

"Of course." She linked her arm through his. "We'll go now."

"Coming?" Asher asked Lynxx and me.

"Darn," I said, feigning annoyance. "I left my backpack under a tree. I'll go get it and meet you guys back at camp."

"You can't wander around alone, Kass," said Asher. "There could be krols in the area."

"I'll be fine."

Asher surveyed our group of five, taking stock. Like me, he carried a sword and gun. None of the others did.

As I expected, he told Lynxx to go with me. Asher's choice seemed logical. Split up the resistance fighters—himself and me—so both smaller groups were protected. Or was he subconsciously choosing Willow over me?

As the others disappeared into the forest, Lynxx quietly said, "You didn't bring a backpack."

"Asher doesn't know that. Where's the vaccine?"

He pulled the metal tube from his pocket and unscrewed the cap. A vial of yellow liquid slid onto his palm. "It's not a lot, Kassia."

"As long as it's enough to protect you."

"You mean protects *us*." He passed me the vial. "You drink half first."

"What are you talking about? It won't work on me. I'm not a hybrid."

"You have hybrid blood in you, enough to give you some hybrid powers."

The vial in my hand felt hot and cold, which was physically impossible. Then I realized *I* was the one feeling hot and cold—emotionally. Part of me wanted to be totally human. Another part knew that Lynxx's hybrid blood in my veins had kept me alive. It had also given me mental powers that were both frightening and exciting. "Xavian gave it to you—"

"And I'm sharing it with you."

"—on the understanding that you'd protect Willow."

"We'll *both* protect her."

"Or we'll both die from the Threads," I pointed out. "You heard Xavian. You have to drink the whole vial to be protected."

Lynxx's tone firmed. "Either we share this vial or we hand it back to Xavian."

I hesitated. "Okay." Uncapping the vial, I reluctantly drank half of the bitter liquid. He drank the rest.

In silence, we headed back to camp. With each footstep, hope and guilt warred within me.

Had Lynxx just saved my life—again? Or had I condemned him to death?

59

Disappointment sliced through our group, sharp as a scalpel.

Sergeant Thorne's mission had failed.

The soldiers exited their Templar the next morning, defeat in their slumped shoulders.

Soon everyone knew the story.

Thorne and his men had crept up to the Outriders' reported location, but the camp had been deserted. No tents. No vehicles. No signs of anyone around. The campfires' wisps of smoke and warm ashes showed they'd missed Bone and the Brethren by minutes.

The soldiers had scoured the area for hours before accepting defeat. Back in our camp, they sat apart, glumly cleaning their weapons.

"They don't look happy," Pepper noted.

Booker closed his fantasy novel with a loud snap. "The Outriders were lucky to have left before our soldiers arrived."

"Maybe they were lucky." Lynxx's gaze met mine. "Or maybe they suspected we were in the area." He glanced at a distant pine.

A brown falcon watched us from a branch. I couldn't tell if its eyes were silver, and when Lynxx casually wandered toward it, the bird flew off.

When he returned, I murmured, "Was it mind-blended with a hybrid?"

"Possibly. Too far away to tell for sure."

The convoy resumed its journey to Miami. We peered through the windows, watching for movement alongside the road: A glimpse of gray clothing among the green trees. A flash of sunlight on guns. A clandestine shift of branches as Outriders prepared to attack us.

Nothing.

We knew Bone could be anywhere, but as the hours passed without incident, people began to relax. Behind the wheel, Booker used headphones to listen to a mystery novel on a disk. In the front passenger seat, Asher studied various maps of the area.

I gazed out of a side window at the countryside. Beside me, Rusty leaned into the back section of the Templar, which was cluttered with our packs and Owlfred's cage. For the last half hour, he'd been trying to teach the bird to speak.

"She's an owl, Rusty," Lynxx finally reminded him, "not a parrot. Let poor Owlfred go back to sleep."

Disappointed, the freckle-faced boy replaced the black cloth over the birdcage.

On the opposite bench, Willow held Xavian's arm while he napped. Every so often she'd anxiously study the old man, as if afraid he might slip away in his sleep. Worry shadowed her beautiful face.

Midafternoon, our vehicles paused at a massive clump of tentacle terras that stretched across the highway, blocking it in both directions. The ten-foot black tentacles waved like seaweed—except seaweed wasn't deadly.

"I hate those things," Asher said, grimacing. Consulting his maps, he ordered a detour.

A short while later, our convoy arrived at a large field covered in yellow flowers and ringed by forest. A road cut across the open area, broken by a huge sinkhole in the middle.

The vehicles stopped at the edge of the field and we got out.

"We'll have to avoid that sinkhole in the center," Asher told us.

"Driving across those yellow flowers is a bad idea." Lynxx yanked a flower from the soil. The blossom was only an inch wide, but its roots fanned outward in a network over three feet long. "*Porifera exTerrus*."

"In English," said Asher.

"Sponge terras. They're all over the field, which means their extensive root system will have weakened the soil."

"That explains the sinkhole," Harlem muttered.

Asher cautiously took a step onto the flower-covered ground. Then another. Another. "It seems firm."

"It's fine if you weigh less than six hundred pounds," Lynxx said. "But the Templars will sink faster than a boulder in quicksand."

Asher opened his map. "We need to find another detour."

"Maybe not." Lynxx folded his arms, surveying the field. "I've come across these terras before, at a park in Brooklyn. The flowers are much sparser at the edges, which means the ground is more solid there."

"So we can drive *around* the field to the road on the far side?"

"Yes, if the Templars stay at the edges and go slow. We'll also have to lighten some of their weight." Lynxx pointed to the supply Templar, T4. "You'll need to share its equipment—and the dirt bikes—among the other vehicles. Plus everyone walks except the drivers."

I stifled a groan. The route around the field looked about a mile long.

Willow stepped up to Asher, saying quietly, "Xavian's too sick to walk that far." Her violet eyes were soft with concern.

Asher hesitated, then said, "He can ride one of the dirt bikes and follow the Templars. And since Lisa from Trident Team sprained her ankle yesterday, she can ride the other one."

Willow gave his arm a grateful squeeze.

"The field is long but narrow," Harlem said. "Can *we* walk straight across the field and meet the convoy on the far side. Is that safe, Lynxx?"

"Fine, as long as we go single-file and spread out."

Twenty minutes later, the repacked Templars slowly set off around the perimeter; Lisa and Xavian followed on the two motorized dirt bikes. The rest of us stretched out in a long line.

"Okay, we're ready," Asher said. "Everyone stay alert and stay alive."

Cautiously, we began to cross the sea of yellow petals. Sergeant Thorne and a soldier headed the line, followed by Lynxx; Willow and I were in the middle with the others; Asher and some more soldiers brought up the rear.

With each step, my boots crushed the flowers, releasing a heady smell like warmed bread. On either side, crabben xans skittered over the plants, chasing smaller xan bugs. I tried to ignore the fact that we were walking across non-terrestrial plants, populated by non-terrestrial animals and bugs. Instead, I enjoyed the wafting bread-like scent, the warmth of the sun, the caress of the breeze. All were brief snippets of tranquility in an increasingly dangerous world.

We skirted the enormous sinkhole, glancing at the trio of rusty cars in its depths, and continued on.

Two-thirds of the way across the field, an unexpected sound shredded the afternoon hush.

Startled, we looked around.

A droning noise was coming from the west. Once, this sound had been common, but after the Mist it had almost disappeared.

A small biplane appeared above the trees that edged the field. Through my binoculars, I saw a man in the open cockpit.

The plane roared down the field, spewing a black spray in its wake.

Asher's earlier words thundered through my mind. *The Outriders are going to trial the virus in several locations around the world. The odds of us being infected are incredibly small.*

Incredibly small.

But not zero.

"Is that a Tiger Moth?" Booker gasped.

"It looks like an old crop duster," Asher said.

They were both wrong.

This plane was Death.

<h1 style="text-align:center">60</h1>

AT THE REAR OF our line, Asher shouted, "Everyone, take shelter!"

We scattered, but there was nowhere to go. We were in an open field, our vehicles far away, and even as we fled toward them—

—the crop duster roared past, barely fifty feet overhead. I glimpsed a cadaverous face peering down at me. *Bone.* What was he doing here? I knew our soldiers had been tracking Bone. Had Bone been tracking us back? But why—?

Wavy black lines rained down and the air reeked of sulfur. My throat burned.

The Threads.

The black lines landed on my skin and clothes like ugly black worms. Horrified, I watched the black lines divide into two, then four, eight, more, replicating with incredible speed. Grabbing my handkerchief, I wiped off as many as I could reach.

People crumbled to their knees and threw up.

Clutching his stomach, Asher doubled over, and I ran toward him.

The injustice of it all, the futility, left me stunned. Despite everything—all our pain-filled struggles to survive in this strange new world—we'd just been infected.

We'd fought the good fight.

And we'd lost.

By the time I reached Asher, he was talking into his radio, his voice weak and shaky. "Keep the vehicles at the perimeter," he told the Templar drivers, wiping black threads off his face. "We'll come to you. Out." He gave me a quick hug. "I'm glad you're okay, Kass. Where's Willow? And Harl?"

"I'm not sure."

"I'll find them. Get to the Templars, Kass." He rushed away.

People stumbled toward the vehicles on the far side of the field.

The crop duster had disappeared.

At the sound of an approaching roar, I tensed. *Oh no.* Was the plane returning?

But it was one of our bikes. The lightweight dirt bike roared across the field of sponge terras, Xavian's skinny figure hunched over the handlebars. "Panny!" Ignoring the black Threads, he scanned the grounds. Further back, Lisa rode the other bike toward us.

"Kassia!" Lynxx raced to my side.

"I think we've just been sprayed by the Threads. Everyone's vomiting and—"

"Have *you* been vomiting, Kassia? Are you sick?"

"I'm fine," I replied with surprise. Even the burning sensation in my throat had gone.

"I'm fine too. The vaccine from the Sphere must've worked."

I wiped more Threads off my face, and my handkerchief came away smeared in black. "We need to help the others."

"Of course. But don't look too healthy or it'll arouse suspicions."

"They're too sick to notice."

In the field, Asher lifted a white-faced Willow onto the pillion seat behind Xavian. He draped her arms around the old man's waist, yelling to him, "Go. Get her out of here." Xavian accelerated toward the Templars.

I glimpsed a body on my left. Pepper. She lay motionless, eyes shut, black threads crisscrossing her face. *Oh no.* Was she dead?

My stomach knotted at a familiar rattling sound, like a skeleton jiggling.

Turning, I saw a large tumbleweed terra bouncing across the yellow field.

Memories swept me. *The enormous ball of branches grabbing up Pepper and me. Landing on the side of a tall building.*

Rattling and clicking, the curved branches rolled over the yellow sponge terras and scooped up Pepper's limp body.

Lynxx and I had lagged behind the others as they'd staggered toward the distant Templars. Sick and woozy, they hadn't even noticed the tumbleweed.

"Pepper!" Sword in hand, I raced forward.

As the tumbleweed lifted into the air, I stopped beneath it. Staring upward, I focused on the woody ball with an intensity so fierce that my temples throbbed and my eyes felt ready to burst. The terra hesitated ten feet above me, shook, then slowly rose again.

A strong hand clasped my own. Startled, I looked around. Lynxx stood beside me.

"Together," he said, staring up at the tumbleweed.

I gripped his hand and together we mentally focused on the ball of branches.

Hard.

Harder.

A strange sensation prickled my skin, and I quivered as something invisible burst from me. This energy slammed into a second wave of energy, becoming part of it, yet bigger, like two starbursts melding into one.

The tumbleweed dropped to the ground. Its branches crackled open, revealing a gray-clothed man with a red armband. Gaunt face. Dark, snake-cold eyes. Thinning gray hair—

—and an air of menace that flowed in a poisonous wave from him.

"Bone," I gasped weakly.

Unable to land his heavy crop duster on the field, the man had used the tumbleweed terra to help him travel across the unstable earth.

He held Pepper before him like a shield, his hand gripping her neck so tightly that she could barely breathe. She stared at me, brown eyes bright with fear and pain.

"A *bonusss*," he hissed, giving Pepper a skull-grin. "Need more test subjects." As usual, the hiss of the occasional word sounded like a snake attempting to speak.

"Let Pepper go." Lynxx released my hand and stepped forward. "You don't need her."

"Do. Virus failed." The Outrider leader spoke in his characteristic clipped manner, as though too weak to waste energy on unnecessary words.

"Failed?" I cried. "Take a look around. People are throwing up. They're sick—"

"But not dying. In tests in lab, *humansss* die in three seconds. Quick." Bone scowled. "But Threads in open air much weaker. Humans only sick." He rubbed his chin in thought. "Maybe humans outside still die from Threads. Just take longer."

Exactly what I was worried about.

"Whatever. Need be sure. Understand why slower outside." He lifted a brow at the fleeing, stumbling people, his gesture reeking of calculation. "Need infected humans. Dissect. *Ssstudy.*"

I struggled to control the hatred that rose within me. Bone had kidnapped my sister. Experimented on her. Made her sick.

And now he wanted to do the same thing to my friend, Pepper.

His hard gaze slid to me. "You look like her."

"Who?" I asked between gritted teeth.

"Olivia."

I remained silent, hands balling at my sides.

He studied me. "You and I first met in Pherrit Tower." Feral Tower. "Months ago. You were sickly. Skinny. Poor test subject. Now, Kass, you healthy. Strong. Beautiful. Warrior. Excellent test subject." A corner of his thin mouth twitched upward. "Apocalypse good for you."

Good for me? I'd lost my sister and family, my friends, my world. Fury boiled up, blotting out everything except my need to kill this man. Raising my sword, I stepped forward.

Bone tightened his grip on Pepper's neck, and her eyes flared with fresh pain.

Stopping, I lowered my sword.

"Smart choice." Bone relaxed his grip a little. Pepper gagged.

"You're a monster!" I cried.

"Realist. Time of humans over. Not opinion. Reality."

"This is our planet."

"It *wasss*. Humans are like disease. Spreads across planet. Destroys lower species. Humans believe in right to rule. Even have phrase for it."

Lynxx ground out, "What phrase?"

"Survival of fittest. Now *fitter* species comes along. Now humans bleat. Mewl. Whimper. Call us evil murderers. Not true. We doing same as humanity. We are surviving."

"You're not a survivor," I told him. "You're just an underling, an abomination created to serve your master. You're not Chi'az or human."

"Nor Lynxx," he said with a thin smile. "He hybrid. Like me."

"He's nothing like you. He's good and—" I fell silent as Pepper's gaze flickered between Lynxx and me. Despite her pain and fear, she was listening to every word.

Bone stared at Lynxx and me. "You two hold hands earlier. Combine mental powers. Bring down my tumbleweed."

Pepper's eyes widened with a mixture of pain and betrayal. Months ago, she had suspected I was different, maybe even dangerous, but I'd eventually convinced her that I was normal, and we'd become friends.

Now her earlier suspicions were confirmed.

She knew the truth.

Bone glanced at his watch. "Time to go."

"Then go," Lynxx snapped. "Pepper stays." He took my hand again, preparing to mentally remote-stop the tumbleweed.

Bone glared at our entwined hands and our determined expressions.

"She *yoursss*," he hissed. With one powerful movement, he jerked Pepper's head to the side. I heard bones snap. As he threw her forward, Lynxx and I rushed to catch her.

Bone darted inside the tumbleweed, and its branches closed behind him. With a chilling crackle, it zipped into the air.

Pepper slumped in Lynxx's arms, dead, her broken neck flopping at a terrible angle. Gently he lay her on the carpet of terra flowers.

A breeze stirred up driftings of the dark threads from the ground and they settled on Pepper like a funeral shroud. On her right arm, the line of tattooed stars—red, white, and blue—echoed a flag draping a soldier's coffin.

61

No time to bury Pepper. People were too sick—and afraid that Bone and his virus-spewing crop duster would return.

Despite my tearful protest, Pepper's body remained where she fell. The rest of us piled into the Templars and sped away, leaving her alone in the field of yellow flowers.

I stared through T2's window, dazed with grief and shock. My friend was dead. Murdered in front of me. Another life brutally taken. Another hole for my heart.

Ten minutes later, we found shelter in a near-empty barn large enough to contain our vehicles.

Two members of Trident Team checked inside, then reported, "Lots of harmless velvet-vine terras, plus the usual xan bugs and insects."

The four drivers of the Templars, who'd been protected from the Threads, were posted outside to keep guard. The others slumped inside the barn, ill, but as the Threads fell off their skin, they slowly began to recover—except for one person.

Xavian.

Chest heaving, struggling to breathe, the old man lay on a blanket in a leafy corner. Like the others, the Threads had dropped off him, leaving his wrinkled skin free of the black lines. Willow stroked his hand as Asher cooled his forehead with a wet cloth. Lynxx and I lingered nearby, helpless to ease Xavian's suffering, but staying close in case he needed anything.

Quietly, I suggested to Lynxx. "What about giving him some of the Lazarus tonic?"

"It's worth a try." He hurried across to T2.

A strong smell filled the barn from the velvet-vine terras. Normally I loved their faint lavender-like scent, but today they smelled like flowers at a funeral.

Willow fought back tears. "You'll be fine, Xavian." She patted his hand over and over again. "The others are recovering. You will too. You're just taking a little longer because you're older."

"It's okay, Panny," he croaked. His kind eyes were bloodshot, and his skin held a gray tint, as though Death had marked him with its breath. "If it's me time, lass, I'm ready. You won't be alone. Asher will take care of you. Lynxx too."

Willow's facade shattered. Tears streamed down her cheeks. "Hold on! I know you'll get better."

"The cancer's too far along, lass."

"Cancer? You don't—"

"I do. Figured I had a few weeks left. But those Threads today changed things right round."

Guilt clutched my heart. If Xavian had taken the vaccine instead of giving it away, he might've survived the Threads.

The scent of lavender mutated into a sour odor.

The old man gave me a sad smile. "No one's fault. I made the gold-star right decision." He squeezed Willow's hand. "Panny, you've been a rare light in me life, the daughter I never had. So precious."

His eyes closed. His heaving chest fell still and his breathing stopped.

"Xavian. No!" Willow's cry seemed ripped from her soul.

Lynxx halted a few yards away, a bottle of Lazarus tonic in his hand.

Leaving Asher to comfort the grief-stricken girl, Lynxx and I slipped away. Plastering fake queasy expressions on our faces, we moved through the barn, past groaning friends and colleagues.

Outside, Lynxx told the soldier on guard, "Kassia and I are going to search for supplies."

As we crossed to a nearby farmhouse, I murmured, "Poor Willow."

"Yes. She loved that old man."

"I liked him too. A lot."

He nodded. "Same here. Still, we had to get out of that barn before anyone noticed how not-sick we were."

"Let's find some supplies."

Inside the farmhouse, more velvet-vines wallpapered the rooms. When Lynxx winced at the terras, I reminded him, "Velvet-vines are harmless."

"Nonaggressive and nontoxic, but not harmless." Lynxx ripped a length of vine from the wall, revealing long cracks in the plaster. "Their roots cause a lot of cumulative damage. In ten years, this house will collapse. The same thing will happen in buildings all over the world."

A quick search of the rooms unearthed canned food, meds, boots, clothes, socks—and half a dozen piles of decomp-dust. We filled canvas shopping bags and placed them by the front door, along with bottles of water and toiletries.

Lynxx paused at a vine-netted bookcase in the living room. "*Harry Potter and the Goblet of Fire.*" He took the dusty volume from the shelf. "I remember you reading this to me in the subway bunker, Kassia."

"What? Oh. You mean, when you were Mousy?"

"Yes. Things were much simpler back then. Just you and me in our own world. The Dynamic Duo." A wistful yearning laced his words, as though he longed to return to the days when I loved him—at least, the Mousy-him.

"Those days are gone forever," I said. "Just as Olivia's gone forever. I'm no longer that sick girl hiding in a dark subway, waiting for my sister to return each evening."

"I know." His voice dropped to a whisper. "It's just that …"

"What?"

"Xavian's death reminded me of how fragile life is. When he gave me the vaccine, he thought he had weeks ahead with Willow. Instead, it turned out to be hours."

"We didn't know the Outriders were going to target us today."

"Exactly. We can't predict the future. We need to make the most of the present. There's only now." Carefully tucking the Harry Potter book inside his jacket, he stepped forward and took me in his arms.

Flustered, I pulled away. "I'm with Asher."

"But is he with you?"

"What do you mean?"

"Haven't you seen the way he looks at Willow? It's like he's found a rare diamond."

"That's normal," I said, trying to convince myself as much as Lynxx. "He thought she was dead, remember? Before the Mist, they were very close."

"He was in love with her. She's still in love with him."

"He *was*. She *is*. There's a difference."

"And if his *was* turns to *is*—if he falls in love with Willow again—what then? If he wasn't in your life, could you love me then?"

"I already love you, Lynxx, as a friend."

"That's not what I'm asking."

Silence weighted the air as I considered his question. Could I ever love Lynxx the way he loved me?

Long seconds ticked by. Finally, I replied, "You're so many things a girl looks for in a boy. Intelligent. Brave. Sensitive. Good-looking. Loyal."

"But?" His single word was ice-cold.

"But ..." How could I say it, after everything he'd done for me? How could I even think it?

He snapped, "But I'm still a hybrid, right? The enemy."

"Never my enemy."

"But always a hybrid."

"We're from two different worlds—literally. Even if Asher wasn't in my life, you and I could never work as a couple."

He studied me, his golden eyes dulling with resignation. "Fine." He withdrew the Harry Potter novel from his jacket and dumped it in a wastebasket. "I'm out." Somehow, his last two words sounded like a key locking a door, never to be reopened again.

"Out?" I asked.

"When we return to New York, I'm leaving the garrison."

62

My heart jolted as though I'd accidentally missed a step coming down some stairs. "You don't mean that, Lynxx."

"I do," he replied flatly. "Don't worry, I'll drop off a bottle of Lazarus tonic at Weston Tower each week. I just won't be hand-delivering it to you anymore. I've had enough. For too long, I've been hoping you'll ..." His voice cracked, and he paused before continuing, "Whenever I was with you, I used to feel warm, as though you were sunlight."

"Lynxx—"

"Now I just feel cold."

Wooden planks on the front porch creaked and a voice said, "A guard told me you were both over here."

Asher entered the living room. He gave Lynxx and me a strange look, and for a heart-stopping moment I thought he'd overheard part of our conversation.

Sighing, he sank onto a dusty couch. "What a terrible day. Attacked by Bone and doused with his toxic Threads. Pepper murdered by Bone. Now Xavian's dead." He sighed again. "Willow's so upset that Soo-Yun had to sedate her."

Lynxx directed a pointed frown at me. "Willow really loved Xavian, even if he was a *hybrid*."

"I get it," Asher said wearily. "Not all hybrids are evil. Some are genuinely good, like Xavian. When everyone else was trying to get away from the Threads, he rode straight into them, desperate to save Willow. He was a decent guy."

I murmured my agreement.

Asher turned to Lynxx. "So, why didn't you get sick?"

"Excuse me?"

"I saw you during the attack in the field. Everyone was throwing up. But you didn't get sick. Why not?"

Lynxx hesitated. "I'm like Xavian."

"What do you mean?"

"I'm one of those good hybrids you've heard about."

I gaped at him, stunned that he'd openly admitted his secret to Asher.

"I see," Asher calmly said. "You're a part of the Sphere."

"No. Not every humanized hybrid is a Sphere member."

"Still, you claim you're a hybrid like Xavian. Yet a little while ago *he* died from the Threads."

"He was much older than me and terminal with cancer."

"It doesn't explain why you weren't affected."

Lynxx admitted, "Xavian gave me his dose of a vaccine."

"What vaccine?"

"The Sphere developed it to protect themselves from the Threads."

"Can it protect humans as well?"

"Only hybrids."

"Are you sure?"

"Absolutely."

Asher remained silent for a long minute. Then he tiredly said, "You've done a lot for us, pal, but I can't keep your secret. I have to tell the others."

Lynxx shrugged. "Fine. I really don't care anymore. I'm going back to the barn."

Numbly, I watched him leave.

Asher turned to me. "And you're a hybrid too." It was a statement, not a question.

"What? No! Why would you think that?"

"For one thing, you didn't get sick from the Threads either. Also, there's your cheek."

"Excuse me?"

"When you escaped from the onion terra a few days ago, you had a long cut on your cheek. With everything that's been going on, no one's noticed how quickly it's healed. But I noticed." Anger simmered beneath his words. "Your skin is perfect again. Not even a scar. That's not normal—or human."

My heart pounded. Did Asher think I'd tricked him into having a relationship with a hybrid? Unable to hide my secret any longer, I blurted out, "I'm human. I just have some hybrid blood in my veins." I detailed the incident with the buckshot terra pod at Grand Central Station when I'd first met Lynxx, and I explained how I'd pressed down on his bleeding thigh with my injured hand.

Stonily, Asher asked, "When did you find out that Lynxx was a hybrid? And that you have hybrid blood in your veins?"

"On the Night of the Blue Meteors, up on that skyweb terra. That hybrid, Bone, told me about Lynxx."

He stared in stunned disbelief. "The skyweb terra was seven months ago."

"I ..."

"How could you keep such a secret from me for months?"

"I knew you hated hybrids and anything to do with the Chi'az. You would rather starve than eat or drink something 'infected' with non-terrestrial DNA. If you'd found out about my hybrid blood, I thought I'd be expelled from the Weston Battalion."

"You were afraid of being expelled?" His face tightened. "That's what you said when you told me about the Lazarus tonic, the one you drink for your leukemia."

"Why are you angry? The exploding buckshot terra pod at Grand Central wasn't my fault."

"I realize it was an accident. I don't blame you for being infected with hybrid blood."

He didn't? "Then why are you angry?"

"Don't you get it? When you finally told me about your leukemia and drinking the Lazarus tonic, I made it clear that I didn't care about either of those things. I only cared about you. But I asked one important question. Do you remember what it was?"

How could I ever forget?

I felt as if I were on a runaway horse racing toward the edge of a ravine, unable to stop. Panic gripped my throat, keeping me silent.

The repulsive stench of lavender was thicker now, almost suffocating.

"I asked if you had any more secrets. You told me *no*." Asher's eyes flashed with anger and betrayal and hurt. "You lied. Obviously I can't trust you anymore."

Weariness and resignation filled me. "I'm sorry."

"That's not good enough."

"I'm sorry for keeping things from you," I said, my voice a little louder. Firmer. "I'm sorry I'm not the person you thought I was. And I'm sorry I've destroyed our relationship."

His anger evaporated, leaving only betrayal and hurt. "You haven't destroyed us. But we're damaged. And we're both tired of the arguing. Maybe we need a break, just for a while."

A break? His suggestion should've left me numb with despair. Instead, I felt as if a boulder had been lifted from my shoulders. I, too, was tired of our arguing and tired of hiding my secrets from him. "A break is fine with me. Or do you want to split up permanently?"

"No. Not at all."

"What about seeing other people?"

"Is that what you want?"

"We should both have the option. That's what people do when they take a break."

"I guess so," he said, stiff and guarded. "Hopefully, after a while, we'll know what we want."

"And *who* we want," I added. "Meanwhile, we'll still work together."

"And we'll still be friends," he said. "For now."

63

WE BURIED XAVIAN ON a rocky hilltop at dawn. His grave was rough and shallow, but a sobbing Willow had insisted he'd love the view of the lake and ducks below.

At Xavian's gravesite, Asher briefly announced that Lynxx was a hybrid, stressing that he was a good hybrid like Xavian. His revelation was met with hostility from some people and disbelief from others. Thankfully, no one questioned Lynxx about his earlier role during the Mist, when he'd calmly taken notes as people died; they assumed he'd always been a humanized hybrid.

As we walked down the hill after the funeral, I managed to get Asher by himself.

"You outed Lynxx as a hybrid," I murmured, "but you didn't tell them about the hybrid blood in my veins."

"It's just blood, Kass. They've got enough to deal with." He walked away from me.

The convoy continued onto Eldron, now only hours away. Everyone had recovered from the Threads, and the interiors of the vehicles had been cleaned of vomit. Still, I found the atmosphere inside T2 almost unbearable.

Lynxx grunted short, icy responses to my comments. Asher buried himself in paperwork and hardly looked at me. Rusty's loathing of Lynxx was clear, while Booker gaped at the hybrid with the incredulity of someone discovering a rare and wondrous insect. Willow quietly grieved in her seat, clasping a bunch of velvet-vines and taking comfort from their lavender scent—but to me, their scent reeked of death, misery, and rejection.

Most of all, Pepper's empty seat screamed of my friend's death.

By the first rest stop that morning, I couldn't stand it any longer.

"Lisa, do you want to swap vehicles for a few hours?" I knew the Trident Team girl had a crush on Rusty.

"Ooh! Yes please."

Inside T3, Trident Team was still discussing the revelation that Lynxx was a hybrid. Everyone in the team had liked hybrid-Xavian. They'd been impressed by his self-sacrifice when he'd rescued Willow during Bone's attack with the Threads. And since Lynxx's knowledge of terras had saved many members, the team eventually decided that he was okay too.

I stared out of a window, still grieving Pepper's death, and mourning my break with Asher. I replayed part of my recent conversation with him.

You didn't tell them I had hybrid blood in my veins.
It's just blood, Kass.

He didn't realize it *wasn't* just blood. I'd inherited some strange powers as well.

Asher had always hated all hybrids until he'd met Xavian. Now he admitted that some of them, including Lynxx, could be decent and trustworthy. He also reluctantly accepted my "tainted" blood. However, I was pretty sure those two concessions were his limit.

Yet I was now planning to push him further.

Asher was right. I couldn't keep hiding my mental powers from him—but I also couldn't expose Lynxx's mental powers without his consent. Once he agreed, I'd reveal the rest of my secrets to Asher. If telling him the truth shattered our new, tentative "friendship," so be it.

When T4's engine started giving problems again, our convoy stopped at Vincent's Corner, a sprawling town north of our destination, Eldron.

A soldier stood watch as two men worked on the engine. Lynxx went off to get more terra samples, protected by another soldier. The rest of us broke into teams, each assigned a soldier. Harlem's group searched for fresh food. Another refilled our water bottles. Two teams scavenged for canned food and toiletries.

I was assigned to a scavenging team that consisted of Asher, Willow, and Rusty—and with Sergeant Thorne accompanying us.

Great. More tension.

We parked T2 in the shopping district, then headed down Main Street.

Vine-bridges stretched between multistoried buildings. Sinkholes dotted the roads and pavements, some large enough to swallow buses. Gold terra vines coated the storefronts, their round leaves murmuring in a warm breeze.

"Hades terras," Asher told Willow, indicating the gold leaves on the stores. "Highly flammable. They'll burst into flames if you break their stems."

"I know. Xavian told me about them." Her flat voice matched her grief-filled eyes.

"We've dealt with them a few times," he continued, trying to raise a flicker of interest in her. "Once, I was trapped by swarmers in an alley lined with them."

"Okay."

I added, "Asher and I broke some stems. This set the Hades terras on fire. You should've smelled the smoke, Willow. It reeked like burned sugar. The swarmers headed for the hot smelly flames instead of us."

Finally, a wisp of interest. "You were there too, Kass?"

"Yes. It was the first time I met Asher. He saved my life that day."

"I'm glad." She sounded like she meant it.

Sergeant Thorne turned to Lynxx, who was inspecting some terras, protected by his assigned soldier. "Hey you, hybrid-boy. That old hybrid, Xavian, said that you things don't have black marks on your earlobes."

Lynxx shrugged. "That's correct. It's a myth."

"So you creeps look exactly like us?"

"Well, our DNA is different."

"Shoot. I don't walk around with a microscope in my hands." When Lynxx shrugged again, Thorne's eyes bulged, as though he was about to explode with rage. With an effort, he controlled himself. Turning to us, he snapped, "I don't like being in the open." A suspicious sidelong glance at Lynxx. "We don't know *what's* out there."

Lynxx addressed the soldier assigned to protect him. "I need to get some samples of the blue terras down here." They headed into a side street.

The rest of us continued along Main Street, looking for stores free of Hades plants. Asher and Sergeant Thorne veered into a café.

Willow quietly said to me, "I'm sorry that you and Ash are having problems. I hope I'm not the cause."

"You're not," I replied as we detoured around a wide sinkhole. Across the road, Rusty peered through the cracked window of a boutique. "Has Asher told you that we're taking a break?"

"From what?"

"Each other."

Her violet eyes widened. "I didn't know." Although she tried to hide it, I heard the relief in her voice.

Outside a community center, three rabbits grazed on a clump of angel-vine terras. Pausing, they watched us, long ears rotating, noses twitching. A flock of sparrows landed on a yellow patch of sponge terras. Overhead, two crows wheeled in the sky.

The breeze faded away. The rustling leaves fell silent.

My heart began hammering.

Sword drawn, I scanned the area. It appeared peaceful—and yet my grip tightened on the hilt of my sword.

At the corner of my eye, something stirred. I jerked around. Saw the rabbits bounding away. Saw the crows fleeing. Saw the sparrows shooting upward, wings beating furiously.

Uh-oh.

In the sudden silence, my heart pounded like a drum. What was—?

A savage shriek sliced the hush.

Gun drawn, Rusty rushed across to Willow and me. "What was that noise?"

A shape moved inside a nearby store netted with burned Hades vines. An instant later, an animal burst through the open doorway. It moved upright on two legs, its overlong arms almost scraping the ground. Four feet tall. Black skin. Upright pointed ears. Snarling bat-like face. Skull pointed at the back.

Krol!

With a nerve-shredding screech, it loped toward us.

Six others barreled from the store, whooping and snarling.

I gaped at the oncoming xans, unable to move. My sword suddenly weighed a ton, too heavy to lift.

"Krols!" Asher yelled as he and Thorne bolted from the café.

Snapping out of my shock, I looked around. Willow fumbled for her gun with shaking hands. Rusty seemed frozen with horror.

My sword's heaviness suddenly vanished, and it felt featherlight again.

A krol leaped over a bench. It lunged at Willow, its clawed hands outstretched, ready to rip her throat—

I remote-pushed. Hard.

The krol spun left, as though kicked by an invisible giant. It tumbled to the ground, then scrabbled upright, growling. Furious black eyes darted to me.

Willow shoved her gun back in her belt and withdrew her sword, her delicate features transformed by determination.

The krol sprang at me, screeching.

Time to end this beast. I swung my sword. Slashed the creature's stomach. Watched it collapse in a gush of blood. *Good.*

Shouts and gunshots rang through Vincent's Corner. The others were under attack as well. Was Lynxx okay? What about Soo-Yun and Harlem and—?

Survive first. Help them later.

The peace of Main Street warped into a noisy battlefield. Humans versus krols. Shouts and screeches tore the air. Guns blasted. Swords slashed. Claws ripped.

Blood sprayed the air, falling in crimson showers.

Asher tried to position himself in front of Willow, attempting to protect her. To my surprise, she ignored him. Wielding her sword like a professional, she fought a hunchbacked krol, her movements filled with the confidence and skill of—

Pandora. Of course. She'd learned sword fighting on that TV show, honing her skills in battles with various mythological enemies.

Razor-sharp talons lashed at Willow. She darted right, then feinted left. When the krol swiped left, she thrust her blade deep into its chest.

Despite Willow being an accomplished swordfighter, Asher remained by his former girlfriend's side.

Not my side.

Willow's side.

Cursing, Sergeant Thorne slashed at his attackers. One fell to the pavement, clutching its spilled intestines.

Another krol crouched over the body of Rusty. I rushed forward, weapon raised. Asher bolted toward the fallen boy, shooting the krol. Gushing blood, it dropped to the pavement.

Rusty stared upward in dead horror, his throat shredded into a red mess.

Another cry from behind.

Turning, I saw Willow lying at the bottom of a shallow sinkhole.

"I think I twisted it," she cried, clutching her ankle.

"Hang on," Asher shouted as three krols charged him. He yelled to Sergeant Thorne, "Get Willow back to the Templar."

Thorne blasted a krol. "But—"

"Do it now!"

Swearing, the sergeant scooped up Willow and retreated down the street. By the time Asher and I had killed the remaining krols, Thorne and Willow had disappeared around a corner.

Asher squatted beside Rusty's body. Felt for a pulse. "Nothing."

Further down Main Street, a new group of krols howled in savage anticipation as they spotted Asher and me.

"We gotta go, Asher."

We fled into an alley, then swung into another street that—

Oh no.

64

A MASSIVE SINKHOLE GAPED in the ground.

It had swallowed a block of buildings, so deep that its depths were pitch black. High above the void, skinny vine-bridges linked buildings on either side of the sink-hole. Around the edges, broken pipes angled downward, like crooked teeth rimming an open mouth.

The howls of our pursuers grew louder.

"They're coming, Asher."

We were trapped. Nowhere to go except—

"Up." He grabbed a cable from his backpack and clipped its end to a four-pronged hook.

The howls sounded closer.

"They're in the alley, Asher!"

"Just a few more seconds."

The strain between us had vanished. Right now, we were simply two people trying to survive.

He twirled the pronged cable like a lasso, then threw it toward an overhead vine-bridge that extended across the sinkhole. When the hook snagged on the twisted growth, he yanked the cable, making sure it was secure. "Good." Pulling me against him, he cried, "Hold on tight!"

The krols burst from the alley. Screeching, they loped toward us, their ugly faces contorted.

I wrapped my arms around Asher's neck.

Gripping the cable, he pushed off from the edge and we swung through the air.

The krols stopped at the rim of the pit, hooting with rage.

We continued swinging onward. Under the vine-bridge. Past it.

Then we swung back toward the rim.

The krols craned forward, long arms outstretched—

"Asher!"

—but their claws missed us by inches as we swung toward the middle again.

Finally, the cable stopped swinging, and we dangled beneath the vine-bridge. The sinkhole's snaggle-toothed mouth gaped below us, its breath stinking of animal droppings and decay. In its dark depths, I glimpsed movement and flickering red eyes.

What was living down there?

"Kass, start climbing up to the vine-bridge. I'll follow."

"Okay."

As I reached for the cable, it suddenly jerked upward a foot. Then another foot. Something was slowly reeling Asher and me in.

A krol peered over the vine-bridge, its clawed hands hauling up our cable.

Only twenty feet separated us from it.

The creature was creepy. Ugly. Its head rested on a thick ring of purple flesh, making it look neckless. Dark eyes glared on either side of its snouted bat-like face. An overhanging brow was splotched with pus-yellow markings. Its mouth was a long thin slash surrounded by wrinkled black skin.

No hair.

No fur.

It opened its mouth and snarled.

Lots of sharp teeth, though.

Only seventeen feet separated us from it.

I looked down. A network of terra roots crisscrossed the sinkhole like sinews in a monster's mouth.

"Those roots look strong and thick," Asher said. "We'll have to jump."

Fourteen feet.

Above us, a second krol was helping to pull up our cable. Could I remote-push them off the vine-bridge? But if they fell on Asher and me, we'd be knocked to our deaths below.

Ten feet.

"What if we miss the roots, Asher?"

Three more krols scurried across the vine-bridge and joined the pair at the cable.

A long rope of saliva dripped from the first krol's mouth, onto my upturned face.

Dis-gus-ting!

"We can't stay here, Kass."

Six feet.

Saliva Mouth bent forward, trying to claw me.

"Let's go." I shook the drool off my cheek. "Say when."

"Now."

We let go of the cable and dropped.

Down.

Down.

We thudded onto a terra root.

It snapped apart.

We fell further. Landed on another terra root, woody and gnarly, but solid. Groaning, we scrabbled to our feet.

"Let's go, Kass. This root ends on the far side of the sinkhole. No krols over there."

Yet.

Skinny brown tendrils sprouted along the wide terra root. As we ran, they clutched at our legs like the hair-thin strands up on the skyweb terra last November.

The thick root shuddered beneath us. Once. Twice. We glanced back. Two krols had leaped onto our terra root. Long toes gripping the woody surface, they scampered after us.

Across the sinkhole, more terra roots stretched in all directions at different levels.

"Asher. Down here." I stepped onto a gnarled root at right angles to our current one.

Clouds rolled in from the east, tinting the air with a strange orange hue.

Gunshots again echoed further in the town, followed by a high-pitched cry, alien and urgent.

The group of krols at the edge of the sinkhole stiffened, their bat-like ears swiveling. Hooting and barking, they turned and raced toward the gunshots.

The two krols on the terra root hesitated.

Asher opened a radio channel to the others. "Guys, a pack of krols is on the move, possibly heading your way. Get ready." After they acknowledged his warning, he switched off the radio.

The two krols charged toward us, snarling.

We jumped from root to root, altering directions, changing levels, struggling to keep ahead. Somehow Asher and I became separated, and by the time I realized it, the two krols had zeroed in on him.

He stood in the middle of a long root, with nothing nearby to jump onto. On either side, a krol slowly crept forward, trapping him between them.

Withdrawing my gun, I ran to help him. "Shoot them."

"No bullets left." He waved me away. "Get out of here. Save yourself."

"You wouldn't leave me to die." And he wouldn't. Despite the problems between us, I knew he still cared about me.

And I definitely cared about him—

—enough to risk everything for him.

No way was I going to stand by, hiding my powers while he was slaughtered.

I closed in on the first krol. It whirled to face me, growling like a rabid dog.

Oh, shut up, Creepoid.

I shot at it. Missed. No matter. I remote-pushed the beast, hard. Yowling, Creepoid stumbled and fell into the sinkhole, long arms flailing.

Asher had been watching the second krol, still some distance away. At Creepoid's yowls, he glanced over. A brow lifted in surprise. "Good shot."

Far below, snarls erupted from the darkness-dwelling creatures, a fierce and strangely hungry sound. Creepoid's screams abruptly ceased.

The second krol barreled forward, spittle spraying from its ugly mouth, claws raised, eager to slash Asher into pieces.

Bad decision, Uggo.

Another ferocious remote-push. Another yowl of fear as Uggo toppled from the root, into the blackness.

More snarls and shrieks from the sinkhole.

Then silence.

Breathing deeply, I turned to face Asher—and the consequences of my actions.

He blinked at the black pit. "We need to get to solid land." Waiting for his accusation, I followed him along the thick vine, across the sinkhole. "Did you see it, Kass? You shot one krol. The other just fell." A broken pipe angled down from the road. As he helped me climb it, he shook his head, bewildered. "Maybe that's why the rest of the krols didn't jump onto those roots. They're not as sure-footed as they seem."

"Yeah," I managed to say calmly, relieved at his wrong assumption. "We got lucky."

Actually, *I* had.

This time.

We had just reached street level when T2 screeched to a halt nearby. Behind the steering wheel, Sergeant Thorne shouted, "Get in. The others are in trouble."

Willow's worried face stared at us from the back cabin, her twisted ankle red and swollen.

As Asher and I piled into the vehicle, another volley of gunshots sounded in the distance.

Frantic.

Desperate.

65

BY THE TIME WE reached the location of the gunshots, it was over.

T2 pulled up and we rushed from the vehicle, except for the injured Willow.

In a parking lot beside a shopping mall, seven dead krols lay near T3. Blood pooled around the gutted body of Lisa, the girl who'd had a crush on Rusty.

"No!" Sergeant Thorne bent over one of his men sprawled on the asphalt. Hazy's head lolled to the side, his throat slashed into strips of flesh.

Another soldier, Buzzard, slumped nearby, clutching his bleeding shoulder. Greta from Trident Team sat dazed as blood streamed from a gash on her forehead.

Soo-Yun kneeled beside Alan, also from Trident Team. Her hands were pressed to his chest as she tried to stop his blood from soaking through a wad of bandages. Blinking back tears, she looked up. "He protect me from krol, but it rip his chest. Many much blood, but he still alive."

I asked, "What about Lisa and Hazy? Did you—?"

"I check each two time." She swiped her brimming eyes, leaving red streaks around them. "Much dead."

Asher ripped a loose board from a store window. "We can use this as a stretcher, Soo-Yun."

"Is Harlem much good? Not hurt?"

"I'll radio him in a minute."

Elsewhere in the town, a series of high-pitched whoops sliced the late morning peace.

The hairs on my arms prickled. "More krols."

Quickly Sergeant Thorne, Soo-Yun, and I stretchered Alan onto the back seat of T2. Asher contacted the others. Although his shoulders sagged at their reports, he calmly ordered all teams to leave the town and meet at a gas station further down the road.

Was Lynxx okay? The question lodged in my throat like a stone, and I found it difficult to breathe.

"Sergeant Thorne, you'll need to drive T3," Asher said. "I'll drive T2." He turned to Soo-Yun. "Harl is all right."

She gave a trembling smile.

Thorne hesitated, his face washed by rage and confusion. "How are my men, Weston?"

"IronHead's injured. MeatMan's dead. Everyone else is okay."

I heaved a guilty sigh of relief. We'd lost another team member—but at least Lynxx was okay.

"Let's go," Asher said.

The sergeant pointed at Hazy's body. "We have to bury him."

"No time." Asher slid behind the wheel of T2. "We need to leave Vincent's Corner. Now."

Another screech shredded the air, closer than the last ones. Thorne glanced at Hazy, then bolted across to T3.

I took the passenger seat beside Asher. "What about T4?" I asked. "Is it drivable?"

"Yes. Just a minor problem this time."

I twisted around in my seat. In the back, Willow was helping Soo-Yun bandage Alan's chest. Buzzard groaned as he held his slashed shoulder. Blood continued to seep from the deep gash on Greta's forehead, trailing down her ashen face and leaving her even glummer than usual.

"Are you okay, Greta?" I asked.

Hand shaking, she pressed a handkerchief to her forehead. "The krols tried to kill me. They're like something from a nightmare."

"You're alive."

"For how long?" Greta's ashen face was curiously expressionless, her voice flat and resigned. "Sooner or later, the terras or xans will kill us all. They outnumber us by millions. We can't win. We're all doomed."

"But—"

"Don't you get it? It doesn't matter how hard we train and fight and struggle, we're all doomed."

I lapsed into an uncomfortable silence.

Fifteen minutes later, T2 and T3 turned into an abandoned gas station, where the other two Templars were already parked. Clumped together for safety, we tended the wounded and grieved our dead. People jumped at every sound and scrutinized the shadows for lurking krols.

Lynxx's grim expression had lightened a little when he'd seen me, but he'd quickly turned away, somber once again. Obviously, he was still upset by my recent rejection when he'd tried to kiss me; to make matters worse, I had backed up my rejection by saying I could never love him because he was a hybrid.

Asher addressed our shrunken group. "Soo-Yun is patching up Greta and Buzzard in T2. Harlem is bandaging Willow's ankle. Alan's badly injured and needs a real doctor. Eldron's only a short distance away—and it has a doctor."

"We've been on the road for weeks, boss," Booker said, running a distracted hand through his tousled blond hair. "What if something's happened to Dr. Tran? He could be dead by now."

"We won't know until we get to Eldron."

"Aren't we in radio contact with them?"

"We were, until yesterday. Then they went silent."

Aghast, Booker asked, "You mean they could *all* be dead by now?"

"They might just have a problem with their radio."

"Or not," Sergeant Thorne interjected. "What if we're driving into a trap? This whole trip has been a disaster."

The shock of the krol attacks quickly turned into burning anger, especially among Thorne and his men. Comments and complaints flew thick and fast between them.

"We shouldn't have come down here."

"Is this trip worth it? Four people dead—"

"Six. Don't forget Davey and Pepper."

"Actually, seven," said a soldier, Rogue. "I know Xavian was a hybrid, but he seemed like a good old fellow."

Thorne growled, "The only good hybrid is a dead hybrid."

"What about Lynxx?" Rogue reminded him. "He's helped us in the past."

"He's still a hybrid," Thorne snarled. "He doesn't belong on our planet. He's the enemy."

With an effort, I stayed silent, aware they were too upset to listen to reason.

"So many of our people are dead—"

"—and injured—"

"—just to rescue a bunch of strangers."

Stung, I finally said, "Those strangers need our help. We're human, aren't we? Isn't that what people do? Help each other?"

"You heard Commander Powell," said Rogue. "There's a limit to what we can do these days."

"Anyway," Sergeant Thorne snapped, "this isn't about rescuing a bunch of strangers. Powell sent us down here to collect Dr. Tran. He's our mission."

"Yeah, sure, we need a doc at Weston Tower," Rogue admitted. "But is one doctor worth seven lives?"

"Eight if Alan dies," Thorne corrected.

Asher raised his voice, speaking to the whole group. "We leave in ten minutes. Make sure you're armed and ready. If you need a bathroom break, take it now. Once we're on the road again, we won't be stopping until we reach Eldron."

As the others dispersed, I saw Lynxx give Asher a small bottle containing a purple powder. "This might help Alan."

Asher frowned. "What is it?"

"Powdered Lazarus terras."

Asher's frown shifted from Lynxx to me. "Aren't they the terras you drink each week, Kass?"

"Yes," I replied. "The powdered form has healing properties too."

"If you sprinkle this on Alan's chest," Lynxx said, "it'll stop his wounds from getting infected. He'll heal faster too."

Quietly, I admitted, "It's helped my own injuries a lot."

Asher's face tightened. "You claimed you were a quick healer."

"I am—with the powder's help."

"Didn't we agree to no more secrets?"

"This wasn't a secret," I said, skating on the edge of truth. "I've admitted to using the Lazarus tonic to stay alive. The powder is from the same terras."

Wearily, he shook his head, too tired to argue. Thrusting the bottle back at Lynxx, he told him, "Okay, use it on Alan and anyone else it might help. Go in T2 with Soo-Yun and the injured. Kass, go in T3." He hurried away.

I took a relieved breath. Asher was almost resigned to using terra plants as substitute drugs. Good. Our previous pharmaceutical river of medicines, lotions, and pills had dried up since the Mist. These days, we had to use whatever worked—and hope there were no terrible side effects.

"Thanks for offering the Lazarus powder, Lynxx," I said, joining him. "Before, you've always been annoyed when I've wanted to use your terra drugs on the others."

"What are you implying?" he asked coolly.

"Hey, it's good that you're helping other people besides me. It shows you're changing."

"Perhaps I'm just waking up." His cool reply was thick with reproach. "Alan's a decent guy who welcomed me into the Weston Battalion weeks ago. Even when he found out I was a hybrid yesterday, he didn't care. He accepted me for *who* I am, not *what* I am."

Suddenly ashamed, I watched him climb into T2. For years I had hidden my leukemia, afraid people would reject me because of it. And now I was mirroring a similar behavior with Lynxx by rejecting him because he was different. He hadn't chosen to be born a hybrid, just as I hadn't chosen to get leukemia.

"I'm so sorry, Lynxx," I whispered to thin air.

As the convoy set off, I stared at the passing countryside. The earlier sunshine had disappeared behind a growing bank of clouds. Two massive onion terras dwarfed overgrown houses. An unseen animal uttered a long, savage howl that I struggled to identify. Wolf? Coyote? *Xan?*

The land seemed thick with threats.

Was Greta right?

Were we all doomed?

66

Two hours later, our convoy finally trundled into the seaside town of Eldron.

We drove toward a large open square surrounded on three sides by low buildings and fences, with a razor wire barricade on the fourth. Armed guards in scruffy camouflage gear stopped us, spoke to Asher, then eagerly waved us through. "Man, we're mighty glad you guys made it."

A young boy ran from a building, calling out, "They're here! They're here!"

By the time we parked in the square, more than twenty people had appeared. They had the dirty garments, lank hair, and drawn faces of people struggling to survive. Many had eyes dulled with shock and something else—a desperate resignation, as though waiting to die.

Asher flung open the door of T2 and lifted out Alan, still unconscious. "I need a doctor."

"Dr. Tran's over there." Several strangers ferried the injured across the square. Asher, Soo-Yun, and Lynxx accompanied them into a two-story clapboard building with a red cross painted on its door.

An attractive middle-aged woman approached our Templars. She scrutinized us, her deep brown eyes sharp with intelligence, but also cool and detached.

"I'm Nila Torres." Her husky voice held the confidence of a leader. She was trim and fit, with olive skin bare of makeup and brown hair cut short, as though she didn't have time to style it. No jewelry, just a large men's watch. Scruffy jeans, a crumpled white T-shirt, and hole-speckled sneakers tied with string. Her functional outfit and brisk manner suggested a person on a mission, uncaring of looks. "Did you bring the engineer?"

"Here." Bevan waved a hand.

"Good. Get your tools and go with John's team to the dock. We're running out of time."

Gray-brown clouds swelled in a darkening sky, and I thought I heard loud hisses.

As Bevan and three men headed off, Nila turned to Sergeant Thorne. "Are you in charge?"

"That'd be Asher Weston." Thorne's reply held a simmering anger, and he cradled his rifle as he gazed around. "He's at your hospital with our injured."

Little whirlwinds scurried around the square, gathering leaves and paper in their spinning embraces.

More hisses, louder this time.

Wary, I looked around. "Are there snakes in this place?"

"Probably. Be careful." A breeze caught Nila's short brown hair and fanned it around her head like a dark halo. "I need to talk to Asher Weston." She glanced at her watch, then crossed to the hospital.

The small, rustling whirlwinds skittered off. The hissing stopped.

Still wary, I scanned the area.

Around the open square, low wooden buildings bore shattered windows and large holes in their walls. Toppled trash cans had vomited their contents onto dislodged lids. Dried pools of blood splotched the ground. Bullet shells dotted the pavers, and an acrid odor wafted on the swelling wind.

By comparison, our Weston Tower back home was a paradise, with its solar-and-wind-generated electricity, indoor farms, and clean dormitories.

Harlem surveyed the damaged buildings and bullet-littered square. "What happened here?"

"We were attacked. Again." A stocky ashen-haired man in his thirties stepped forward. "I'm Wayne Smithers, second-in-command. You guys were lucky you arrived during a lull. They don't happen very often." He pointed to a nearby warehouse with an open garage doorway. "You need to get your vehicles under cover ASAP. We've already cleared a space for them. Hurry."

Sergeant Thorne peered around, raising his rifle. "Expecting another attack?"

Among the buildings, tall wooden poles held tattered flags that fluttered in a newborn wind. Nervously eyeing the flapping flags, the crowd of ragged welcomers broke up and scurried indoors.

"No, not an attack," Wayne replied. He shot a worried glance at the billowing clouds. "The krols are too smart to be outside during these storms."

I peered around, alarmed. *Krols? Here?*

Increasing in strength, the wind snapped the flags on the poles.

Sergeant Thorne pointed at Harlem, IronHead, and Rogue. "Get the Templars under shelter. I'll drive T3." He turned to the rest of us. "Everyone else go with this guy."

"Hurry," Wayne cried, practically running as he led the way to a wooden building. "We're almost out of time."

We followed him across the square, our heads lowered as the howling wind battered us.

Inside the dusty community hall, rows of camping cots crowded the dirty floor. Smoking candles lit the room, their flames flickering in stray gusts that blew through the cracked walls. Rafters groaned and unseen rats squeaked in alarm.

"Hope you like the accommodation, folks," Wayne said proudly. "It's the best in town."

The best? Wow. What's the rest of Eldron like?

A peculiar odor filled the room, like burned metal mixed with earth. I'd noticed it outside, but in the past couple of minutes it had grown stronger. The air felt heavy with dread, as though this town's inhabitants were bracing for something.

"The air smells weird," I said to Wayne. "Is there a bad storm coming? Is that why everyone's so jumpy?"

Before he could answer, Nila Torres entered the hall in a blast of wind. "Where's Kass Madison?"

"Here." I hurried across to her.

"Lynxx sent me. He needs more Lazarus powder. He says you might have some."

I grabbed my backpack. "Did Lynxx tell you, Nila, that this powder is made from terras?"

To my surprise, she dismissed my revelation with a toss of her head. "I don't care if it's made from crushed dinosaur droppings. If it heals someone, I'll use it."

"Good to hear." I headed for the front door.

"Where are you going?"

"To the hospital."

"No need." She held out a hand, impatient and demanding. "I'll take the powder."

"One of my colleagues is injured. Greta. She has a cut on her forehead. I want to see how she is."

"You're safer in here."

Greta's words whispered through my mind. *We're all doomed.*

"I'm coming with you, Nila."

She flung open the front door. "Do you really want to go out in that?"

I stared at the scene outside.

An early twilight had descended, along with a wild storm that spun and howled and churned. The yowling wind snatched up pieces of trash and hurled them in all directions, turning innocuous objects into bruising missiles.

"I'm still coming with you," I said, somehow keeping my voice steady.

"Fine, but you have to obey my instructions. Otherwise you could die."

We're all doomed.

I nodded.

"Stay close." Nila hurried down the steps.

I followed, shoulders hunched against the wind.

A few yards across the square, she abruptly halted. I stopped behind her.

"Wait for it," she told me.

A flash of lightning lit the area, followed by a swell of loud hisses. From around the square and between the buildings, jets of glittering green sparks spurted from the ground, high into the air, like giant Roman candles in a fireworks display. The blazes smelled like burned fertilizer.

"Terras?" I said, trying not to gag at the stench.

"Yes. I call them Roman-candle terras."

Ha. Great minds.

Nila continued, "They grow at the bottom of holes, and their sprays are triggered by lightning."

"Why? What's the purpose of them?"

"The sprays contain terra seeds that are scattered by the wind. The sparks' heat cracks open the seeds, allowing them to germinate more easily wherever they land. Until this place, I've never seen terras use fire before."

"I have. Hades terras. Are these Roman-candle terras dangerous?"

"Very—especially if you step on a hole just as it erupts. The holes are small. Hard to see. I lost three people before I figured out a system." Staring across the square, she lifted a hand for silence.

More bolts of lightning flashed from the clouds. They flooded the area in a hard silver light that highlighted the perimeter's battered buildings—and revealed two shapes a short distance away.

The xans paused, baring their jagged teeth at Nila and me, huge dark eyes savagely glinting.

Krols.

67

"Stay still," Nila snapped, watching the two xans. "Wait."

Wait for what? I wondered, swallowing. *For them to rip us apart?*

The krols loped across the square, long arms and clawed hands grazing the pavers.

The creatures were twenty yards away.

Nila raised her voice over the wailing wind. "I've never seen them out in a storm. Usually they shelter until it's over."

"Maybe we should go back."

Fifteen yards.

"Don't move, Kass."

Ten yards.

My heart pounded in my chest. Was I strong enough to remote-push two savage krols—

Five yards.

A blast of green sparks shot from the ground. The krols stumbled back, engulfed in flames. They fell, writhing and shrieking as they burned.

Nila ignored the living bonfires and scanned the square again. "I can't see any more krols." A shrug. "But that doesn't mean anything."

"Why were those two outside in the storm?"

"They probably saw your convoy arrive and were curious. Let's go, Kass. Stay close. Do exactly what I do."

We hurried toward the hospital, through the howling wind that pelted us with trash and leaves and grit. Nila moved in a strange pattern, and I followed behind, copying her. We darted left, paused, then swung right. In our wake, two Roman-candle terras gusted upward with loud hisses, turning toppled trash cans into blazing pyres. Stepping cautiously, Nila detoured around holes that sizzled and threw off green glows; she zigzagged and veered and avoided, knowing which spots were dangerous and which were safe.

"Made it," she cried, darting up the steps of the makeshift hospital. "These storms are getting worse every week."

"So why do you stay here?" I asked, panting.

"Because of the storms." She closed the front door behind us, lowering the shrill of the wind. "Two months ago, Eldron started getting hit with lightning storms. Each one lasted for three days. We quickly realized that the storms and the Roman-candle terras provided a built-in deterrent to the krols. Sort of."

"Sort of?"

The woman picked up a lit oil lamp and moved down a dim hall. "There's an eight-hour break between each three-day storm. The krols have learned to attack us during those breaks. Our ammunition is running out and we're down to minimum rations. People are getting too weak to fight. It's only a matter of time before the krols wipe us out completely."

"Is that why Isabel and the others flew to Manhattan for help?"

"Yes. Our radio doesn't always work during the storms, but every so often we can talk to survivors around the world. Your resistance cell in New York is the closest one to us. We knew we'd never make it by land, so we started outfitting a trawler to take us by sea." She picked up a clipboard, read the itemized list, and signed it. "Then we had an engine problem and no one to fix it. We needed help. Isabel found it." She paused. "Your commander told us what had happened to the others on her flight. Very unfortunate."

"I'm sorry for the loss of your friends," I said. Three people had died in the Cessna crash, and two more had died while crossing a vine-bridge terra.

Nila and I stopped in an open doorway. Over two dozen army cots crowded a large room, each occupied by a patient. Despite her bandaged ankle, Willow held a tray of medical instruments as Soo-Yun stitched the deep gash on Greta's forehead, while Lynxx changed the bandages around Buzzard's shoulder. Other members of Nila's community tended to their sick and injured colleagues.

Through an open doorway, I saw a makeshift operating room. A middle-aged Asian in a blood-smeared white coat leaned over Alan's unconscious body, stitching a wound. Asher stood nearby, a mask held over his face as he watched.

Outside, the wind slammed the wooden shutters on a window, and I flinched at the storm's strength. Were we stuck in this town for three violent, lightning-filled days and nights? "It wasn't storming when we arrived, Nila. Was that the end of an eight-hour break?"

"It was just a one-hour lull. It happens now and then. The next longer break starts tomorrow."

"What time?"

"Around nine o'clock in the morning. We need to get everyone on the trawler before that deadline, even if the engine isn't fixed." She scowled at the cobwebbed ceiling, and for a moment her gaze seemed haunted, as though viewing a long line of bloodied ghosts. "We can't stay here any longer."

"You sound worried."

"I am. Boarding the trawler will be difficult. And incredibly dangerous."

68

ONLY THE BABIES AND young children slept that night.

My team helped Nila's weary group prepare for the up-coming journey by packing supplies and blankets. Conversations were subdued as everyone waited for the one message that would bring hope for a new life.

Outside, the lightning and wind had been joined by heavy rain. The Roman-candle terras continued to brighten the night with their beautiful, deadly sparks. In the square, the two burned krols remained as grotesque warnings to their pack.

By 6 a.m., we were ready. Some people napped. Most were too restless to sleep. We watched the clock and waited, listening to the wind as the minutes crawled past dawn. According to Nila, the storm would stop around 9 a.m.—and the krols would attack.

I watched Nila bustle around, arranging things, reassuring her people. She acted like a good leader, but her eyes were distracted and her comforting words were brief and mechanical. The woman seemed distant from her group. I had the impression that she didn't genuinely care about them; instead, she was with them for another reason. Convenience? Food? Shelter?

Finally, at 7:40 a.m., the message we'd all been waiting for arrived. The engine was fixed. Carrying or supporting the sick and injured, people hurried through the wind and rain to the vehicles, trailed by Willow, who hobbled on crutches.

Thirty minutes later, our expanded convoy trundled onto the wooden dock alongside a large trawler named *DeepSea*. Although the rain had stopped, a layer of thick gray clouds remained, along with the wind and lightning.

People exited the cars and vans and Templars, excited—and afraid. Had the krols seen us leave? Even if the xans were sheltering from the storm, had they heard our vehicles rumble down the streets? Or had the howling wind muffled the sounds of our flight?

Once the Templars were emptied of their passengers and supplies, they were driven alongside the trawler. A crane operated by Wayne Smithers, Nila's second-in-command, began loading them into a hold.

Sergeant Thorne and the remaining soldiers positioned themselves in front of the boat, guns ready. Armed members of Nila's group also stood guard as the children hurried up the narrow gangway. The sick and injured were next to board. The healthy stood to the side, anxiously awaiting their turn.

As Alan passed by on a stretcher, I marveled at his improvement. His face had color, his breathing was regular, and Soo-Yun had told me that his chest wounds were starting to heal. She followed Alan to the gangway, fussing over him and tending to his near-fatal wounds with a vigilance born of guilt.

"Alan many much better." She smiled at me, pretty face bright with relief. "Dr. Tran plus Lazarus powder make much good medicine."

Lynxx hurried across to Soo-Yun. "Can you take Owlfred on board?" He thrust his covered birdcage into her arms. "I need both hands free in case of trouble."

"Much yes." Soo-Yun cradled the cage as she accompanied Alan onto the trawler.

Nila had warned everyone about the glow-lotus terras on the far side of the walkway. Even in the gloomy morning, the luminescent blooms were glorious. Shuddering, I turned away from them.

The wind faded into stillness, and only the occasional bolt of lightning stabbed the sky. Seagulls screeched overhead, drawn by the stench of old fish that wafted from the trawler. The vile smell didn't worry me. After weeks of being cooped up in a Templar, I was looking forward to standing on the deck, gazing at the ocean, and feeling the sea breeze on my face.

First, though, we had to complete our escape from Eldron.

I crossed to Nila, who stood on the dock, cradling a large potted plant. The gold plant had long thin leaves immobilized by plastic wrapping. "What? Is that a zap terra, Nila?" These terras gave off electrical shocks when touched.

"Yes. Don't worry, it's harmless when its leaves are bound in plastic."

"Why are you bringing a zap terra on board?"

"I need it."

"Why?"

"Don't worry about it, Kass."

Her evasive answer cut off my questions. Like me, Nila seemed to have her secrets.

"You're organized," I said to her.

"Excuse me?" Her grip tightened around the potted zap terra.

"The crane."

"Oh. Right." She relaxed a little. "When Isabel radioed us after reaching Manhattan, she said that Commander Powell wanted the Templars returned. Luckily, we'd already started preparing this boat. It has a large opening in its hold, big enough for the Templars."

Hand resting on my sword, I studied the trawler. *DeepSea* was over two hundred feet long, with four levels and a wheel-house at the rear. "It's bigger than I expected."

"Freezer trawlers are bigger than most regular fishing trawlers," she said, distracted. She watched the thirty or so people on the dock, and the two dozen patients slowly boarding the boat.

Nearby, several smaller vessels bobbed on the water, rotting from neglect and terras. Green velvet-vines grew over their decks and hung down their sides like tattered curtains.

I studied *DeepSea* again, noting only a few patches of velvet-vines. "I'm surprised there aren't more terras on the hull."

"Originally there were many more." Nila flinched as a huge bolt of lightning struck the ocean. "My people spent weeks clearing them off, even working in the storms. Then the krols moved into this area, and we had to stop. It was too dangerous being in the open."

"Do the krols know about this trawler?"

"I don't think so."

Willow's sprained ankle had placed her last in the line of patients. Finally it was her turn to board. As she hopped forward on crutches, Asher hurried over.

"I'm okay, Ash," she said. "I can do this by myself. Lynxx put some terra cream on my ankle last night. It's a lot better."

Ignoring her protests, he slipped an arm around her waist and helped her up the gangway. Relaxing, she gazed at him, her expression filled with longing and love.

I looked away. What was the status of my relationship with Asher? Since our brush with death at the giant sinkhole, he'd been friendlier to me. However, things had been hectic in the past couple of days and we'd had no time alone. I wondered if Willow had taken first place in his heart again.

With a strangled cry, Nila pointed across the dock.

69

A MAN YELLED, "LOOK!"

The murmur of conversation in the waiting crowd abruptly died. People glanced around, wary, fearful.

On the far side of the dock was a row of low stores. On their roofs, a dozen krols stood upright, watching us. Each grasped a rough weapon—either a long wooden stick sharpened to a point, or a short club-like branch.

Harlem gasped, "When did they start using spears and clubs?"

Oblivious to the wind and lightning, the krols stared down at us with dark, hostile eyes. One raised a spear and uttered a sharp cry. The xanimals leaped from the roof, onto the walkway, then charged forward, shrieking and whooping.

Nila shouted, "Everyone on the trawler. Now!"

The orderly evacuation shattered into chaos.

People scattered, screaming. The trawler shuddered as the engine groaned into life. Something whizzed past me and a woman crumpled to her knees, a wooden spear jutting from her stomach. Gunshots blasted, and a couple of oncoming krols fell, blood spurting from their chests.

Gripping my sword, I jumped aside as a club missed me by inches. Before the krol could swing it again, I gutted the xan with my sword.

More screeches from my left as a second pack of krols raced toward us.

In the crane's cabin, Wayne pulled on levers and, as four xans scurried by, he released the chains supporting the raised Templar. It crashed onto the screaming krols, crushing them.

The ongoing bedlam allowed me to remote-push without being noticed. I saw Lynxx mentally pushing people out of the path of wooden spears as well.

Sword drawn, Asher leaped over the trawler's railing, onto the dock. A snarling krol aimed its spear at him. *No way!* I remote-pushed the hairless black arm, and the spear zipped harmlessly over Asher's head. He lunged at the krol, gutting it.

I glimpsed people running up the gangway as a couple of men threw off the mooring ropes.

Empty-handed, Greta stood in the middle of the battle, dazed.

"Greta," I screamed, dodging a krol's spear. "Defend your-self."

She didn't move.

I thrust my sword into a krol's stomach, dropping it to the ground.

Another krol leaped at Greta, its upraised club about to crush her skull. She stood there, unmoving. Running forward, I remote-pushed the krol. It tumbled in front of Sergeant Thorne, who blasted its head into a bloody mess.

"What's wrong?" I cried, grabbing her by the shoulders. "Are you injured?"

She didn't look injured—or aware. She just stood there, silently staring through me.

I didn't have time for this.

"Sergeant Thorne, can you get Greta onto the boat?"

"I'm needed here," he snapped. He shoved her toward Book-er, who was clutching his bloody shoulder. "Take her aboard. Now."

Booker grabbed the dazed girl's arm and pulled her up the gangway.

As I turned back to the battle, a club swung toward me. Instinctively I tried remote-pushing it away, but it grazed the side of my head and bright lights flashed in my eyes.

Stunned, I crumpled to the ground.

Two shots rang out.

A krol holding a club thudded down beside me, dead.

Gun in hand, Nila pulled me to my feet. "You all right?"

"Yes."

"Good." She returned to the battle.

Gingerly I touched the side of my head, wincing as my fingertips came away covered in blood.

Lynxx grabbed up a fallen sword and impaled a charging krol. It slumped down, blood gushing from its twisted mouth. "You're bleeding, Kassia."

I shook off his concern. *He's going to leave me when we get back to New York.* "I'll live."

At a scream, we looked around. Five krols were scaling the sides of *DeepSea*, their long black arms and legs reminding me of giant spiders. Trying to ignore my throbbing head, I ran with Lynxx toward the vessel. Together, we managed to remote-push three of the xans into the water, but two reached the top and scrambled over the railing.

"Lynxx," I gasped, "the krols are on board with the kids, the injured, and the old."

"*Help.*" Outside a store, Maya, a teenage girl from Nila's group, ran from a krol.

"You kill the two krols on the boat," I told Lynxx, blinking as my vision blurred, then sharpened again. "I'll help Maya."

"Okay." He raced toward the gangway. "Be careful."

"Always." As I rushed toward the stores, the krol threw a spear at Maya. Desperately I focused on the airborne projectile—

—and it missed her by an inch.

Maya darted between two rows of outdoor tables, then jumped over the corner of the glow-lotus patch. But I could see she wasn't going to clear them. I remote-pushed her. Hard. Back arched as though she physically felt my mental shove, she skimmed the flowers at the edge of the patch and landed on the wooden boards. She stumbled. Fell. "Oww! My knee."

The krol leaped over the bright plants, long claws twitching in anticipation—

I remote-pushed.

—and the krol suddenly flew left. It rolled into the patch of glow-lotus terras, an ugly black monster among the radiant blooms. Snarling, it tried to stand, then shrieked, staggered back, and collapsed onto the flowers. By the time I reached Maya, the creature lay dying among the luminous terras, pinned down by iron-strong stems that had sprouted with incredible speed through its body.

Eighteen months ago, I'd accidentally knocked a young woman, Sophie, into a patch of glow-lotus terras. Today, I'd saved a girl from some glow-lotuses. Did today's rescue balance out that earlier terrible death?

Asher joined us, breathing heavily, his sword dripping blood. "Are you okay, Kass?"

Swaying a little, I pulled Maya to her feet. "I'm fine, but she's hurt." Why was I so dizzy?

By now the others were aboard, leaving the battlefield strewn with a dozen broken krols and five fallen humans.

"We need to get on the boat." Asher hurried toward the gangway, supporting Maya as she limped beside him. "Come on, Kass."

Nearby, I saw a pair of boots poking from between two decorative barrels. "I'm right behind you, Asher." I headed for the barrels.

Sudden screeches cut through the howling wind. Down the walkway, a third pack of krols emerged from an alley, brandishing more spears and clubs.

DeepSea's engine grew louder, eager to be off.

I rounded the barrels and saw a stocky ashen-haired man sprawled on his back. Wayne Smithers, Nila's second-in-command. Gaping stomach wound. Sightless stare. Dead.

My surroundings blurred, then spun in a crazy whirlwind of flashing lights and motion.

I swayed.

Tried to stay upright. Couldn't.

I fell.

70

Helpless, I lay facedown, head to the side. Through my blurred vision, I saw the new group of krols scrabbling toward me.

Go, I silently urged the trawler. *Get everyone to safety.*

Two strong hands reached down and swept me up. Asher cradled me in his arms as he bolted for the boat.

The oncoming krols shrieked in rage. They were close. Too close.

"No," I murmured, my mouth against Asher's ear. "Leave me or you'll die too."

He held me tighter. "You wouldn't leave me to die," he said, echoing my words back at the giant sinkhole.

Willow, Harlem, and others stood at the railing, shouting at us.

"Hurry!"

"Faster."

"One's right behind you!"

Gunshots boomed from the trawler. Behind us, krols shrieked and I heard thuds as they fell.

Still carrying me, Asher raced up the gangway. The second we were on board, Harlem kicked the top of the gangway, sending it crashing below. The engine roared and, with a shudder, the trawler pulled away from its mooring.

Over Asher's shoulder, I saw Lynxx emerge from below the deck. Seeing me, he raised both thumbs. Good. He'd killed the two krols which had climbed aboard.

Despite my raging headache, my vision slowly returned to normal, and I began to feel better.

"What happened?" Asher asked me. "Why did you fall back there? Is it your leukemia?"

"I don't think so. I just felt dizzy. I'm okay now, though. I can stand."

"All right, but I'm going to keep my arm around your waist in case you fall again."

"Good idea." I gave him a weak smile.

He set me down beside the railing, still holding me close. "You've got blood on your head."

"A krol clubbed me."

"Ah! That would explain your fall. You could have a concussion. Dr. Tran needs to check you out. Wait here. Hold on to the railing if you feel dizzy again." He left and returned a few minutes later, his face subdued. "Dr. Tran and Soo-Yun are flat out treating today's injured."

"Are any of them ours?"

"Two. Booker's got a slashed shoulder and Rogue took a spear in the side. They'll both survive."

"What about the five bodies on the dock?"

"Dead. All from Nila's group." For a long, heavy moment he remained silent. Then he gestured to my bloodied head. "Are you sure you're okay?"

"It's just a graze. I'll heal."

His blue eyes met mine. "I'm sure you will—with the help of the Lazarus powder." His voice wasn't accusing or angry. He sounded accepting.

DeepSea plowed through the waves, trailing a frothy wake. From the deck, I watched the krols reach the toppled gangway. Enraged at our escape, the xanimals leaped up and down, shrieking and waving their weapons in frustration. Some threw their spears at the vessel, but the projectiles arced harmlessly into the water.

As we headed out to sea, people began complaining about the trawler's strong fishy smell, but I just shrugged, happy to be alive. Besides, I'd smelled worse … maybe.

"We're on our way home, Kass," said Asher. "We're going to be okay."

We're going to be okay.

Did he mean the group in general?

Or was he referring to us as a couple?

71

I was in paradise.

To my immense relief, we had left Eldron and the storms far behind us. Standing at the deck railing, I reveled in the smell of salt spray, the wind in my hair, and the sight of a blue ocean that stretched in all directions.

Yesterday, our ship's engineer had told us that *DeepSea's* old, rusty engine would need about a week to travel to New York.

A week where we wouldn't see land—or terras and krols.

A week without worrying about Bone and his Brethren cult.

A week of rest and peace.

Paradise.

Asher joined me at the railing. "You're looking better."

"I feel better," I replied, watching seagulls circle overhead. "Dr. Tran said I only had a mild concussion. If I rest for a few days, I'll be fine."

"This trip will give you that rest."

"We probably all need a rest, especially you and Nila." Since the trawler had left Eldron yesterday, Asher and Nila had been busy. They had assigned makeshift quarters, distributed supplies, set up security shifts, and visited the patients under Dr. Tran's care.

Harlem appeared further down the deck. "Hey, bro, we've finally got Commander Powell on the radio."

"Gotta go, Kass."

I watched him hurry off. Lately, Asher and I had been more relaxed around each other. Although busy, he occasionally stopped by for a quick chat, and the strain between us had eased.

So why did I feel unsettled? Was I still a little concussed? Or was I unsettled because of—?

Lynxx took Asher's place at the railing. Coolly, he asked, "How are you feeling?"

"Fine. A lot better than yesterday."

"Are you sure?"

"Why do you sound surprised?"

"Because it's been eight days since your last dose of the Lazarus tonic."

"Really? But I usually start to get sick on Day 7. And yet I feel okay. I'm not even seasick like some of the others."

"Don't get too excited, Kassia. You went thirteen days without being sick a while ago. And then you were ill again."

I sighed, remembering my collapse in the ruined church. "You're right. I still have leukemia."

"Maybe not. I've tucked away your bottles of Lazarus tonic. You can drink one today. Or you could hold off for a while longer. See what happens."

"Why bother? I'll just get sick."

"Not necessarily. You might be like some of those patients who used to get chemotherapy."

"Excuse me?"

"They got dose after dose after dose. And then many of them no longer needed the doses because the chemo had finally killed the cancer."

"Really?"

"A scientific fact. Do you want to hold off on taking your next dose?"

"Definitely."

His voice softened. "I truly hope you're leukemia-free."

I gripped the rail, heady at the wonderful possibility of being cured. "Imagine if I didn't need the Lazarus tonic anymore."

"Then you wouldn't need me anymore. I could move out of Weston Tower without feeling guilty. You'd never have to see me again."

"What?" As he turned and walked away, I stared after him, struck by a sudden realization.

Lynxx. He was the reason I'd been feeling unsettled earlier.

A few days ago, he'd told me of his plans to move back to his old penthouse apartment when we returned to New York. I hadn't wanted to believe it then. And I didn't want to believe it now. The thought of never seeing him again left an ache in my heart.

Did I have deeper feelings for Lynxx than I realized?

My thoughts were interrupted by Greta, who was zombie-walking along the deck. *Zombie-walking.* That was Sergeant Thorne's description of her recent behavior—cruel but sadly accurate. Her head remained bandaged from the krol attack at Vincent's Corner, and she still wore the same dazed expression from yesterday's battle.

"Hi, Greta," I called out. "How's your forehead?"

She stared at the waves, fiddling with her bracelet.

The beaded band around her wrist looked familiar. "Wasn't that Lisa's?" I asked, joining her.

Voice flat, she replied, "I took it off her body after that monster murdered her." Greta trembled, as if remembering the sight of her friend lying in a pool of blood, her stomach ripped open. "She was my friend."

I struggled to find the words to comfort her. "I know how you feel. Pepper was my friend, and she's dead too. I miss her a lot." I gestured to her bracelet. "Wearing that is a nice way to remember Lisa."

"That's not why I'm wearing it."

"Oh?"

"I wear it to remind myself how Lisa died and how fragile our lives are. Everything's changed. The world, our country, us. We're all doomed. Doomed." She walked away, moving slowly like a zombie. One of the living dead.

I wanted to go after her, tell her that there was still beauty in our world, plus family and happiness and love. However, I guessed that she wanted to be alone. Greta had seen her friend gutted by a krol. She needed time to process Lisa's death and to start healing.

Early the next morning, I stopped by the rough quarters Greta shared with three others. She wasn't there. One of her companions, half-asleep, told me that she'd gone for a walk on the deck.

When I went up on deck, though, there was no sign of her. Nor was she in the galley, mess, restrooms, or the other common areas. Worried, I spoke to Asher, who ordered a more thorough search of the boat.

By the time we realized Greta wasn't on board, the mild weather had shifted into a light rain. It was assumed that Greta had either fallen overboard—or, depressed, had jumped.

"How long has she been missing, Kass?" asked Asher as we gathered in the galley.

"No idea. We need to turn the trawler around and search for her."

He shook his head. "We wouldn't know where to start looking."

"Plus," Nila said, her face strained, "we don't have enough fuel to mount a search."

"Sorry, Kass," said Asher.

Even as I argued with them, I knew they were right.

Back on the deck, uncaring of the rain, I stared at the slate-gray ocean. The last time I'd seen Greta, she had been wearing blue jeans and a gray top—colors that would blend her into this wet blue-gray world.

"Any sign of her?" Lynxx asked, joining me.

I shook my head, anguished at the thought of Greta alone in the ocean, struggling against the waves. "I should've guessed she was depressed. The way she spoke. What she said. I should've done something."

"Maybe it's not too late." Wiping raindrops off his face, Lynxx looked around. Most people had abandoned the deck, preferring the fishy smell below to getting wet. "Meet me on the left side of the wheelhouse in five minutes. Make sure no one sees you."

"Why?"

"You'll see."

72

THE AREA BESIDE THE tall wheelhouse held three lifeboats stacked on top of each other, leaving barely any room to squeeze past. I stood in front of them, scanning the distant waters again. Nothing. Just the fleck of rough waves, and the ever-present seagulls that followed the trawler and its fishy smell.

Lynxx rounded the lifeboats, with Owlfred perched on his shoulder. "Did anyone see you, Kassia?"

"No. But I'm guessing *you* caught a few eyes by wandering around with Owlfred on your shoulder."

"Almost everyone is belowdeck, keeping out of the rain. And I made sure the guards, fore and aft, didn't see me."

"What are we doing here?"

"I need you to stand watch."

"Over what?"

"This way," he said. "Keep your voice low."

I followed Lynxx and Owlfred into a small area behind the stacked lifeboats. Barely eight feet square, it was dirty and smelly and hidden from view. He shooed away some seagulls perched on a pipe. Then, murmuring soothing words, he placed Owlfred on an old barrel.

As he stretched out on the dirty boards, I guessed his plan.

"No, Lynxx," I whispered, horrified. "What if something happens and you're out there alone?"

He threw me a reproachful look. "I've mind-blended with Owlfred lots of times over these past few weeks. On every occasion, I was always 'out there alone.' How is this different?"

"Those times, I didn't know you were mind-blending. Also, I had no idea how dangerous it was." I trembled beneath a surge of memories. My mind-blend with the frog, Hopalong, still gave me nightmares, and sometimes I woke up in a cold sweat. "Even if you find Greta, you can't do anything. You'll be an owl."

"I can fly back here, leap into my body, and tell Asher to turn the vessel around, pretending I saw her through my binoculars."

"Even if Owlfred-you find her out there, how will you pinpoint her location?"

"I'll drop this down to her." He held out a small black cylinder with a blinking red light. "It's a tracking device that floats. Once I'm back in my own body, we can use it to locate Greta again."

"It sounds like a long shot."

"It is, so don't get your hopes up." Lynxx regarded me, his golden eyes bright with concern. "Greta's disappearance is ripping you apart. I have to try to find her—for you."

Seconds later, his outstretched body went limp.

Owlfred's yellow eyes turned silver. She fluttered onto a metal pipe beside my face, the tracking device clutched in one claw. Gently, she pressed her soft feathered head against my cheek, the gesture brief and tender.

A twinge shot through my heart, unexpectedly painful. "Be careful," I whispered. "Make sure you come back."

Then, with a flap of wings, the bird was gone.

I looked down at Lynxx's body. His eyes were closed and his breathing was shallow, as though asleep. But this was just his shell. Lynxx's real soul and personality were now merged with a bird. And he was out there alone.

Quickly, I moved to the side railing, watching as Owlfred disappeared into the distance.

For an hour I peered through my binoculars, scanning the sky, waiting. I knew Lynxx would use Owlfred's hyper-sharp vision to search the waves for Greta. The fact that he hadn't returned within a few minutes meant he was having trouble finding her.

With each passing minute, the odds of finding Greta alive grew smaller.

Dejectedly, I stretched my stiff muscles, then looked in on Lynxx's hidden body. He was still non-conscious. Restless, I headed toward the rear of the trawler. As I turned the corner, I glimpsed Sergeant Thorne wearing a raincoat.

Stifling a gasp, I jerked back, out of sight.

I'd forgotten Thorne had guard duty today. During our trip to Eldron, he'd proved to be a brave fighter and loyal to his men, but he was also a creep and a bigot who made my skin crawl.

A gunshot broke the morning peace.

I rushed around the corner. Thorne had his pistol aimed at Owlfred, who was flying a short way off the stern.

"Stop!" I shouted. "What are you doing? That's Lynxx."

"I know it's Lynxx's owl." Thorne spat on the deck, hatred distorting his face. "Since Asher won't let me shoot the hybrid, I guess I'll have to settle for his stupid bird."

Owlfred dropped twenty feet through the air, then rose a couple of feet, struggling to fly.

"I think you hit him ... her."

"Good. I hope it dies. Let the hybrid feel how it is to lose something he loves, even if it's his dumb bird." Thorne stomped away. "I'm going forward. Fewer bleeding hearts up there." He disappeared around the far side of the boat.

Owlfred flapped and dipped, trying to remain airborne.

"Hang on." I grabbed a red life buoy and threw it into the ocean. As it floated on the choppy water, Owlfred fluttered down and landed on the red ring. Her claws were empty. No tracking device. Through my binoculars, I saw that her feathered chest was bloody—and her eyes were silver.

My heart leaped with relief. Lynxx was still mind-blended with the bird.

Could I persuade the trawler's pilot to turn the boat around? *No way.* If the trawler hadn't been allowed to go back for Greta, a sixteen-year-old human, it would never go back for an owl.

Could Lynxx mind-hop into another creature? Doubtful. The nearest seagulls were perched on *DeepSea*, which was powering away from the red buoy. And if Lynxx blended with a fish, what then? It'd still be impossible for him to catch up with the trawler.

By now the life buoy was a shrinking red ring on the gray ocean.

At any moment, Owlfred could die from her gunshot wound. If that happened while Lynxx was still mind-blended with her, he would die too. What could I do? Should I ...?

No. Impossible. Unthinkable.

But even as my stomach roiled in fear, I knew it was the only way.

73

NO TIME TO THINK it through or talk myself out of it.

I rushed back to the small secluded area where Lynxx's non-conscious body lay. Unless I acted quickly, his body would remain empty.

Clearing some space, I lay down beside him and scanned the line of birds perched on the nearby pipe: two seagulls—and a huge white seabird with a hooked beak and enormous black wings. An albatross.

"Okay, Wings, you're it."

Trembling, I focused on the albatross and desperately threw my mind toward it.

Exploding stars. Whirlwinds of light. A horrible sensation of pushing against something gray and spongy—

The frog, Hopalong. The terror of the click xans. The agony of my broken frog-leg.

—and then I was there. Inside.

Frantically, I shoved my panic and claustrophobia away—*I'm okay, I'm okay, I'm okay*—and grabbed hold of the small intelligence with me in the spongy grayness. I opened its ... *our* ... eyes and saw a huge, different world. New colors. Strange smells. Foreign sensations.

No time to dwell on my mind-blend with the seabird. Lynxx could be dying. Or dead.

I threw myself ... albatross-me ... up, half-expecting to drop onto my own soulless body lying below.

Instead, albatross-me lifted into the air and, with a beat of wings, I was off. Around the lifeboats. Above the deck. Beyond the trawler.

I was flying. It should've been a fantastic experience, but it was as frightening as juggling live grenades.

The rain battered us like needles, but Wings-me didn't care. Twice, my hold on the seabird's mind slipped and the bird faltered midair, almost falling. Both times I hurriedly tightened my mind-grip, terrified of losing control. I was flying high above the waves, far from the trawler. If the albatross threw me out of its mind, what would happen? Would I be flung into nothing?

Would Lynxx and I both die today?

Please, no.

At first awkwardly, then with more strength and confidence, Wings-me flew over the water, searching for the red buoy. The bird's eyesight was far sharper than my own human vision and—

Abruptly, the albatross dived toward a school of fish far below, beak open, ready to snatch one up.

Eat later, greedy-guts.

Frantically, I pushed us away from the water. When the bird resisted, I pushed harder. Annoyed, the albatross flew upward again, and I resumed our search.

Minutes later, Wings-me spied a speck of red amid the waves.

The life buoy?

Yes.

I landed on the bobbing red ring. Opposite me, a bloodied and weak Owlfred grasped the life buoy's rope with its claws. Two silver eyes stared at me in shock and disbelief as Owl-fred-Lynxx gave a soft anguished squawk, clearly distressed at seeing *my* silver eyes in the seabird.

Movement flashed overhead.

A large brown bird arrowed down, intent on snatching up the bleeding owl.

Screeching, Wings-me shot into the air, straight at the brown bird. Nails slashed amid a whirl of beaks and squawks. Wings-me tasted the tang of blood. Felt nails scrape my feathered stomach. Knew this battle was life and death.

The conflict was frantic and intense. Finally, with a pained flutter of wings, the brown bird took off, angry and defeated.

In the distance, another large bird flew toward us.

Time to go.

Wings-me swooped down. Since my webbed feet were useless for gripping anything, I carefully scooped up Owlfred with my hooked beak and flew off. She was surprisingly heavy for such a small bird, but thankfully she didn't wriggle in my beak as we headed toward the trawler.

Was Lynxx still blended with Owlfred? I hadn't checked the color of the bird's eyes before lifting her up—but the smell of blood was much stronger. Owlfred was bleeding out. If she died before Lynxx could leap into another body, he would die too.

Must fly faster. Faster.

Slowly we closed in on the trawler. The wondrous aroma of old fish filled the nostrils in my yellow beak, along with the fragrant scent of oil and grease, plus smelly humans.

My head ached from Owlfred's weight, and I struggled not to drop her into the water. A glance down set my small heart beating even faster. A long black shape was gliding through the waves, its triangular dorsal fin jutting up.

Shark.

This predator could gulp Owlfred down in one bite. Should I swoop down closer so Lynxx could mind-leap into the shark? But what if, instead, the shark leaped out of the water and ate us all?

Keep going.

Minutes later, aching and afraid, Wings-me flew behind the trawler's lifeboats, where two soulless bodies lay hidden.

Exhausted, I placed the bloodied owl beside Lynxx. The bird was limp, her eyes closed. Was Owlfred—*Lynxx*—dead?

Wings-me fluttered down to my own body. Shaking, I finally released my mental grip.

More stars. Whirlwinds of lights. Flashes. A tremendous sense of being home ... of being *me*. I was in my own body again.

With an annoyed beat of wings, the albatross took off.

Was Lynxx dead?

Heart pounding, barely able to breathe, I looked over.

He stirred. "Kassia?"

"You're alive!" A tangle of emotions swept me. Repressed panic at my mind-blend. Horror at the thought of losing Lynxx. Relief that he was okay.

Overwhelmed, I leaned over and kissed him on the lips. For a moment, he stiffened in surprise. Then he drew me closer and our kiss deepened as our bodies melded together. I could feel the racing of his heart against my chest, and the warmth of his hand pressed into the small of my back.

Eighteen months ago, when he'd embraced me in Central Park as Loner, his kiss had been firm and hot and passionate. This time, his kiss was soft and gentle and filled with love.

A weak squawk jerked us apart.

"Owlfred." Hurriedly, he gathered the dying bird into his arms. "I'm so sorry, girl. Sergeant Thorne shouldn't have shot you."

His kiss lingered on my lips. "Can you fix her, Lynxx?"

"I wish I could."

"What about the Lazarus tonic?"

His eyes swam with grief. "It's too late." Cradling Owlfred, he stroked her feathered head. Moments later, the bird's small chest fell still.

Glumly, Lynxx cradled the lifeless bird as we made our way to his cabin. "Thanks for saving my life." He spoke evenly, with no sign of the coolness he'd shown over the past few days. "I know how much you hate mind-blending."

"Turns out, I hate the thought of losing you even more."

He looked at me for a long moment. "You kissed me."

"Yes."

"Why?"

"I was emotional. Upset. I thought I'd lost you."

"What did the kiss mean?"

Struggling to understand my own feelings, I replied, "I honestly don't know."

Disappointment flashed across his face and he stared into space, pondering my words. Then, with a sigh, he moved on. "I'm sorry I couldn't find Greta."

"Thanks for trying. I know she's dead." Just one more loss in a long line.

We found a large empty cookie tin with a lid, lined it with a soft cloth, and placed Owlfred's body inside.

"I'll bury her back in New York." He packed the tin in a burlap bag. "She deserves to rest in peace, not get tossed overboard—or gulped down by a shark."

"So you saw it?"

"Yes. Big ugly brute. Trash can of the ocean."

"I almost flew down so you could mind-hop into it."

He grimaced in disgust. "No, thanks. I dislike sharks."

"I thought you wanted to live."

"Not as a shark!"

Together, we went to breakfast.

Neither of us mentioned the kiss again.

74

Home.

As the trawler, *DeepSea*, cruised toward Lower Manhattan, I studied the once-familiar sights. The one-armed Statue of Liberty was almost unrecognizable beneath her coat of gray terra vines, and most of the skyscrapers were smothered by blankets of green. Everywhere I looked, the jungle was tightening its grip on the city, as though hundreds of years had passed.

But it had only been a year and a half since the Night of the Red Mist.

Asher joined me at the railing. "You look upset."

"I can't believe how much the city has changed."

"Yeah. I hate to admit it, but we're losing the battle."

"So why do we keep fighting?"

"We can't save the world. Still, we need to keep small parts of it safe for humanity."

"Harlem is right. You *are* a Don Quixote."

"Is that bad?"

"No," I replied gently. "Now more than ever, the world needs knights who'll keep fighting the good fight."

At Nila's call, he moved off to help supervise our disembarkation.

With a rumble of engines, *DeepSea* pulled alongside a dock. Two men grabbed the mooring ropes. When the engine stopped, I heard silence for the first time in days.

No, not silence.

A coyote howled in the distance. The cackle of hyenas echoed in a city canyon. Elsewhere, a gorilla roared. Although none of these wild animals belonged in New York, their cries were vaguely reassuring, as all were sounds of Earth animals.

It was the other sounds that worried me. The rustle of the gold Hades vines at the end of the dock. The strange creak-hiss of some unseen xans. The weird crackle of something.

The soldiers spread out on the dock, cradling their rifles. Scowling, I watched Sergeant Thorne survey the area, alert for trouble. When Lynxx and I had told Asher and Nila that he'd shot Owlfred, Thorne had claimed he'd "mistaken" the bird for an attacking vulture. Since we couldn't disprove his ridiculous lie, the matter had been reluctantly dismissed.

At Thorne's "All clear," the injured and their caregivers disembarked from the trawler. Despite the warm sunshine, they stayed bunched together, nervously scanning their surroundings.

Lynxx placed his backpack and burlap bag on the deck beside me. "Did Asher reach Commander Powell?"

"Yes," I replied. "They should be here soon."

"What's holding them up?"

"Powell ordered the vehicles to stay together. So when one got a flat tire, they all stopped while it was changed."

"Makes sense," he said. "I hope the commander's in a good mood when he learns I'm a hybrid." He sighed. "How are you feeling this morning?"

"Fine. No nausea at all."

"That's encouraging."

"Fifteen days without a dose is amazing. Do you think I'm cured, Lynxx?"

"We'll know for sure in a few weeks."

"I guess." My gaze shifted to his burlap bag. "Is poor Owlfred in there?"

He nodded. "Still sealed in the cookie tin."

"Where are you going to bury her?"

"I'll find somewhere nice."

"She was a good bird."

"The best."

Nervously, I cleared my throat. "Are you still leaving Weston Tower?"

He gave me a long look. "Probably."

We both fell silent. During the past few days, neither of us had mentioned our kiss again. Yet the memory of it left me restless, and I could still feel the warmth of his lips on mine. From the way Lynxx was looking at me right now, he was clearly wondering what my kiss had meant.

I couldn't tell him because I didn't know.

"I'd better lend a hand." Lynxx picked up his bags and left.

At a chittering sound, I turned. Five crabben xans scuttled across the dock. Each crablike xan carried a gold leaf, probably taken from the Hades terras that grew over a nearby store. I wondered how they had cut off the leaves without setting the plants on fire. Did those xans have a symbiotic relationship with the Hades terras, one that benefited both the crabbens and the plants? Was that why they could harvest the highly flammable leaves? Maybe Lynxx would have some answers.

Asher returned and passed me a large pair of bolt cutters and a flashlight. "Can you give this to Drake? He's in the forward hold."

"Sure."

I descended a long set of stairs into the bowels of the trawler. On the walls of the forward hold, scattered globes created weak patches of light. Our three remaining Templars were parked in the dimness, secured by thick chains to large rings on the floor.

The stench of old fish roiled in my throat. Holding a handkerchief over my nose, I called out, "Drake, I've got the bolt cutters."

No reply.

I moved further into the hold. "Drake?"

Nila clattered down the metal stairs behind me. "Ahh. *You've got the cutters, Kass. Good. Drake needs to cut some chains.*" She headed back up the stairs.

"He's not here. I've called out a couple of times."

"I just saw him a few minutes ago."

"Drake." My voice echoed in the metal hold, a lone sound in the gloom.

"Maybe he's unwell again. He's been seasick." Switching on her flashlight, Nila moved further into the hold, past the first chained Templar.

Gripping the bolt cutters, I followed her.

"Drake," she called. "Drake."

Still no reply.

She sighed. "I knew I should've kept him in the sick bay for another day. But he insisted he was fine."

As Nila and I rounded the last Templar, we jerked to a halt.

In the dimness, a body lay on the floor. Bits of flesh clung to the bones, and the shredded clothes were covered with dried blood.

Nila snatched a gun from her waistband. "Drake!"

"I don't think so," I whispered. The skeleton was about five and a half feet long. "Drake's really tall." Why had I left my gun and sword in my cabin?

On the floor near the body, a dozen tiny round objects glinted in the flashlight's beam. *Oh no.* They were small colored beads from a broken beaded bracelet.

"It's Greta." My friend hadn't jumped or fallen overboard after all. Warily, I looked around. A few yards away lay a man's body. Tall. Midforties. Throat slashed. "Nila, I think that's—"

A dark shape leaped at me from the shadows. Long claws. Savage teeth-lined mouth. Dark eyes.

Krol.

75

SHOCKED, I RAISED MY bolt cutters and—

—the creature flew left. A loud crack sounded. The krol slammed into the hood of a Templar and toppled to the ground, dead, its neck hanging at an unnatural angle.

I stared at Nila.

My mind flashed back a couple of weeks.

Trapped in the enormous onion terra with Xavian and Willow—and a huge rattlesnake.

Nila switched her flashlight to high beam and swept it around the hold. Gun drawn, she gestured for me to go right while she went left.

Heart slamming, I gripped the bolt cutters like a club as I crept forward, watching for more krols. At the same time, I tried to keep an eye on Nila.

In the onion terra, the twelve-foot rattler swims toward Willow.

Chained to the floor, the three remaining Templars were spaced across the trawler's hold. Nila and I looked inside the vehicles and shined our flashlights underneath them.

All clear.

We swept our beams across the hold's walls, into the gloomy corners, and behind the metal stairs.

Nothing.

No more krols.

Nila adjusted her flashlight to low beam. "That thing must've been hiding down here since we left Eldron."

The rattlesnake suddenly jerks and dies, as though touched by a tiny bolt of lightning.

"Yeah," I muttered, inching away from her. "Lynxx and I saw two climb aboard. He killed them both, but there must've been another one that we didn't know about."

Gun in hand, she said, "You don't need to be afraid."

I glanced at the xanimal with its broken neck. "I'm not afraid of the dead krol," I muttered, wary of her. I kept my bolt cutters raised like a club.

"Then why do you keep backing away from me?"

Xavian remote-killed the rattler in the onion-terra.

My gaze flickered to the revolver in her hand. "Why do you still have your gun drawn?"

"In case I'm wrong."

"Wrong about only one krol left aboard?"

"Wrong about you, Kass."

"What are you talking about?"

"You saw what happened to that krol, didn't you?"

With a super-casual shrug, I said, "It lunged at me, missed, hit Templar 3, and broke its neck." A lie. The krol's neck had been snapped in midair, *before* it had slammed into T3.

Nila had remote-killed it.

"You're a terrible liar, Kass."

"And you're a hybrid."

"Okay," she said calmly. "Now our cards are in the open."

"Are you going to kill me?"

"Why would I?"

"Because you're an Outrider spy."

Now it was her turn to gape. "*You're* the Outrider spy, Kass."

"Me?"

"Last week, during our battle at the dock, I saw you and Lynxx remote-pushing those krols. It's common knowledge in your group that Lynxx is a humanized hybrid. But no one's mentioned you being a hybrid, which means you're hiding your identity. That's something an Outrider spy would do."

"No one talks about *you* being a hybrid either, Nila. Does that make you an Outrider spy?"

She hesitated. "Good point."

Lowering my bolt cutters, I told her, "I'm human." Briefly I explained about the incident in the courtyard near Grand Central Station, when Lynxx's blood had mixed with mine.

"Incredible." She holstered her gun. "I haven't heard of a human gaining mind powers that way."

"And I thought all hybrids were named after inanimate objects like steel, gun, blade, and so on."

"My given name is Nail. When I started identifying more with humans than hybrids, I rearranged the four letters. Nail is a cold, hard name; Nila's more acceptable."

"I agree."

Metal creaked overhead as the hold's large hatch opened and sunlight poured in. Glancing up, I saw a man bending over the side. A hook and cable dangled from a crane's arm above him. "Nila," he said, "we're ready to unload the Templars."

"Okay," she called up. "Get Asher to meet me on deck, Ben."

"Will do."

As Nila and I hurried past the vehicles, I asked, "Are you going to tell Asher about you being a hybrid?"

"Absolutely," she replied. "I was planning to let him know once we reached New York. Also, I need to talk to Commander Powell about the Sphere."

"So you're part of the Sphere?"

"I am."

I hesitated. "Okay." I followed her up the stairs. "Asher knows about my blood being mixed with Lynxx's blood. But I haven't told him about my mental powers yet. I will at the right moment."

"I understand."

"Also, he doesn't know that hybrids can remote-push and so on."

"Are you suggesting I keep that from him, Kass?"

"Just until he gets to know you a bit. Asher's fiercely anti-hybrid."

"Except for Lynxx."

"That took some time," I said. "And Asher only accepted him because he knows how much Lynxx has helped the Weston Battalion."

"I'll think about it. Thanks for the heads-up."

"I should be thanking *you* for saving my life from that krol a few minutes ago."

"You're welcome." She gave a thin smile. "Again."

"Again?"

"Back at Eldron, during that battle on the dock, a krol clubbed you to the ground."

"And you shot it," I said, remembering the incident.

"Actually, I'm a terrible shot. Couldn't hit the side of a barn."

I blinked at her. "You remote-killed that krol?"

"Had to."

"Wow! Thanks."

Back on the deck, we joined Asher as the crane unloaded the Templars. Nila gave him an edited version of what had happened in the hold. Immediately, he ordered an armed team to do a thorough sweep of the trawler. Others were dispatched to remove the two bodies from the hold.

Nila said softly, "The krol had been feeding on Greta's body for the past week, Asher."

He winced. "When we were looking for her, we never searched the hold."

"Why would you? Young girls usually don't wander around dark, stinky holds."

"Maybe if we had—"

She shook her head. "My guess is the krol killed Greta on the deck. It then took her body back to the hold, where it could feed on her in peace."

Engines growling, a convoy of familiar vehicles, including three ambulances, drove onto the dock and pulled up alongside *DeepSea*.

"They're here." Asher turned to the gangway.

Nila touched his arm. "I need to speak to you."

"Is it urgent?"

"Not exactly. But it's important."

"Can it wait?" he asked, distracted. "I want to get everyone to Weston Tower. It's dangerous out here. We've no idea if the Outriders have returned to New York. Or what's been going on here."

A muscle twitched beneath Nila's left eye. "I can wait."

Half an hour later, the three remaining Templars had been unloaded from the trawler, and the sick and injured had been placed in the ambulances. Alan, from Trident Team, had made a strong recovery after Dr. Tran had operated on him, followed by Soo-Yun using a terra powder on his chest injuries. Smiling and walking gingerly, he entered an ambulance unaided.

The convoy set off for Weston Tower.

Nila had arranged for T2 to hold only herself, Lynxx, Asher, and me. Our vehicle was last in line. As Asher drove down the streets, he scanned for danger. Terra vines covered most of the buildings, and unfamiliar animals darted among the undergrowth. Even through the reinforced windows, we could hear a medley of strange sounds. Terras? Or xans?

In the front passenger seat, Nila cradled her potted zap terra as she studied the overgrown structures. "Finally, New York. Not as impressive as I'd imagined."

Asher leaned over the steering wheel and peered through the windshield. "You should've seen it before the Mist, Nila. Busy, vibrant, full of people. The skyscrapers stretched to the heavens, their walls clean and windows bright in the sunshine. The place was noisy too, with horns blaring, music playing, machinery rumbling at construction sites."

"That city's gone forever," I said, sitting next to Lynxx in the rear seat.

"It's still our home, Kass."

"Parts of it are ours," Lynxx said. "And parts of it belong to *them*." The terras. The xans.

Asher lapsed into silence, then glanced at Nila beside him. "What did you want to talk about?"

She drew in a deep breath. "I need to speak with Commander Powell as soon as we get to Weston Tower."

"What about?"

"I have a proposal from the Sphere."

Beside me, Lynxx stiffened with surprise.

"The Sphere?" Asher repeated, voice sharp as a blade. "What the heck? Are you a hybrid, Nila?"

"Yes." She glanced back at me. "Sorry, Kass. My information is too important to wait."

Asher glared at me in the rearview mirror. "*You* knew that Nila was a hybrid, Kass?"

"Only for an hour."

"Why didn't you tell me?"

And I suddenly realized my mistake.

I'd kept quiet because Nila had wanted to tell Asher in person that she was a hybrid. I'd chosen to respect the wishes of a stranger I'd only known for a few days, but in Asher's eyes, my loyalty should've been to him—someone I'd known and worked with and cared about for over a year.

And he was right.

Why had I chosen Nila? Was it because I empathized with her hybrid background, so similar to Lynxx's?

I floundered for an answer. "I was going—"

Something large and bright streaked down from the sky and struck the ambulance in front of us. The vehicle catapulted into the air, flames and black smoke billowing from its engine.

374

76

ASHER WRENCHED THE STEERING wheel. Tires squealing, T2 swerved left.

On the road ahead, the ambulance crashed down, rolled over, and collided with a storefront.

Soo-Yun. Was she inside that vehicle?

Asher braked the Templar, shouting, "Everyone wait here. I'll go—"

I flung open the door and raced down the street. "Soo-Yun!"

The ambulance blazed beneath roaring flames. Their scorching heat drove me back, and I remote-pushed the fire again and again, trying to extinguish it. No effect. Brow furrowed, I attempted to remote-push a path through it.

Lynxx raced up. "Get back, Kassia. You're too close."

"Help me put out the fire!" I grabbed his hand.

He pulled his hand free. "Even if we combine our mental powers, we can't remote-push fire. It's impossible."

"Someone needs to help them."

The rest of the convoy had disappeared around a corner, unaware of our accident.

By now, the ambulance was a raging inferno, and I gagged at the stench of burned flesh. The driver and passengers had been roasted alive.

Asher ran up with a fire extinguisher. At the strange look he gave me, I flushed. Had he seen me take Lynxx's hand?

He aimed the extinguisher at the ambulance, and a white cloud gushed out, then fizzled away. After shaking the extinguisher, he tried again. Nothing. "It's broken—or empty." He gestured to the burning vehicle. "Who was in there?"

"My people," Nila answered.

"Dr. Tran? Soo-Yun?"

"No. They're in the first ambulance."

My shoulders sagged in guilty relief.

Another burning ball arrowed down from the sky. It struck a nearby building with a deafening impact, exploding chunks of concrete and metal in all directions.

"Everyone back to the Templar!" Asher yelled.

We piled into the vehicle and snapped on our seatbelts.

"What's happening?" I cried as Asher planted his foot on the accelerator.

"I don't know." He turned the steering wheel and veered around the burning wreck.

We sped down the street.

"There's another one!" Lynxx shouted, pointing.

A third ball of flames struck the road ahead of us, creating a huge hole. Asher yanked the wheel violently, too violently—and T2 smashed into a lamppost. The hood crumpled like paper. Steam gushed out, white and hissing. Again and again, Asher tried to restart the engine. No luck. It was dead.

More flaming balls rained down, bombing the buildings.

"I think they're meteors," I cried, dread icing my veins.

The "meteors" on the Night of the Red Mist had spread terra plants across Earth. The Night of the Blue Meteors had populated the continents with non-terrestrial animals. And now the "meteors" were back again.

What are they bringing this time?

A small ball of fire smashed into T2's engine, and flames gushed from the hole.

"We can't stay here," Nila cried, unbuckling her seatbelt. "We need to go. Where's my zap terra?"

"Leave it," Asher shouted, shoving his door open.

We bolted along the street, shoulders hunched. More fireballs streaked down and slammed into the buildings around us, filling the air with the stench of twisted metal and burned materials. Shrapnel nicked my arm, and my throat felt scoured by sandpaper as I breathed in cement dust.

"Watch out!" Lynxx pushed Asher aside.

A decorative stone gargoyle crashed down, smashing into pieces and spraying bits of concrete everywhere.

Asher touched his bleeding forehead. "Thanks, Lynxx. That was close."

Nila pointed to a hotel across the street. "Over there."

We raced to its recessed doorway. A pair of broken glass doors revealed a lobby clogged with thick, flammable Hades terras. Here and there, crabben xans scurried among the gold leaves.

Lynxx stepped back from the entrance. "We can't go inside. The second we break any of those Hades leaves, that lobby will go up in flames—and us too."

We huddled in a doorway as Asher tried to contact the rest of our convoy. No answer. He shook his radio, frustrated. "Is this thing even working?"

Nila suggested, "Maybe they're busy ..." Her sentence trailed away, leaving the rest of her words unsaid.

... busy fighting to survive. Or they're dead.

At the corner, a collapsing wall spilled office furniture onto the street in a deafening waterfall of debris.

"Do you think Willow's okay?" Anguish filled Asher's blue eyes. "Harl? The others?"

"They'll be taking shelter like us," I said, trying to sound reassuring.

The deluge of meteors thinned to a trickle. Then, a few minutes later, it finally stopped. The smell of smoke and ashes clogged the air, and scraps of paper floated like confetti from maged offices.

Warily, I peered at the sky. "It's clear. No more meteors."

"I don't think they were meteors," Lynxx said. Using his handkerchief, he picked up a small smoldering object from the ground. He waved it around, cooling it before placing it in his palm and showing us.

It was a burned section of an electronic panel.

"Chi'az electronics?" Asher asked.

Lynxx rubbed at the blackened metal, revealing letters. "Not unless they write in English. I think it's a piece of satellite. Ours."

"Are you saying one of our satellites crashed to Earth?"

"Exactly, Asher. It broke into hundreds of small pieces on entry into the atmosphere." He pointed. "Look!"

In the distant sky, dozens of flaming pieces were streaking downward like missiles.

"Is that a second satellite breaking up?" I gasped, confused.

"Probably more than two, Kassia. Dozens. Or hundreds."

"We'll survive," Asher said reassuringly. "It's not like we use them anymore, anyway."

Lynxx's eyes darkened with worry. "You don't get it. I think the Chi'az are destroying our satellites. They're preparing for the Final Wave."

I blinked in shock. "The Final Wave?"

Grim-faced, Lynxx watched the distant debris fall in a rain of fire. "It may not happen for a few months, but the Chi'az are definitely getting ready."

"For what?" I asked him.

"For their invasion."

**Don't miss *Phoenix Rising*, the final book in the
Girl on Fire Series. Available now.**

As the Weston Cell prepares for the upcoming battle, Kassia uses her newfound abilities to become a unique resistance fighter. But the price is high. She endures physical and mental traumas as she struggles to turn the tide against their enemies. And emotionally, her relationships with Lynxx and Asher are in tatters.

The final conflict begins. Humans versus Outriders. Good versus evil. Life versus death. The winners of this epic struggle will claim Earth. The losers will be crushed into oblivion.

With time running out, Kassia risks everything she has—and everyone she loves—in a battle that's impossible to win.

Get your copy today!

THANK YOU

Thank you for reading *Embers Burning.* I hope you enjoyed the book. If you did, I would be very grateful if you would tell your friends and consider leaving a review online—it can be as short or long as you wish.

Not a fan of writing reviews? That's okay. A rating (where you just leave stars) online is also much appreciated.

Reviews and star ratings are like life buoys. They help my book float on the surface of a gigantic ocean of books. From there, other readers can see it.

Without reviews and star ratings, my book will sink out of sight, dropping to the pitch-black bottom of the ocean. This is a graveyard for books.

Please help save a book today.

Happy reading!

Eden Hart

Also By Eden Hart

The complete *Girl on Fire* Series:

Girl on Fire Book 1

Ashes Falling Book 2

Embers Burning Book 3

Phoenix Rising Book 4

About the Author

There are several authors named Eden Hart, who write in a wide variety of genres.

So far, the only books I've written are the 4 books in the *Girl on Fire* series.

My dystopian post-apocalyptic novels focus on compelling characters caught up in extraordinary events. They are laced with romance, action, sci-fi, and suspense, and aim to create immersive worlds that stir the imagination and enthrall the reader.

Along with writing, I'm passionate about travel. I've explored the crater of a mildly active volcano in Hawaii, abseiled down cliffs in Australia, trod the ruins of Pompeii, breakfasted with an orangutan in Asia, and crawled through the tunnels of an ancient subterranean city in Turkey.

Some of my less enjoyable experiences include flying on a broomstick-like ultra-light, having a ten-foot snake draped around my neck, and traveling in a plane whose engine burst into flames over the Indian Ocean.

Books are now my preferred way of adventuring!

I love hearing from my readers and can be found at:
Facebook Page: "Eden Hart - Author"
Email: EdenHart77@outlook.com
Website: www.edenhart.com.au

9 781922 838025